W9-ADX-596

THE COMEBACK

Ed Vega

Arte Publico Press
Houston
1985

This volume was made possible through a grant from the National Endowment for the Arts, a federal agency.

Arte Publico Press
University of Houston
University Park
Houston, Texas 77004

ISBN 0-934770-29-8
Library of Congress No. 83-072579

Printed in the United States of America

MUSIC

MUSIC MUSIC

THE COMEBACK

A

NORTHSTAR-VEGA PRODUCTION

PRODUCER: PATRICIA NORTHSTAR

ARTISTIC DIRECTOR: SUZANNE CALYPSO

RESEARCH: ALYSON RADCLIFFE

SOUND EFFECTS: MACHU L. KABONG

SETS: LIGHTNING TIM TOBAN

DIRECTOR: EDGARDO VEGA YUNQUE

To my wife
Patricia Northstar
A hell of a tough Indian!

INTRODUCTION

Edgardo Vega Yunqué, which is my real name except, that people, including myself, shorten it and call me Ed Vega because it's easier to pronounce in English. This whole business of a name has always given me problems in the United States. Vega is my father's family name and Yunqué my mother's. Vega Yunqué is not a hyphenated name. As such, you may call me Edgardo Vega, Edgardo Vega Yunqué, Vega, Vega Yunqué, Edgardo, Eddie, Ed or any other combination which pleases you. One thing which you must not do is call me Yunqué. Using solely your mother's maiden name is considered gauche among Latins. I imagine excluding one's patronym is a symbolic rejection of one's masculinity. In truth, I feel more comfortable with just Ed Vega, but then I often wish I could play left wing for the New York Rangers and not be expected to produce works of lasting literary significance or whatever it is I'm supposed to be doing before cashing in my chips or singing good night to Irene or some such euphemism for dying. Seriously, adjusting one's name to the rhythm of a language is often necessary, but on a purely artistic level, the transnomination from Edgardo Vega Yunqué to Ed Vega is akin to Federico Fellini calling himself Fred Fell.

This is not to say that Fred Fell isn't a nice name, but that it's better suited to someone selling insurance or hardware at a department store or maybe if you wanted to inform your mother that you pushed your brother the time he was bugging you about the baseball cards. I've even heard there is a publisher named Frederick Fell, so the name definitely has some potential.

The name Fred Fell, however, is just not suited to a giant of the cinema, much as Ed Vega is not suited for conveying my stature as a giant of the mickey.

I'm not going to explain why it's impossible to present THE COMEBACK in any way but as a Multiple Inter Channel Kinetoscopic Experience (MICKEY), which is my own invention born out of extreme dissatisfaction with the existential dilemma, my hard luck in affairs of the heart and the inability of the New York Rangers to win the Stanley Cup since 1940. Eventually someone will come along and write a novel, make a movie or a TV special based on the material, but none will be as good as the mickey.

Although a mickey has elements of both cinema and television, it is neither. The similarity to movies inherent in a mickey is having to sit there like a cluck and suffer because you've paid a certain amount of money and people you trusted suggested that you see it.

For example, I once heard a critic say that a theater was charging $6 admission to "The Great Gatsby," and that the movie stunk and Robert Redford "wouldn't want to put that one on his resumé." This may or may not be true. In Redford's case the matter becomes academic, because a blind man would want to go see the movie if you told him what Redford was like in "Butch Cassidy and the Sundance Kid" or any of his other movies, like "The Sting" or "The Way We Were."

Apropos blindness, an illness suffered by all humans in some degree or another, a mickey can be converted to braille, an obvious failing of movies and television.

As you can see, I'm partial to Robert Redford. At one point I was tempted to offer him a part in THE COMEBACK. It was a small part and I didn't want to insult him. Of course, my children, inveterate cultists that they are, were furious and thought me inconsiderate for not even approaching him. I'm certain it was for the best. The role was that of the young man who plays center for Frank Garboil's line on the New Amsterdam College hockey team.

I shouldn't have to tell you how difficult it is for people to participate in new things. Getting people to work in a mickey is almost impossible. Individuals begin to see themselves as they truly are and then it's therapy time. For this project I needed people with both acting and hockey experience. I suppose I could've asked Ryan O'Neal, who's had limited experience in hockey and can definitely act, but he might've been doubly insulted if I brought up the skating.

I have to digress momentarily and inform you that, whereas "Love Story" was peripherally a hockey movie, THE COMEBACK is a hockey mickey and therefore better. Eat your heart out, Erich Segal. The people in THE COMEBACK can really skate. There won't be any long shots of the leading man, so that it's obvious someone else is doing the skating. Truth is absolutely essential in a mickey. For this reason I've given the lead to an unknown. He looks like Elliot Gould and can skate as well as act. I'm confident that my decision won't cause too much of an uproar and I apologize to my relatives, friends, and acquaintances for not even considering them for parts. Many people will no doubt be disappointed by my choice and wonder whether I've finally gone off the deep end. My response to that question is: The deep end of what? The other question which will probably come up among some of my friends is whether the person I chose to play the lead is a Puerto Rican or not. This concern will mainly be voiced by my very political Puerto Rican friends for whom politics takes precedence over esthetics. I frankly don't feel I have to answer that question and I leave it up to the viewer to decide whether the lead is being played by a Puerto Rican or not. I'm sorry, guys, in this one I'm calling the shots.

The element shared with television by a mickey lies in the remarkable phenomena of channel switching and video taping. Through these devices you'll be able to do your shopping subliminally, get news, and the weather (particularly regarding tropical storms and, possibly, which way the wind is blowing) while being exposed to a smattering of intellectual stimulation and spiritually uplifting morality in the form of lightly plotted stories, situation comedies, soap-opera romance and civil service heroes in dire straits.

I believe it's quite important that you understand all of these elements before you plunge into a mickey, so that later on you won't scream and yell and complain about what you expected or hoped to get out of the experience.

A long time ago, when time was slower and people thought and felt, authors would write apologies to their works. This, I believe, is a fine and honest thing to do. I feel all human work should carry an apology. Movies, TV shows, books, cars and chocolate bars should all have apologies, instead of guarantees, warnings and ratings.

By way of an apology I'll reveal some things about myself which may be of interest. Thus, if you're not completely satisfied with THE COMEBACK, you can at least tell yourself, well, the guy's no Dostoevsky, but at least he's a gentleman and not a con-artist.

I've been writing for a few years, but it's hard work and I'm basically of a contemplative nature. Besides, after a while, I become emotionally involved with the characters and late at night I split off so that it's impossible to tell whether I'm in the scene with the characters, at the typewriter or standing behind myself watching the entire process.

I once walked up to Rollo May (who doesn't know me from Adam) after he had lectured on his self-therapy and told him about my experiences and that I viewed schizophrenia as the natural state of humans, but that what was difficult to accept was that, rather than two personalities, the division was into three. Dr. May smiled kindly as if he understood what I was talking about. I was very young at the time, but I was left with the feeling that my perception, in spite of Dr. May's perplexed look, had been accurate. Writing was an extremely dangerous profession and one I should avoid at all costs.

But I didn't heed my own advice, and late at night when I was working and this triple awareness occurred, something of myself remained behind after I was finished. It was nothing like "The Three Faces of Eve," and never quite as frightening, but I felt then, talking to Dr. May, that one day I would remain in one of my own scenes and never return to what most of us in the western world understand as reality.

My concerns led to the next logical question, that of identity, which of all the problems attendant to writing can become both an obsession and a supreme escape from doing any work. My fear of losing a part of myself in my writing and the question of identity continued to plague me. I, nonetheless, continued to write, albeit with great trepidation. Like all things, however, this too passed, or at least I believe it has, which is quite different. I no longer concern myself with who I am, who I've been or who I'll be. These are the three stages of consciousness, and dwelling on any one of them individually for any length of time can cause extreme psychic and emotional pain. This is particularly true if you're not very happy with your life; if you spend a lot of time and considerable effort regretting your actions or planning what you could be if only circumstances would permit it, and not enough time watching light changes to avoid denting people's automobiles with your body. Myself, I don't much care who I've been, who I am or who I'll be. If I become someone else or something else, I'm sure it would be Bugs Bunny or maybe an unsuccessful camel trader in the time of Ghengis Khan, (my favorite historical name, not for his deeds but for the sound of it). I love the sound of words and I have favorites in every category. My favorite scientific element is plutonium. It has a sense of finality and, at the same time, is such a comical word, even without the association with Mickey Mouse's dog. My all-time favorite, however, is a geographical location. You can have Katmandu, Oshkosh, Sidi Slimane and any other place you wish. Mine is Herzegovina. What a great sound! "Hey, what's happenin', man? Where you from?" "Me, bro? I'm from Herzegovina."

Anyway, people always said nice things about my writing and told me I should keep working at it and send my stories to *The New Yorker* or *Atlantic Monthly*, which I did for a few years. But it gets depressing collecting little printed notes and comparing them with other writers. The worst part of the ritual is that you start depending on the rejections. You begin assigning value and status to the rejections on the level of tolerance shown by the editors. Pretty soon you reach the point where you want to start trading them like bubble gum cards. You know, one of my "We will be more than happy to see more of your work" from the *Atlantic* for five of your "The material submitted does not fit our needs at the moment," from *The New Yorker.* Like the words "at this time" should offer some measure of hope. Well, they don't.

I gave up sending out my short stories. I still wrote them, but I began putting them away with the hope that someday they'd be discovered and critics, academicians and the general public would weep over such a superb story teller having been rejected. Oh, well.

Pretty soon I was writing novels. I started three, but never finished them. And then just to prove something to my wife, who'd left me over my real or fabricated madness, I finished one. I soon had an agent and he said I could really write and just had to keep plugging away. The novel was rejected by some twenty publishers, or so my agent said. It's really a beautiful book, but people wouldn't buy it. I know. You're probably thinking I should turn it into a mickey. Impossible. It was a novel and not at all suited to Multiple Inter-Channel Kinetoscopic Experience treatment. And I kept thinking. These fucking people want me to write a down and out immigrant book about the oppressed. They want me to write something full of ethnic flavor and sociological significance which glorifies struggles over insurmountable odds for a piece of the pie. Buzz off and take your mother with you! Okay? Gimme a break!

You see, I came to the United States from Puerto Rico when I was twelve. But I'm not an immigrant. Some of my ancestors have been on this continent, in this hemisphere, for thousands of years. The fact that Puerto Rico is part of the United States should eliminate that argument of my being considered an immigrant, but it doesn't, because if you don't look, act and speak a certain way, you don't really belong here. The truth is that Puerto Rico is part of the United States by theft, but that's another question. It was kind of hard for me to figure out if I was an immigrant or not until I realized that you could be born in the United States and have a family tree going back a couple of hundred years and still feel unwanted and like you didn't belong. Don't try to argue that one, because you know it's true. I haven't figured out why this is so, but it is. People talk to me about the advantages of living in the U.S., but it's still a shock to me how blacks are treated in this country and how being white is such a big deal.

And all along, as I dealt with these problems, I kept writing just as I had since I was about ten years old and before I came to the U.S. had already made a movie. It was the only movie I ever made and a complete failure, both socially and in every way possible.

At that time my father, who was a Baptist minister, was the head of the Civil Defense in our town. Oh, I thought Puerto Rico was a Catholic country. It was until the Spanish-American War in 1898 and then the Island became a spoil of war and one of the first things the United States did to spoil it was move in the missionaries. They took a perfectly good country, with superficial appearances of Catholicism and a deep cultural heritage based on superb pagan rituals from Spain, Africa and the Amerindian continent, and introduced Protestantism with its silly beliefs in salvation through self-denial. The U.S. gave the different Protestant denominations an equal chance by dividing the Island into sections and assigning them to Lutherans, Presbyterians, Menonites, Methodists, Baptists, Episcopalians, etc. in order that these good people save the poor fuzzie-wuzzies from eternal damnation, as they were doing all over the world. Don't be shy, fellas. Dig in. Here, you guys take the northeast. C'mon. You, John Calvin, take the southwest. And so on. It was a Protestant pizza party, with everyone getting a slice of this delicious heathen pie. I have rejected all that silliness and feel great. In my most grandiose moments I don't feel I'm a writer, but a 5'll", 200 lbs poorly digested anchovy sitting in Uncle Sam's stomach, giving him gas. Big deal! Eventually I'll be purged and pass on. So my father, orphaned at an early age and in sore need of a father-figure, was befriended by a Puerto Rican man who was the Baptist minister of his hometown. The man was very kind and eventually, as my father grew up, encouraged him to attend the university and then the Baptist seminary. My father followed the advice, became a minister, married my mother and I came along to bring them untold happiness, they thought. But I was a little weird.

We lived in a small mountain town in the center of the Island. My parents, as devout Baptists, would not let their children smoke, drink, or gamble, pretty common for any parents to demand from their children. However, on top of those restrictions, we were not allowed to dance or go to the movies. The dancing part was okay, because dancing was for girls and older guys, so they could feel girls up, which at the age of eight I didn't think was so big a deal. But not being able to go to the movies? Torture. My friends constantly talked about the latest movies and how Bob Steele had done this and Tim McCoy had done that. Until I was about seven and snuck off and took a look at photographs of the cowboy stars in the lobby of the theater, I had no idea what they were talking about. Not being able to go to the movies was cultural deprivation at its worst. The restriction muzzled my creativity and made me a laughing stock among my peers. One maintained his status in the group by being able to recount entire scenes from the movies and then acting out the scene with the teller playing the hero. Wishing to be part of the group, I was often pushed to the limit and could only draw on my experiences as a Baptist. Feeling sorry for me the other boys would agree to play David and Goliath from one of the Sunday-school stories. The other boys thought I was a sissy for wanting to play that particular game and the only way they would go along was for me to play Goliath to their gang of Davids, employing mango pits as missiles, but oftentimes using slingshots and actual rocks.

All of this took place during the Second World War and my father, who was head of the Civil Defense and on the rationing committee, had a huge crate delivered to our backyard. He wouldn't let us do some of the things other boys and girls did and was very srict and serious, but once in a while he'd give us things which made every kid in town jealous as hell. Like I was the first kid to have my own Sears & Roebuck catalog. Anyway, this crate was enormous. I could walk in and out of it like it was a house and could get ten of my friends in for clubs and war games. War games were the worst. The other kids always wanted to be the Americans and I had to be the Jap. If I refused, they threatened to leave and play somewhere else. I really needed human companionship, so I went along and played the Jap. This was the real threat in Puerto Rico at the time. I don't think I ever heard anyone mention Germans or Italians. It was always "*los japoneses*."

The process by which I came to make my first and only movie is worthwhile telling, if only to illustrate how a truly fine but silly mind works. One Sunday afternoon after my father had quite skillfully wrung a chicken's neck and handed it to me to bring to my mother for the evening meal, I lay down on the floor to read the Sunday funnies. It was then that I decided I'd have my own movie house. To this day I don't know what inspired such a mad scheme. I immediately began cutting out comic strips and making them transparent with water paste. When they dried, the comic strip on the reverse side was not visible. I next obtained a shoe box, cut a hole in it and mounted a magnifying glass in the hole. I then cut a slit in the shoe box and, by sliding the comic strip through in back of the magnifying glass and shining a candle behind the comic strip, I was able to project the images onto a pillow case inside the crate. This process was neither drawn out nor injurious to the brain. It came quite naturally, arriving in a flash. Although the process took most of the afternoon to complete, by the time the sun had set, I had figured out that the strips had to be inserted upside down into the slit in the shoebox. That evening, between dinner and the evening service, I demonstrated the invention to my sister by showing her a Mutt and Jeff comic strip.

Years later, in college, I saw the notebooks of Leonardo Da Vinci and found a sketch for the design of the contraption I had invented at the age of eight. Having found proof positive of my high ranking among history's great thinkers and entitled to rub elbows with them, the next logical step in my thinking was to deduce that I had been a film genius and had made a superhuman leap in creativity at that tender age. This exercise in full-blown narcissism was accomplished notwithstanding the fact that my father owned a magic-lantern-type slide projector on which he showed, at least monthly, black and white views of the Holy Land; that he was a scholar of sorts with numerous obscure books in his study; that he had varied interests, including the careful breeding, along genetic lines, of rabbits, guinea pigs and pigeons (not to each other of course), and the fascinating hobby of making plaster death masks of people in the town, so that on Saturday afternoons there were people lying down all over the house with goop on their face and macaroni sticking out of their nostrils. It is quite possible that in this semi-fertile creative environment the seed for my invention may have been sown when I saw the Da Vinci design in my father's study. I don't recall doing so, but if I did copy the design subconsciously, I find the feat remarkable and hardly minimizes the accomplishment, although somehow taints it, at least in my mind.

But back to the movie-house project. It wasn't long before one of my friends began collecting an admission fee from the other kids. The penny admission to the backyard included a small glass of lemonade, the opportunity to possibly catch my father's rabbits screwing (as rabbit lovers know, a phenomenon ranking in viewing length with that of a shooting star, but which we found hilarious) and cramming into my crate to see a "movie."

The cinematic program opened with something light, such as "Mutt and Jeff" or "Alley Oop," which in Spanish were translated as "Benitin y Eneas" and "Trucutru," followed by something serious: "Terry and the Pirates," "Red Ryder," or "Dick Tracy," all of which appeared in the newspapers in Puerto Rico, in Spanish and in color. Oh, the joys of being a colony. The best part of the performance was that the audience could either take one of the speaking parts in the comic strip or it could do a class recitation, as we often did in school. But I wasn't satisfied. I was an artist and born to suffer.

Success, oh vile goddess, why dost thou haunt my dreams! Don't strain your brain trying to figure out which Shakespeare play the quote is from. It isn't, or at least I hope not. No, it doesn't sound right. Don Guillermo would never call a goddess vile. Anyway, my success spurred me on to bigger and better things. Once the original flash of creative energy had subsided, I began to feel restless. In school my mind wandered and at home I couldn't keep still. As in every Puerto Rican family, I was suspected of suffering from *el baile sambito* or St. Vitus Dance. Something inside me burned with such intensity that I thought my body had been possessed, a type of affliction strictly reserved for Catholics and totally impermissible to Baptists.

In another burst of brilliance I decided that what I needed to do in order to quell this feeling of unresolved creativity was to launch a full-length production. I was great as a kid, a budding impressario, precociously conscious of advance publicity. I made announcements in school and pasted signs up around the plaza. Soon, even kids from the other end of town began coming around to inquire.

When the time came for the premiere of my spectacular, our backyard was teeming with activity. Even the rabbits joined in and seemed more active than ever. It was Friday and no one had to be home early. There was, however, tremendous tension in the air. Most of my customers were my religious enemies, or so I was led to believe by my father's moving sermons. Perhaps those poor Catholic boys thought my ultimate purpose was part of an elaborate plot by which they would emerge from our backyard as Baptists and be forced to attend Sunday school, Sunday evening services, Monday prayer meetings, Tuesday choir practice, Wednesday Bible study, Thursday Young People's Fellowship meetings and on Saturdays visit the wayward and sickly. I never understood why we had Fridays off but I suspect the Baptists reserved that day to watch the Catholics suffer because they couldn't eat meat. Big deal! Meanwhile, the rest of the week they had a ball and didn't have to be in church listening to boring stories about sheep.

But Catholics are not easily intimidated. They fought Moors, kicked the Jews out of Spain and invented the Spanish Inquisition. They made religious promises that emulated Christ's sufferings, walking all the way from the mountains on their knees, so it took them two or three days to reach town. Covered with ashes and their blood trailing them as they kneed along the street, they then went into church and prayed for hours on end. So as I saw it, they were a hardy breed. They paid their penny, drank their lemonade, thought the rabbits were boring and went into the crate. Everything seemed fine. One group went in and another waited until that one was finished and then entered. Around the fourth showing, reviews had been put out by an insensitive critic and the audience, predisposed to hostility from having abstained from meat, became restless. Halfway through the performance, someone began booing and others began rocking the crate and finally managed to knock it over, causing an argument and several fist fights to ensue. One thing I learned early on about Catholics, is that they did not read the same Bible we Baptists read and, although it was obvious that they had two cheeks as we did, they rarely resorted to turning either as a way of dealing with violence.

My problems were far from over. On top of having my film break-through rejected by a hostile, insensitive and brutish audience, and having to return the admission price to several people, my father came out to investigate the source of the commotion and of certain language being employed which was not permissible to Baptists. He discovered that not only was I responsible for so many children being in the backyard, but that I had gone beyond the bounds of creativity into the area of common and petty destructiveness. This is the feeling I was left with, because I don't recall my father's actual words, perhaps a protective psychological device to preserve my image of him as a perfect father. It is very likely that on that occasion, my father may have employed vocabulary strictly reserved for Catholics.

Behind the fiasco and the eventual curtailment of my career in films was the fact that a year prior, I had been given a collection of beautiful books. A THOUSAND AND ONE NIGHTS, TREASURE ISLAND, SWISS FAMILY ROBINSON, etc. The books had been published in Spain and they were big, leather-bound volumes with delicate gilt-edged pages and color illustrations which kept you staring at their remarkable detail for hours. In my enthusiasm to share with others what I had gained from the books, I cut out over twenty illustrations, prepared them and wrote a screenplay in which Ali Baba and his forty thieves fight the Robinsons for control of Treasure Island, or somesuch combination. The subsequent experience at my father's hands was so traumatic that I don't recall all of the details. I am still convinced, however, that my work was one of true genius. As often happens with artistic endeavor which is far ahead of its time, my father chose to ban it, a common practice among people of his religious persuasion.

It was then that I began writing in earnest, in Spanish of course, because it was the only language I knew at the time. I believe I did so, as I've done many things since, out of a sense of guilt, Protestant guilt, Baptist guilt, out of a sense of duty and as pennance for the damage that I had inflicted on those beautiful, innocent books. In committing myself to right this grievous wrong, I realized that I wanted to write books more than I did to make movies. Writing, it turned out, was what I truly loved.

I also wanted to be a hockey player three years later, after I was introduced to the game in the streets of the South Bronx and through my mother's good fortune. She, responsible citizen that she was, being in the U.S. only a year, but a year well spent learning the English language, entered a contest sponsored by Alexander's Department Store in the Bronx. "Your Favorite American President," in twenty-five words or less. She chose Franklin D. Roosevelt. Good for her. My favorite American president is Lester Young.

Anyway, the prize was a television set and she won the damned thing. I still don't believe it. It was an eight-inch number with, no kidding, a magnifying glass which made the picture bigger, even though from the side the figures on the screen appeared bloated. I still have a photograph of my mother, my aunt, my brother and me around the TV set. The two ears of the antenna make a "V" within which sits a large, framed picture of Jesus praying fervently at Gethsemane, looking, I always thought, rather worried, which he had every reason to be. Symbolism is the purview of readers, so please figure it out. It doesn't interest me in the least.

But TV was great. Wow! What wonders! "Foodini and Pinhead," Jack Bellamy in "Man Against Crime," "The Lone Ranger," "Suspense," Notre Dame against North Carolina, which meant Leon Hart against Choo-Choo Justice. Of this pioneering TV fare, what most intrigued me was the game of ice hockey. The New York Rangers of the early 1950's. In retrospect I now realize they were terrible, but I suffered with them and they were my heroes. Joe DiMaggio, Duke Snider and Willie Mays were all right and Buddy Young running back a kickoff for the New York Football Yankees was sheer poetry, but none of those names had the magic of Wally Hergersheimer, Nick Mikoski, Black Jack Evans and Chuck Rayner. I was a hockey nut when the phrase had yet to be coined. I still shock people around hockey when I tell them I once saw a Chicago Black Hawks player score 3 goals in 21 seconds against the New York Rangers. No one believes me until they go into the record book and find it. It was Wild Bill Mosienko and I still feel deep shame.

This fascination with hockey, a sport foreign enough to citizens of the United States in those days, but totally unheard of by Puerto Ricans, is the biggest deviation from socialization I've ever encountered, other than Romulus and Remus. The U.S. has a way of getting your attention one way or the other, once you get here, and here we had come in 1948.

Upon coming to the United States, my father became the minister of a Spanish-speaking congregation housed in an old, very stately, German Lutheran mini-cathedral with stained glass windows, a choir loft and pipe organ, and an altar and pulpit better suited for a six-foot Saxon than my five-foot-four Puerto Rican father. Exploring the basement and subbasement of the church, I found an extensive collection of Nazi propaganda written in English. I even found a German helmet, a bayonet, and Iron Crosses painted on the walls during my exploration of the labyrinthian confines beneath the church. Curious child that I was, I immediately began to ask questions and learn what had taken place in Europe during the war. I knew enough about Japan's role, but now I needed to know Germany's part.

My father was very knowledgeable concerning the persecution of the Biblical Israelites and told me about Hitler's atrocities. I read voraciously on the subject. Shocked, frightened and outraged by the inhumanity, each account I read angered me more and led me to wish to avenge wrongs against defenseless people. I read and read of the persecution of the Jews in Europe and had terrible nightmares of being burned alive by people in those terrible helmets. Eventually, my mother made me throw out the helmet which I had found in the basement of the church.

My father's church and adjoining house was in the South Bronx, at that time a predominatly Irish Catholic, German and

Jewish neighborhood. Once again my curiosity got the best of me. I did not enjoy being a Baptist, I had found that Catholics were no better off and I now became curious about the Jews. Up the street from my father's church, on Beekman Avenue, there was a synagogue. I watched people go in and out of the building for days. Everyone was dressed in black and the men had beards and big hats. They looked as unhappy as the people in our congregation or the ones coming out of the Catholic church. I figured their sadness was understandable, given what they had suffered under Hitler. One Saturday I finally worked up the courage to walk into the synagogue, hoping I suppose, to explain to them that I sympathized with their plight in Europe. My presence in their place of worship caused a tremendous commotion and a couple of black-hatted, bearded men grabbed me by the arms and ushered me out into the street. I was hurt by the rejection, but rationzlized their actions by deciding that, because our family lived in the German church, they suspected us of siding with the Nazis. I asked my sister's girlfriend from school why I hadn't been allowed into her church. Gertrude, who was a member of the synagogue, explained that you had to be Jewish to go to the synagogue and that you had to be circumcised. I was thirteen and Gertrude was eleven, my sister's age. Although I spoke sufficient English, I didn't know what she was talking about, but assumed the word represented what baptism was for us. We were in the basement of our house and my sister had gone upstairs. I believe in all innocence, Gertrude and I wandered off to the basement of the church, which was connected to the basement of our house, and found ourselves in back of the boiler. She still wanted to know if I was circumcised. I shrugged my shoulders and she pointed and said I should show her. I shook my head and stepped back, but she insisted and I finally gave in. She took a long time examining me, but finally shook her head and said there was no way I could go into the synagogue. I was crushed by the added religious rejection. Gertrude, however, made up for it by becoming increasingly more curious about our anatomies, all of it very pleasurable and innocent, but tremendously guilt-producing, since we usually met in a basement room beneath the pulpit from which my father addressed his congregation on the evils of the flesh.

At night I was tortured with dreams in which Gertrude and I, each in our own hells, hers Hitler's ovens and mine the fire of eternal damnation, burned incessantly. The pyres of the Spanish Inquisition were nothing compared to the torture I felt each night as I turned away all manner of sexual thoughts. I finally overcame my obsession with Gertrude by concentrating on street games, football, hockey, learning English and explaining to the Irish kids why I spoke with an accent and was not Catholic, a fact which they treated as a mystery.

Finding refuge from my passion for Gertrude in sports, I didn't think very much about writing, except for the little I had to do in school. From that time until I was twenty years old and came across a pornographic work published by Olympia Press and whose title and author I have forgotten, I did no writing. It was a green pocketbook about cogitating.

Upon finishing the book, I thought to myself: I can do better than this. As usual I ran into problems. The people I wrote about kept having similar problems to the ones I encountered and saying awkward things to each other. Worst of all, they were always looking to fall in love and didn't screw unless they were deeply committed to each other. This romanticism clashed violently with my actions at the time, since I had determined to seduce any and every female who exhibited even the slightest interest in me. But I was shattered once more by my inability to create. More crushing was the disappointment I felt in having failed my friends whom I had promised a "real" dirty book.

This happened in Athens, Greece while I was in the United States Air Force. I'd enlisted after high school in order to get away from New York, where nothing good was really happening for me, and to escape my parents and religion. I was having unnatural thoughts about most women, including my mother, my sister and members of my father's congregation, both single and married. I knew if I didn't get away, I was going to disgrace my family. In Greece I was able to let go a bit and learn some things about women. After a while I felt more at ease, which for me is like an elephant playing ping-pong if he could hold the paddle and keep his trunk from getting in the way.

Greece was magnificent. The sea, the sun, the sky, retsina, ouzo, Fix beer, outdoor movies, fried squid, souvlaki and girls who apparently had not been affected by religion. I fell in love with a girl. Her name was Melpomene. Everyone said she had a strange name, but no one would explain. Melpomene is of course the muse of tragedy. Fittingly, I had my heart broken, although I didn't find out Melpomene was the muse of tragedy until I took a Classics course at N.Y.U. More curious yet, such was my emotional retardation that I didn't realize I had been in love with Melpo until ten years after I left Athens and was already married to my wife. When I got out of the Air Force, I went to school in California under the G.I. Bill. I took up with a girl even more confused than I was. Like myself, she believed I could write. I received some encouragement from an English teacher who was totally crazy and got pissed off one day because his kids wouldn't listen to him and all they did was watch television and so he went out into his garden, picked up a big rock, told his kids to clear out of the living room and he pitched the rock right into the tube, causing a tremendous explosion and knocking out all the lights in this one section of Malibu. Three years later I returned to New York with a wife and a child, was accepted into N.Y.U. as a transfer student, got good grades, a scholarship, a prize in the study of Portuguese that I went to accept at the Brazilian consulate the day John F. Kennedy got shot in Dallas, which made me cry and spill coffee all over the Consul's rug. She held my hand through the apology. This made me feel better because she was one of those beautiful, well-bred, elegant women who have sex appeal even when they're sixty. After that I didn't want to be in school anymore. I had only one semester to go, but all the confusion of that Dallas weekend threw my life into turmoil. Additionally, I was to graduate Phi Beta Kappa, had been nominated for a Wilson scholarship, was accepted into several Ph.D. programs, had set my mind on teaching at the college level and yet, when I went up to discuss my plans with the Dean of Washington Square College, I was told that I should really think about returning to my community to teach junior high school. Cold water bucket time. I didn't even inquire as to his reasons for making this judgment. I wasn't good enough to teach college. There was something missing. I spoke without an accent, wrote brilliant papers, made the Dean's List and all sorts of other things, but was not college-teaching material. Okay. I eventually taught college for a number of years and found out I didn't care for it, so maybe it was all for the best.

Things sort of fell apart for a while. I went to work in the War on Poverty. I suppose, to do pennance for my inability to pass muster with the dean. I did "undercover" work for the Office of Special Investigations of O.E.O., arriving at Job Corps camps at night, changing into teenage clothes and mixing in with the internees, only to leave at the end of the weekend to write reports on suspected homosexuality, drug abuse and black-market activities. A real fink's job, but I had to feed a family. I gave all that up and went to work as a community organizer.

I continued writing stories, sending them out and building these enormous literary sand castles which crumbled each time I received a rejection slip. But I kept plugging away. I started thinking about writing a book, a novel. And then it hit me. I was going to be expected to write one of those great American immigrant stories, like STUDS LONIGAN, CALL IT SLEEP or FATHER, which was written by Charles Calitri, one of my English teachers at Benjamin Franklin High School. Or maybe I'd have to write something like MANCHILD IN THE PROMISED LAND or a Piri Thomas' DOWN THESE MEAN STREETS, which threw me for a loop when I read it, because

Piri lived at 109 East 104th Street and my father's next church after we left the Bronx was the Second Spanish Baptist Church at 110 East 104th Street and to have the coincidence of two writers from a Puerto Rican background living on the same block at the same time had to be too much for any literary establishment to accept.

Things on that block were exactly as Piri said they were, although I don't remember him. The whole street scene scared the hell out of me. Some of the stuff that happened to Piri didn't happen to me, so I can't give you the great American immigrant story full of ethnic color, sociological significance and soul-bearing reality. It would be a lie. Not fiction, but a lie.

Life was rough the same way life is rough for anyone growing up. I had the normal amount of pimples, erections, broken hearts and failures. But I guess I was lucky. My parents shielded me from a lot of horrible things, although for a long time, and to a certain extent still, I felt that I didn't belong. I didn't smoke cigarettes until I was eighteen, didn't smoke pot until I was twenty-seven, fell down the stairs with my one-year-old son and quit. Anyway, I liked sports and that was a different crowd altogether. I was big enough in size to talk myself out of a lot of fights by the time it was important. To make matters even safer for me, my head was always in the clouds. Most people thought I was a strange kid and no matter how bad the crowd, no one bothers strange people. They're the butt of a lot of jokes and verbal cruelty, but no matter how insensitive or rough the group, strange people are tolerated for the most part.

So I never shot dope nor had sexual relations with men, didn't for that matter have sexual relations of any significant importance with women until I was about nineteen and in the Air Force stationed in the Azores where it was common practice for the airmen to visit houses of pleasure. And I never stole anything, except once when Benjamin Franklin was playing in the city basketball finals at Madison Square Garden and my friend Jimmy Webb was on the team (How you doin', Jimmy Webb, wherever you are), and coming out of the Garden, everyone was going wild and I took an apple from an old man who was selling them. I didn't go a block before I started feeling sorry for the old guy. It was like every Mother's Day I would start thinking about kids who were orphans and I'd cry. The apple wasn't heavy in my hand or anything like that, but I went back and paid the old man for it. It only cost a nickel anyway. I was a real jerk. Aside from some fist fights, I've never shot anyone, although I've felt like it. It seems pretty far-fetched to me that I would ever want to really do permanent physical harm to anyone. It is equally repulsive for me to write an autobiographical novel about being an immigrant. In fact, I don't like ethnic literature, except when the language is so good that you forget about the ethnic writing it.

So before you read this mickey, I'm going to warn you. There are parts of it even I don't like too much. I've left them in because they're necessary to the overall kinetoscopic effect and what they represent are things that some people are afraid to say and it's on me to say them. If you don't like them either, you're stuck, which is in part the idea of a mickey. Once you're in for a couple of bucks, you might as well finish it. You're welcomed to boo, throw the mickey down, turn the lights off, go to sleep, or curse, because you might view the mickey the way my agent did. He said one day: "This oughta be either a serious work or a romp, but it can't be both," and we argued and he got some boob editor friend to say some nasty things about THE COMEBACK, which it was obvious he hadn't read in its entirety, and I recalled my ambassador and he recalled his when I found a note written by one of his readers saying that I had to cut out all the Marx brothers stuff. I laughed in their faces and told them that if they didn't understand the deeper philosophical implications of the Marx Brothers, I felt sorry for them and considered them, both he and his precious reader, a notch below cretins.

So some of the stuff is slapstick and sometimes there are bad jokes and some of the people are stereotypes. So what! I didn't write the damned thing to win the Nobel Prize for Literature or get a book award or even a Finn for Best Mickey. I wrote it becuase I felt like it. It came to me and I thought there were some things that needed to be said. In any case, I wrote it and not you and I know what I'm trying to do and it's for you to figure out, otherwise what the hell do we have here, with readers and critics trying to write the book for the author already? I can promise you one thing. When you're finished reading THE COME-BACK, you may not put me up on a pedestal, but you'll feel like you got your money's worth, and it may give you a little more courage to attempt something of difficulty, rather than bouncing off walls for the rest of your life.

Oh, I was told this mickey was too long and I should cut it down. My friend Dan Evans, a writer and painter, said maybe it should be longer, so who do you listen to? Longer or shorter, who cares! What are we talking about, curtain rods, fabric? What? If you feel the thing shouldn't be so long, edit it. If you feel it should be longer, write a few scenes yourself. Once you have it, you can rip out pages at your leisure and arrange them differently. You can even change the dialogue to fit your taste. You can also get angry, because I'm poking fun at your people or anything else you wish. Whatever happens, though, I'm going to put a smile on your face once in a while and make you think a little and maybe even cry, which is what it's all about, and not about being Puerto Rican or Jewish or Black or Irish or Italian or even Herzegovinian. Except that it is in a roundabout way.

I was a person before I was anything else.

I came on the scene free and no matter what, I'm going out in the same condition.

I'll tell you one thing, though. If this mickey is a success and I can make more than just a little bit of money, I'm going to turn this country upside down with the stuff I got in my files. This ain't a one shot thing, folks. However many you want, I have them: already written, halfway through, a few chapters here and there, in outline form, sloshing around in my brain. Lots of stuff, relevant and irrelevant, reverent and irreverent, whatever your choice. My aim is to do with the pen that which is abhorrent for me to do with the sword, to help in any way that I can to free my country. It may be an odd and unconventional way to go about it, but I'm doing it anyway.

Like I said: I'm free and if that bothers you, try locking me up in one of your little head prisons. If you're a mind guard or head warden, please disqualify yourself from passing judgment on mickeys.

If you understand what I'm doing, thank you very much.

A Poem

Faceless shadows we are
We watch each other and pretend not to see
Our laughter is hollow like the rattling in
an old man's chest
Our journey is to nowhere
Our words have been stripped of magic and the
sounds they make are ones of anguish
Like a wounded bird, the heart flutters
weakly and the spirit wanes
Our future was yesterday, but the time is gone and
we nostalge gracelessly in order to forget
Children we are, lost in a game to stave off
execution
We try to be and are not
We cry and know it's an act brought on by boredom
We ask the question, but it's been laughed out of
vogue and in its place there's fear
And yet the masks go on and we step out on the
stage to make believe
Somewhere, a fool turns from channel to channel,
laughing one minute and crying the next, never
knowing which is real and which not,
as if that were the measure of life.

-The Poet-

CHAPTER 1

In which it is shown that a rodent can exist anywhere and, if given the opportunity, can eat you out of house and home, make you paranoid about your closest friends, and even force your wife or girlfriend to commit unnatural acts against her will.

The skin of his face was the texture and color of uncooked pizza dough left out a few days so that it becomes cracked and yellowish. This uncommon pallor, a losing battle with acne during his teenage years and his small body and pronouncedly narrow face conspired to make him resemble a wet, exotic rodent as he moved through the steady winter drizzle of Manhattan, which during this time of the year, the island being mostly asphalt and stone, evokes, particularly in the evening, a feeling of murkiness about life's ultimate purpose. But this viscacha or acuchi or pacarana or tucotuco had a purpose, ultimate or not, so that here in El Barrio, near the river, with the streets shiny-black from the mixture of rain and snow which had been falling since morning, he scurried on.

Out on the water, downstream from the confluence of the East and Harlem Rivers, at a place called Hell Gate, because of its treacherous crosscurrents, a tugboat sounded its foghorn as it cut through the night. Onshore an alley cat, anathema to common rodents, recalling some ancestral danger, dashed to the safety of a burned-out building and away from the dark trumpeting.

It should come as no surprise, therefore, that on this cold, gloomy night at the beginning of 1971, John Chota of the rodential mien, born and raised on this huge funny farm called the United States of America, and in spite of being one of the People and fluent in their language, that is, the language of Cervantes, coded for protection against intruders, linguistic and otherwise, and attired at all times for Latin dancing, found the circumstances of his background and its traditions irrelevant.

As he moved through the cold drizzle and because of his purpose, Chota's mind was divided between concern for his safety and the warm breasts and thighs of a near-sighted Polish-American topless dancer from Weehauken, New Jersey, with whom he had recently found favor. As the tugboat moaned in the night and the frightened cat crossed his path, Chota's image of his dancer dissolved and only a cold, liquid fear remained in his groin. Oh Christ, he thought, they'd sent the cat after him. A black cat crossing his path on such a night was bad enough, but that it was their cat and he was once again under suspicion, made him, for the first time, seriously consider computer programming or some such profession as a healthier, less anxiety producing way of earning his living. He would have to discuss his career plans with Mullvaney at some point.

At 116th Street and Pleasant Avenue, Chota stopped under a street lamp, folded back the edge of his left glove and checked his watch. Five minutes to nine. He was still on time. Before moving on he pulled the black beret a bit further down on his forehead, ran his fingers along the zipper of his leather jacket to ensure full protection against the cold, and turned north. At the next corner he crossed Pleasant Avenue and headed east towards the river. The combination of rain and snow still fell in a fleecy mist.

Halfway down the block, composed mostly of abandoned buildings and warehouses, Chota stopped suddenly and looked behind him. Nothing. The street was deserted. But he'd felt something behind him. It was like the rustling of cloth, the flapping of wings, a thin whistle or the tinkling of glass. He did not know which but each one was the indication of a spirit not at rest. Oh Jesus. The fear in his bones made his teeth chatter.

He shuddered involuntarily, took a deep breath and headed down the stairs to a basement. As he descended the wet metal steps his heart beat more insistently, the anxiety mounting and his palms sweating inside the leather gloves. He knocked twice on the door and waited. Instinct told him that something big was in the making. The feeling would not leave him. Up to then it had been all talk. Yesterday afternoon, however, there had been something different in Maritza Soto's voice when she called.

When a young man finally opened the door Chota stepped quickly inside. As he brushed the moisture from jacket and beret he felt strangely at home. The whitewashed walls and steam-pipes of the basement apartment, the cheap linoleum floor, the national flags on the walls, the posters and photographs had all formed part of his life for more than a year. Together they created a protective environment, tenuous as it had always felt to him. Several young men greeted him but no one smiled. It was always this way, he thought. Laughing was frowned upon as frivolous, smiling a sign of relaxed commitment. The others greeted him by the name he'd given them: Pancho Miranda. After several perfunctory nods he removed his jacket, hung it on a hook, adjusted his beret at the correct, accepted angle and joined the others in moving chairs into a circle in the middle of the meeting room. Even in carrying out this simple task the dozen or so young men appeared angry. Each one wore a black beret and like his, their hair was long, either to their shoulders or in huge bonnet-like afros. Like birds of prey, their eyes were quick one minute and penetrating the next.

As he unfolded his second chair, Chota noticed four strangers in the room. For a moment he felt as if his instincts had failed him. Had he been asked to attend an innocent celebration for an elderly relative of a group member? On the other side of the room, standing together in front of the flags, were four old men. Each one around sixty years of age, they looked no different than the men who sit outside bodegas, playing cards or dominoes in warm weather. His initial urge was to ask someone about them.

Considering his stage of agitation he decided against it. Let the evening unfold naturally and he'd find out. Upon closer examination, however, he noted that the old men were as serious as the young. So something was up.

Chota did not bother greeting the three young women working at a mimeograph machine on the other side of the room. Unlike Lena Kojinsky from Weehauken, New Jersey, they had each rejected his amorous advances even though during the past year he had seen each one change sexual partners at least four times. Privately, he referred to them as the Undress Sisters.

When the task of arranging the chairs was completed, Chota made his way to the kitchen at the back of the apartment. Maritza Soto had just finished brewing coffee and was kneeling on the floor, petting a large black cat as it lounged in front of the stove. The cat looked sullenly up at Chota, yawned and then haughtily turned to grooming itself. Its fur appeared dry but that was no indication that it hadn't been sent out to frighten him. There was something dangerous and evil about the cat. He had always known it. As usual Maritza was dressed in tight jeans and an army fatigue shirt, the top of her breasts visible from Chota's position in the doorway. The drab clothing did nothing to hide her voluptuous figure. Her thick, black hair falling to well below her shoulders and her beret angled off to one side made Maritza more sensuous yet. As he had been upon meeting her in the fall of the previous year, Chota was fascinated by her Indian looks. India he called her in his fantasies. He wondered, as he recalled her nakedness again, how a good kid like her had become mixed up with the trash in the other room.

"How you doing, Maritza?" he finally said, and commented on the weather, adding a stupid remark about it being colder than an Eskimo's widow.

"I'm all right," she replied, ignoring the Eskimo remark. "I'll fix you a cup of coffee if you feed Pantera," she said. "There's some *cuchifritos* on the stove"

"Deal," he said, but hated the idea of getting any closer to the cat. "Has he been out tonight?" he asked, matter-of-factly.

"I don't know," she said. "Why?"

"Nothing. Just wondering," he said and quickly changed the subject. "Listen, who got him started on this shit, anyway?"

"I don't know," she said. "He just showed up one day. Just a scrawny little kitten. I guess we were eating and somebody gave him some *oreja*, you know the stewed ear."

Chota made a face as Maritza went on talking.

"He went crazy on it. We bought him cat food after that but he wouldn't touch it. Just *cuchifritos*, that's all he'd eat."

Chota laughed but it wasn't really laughter. It was more like what he thought laughter should be under the circumstances.

"I guess he really goes for pigs, right?"

"Only four-legged ones," she said as she stood up.

She was a head taller than him and the difference always disturbed him. In his fantasies she was much shorter and therefore easier to overpower.

"He's a real P.R. cat," she said, running water in the sink.

"Why, because he likes *cuchifritos* or because he doesn't dig two-legged pigs?" Chota teased.

"Both," she replied coldly.

Chota didn't answer her. His mind was on the previous fall when he'd seen her and Martinez going at it. The images of the naked bodies writhing against each other still disturbed his sleep. How could a good, decent kid like her, he again wondered as he watched the curves of her body, act like such a *puta*?"

Jesus, at one point she had been on top of him, her body bent back so that her breasts were pointing straight at the ceiling. Her moans were like those of an animal in pain. The thought of being inside of her like Martinez had made him lightheaded and nauseous. Now that Martinez was safely out of the way he'd have her. Fighting the nausea, now compounded by his disgust of the food, he gingerly placed the stewed stomach, ears and assorted entrails into a bowl. The cat, growling as if he were about to engage in mortal combat, rushed past his leg.

"Go to it, champ," he said, controlling the fear as he recalled the black cat crossing his path earlier. "Get yourself straight for the ladies. In this weather you might have to wait a long time for them to come and party."

Maritza handed him a cup of coffee and, as he sipped from it, he watched her, undressing her in his mind. Maybe he'd have to hold a gun to her head or even knock her out, he thought. He wanted her and hated her at the same time so that his mind felt like a ping-pong game. She made him so angry that his only wish at that point was to rip into her even without being erect. For a moment his mind went blank and only a red film of anger was present as awareness. Would she moan and scream as she had with Martinez?

"Maritza?"

"What?" she replied, looking up from filling a sugar bowl.

"Do you believe in spirits?"

She looked at him suspiciously.

"No, do you?"

He shrugged his shoulders noncommittally.

"I felt something outside," he said.

"Maybe it was the wind," she said.

"No, there was no wind," he said. "It brushed past me from behind. I'm not kidding, it touched me. I don't know. Like a spirit or something, you know. I should go and talk to somebody. It wouldn't hurt, right?"

"That's all superstition," she said.

"But I felt it," he insisted.

"Okay, so you felt it," she shot back, becoming annoyed. "What's it mean?"

"I don't know," he said, seriously. "That's why I should go and talk to somebody. It was like a...I don't know...like a..."

"Like a what?" she demanded impatiently.

"I don't know. It was behind me so like I didn't get a chance to see it. But it was like a bird or something."

The tension of the past few weeks, the upcoming meeting's importance and her natural reserve suddenly dissolved and uncharacteristically Maritza snickered. She covered her mouth immediately and peeked out of the kitchen, hoping no one had noticed her transgression.

"Really, it's true," he said.

"Gimme a break, okay, Pancho!" She was angry at herself for allowing him to see her laughing. "Like a bird, right?"

"No, not like that friggin' thing on TV. You know, a real bird, flying real fast and dangerous."

A curious look came over Maritza's face.

"That's possible," she said, cryptically.

"Then you believe in stuff like that," he said.

"Hell no," she spit back at him. "Not like spiritualists with all their mumbo-jumbo and plants and oils and the rest of the junk, if that's what you mean. They don't do anything but rip people off, selling love potions and bullshit. But like things have their own space and presence and like some folks have ESP and what-not. Maybe you did feel something. What sign are you?"

"Gemini," he said.

She thought a moment.

"Yeah, maybe," she said, nodding as she spoke.

"Sometimes it means death," he said.

"What does? Signs?"

"No, birds."

"Bullshit."

"No, listen," he said. Don't laugh. I had this dream about my cousin, right? In the dream I was at my aunt's house on Simpson Street up in the Bronx and this huge black bird came and sat on my cousin's birthday cake from Valencia Bakery. Two weeks later my cousin, Pito, was coming from school. He went to Aviation High School, right? So, he was like high and riding between the cars on the Lexington Avenue Express and he fell and the train ran over him. So, like I told my mother about the dream and she said we had to go over and see her *comadre*, Doña Crispina, who's into spirits, right?"

"Yeah?"

"Like I didn't believe in the shit either so I told my Moms that I didn't wanna go see old Mrs. Snap, Crackle and Pop, which is what we called her, right? Get it?"

"Yeah, I get it."

"You know, Rice Crispies."

"I said I got it, go ahead."

"Well, like my Moms didn't dig me coming down nasty on Mrs. C and she'd smack me. She'd smack me regularly. Just on GP's, but this time she really got off a good one. Stars and little birds and the whole thing went off in my head. And then when my big brother, Angelo, got home, she told him I was acting all funny and he plexed up about his big brother and head of the family bit and told me he'd kick my ass if I didn't do what Moms said. You didn't wanna get my brother pissed off at you. He was like a house, he was so big. One time he was body punching with a guy and hit him in the arm and broke it. I swear. So like I went and old Mrs. C got down very solemn and I told her the dream and like she said any kind of bird means trouble and that if it was a black one it definitely meant death."

"Sure," Maritza said. "Drink your coffee, we're gonna start soon."

He felt crushed by her superior attitude. It was all part of that college crap they fed good kids. His resolve not to ask about the old men had vanished. Why did she have this power over him? He was like a little kid around her. Birds, ghosts, spirits. He sounded like an idiot. But all of it was true. All those things were true. Every time he'd gone to see the spiritualists, things they had no way of knowing came out of their mouths and even in the summer the room got very cold and he shivered. Her arrogance made his anger and hatred grow.

"Listen," he said, mustering up his courage. "Who are the old dudes out in front?"

"Old guard," she replied, absently. "*Plataneros*."

"The what?"

"The old nationalist group. You'll see. We've got it all worked out."

A current of perverse pleasure ran through Chota as he considered her beliefs. They were just as ridiculous and fantastic as she made his belief in spirits sound. To chide her would leave him wide open, but he couldn't help himself. What had gone wrong with her? She seemed like such a nice kid. Had probably gone to Catholic school and always did what her parents asked.

"And they're here for the meeting?"

"Yeah," she said, somewhat defensively.

It was exactly the opening he'd been looking for.

"You're kidding," he said. "They're practically senile. Like what are we getting into, the nursing home business?"

Her reaction was instantaneous. It was as if he had touched her breasts.

"Hey, man," she snapped at him. "That's not very fucking funny, all right?"

"I have a right to ask," he said, taken aback by her fury.

"Just fuck off, okay, Pancho?"

God he hated her when she cursed. What a *puta* she was; a glorious big-titted, wide-hipped *chochona*, just begging for it. The red film had returned to his consciousness. The rage made him dizzy and he held on to the counter top.

"Hey, listen, I'm sorry," he said.

"Yeah, I bet you are," she said and stormed out of the kitchen.

He watched her round bottom retreat and wondered again if she'd put up much of a fight. It would be worth it, fight or not. He took a deep breath, placed his empty coffee cup in the sink and, avoiding the cat, followed her out.

CHAPTER 2

Wherein it is possible, and perhaps profitable, to examine some examples of male chauvinism, old chauvinism, youth chauvinism, anti-Russian communism, stale nationalism, opportunism, sports symbolism, aspirations to media journalism and in which, coincidentally, a tangential question, out of necessity, may be posed: Should not legislation be passed to make politics a contact sport?

An astute, if perhaps overworked, North American captain of industry once suggested that the most efficient method of conducting a meeting was to have neither table nor chairs in the room. This method, he insisted, would produce several effects conducive to increased labor output. Without a writing surface participants could not doodle or take notes and therefore paid closer attention to the agenda. Having to stand created instability of hierarchical position and curtailed intransigence of viewpoint. Lastly, being on their feet united the participants in common endeavor, that of leaving the meeting as soon as possible and returning to the familiarity of their work with a new appreciation of the need for efficiency. This formula is probably applicable to all meetings except political ones. It is generally accepted that at political gatherings there is no need to take notes since the only things of importance to be said are your own. Additionally, intransigence in politics is not only a requisite but a sign of commitment. Lastly, because of the rapacious nature of most people involved in politics, common endeavor is only superficially necessary.

What took place on this cold Manhattan night, deep in the intestines of El Barrio, roughly between 9:15 and 10:30 P.M., illustrates the above point concerning political meetings.

The combination of John Chota's chagrin at being rejected by Maritza Soto and her outrage at his remarks and superstitions, in part, and only in part, fueled what happened. Everyone was already sitting down when Chota finally took his place and Maritza, more loudly than necessary, thanked him sarcastically for his presence. Not being able to tone down her anger, Maritza next broke into the different conversations to ask for a volunteer to stand guard during the meeting. In spite of what everyone perceived as extremely bad vibrations, several people, including Chota and two of the young women, raised their hands. With great seriousness of purpose, but still annoyed, Maritza pointed to one of the young men, who stood up and headed for the front door where he stood legs apart and hands behind his back, his eyes fixed in a menacing stare. Maritza thanked the young man and, fighting to control her rage, welcomed everyone, particularly the guests. She added how honored the group was to have them present. She asked each one to introduce himself individually. When the last one had said his name, made a small speech full of rhetoric and tacked on ceremoniously that he was at everyone's service, Pupi Malave, before the old man had a chance to sit down, raised his hand. The small discourtesy did not go unnoticed by the old guard.

After some polite applause for the guests, Maritza pointed reluctantly at Pupi, who swaggered up out of his seat and began complaining that he hadn't been informed about the guests and that he thought it was really bad communications because all he'd gotten was a call at the jive-ass supermarket where he was busting his hump stacking shelves and told to be at the meeting.

"That's it, man," Pupi exploded. "Be there! Bam! Boom! Be there! No explanations, no I'm sorry, bro, no nothing. Boom! Be there."

He went on venting his anger in seventeen different directions and accusing the group of hypocrisy and elitism for some ten minutes. Throughout the tirade Maritza inspected her workman's boots and kept her jaw clenched, listening and in her mind cursing Pupi Malave. When he had finally talked himself out, Maritza explained that someone should have informed him more thoroughly. She shot a quick angry look at Angel Correa and told Pupi the matter would be taken up the following week at the Central Committee's criticism-self-criticism session. Pupi replied that he could respect the upcoming action of the Central Committee, but still felt burnt by the communications and maybe they all ought to reevaluate the leadership of some of the brothers *and* sisters.

It never failed, Maritza thought, whenever her turn came up to run the meeting, someone caught an attitude and plexed up. After some more grumbling from two other young men, she began reviewing the purpose of the meeting, that of deciding on a course of action concerning the detention of Armando Martinez for psychiatric observation. The word *like* crept into people's vocabulary as would fog, silently, unobtrusively during this difficult time in history. For Maritza Soto, the more difficult a situation became, the more complicated the issues, the greater the emotional tension, the more the word *like* appeared in her speech.

"Like they have him like locked up at Stuyvesant Hospital," she began. "And like let me remind you that imprisonment of our people is like nothing new for the imperialist war mongers. I mean, trumped-up charges are par for the course, but like this new tactic by the capitalist pigs is like an escalation of our oppression. Like Comrade Martinez is being held in this so-called hospital against his wishes and in violation of their own like capitalist constitution and like a team of psychiatrists is like working on his mind."

"Dig that shit!" Dorothy Robles, one of the young women, shouted.

Thankful for Dorothy's support, Maritza continued.

"Let me also remind you that our oppressors know their business. They're well aware that the person in question has very little political sophistication. I tried to see him but they claim he's not well enough to receive visitors. And like check this out. As strange and unbelievable as it sounds, the establishment lackeys and psychiatric running dogs of American imperialism claim that Armando Martinez is someone he's not."

"Run it, sister," said Pablo Irrizary, Dorothy Robles'current boyfriend.

"Right," shouted Maritza, responding to the encouragement and fighting the mounting hysteria. "This is serious, brothers and sisters. Not only is this a first-class lie but something we, as an oppressed people, should not tolerate under any circumstances. Like especially under the present system of colonialism."

Maritza went on to point out that *The New York Times* claimed that Armando Martinez was someone by the name of Frank Garboil and that he was a one time intelligence officer in the United States Army. Her voice rose and fell with emotion as she spoke. "Fine, beautiful, like let them roll out their propaganda machine, okay? Like that's expected, right? But like they're claiming that the brother confessed to this lie."

For the first time there was a sense of outrage in the group. This was an insult. No one doubted the existence of weakness in certain individuals among the people concerning their heritage. Some changed their name from Rivera to Rivers, from Torres to Tower, from Puente to Bridges. There was even the case of an insurance salesman by the name of Victor Colon, who learned that *colon* was not only a punctuation mark but the name of the large intestine. In order to rid people of the latter association he changed his name to Samuel. Whenever he met people he stuck out his hand and said: "Hi, I'm Sammy Colon." All of that could be forgiven. People were under such pressure in the society. But that one of their own would go to the extent of changing his name to Garboil? Impossible. What did he want to be, Jewish, or what? It had to be a lie, a fabrication to discredit their cause. The pigs, the lousy, rotten, imperialist, capitalist pigs.

Maritza held up her hand for order and went on speaking.

"Like there's no need to be shook, brothers and sisters. It's true that Comrade Martinez was in the imperialist army. Like he'll admit that himself, but like it bothers him to talk about it. The brother did a tour in Vietnam before his consciousness was raised in our student group at New Amsterdam College, right? So, like don't get me wrong. He's not like completely politicized, but like he shows promise, especially in the area of economic analysis. Right! Like the tactics of the bourgeois, capitalist pigs is like a new one. What they want to do is brainwash the brother and convince him that he's a yanqui, gringo pig, right?"

"Eggfugginsactly," someone said.

This did nothing to settle Maritza since the agreement came from the group which opposed her leadership.

"Yeah, well," Maritza said, noncommittally. "Like that's all I have to say and like the meeting is now open for suggestions."

It was really useless, she thought. The action to be taken had already been decided and yet they had to go through the charade of getting everyone's opinion. As she scanned the circle a number of hands were already up. Oh well, feeding time at the zoo.

"Yes, Chino," she said, acknowledging a thin, skeletal-looking young man.

Chino stood up, nodded defiantly a couple of times and, punctuating his words with downward stabs of his right hand, said that what was called for was a letter to the *Times* demanding they retract their statement.

"If they don't," he said, "we call for a boycott of the paper by all Spanish-speaking people."

"Right-ons" exploded from the group.

"Thank you, Chino," Maritza said, but inwardly groaned in desperation. Maybe Armando's friend, Vega, was right. Maybe the whole island thing was a front and they were all from another planet. What a mess. I mean where did their ideas come from. How many Spanish-speaking people read the *Times*, anyway? "Yes, Lucky," she said, pointing to a dapper, fashion model-looking young man in a huge afro.

Lucky got up, looked to his left and posing with one foot at an angle from the other said: "Yeah, well, like I know these people at NBC and they're like on top of what's happening and they're like always talking about what a great speaking voice I have, and that I really have a perceptive mind and like keen insights into the issues and like I really should start thinking seriously about a career in electronic journalism and whatnot, and like it's time I call in that little chip, because like they owe us."

"And?" Maritza said.

"And like they should be contacted and asked to investigate the issue."

"Thank you, Lucky. Yes, Ashanti."

"Yeah, like I go along with Lucky," said Ashanti, whose real name was Jesus. "Like not only television but radio. Disc jockeys are like the most powerful people in the world because they play popular music and that is how many cultural messages are transmitted to the people. So like I know this dude and like he can put on a whole hour of music dedicated to the struggle and maybe even interview some of the folks here."

More shouts of right on.

"Thank you, Ashanti."

John Chota listened to the different opinions and wondered what, other than sawdust, was in these people's brains. Mention of Martinez had twisted his gut into knots. What bothered him most right then, however, was that his instincts had proved wrong. The old men appeared harmless. They may have raised hell on the Island in their day, but they had shown up just for moral support to another hot air festival. Not wishing to dwell on his failure, his frustration was once again turned to his hatred for Martinez. What the hell did Maritza see in him, anyway? Okay, so he was over six feet tall, well built and wore his hair long. He didn't have such a big one for a guy that size. What was it with these radical bitches? He watched as one of the old men raised his hand. Maritza recognized him and the old man stood up.

"I don't know how true it is," the old man said. "It may be part of the propaganda these people throw at us, Comrade President." Oh no, thought Maritza, Comrade President? "The talk," the old man went on, "is that this young man, Comrade Martinez, is a hockey player. Is that true?"

"Yes, that is true," Maritza replied.

"Then, it is not a rumor."

"No, it is not a rumor."

"Very well, I have two questions. One, is the infiltration of this sport by our people a new strategy? And two, if that is the case, what does hockey have to do with our independence as a people?"

Maritza restrained herself from rolling her eyes up into her head and explained that there was no strategy involved, but that many different people were needed for a revolution. The old man countered by saying that, with all due respect, no genuine, patriotic son of the Island of Enchantment should be caught playing a game, any game, on ice. In his opinion ice hockey was a symbol of the cold blooded way yanquis had always treated their people. He had seen the game on television and although it appeared very chaotic there was great order and subtlety in its ultimate aim.

"And what is that, Comrade Alfredo?" Maritza asked as politely as she could.

"Yanqui domination," Alfredo replied. "Don't get me wrong. I believe political power comes from the barrel of a gun, and I'm not afraid of any man, young or old, but I also believe that this game is nothing but North American brutality and a way to keep the working class in line. The game is a yanqui enterprise."

"Like what the fuck isn't," whispered one of the young men.

"Yeah, man," said another more loudly. "Why doesn't this old turkey shut the fuck up and sit down."

Maritza shot the two young men a disapproving look and attempted to answer the old man.

"Like you brought out some very pertinent things," she said, which was the standard mollifier in the group when someone's words were less than to the point. "But like I want to remind you," Maritza continued, "that hockey is played in many socialist countries today."

"Not Cuba," the old man said.

Maritza ignored the remark. Even with the respect she had for the old revolutionaries, the old man was beginning to get on her nerves. One of the young men sitting next to the old guard tried to explain geography to one of them.

"Like Cuba doesn't have a cold climate," he said.

The old man ignored him.

"In the Soviet Union," Maritza said, trying a different tack, "the game was not known until twenty-five years ago, and like they're now Olympic and World Champions."

As soon as she began speaking Maritza knew bringing up the Soviet Union was a mistake. Within the group there were a couple of anti-Soviet fanatics. One of them immediately popped up.

"Yeah, well, maybe the old dude is right," he said. "Maybe the reality is that the game's pushed the Soviet Union into being soft on capitalism and oppressing other Socialist nations."

"Not Cuba," said Alfredo, the old man, who had sat back down.

"Wow, like I won't argue that point," Maritza countered, once more ignoring Alfredo. "But like let's get to the core of the issue, right? Like the game has its roots in Indian rituals, and like our own native Indians played a primitive form of the game before the imperialist Spaniards arrived to colonize them."

"Point of order," Alfredo said, bolting back up out of his seat.

"Yes, Comrade," Maritza said.

"There's no ice on the Island of Enchantment," Alfredo said. Someone tried to explain climate to the old man, but he said he knew more about climate than any of the young men. When he said this a couple of whispered boos floated lazily above the circle. When he heard them the veins stood out on his neck. "The important thing," he said through the faint booing, "is that because there's no ice on the Island, the game our Taino Indians played was like baseball. And it was the Spanish who sold the idea to the Yanquis."

"Yeah, and to the Mets," said another of the young men.

This remark did nothing to help the situation. Where had all the respect gone? This generation was nothing but a collection of long-haired *maricones*. In defense of his offended compatriot, another of the older men jumped up, removed his coat, rolled up his sleeves and challenged any of the young men to a fist fight. The challenge produced louder booing and derisive waves of the hand, some of them quite limp and their implication not unnoticed by the old men. Spanish, English and a mixture of the two shot forth from all sections of the circle, criss-crossing in the air like fireworks gone awry. Maritza Soto was now running around the circle calling for order. Not successful in quelling the anger and confusion, she retreated into the kitchen. When she returned she held a broom, which she raised above her head and with all the frustration she felt, banged on her chair. The sound of the broom hitting the metal was loud enough to startle everyone.

"Just shut up, okay?" she said. She was hyperventilating so badly that her face was splotched and her nostrils flared. "Like I wanna point out a couple of facts. One, like whether it was baseball or hockey that our ancestors played, it doesn't matter. Like the thing is that it was stolen from us, right? Two, if that's the case, then like all the brother is doing when he plays hockey is participating in one of our ancient rituals. Three, if the person being held in the hospital is one of our people, and there is no question in our minds that he is one of us, it's like our duty to help him in any way possible and by any means necessary. And four, like we're spending too much time arguing about irrelevant information and losing respect for each other in the process. Like the brother in Stuyvesant Hospital is like, wow, such a symbol of our imprisonment, both here in New York and on the Island."

The basement room had grown quiet as members of both groups reflected on Maritza's impassioned plea. The first one to speak was one of the young men. He tried speaking in Spanish but the words did not come easily and he reverted to English.

"Like the point I wanna bring out," he said, "is that I didn't join the Young Barons so that I could sit around and rap all night and get into like non-productive dialogue and whatnot while them jive-ass honkies have one of our brothers locked up, right?"

"Run it, Pee Wee," someone said.

"Right, so like we have to get our shit together and quit bull-jiving. The old dude was right when he said that power comes outta the barrel of a gun, you dig? In spite of all his off-the-wall shit that we all got plexed up with, the old dude is correct. We have to get into that so-called hospital and blow the pigs away and cut all this rhetorical jungle monkey shit out."

Shouts of "right on" exploded from the Young Barons. The old men appeared a little perplexed by the mixed message. Johnny Chota joined in the cheering in spite of the fact that the cheering and anger made him uncomfortable. Were they testing him again? Another of the old men, who had been sitting impassively during the shouting match, raised his hand and Maritza recognized him.

The old man stood up slowly. Of the four he appeared the most stately, the surest of his place in the meeting. He spoke solemnly, his speech filled with dramatic pauses.

"The first thing I want to do is congratulate the young comrade on his revolutionary spirit and his frankness concerning tonight's meeting. But let me be frank with all of you, young comrades. We must be very careful. Any action should be well planned. Any mistake could be fatal to the entire group."

For the first time that night, the Young Barons listened intently to one of the old *Plataneros*. Some even felt ashamed that they had ridiculed the old men. The feeling did not last. What next came out of the old man's mouth was enough to set back any revolution at least fifty years.

"Wasn't it the great Mao who once said: 'Float like a butterfly and sting like a bee?' "

"Oh shit," said one of the Young Barons.

"Here we go again," said another.

"Sit down and shut up," said a third.

This was too much lack of respect. The same old man who'd stood up to fight before once again jumped up and began removing his coat. His two comrades managed to get him back into his seat, but his face was beet red, that is purple, and he was breathing as if he'd just run up ten flights of stairs. One of the other old men immediately accused the Young Barons of attempting to provoke the man into having a heart attack. The Young Barons countered by saying that the old men were useless.

"If you have the answer," one of the Young Barons shouted, "how the fuck come we're still a motherfucking colony, turkey?"

This was too much for Maritza Soto. If she'd had her piece she would've shot somebody by now. What the hell was going on! Once again she seized her broom and began pounding on a chair. No one in the room paid the least bit of attention to the noise. She did manage to get their attention, however, when one of her downward swings of the broom hit a bare light bulb and sent it shattering against a steampipe above. The subsequent explosion, flying glass and sudden dimming of the lights sobered everyone, although considerable cursing ensued.

When the light bulb had been replaced and everyone was back in place, Chota spoke for the first time. His left eye blinked as he spoke and his voice, as always, was high pitched. The members of the Young Barons listened attentively, stilling for the moment their overriding suspicion that Pancho Miranda was a drug addict. Over a period of a year they had talked to him at length, checked his arms and legs and found no needle tracks. But there was still something not quite right with him. This suspicion caused a heavy silence as he spoke.

"You dig," he began, "I go along with what the brother says about caution, but I also agree with the brother who says we gotta hit the pigs and hit them quick. I'm not bragging or nothing but I know where we can get some automatic pieces and even hand grenades. I'm not saying we should go and shoot up the hospital, but we can use the shit to distract the pigs while we free the brother."

"Right on," shouted the Young Barons in unison.

"Once again Maritza called for order and spoke.

"Comrades, like please consider the implications. Like let's settle down and attack the problem dialectically. Like we're getting disunified again. We invited our older comrades because we thought we could work together towards a common goal, that of the release of our imprisoned comrade. Like the Central Committee did not take into consideration like a generation gap. Like some of our older comrades may not be caught up with all the new developments in the revolution, but like they're the ones who have been struggling all these years without recognition, like."

The Young Barons began grumbling again. It seemed the more they complained the more likes came out of Maritza's mouth. She hated it. What would happen if she suddenly burst into tears. They'd really have a case against her. But she pushed on.

"Like the thing you must understand is that our older comrades never got much media coverage here. And that may work to our advantage, right? Some of you may go on to become television reporters and disc jockeys, but it's the old guard that has sustained the revolution all these years. The *Plataneros,* right?"

"Yeah, the plantains," said a Young Baron.

"Yeah," said a few others.

Maritza ignored the dissent.

"I know some of you never met him because he's been in and out of prison all these years, but the Supreme Commander of the *Plataneros* is here tonight. He escaped last month and, rather than running from the struggle, he's returned to his people. He knows about our situation and the Central Committee has asked him to outline his strategy. That's why we called the group together."

Although astonished by the announcement, the overall feeling of the Young Barons and the *Plataneros* was one of doubt. Sensing this, Maritza put up her hands.

"Okay, all right, like I know you don't believe me," she said. "Just wait a minute and you'll see."

Having said this, she got up from her seat and retreated to the back of the room where she entered a door into the boiler room. As noisy and chaotic as the scene had been up to now, the basement room became hushed, the atmosphere one of reflection. Both young and old thought about their part in the animosity. How could they, within hearing range of such an inspirational and legendary force in their struggle, have behaved this way. How could they atone for their behavior, their disrespect and anger?

As they chastized themselves individually and determined to be better revolutionaries, he suddenly materialized. Before their eyes, svelte and looking taller than his five feet, three inches, stood their leader. Dressed in immaculate white pants and shoes, an embroidered *guayabera* and the sweeping straw hat of the Island's peasants, he resembled someone's invention of a hero more than a man. His face was tanned, highlighting his coal-black eyes and thick, silver moustache. His white hair flowed to his shoulders and he held a golden machete in his right hand. There he finally was: Don Alfonso Del Valle, El Falcon.

Time stopped, hearts skipped, breaths were held and the air seemed to stir as if a wind had gushed through a suddenly opened window. In his seat John Chota broke into a cold sweat and wished to be held by his mother.

CHAPTER 3

Within which we, as it is oftentimes expressed in the vernacular, begin to observe a thickening of the plot, get a glimpse at the lachrymose school of electronic journalism, meet a blonde, and are introduced to the main character as he struggles against the forces of sanity.

The story of Armando Martinez surfaced in a couple of lines written in a sports column of the *Daily News*. According to the columnist the star left wing of the New Amsterdam College hockey team was out indefinitely with what appeared to be deep personal problems. The item went unnoticed for two weeks by the rest of the media. On Christmas Eve Eye Witness News picked up the story. One of its reporters, coincidentally a Puerto Rican, appeared on the six o'clock news. His forehead wrinkled and his eyes filled with the piety that must come when one is about to administer the last rites to the entire Borough of Brooklyn, he pleaded his case.

"In my years as a television reporter, I've never run into anything quite like this story. This is the tale of a young Puerto Rican who recently began his education at New Amsterdam College of the City University of New York after serving two years in Vietnam. His name is Armando Martinez and, from what I've been able to gather thus far, his one love is the game of ice hockey. We weren't able to talk with the young man, but we did talk with his doctors at Stuyvesant Hospital."

And then the reporter, mike in hand, wounded by the calamity, socially concerned in his matching Levi jeans suit, approached two doctors. They were standing in a hospital corridor, outside a large room. Through the glass on the upper half of the door a gleaming white floor could be seen. Periodically a loud thumping was heard within.

"Doctor Kopfeinlaufen, what seems to be the trouble with Armando?"

On the screen appeared a closeup of a sixty year old, pudgy, balding man. Electronically printed, the words *Dr. Dieter Kopfeinlaufen* were momentarily seen at the bottom of the picture. The doctor spoke with a pronounced German accent.

"Well, it's quite simple. It's an identity crisis. The young man is Puerto Rican, and he attempted to play a sport which is basically a northern sport. Finns, Swedes, Norwegians, Germans, Canadians and Russians, because of the cold, adapt quite well to the strain. It's also a cultural matter. Psychologically, there are cultural defenses to deal with, pressures of the game. These seem to be absent in the young man."

The other doctor, who was wearing a blue turban, looked on impassively. The reporter cut into Dr. Kopfeinlaufen's explanation and shoved the microphone under the turbaned doctor's nose.

"Isn't it true, Dr. Kohonduro, that Armando Martinez claims he's not Puerto Rican?"

"That is absolutely correct," said the doctor in a melodic voice.

"And to what is this attributed?" asked the reporter.

The doctor thought for a moment as the camera closed in. Beneath the closup we see: *Dr. Rapudiman Kohonduro*, in green letters.

"It is obvious that he is seeking a resolution with himself. If he is who he claims to be, he does not have to return to his school and face the rigors of playing ice hockey. Somehow, deep in his psyche there is an association between the game and his combat experiences. This dilemma has thrown him into deep psychic conflict, do you see? The more he plays the game, the closer he comes to having to recall combat. It is not uncommon for people under extreme stress to adopt a new identity in order to cope."

"Is there any hope for recovery?" the reporter asked dolefully.

"Oh yes, there is always hope," replied Doctor Kopfeinlaufen. "Just inside is the answer. We have created what I call a TDE. It is one of several in the hospital, each designed to meet the needs of the patient."

"Could you explain the purpose of the TDE. What does it mean?"

"Most certainly. TDE stands for Total Detraumatizing Environment and it was designed to help the patient relive his trauma. It is absolutely sealed and sterile and receives a constant infusion of pure oxygen through specially controlled vents. The oxygen activates the blood and speeds up cathartic output."

"And you say we can't film inside or talk with Armando?"

"No, absolutely not. He is not ready for that kind of exposure. Only yesterday we had a small breakthrough." The doctor chuckled. "It seems minor and rather comic, but it is nevertheless a sign."

"Yes, quite remarkable," said Dr. Kohonduro. "The patient asked for banana ice cream."

The reporter looked from one doctor to the other, perplexed.

"Can you explain further?"

"It's the beginning of an integration process," said Dr. Kopfeinlaufen. "The two cultures at hand coming together at their most primal level, that of oral gratification."

The reporter thanked the doctors, they nodded and disappeared beyond the door of the TDE. There was then a closeup of the reporter.

"And there you have it, folks. From Stuyvesant Hospital this is Reynaldo Nevera, Eye Witness News."

The picture switched back to the studio and a closeup of the reporter sitting at his desk. He was shaking his head and seemingly on the verge of tears.

"If there is anyone out there who has information or is a friend or relative of Armando Martinez, please call this number." The number flashes on the screen as he repeats it. "I promise to meet with you privately. So far no one, relative or friend, has come forth in response to this tragedy. Please help. Even on the eve of one of the most joyous of occasions, the city seems oblivious to the plight of people like Armando Martinez."

The camera switched to the anchorman.

"A Lithuanian cookie bake, another look at 'Further Inside Wanda Lovelass,' and the rest of the sports when Eye Witness News continues."

The screen dissolved into a laxative commercial in which an elderly matron is accosted by a pharmacist.

Frank Garboil's room at Stuyvesant Hospital was not what one might call an average hospital room. For one it was larger than most. In a short period of time the staff assigned to his case had converted the top floor solarium of the hospital into a replica of a hockey rink. The floor had been painted a gleaming white and marked off with the appropriate lines and circles needed in order to play the game. Dasher boards had been built around the simulated ice surface and the temperature kept at a constant forty-five degrees. At both ends of the room regulation size hockey nets had been installed, lending the room another touch of authenticity. The converted solarium had been wired to support a public address system, goal lights behind the boards at each end of the rink, and a scoreboard, operated by Ingrid Konkruka, a rather imposing six-foot-tall Swedish, blonde physical therapist. Nurse Konkruka had been imported directly from one of the most famous clinics in the U.S. at Dr. Kopfeinlaufen's request.

"It is the ultimate confrontation," he'd said to his colleague, Dr. Kohonduro, when she first arrived at the hospital. "The feminine personification of the North. One way or the other, the patient will have to face himself and this hockey business. We must work from all angles. Not only the mind but the body as well."

The public address system was operated by the fourth member of the staff, Helen Christianpath, a missionary turned social worker. She was thirty-five years of age, thin and dry, but with a love more boundless than the universe. She was a virgin, or at least considered herself so, this, after being entered repeatedly each day for a period of two years by the Coolobibo Indians of Brazil's Matto Grosso where she had gone on her first assignment as a missionary. They believed it was their duty to make the thin, odd looking woman healthier, fuller and more alive. In spite of their efforts Helen Christianpath persevered and never once allowed herself to gain pleasure from the experience nor to believe that anything malicious had occurred. For the next ten years she worked in far off places, enduring illness and travail. The Sudan, Singapore, Jakarta, Kuala Lampur, Katmandu and Easter Island. Wherever she was needed, she went. Her fame was worldwide and it was Dr. Kohonduro who had heard of her from English missionaries in Madras and who wrote to the New World Beacon Mission and asked for her services.

"She is a completely tolerant person," had explained the younger Dr. Kohonduro to his colleague, Dr. Kopfeinlaufen. "She knows the complexities of the mind common to the dark people of the world, but most of all she knows the wild, untamed spirit which inhabits it at times."

"Yes, doctor," replied Kopfeinlaufen. "She is also rather undernourished."

"It is only the suffering and tribulation. Did you see Gandhi at the end? He was physically consumed but true in spirit."

"That, my friend, is a different story," argued Dr. Kopfeinlaufen. "Gandhi was a holy man. This woman is virtually an apparition."

"She will work miracles."

"Perhaps. From a dialectical point of view, it is worth a try. She is certainly a contrast to Nurse Konkruka."

"We won't fail," said Dr. Kohonduro. "The spirit, the mind and the body working in harmony."

In the three weeks Frank Garboil had spent in the hospital he had remained silent. Around a week before Christmas he began responding to greetings from Ingrid Konkruka, who had urged him to help her trim a small Christmas tree. At her insistence large posters of hockey stars had been put up on the walls, along with pennants from every National Hockey League team. Garboil began to be secretly amused by the friendliness and enthusiasm of this giant Florence Nightingale and rewarded her efforts with compliance to her wishes.

Now, as the doctors entered the room for their evening session with him, Garboil eyed them with contempt, particularly Dieter Kopfeinlaufen, attired in full goalie equipment. Garboil was suddenly seized with the urge to grab a hockey stick from the dozen near his bed and attack the doctor. Instead he lay back on the bed and resigned himself to the ordeal. He looked almost boyish except for the full, drooping black moustache. His dark eyes seemed unusually sad as he looked at Ingrid Konkruka for support. She came to him and patted his hand.

"Cheer up," she said.

He nodded and watched the nurse glide across the floor to take her place at the scorer's table. Dr. Kopfeinlaufen approached the bed, pulled the face mask down over his face and tapped the goalie pads with his stick.

"When can I go home, Doc?" Garboil asked.

"That's not up to me," replied the doctor. "You incurred the penalty and you must stay in the penalty box. Talk with the referee."

Dr. Kohonduro, second in command to Dieter Kopfeinlaufen, joined the conversation. As usual, he was dressed in his striped referee's shirt and one of his turbans. That night the turban was yellow. The combined smells of ginger, cloves and turmeric were especially strong that night as he spoke. His speech was clipped like that of an Englishman, but with the lilting of his Indian background.

"We'll have the faceoff now, Armando," he said. "You be a good fellow and play a fair game. No penalties, please."

Frank Garboil laughed sarcastically.

"Oh, why don't you cut it out. I already told you. It was all a joke."

From his end of the room, Dr. Kopfeinlaufen chuckled.

"That is very funny. Did you hear that, Dr. Kohonduro? Young man, this is no laughing matter."

Garboil sat up in bed.

"Jesus Christ! Stop it. My name's Frank Garboil and I teach economics at Frick University in Long Island. At least I did. It was just something I had to prove to myself."

Dr. Kohonduro intervened once more.

"Please cooperate, Mr. Martinez. Do be a good chap. Now, when I blow the whistle, start telling us everything that happened. Please direct all your remarks to Dr. Kopfeinlaufen. If you feel any hostility you would do well to direct it at him. As you can see, he is well protected. If I feel you are not being truthful I will blow the whistle to let you know that you have iced the puck, that is, that you have decided to shut off your emotions, or gone off sides, meaning that you are digressing. Is that understoood?"

"Aw go scratch a cobra's ass!" Garboil shouted.

Dr. Kohonduro ignored the remark and signaled Helen Christianpath. The lights dim and the proud musical strength of the Star Spangled Banner filled the room. When the anthem was over, recorded cheering took over, and then Helen Christianpath's voice was heard over the public address system.

"Good evening ladies and gentlemen and welcome once again to the Bronx Ice Palace where tonight the New Amsterdam College Golden Hawks face the Saint Basil College Fighting Saints."

More recorded cheering. The lights went up and the buzzer signaled the start of the session.

"Now, how did this whole thing begin? Was it in Vietnam?"

"I've never been in Vietnam," Garboil said. "I was in the Army for a year in 1957. I was stationed in Fort Dix. Check it out. They'll tell you."

"We did check it," replied Kohonduro, his whistle at the ready. "They have no record of Frank Garboil."

"I was in an intelligence outfit. Code name Paddywhacker."

"They have no record of that code name. We have checked Army intelligence. Why don't you be a good chap and tell us exactly what happened."

Garboil's eyes narrowed with anger and he spit out the words.

"Your sister sucks bandicoot peckers, Doc."

Kohonduro immediately blew his whistle, and for the first time in the case his fine, dark features contorted out of proportion at the insult. He spoke rapidly in Hindi for several seconds but quickly regained his composure.

"Penalty," he said, making a turning motion with thumb and forefinger. "You miss the Rangers-North Stars game tomorrow night. No television."

"Good going," yelled Kopfeinlaufen from his position in goal. He tapped his stick on the ice-like floor in the traditional ice hockey player's applause. Frank Garboil looked at the hockey sticks and started to get up from bed, but thought better of it when Nurse Konkruka winked at him to go along with the treatment.

"All right," he said. "I'll tell you what happened."

"Very well," said Kopfeinlaufen.

"Excellent," said Kohonduro.

Christianpath's look was positively beatific. Konkruka was simply amused.

Frank Garboil slipped further down on the bed, closed his eyes and began talking.

CHAPTER 4

Out of which one may draw certain conclusions regarding the influence of sports on the psyche of males reared in North American society, experience nostalgic indigestion from romanticizing about New York City neighborhood sports and begin superficial explications of the main character's existential dilemma.

I guess what happened to Frank Garboil could've happened to anybody. Every guy who's played sports feels like making a comeback after he retires. Whether he's a professional, an amateur or a neighborhood player, an athlete, after retirement, always thinks he can return to his old form and give it one more try. Take Joey the Moose. That wasn't his real name but everyone called him Joey the Moose. His real name was Joseph Anthony DeMuse. Anyway, back in 1950 around St. Mary's Park in the Bronx there was a group of boys who called themselves the Rebels. Almost every one of them was the perfect street athlete. To a man they had heart and what they didn't have in muscle or skill they made up for in brains. Not that any of them ever brought home an Excellent on his report card. Far from it. Most of them did lousy work the first eight or ten years of school and were constantly in trouble with the nuns at St. Luke's. Later they settled down and with a few exceptions did pretty well, including Frankie, before the whole thing started with him.

The Rebels, though, were something. If it was football season, the Rebels had a team. If the recreation center at St. Mary's Park had a swimming meet or a billiards tournament it was the Rebels who walked away with the trophies. Softball, baseball, basketball, off-the-wall (a game which has nothing to do with attitudes), stickball, stoopball, Johnny-on-the-pony, kick-the-can, chinese tag, played either with a cardboard box or for those not faint of heart with a metal milk crate. You name it, the Rebels were the champs. Even today, if you asked Bones Friedenberg, the big Queens bookie, how he got started, he'll tell you he did it by betting on the Rebels. He'd tell you he could give any odds and still come out a winner.

One year the Rebels even accepted a challenge from Peggy Rattigan's sister, Maureen, to double-dutch because she caught Mousey O'Hara kissing a Puerto Rican girl down on Willis Avenue and threatened to tell Mousey's mother. The only way they could get Mousey out of the mess was to go right to Maureen's power. That was the way the Rebels did things when faced with a challenge.

Of course the guy they picked was Joey the Moose because Joey could do anything better than any of them. He was the true athlete in the group. Truly remarkable. He wasn't the biggest of the Rebels but he always came through with a clutch performance. As long as it was a game, you could count on Joey. And the better or tougher the competition, the more he rose to the occasion. It was a thing of beauty to see him weaving in and out of tackles or watch him scale a playground fence to rob someone of an extra base hit or a homerun.

But the business with Maureen Rattigan was something else. It wasn't that he couldn't skip rope. That was simple. Joey trained for the Golden Gloves every year and once even went into the semis only to come up with a sprained wrist from hitting a kid from Harlem. So Joey could skip rope. It was Maureen Rattigan who fouled things up by insisting that the contest be held in public and thoroughly advertised in the neighborhood.

"P.S. 65, in the schoolyard at lunchtime," she said. "And everybody knows."

The school was right across the street from Mrs. Cohen's Candy Store where the older guys who'd gotten kicked out of school and worked in the neighborhood as apprentices hung out.

They always went to the Polo Grounds and knew Whitey Lockman and Blackie Dark personally. This group included Bones Friedenberg, who, at sixteen, was already taking bets on anything you could think of, whether it was the exact weight of a rock in the park or the color of Kitty Shaughnessy's panties. Anybody of any importance in the world of neighborhood sports would be in attendance.

They tried everything in the book to get Maureen to change her mind and not tell Mousey's mother about Minerva Fuentes, but Maureen refused to budge. The Rebels even promised her a tryout with their softball team but she turned them down.

"Youse guys owe me something and it ain't no tryout," she said, reminding them of the times she had been excluded from games because she was a girl. "Wait till I tell Mrs. O'Hara about My Nervy Fountains or whatever her friggin spic name is."

"Oh yeah?" said Mousey O'Hara. "You tell my mother and I'll beat the shit out of you."

"Oh yeah? You wish. I'll tell my sister, Pegeen, and she'll tell Charlie and you'll get suspended from the team and then I'll beat the shit out of *you*."

Charlie O'Brien was their coach and idol. He'd played tackle at Cardinal Hayes High School for three years and almost got a scholarship to Notre Dame. The only thing Maureen agreed to was that she wouldn't talk to Mrs. O'Hara until the dispute was settled one way or the other. But Mousey had to gain an advantage in order to even things up. Maureen Rattigan, in spite of being a girl, was probably as good an athlete as half of the Rebels. At the age of thirteen, already starting to show the shape she was to have as a woman, she could still outrun and outfight most of the boys her age. But she lacked one thing which most of the Rebels had learned years before—control over their emotions in a tense situation. Any little thing rattled Maureen. Mousey knew this and began working on her.

"Oh yeah?" he said. "You're just sore 'cause even if you was a guy we could beat you at anything."

"Oh yeah?" Maureen said, balling up her fists.

"Yeah," Mousey said. "We could even beat you at hopscotch."

Maureen's eyes lit up for a moment so that green flecks of fire seemed to jump out of them, scaring Mousey, except that he wouldn't let on.

"You see," said Mousey in an apparent nonsequitur, but playing his cards carefully. "Your're already pissing in your pants you're so scared."

"Yeah?" Maureen said. There was an evil look in her eyes that made Mousey think of his mother blocking out the light from inside the apartment when she stood at the door threatening to kick him out of the house once and for all. "What about double-dutch?"

The words knocked Mousey off balance for a moment.

"Double dutch?"

"Yeah, double dutch, moron," Maureen replied.

"With my eyes closed, Rattigan," Mousey shot back.

"In the school yard at lunchtime," Maureen said.

"In the park after school."

"Yeah, wise guy?" Maureen said through clenched teeth. "You wanna have it in the park at night with all the guys there so nobody knows and you can come back and tell the whole block you won. In the school yard at lunchtime, or I go up and tell your mother how you was french kissing that niggah."

"She's not a niggah," Mousey replied. "She's a spic. I told you already. There's a difference."

"Not if you're mother finds out," said Maureen Rattigan and walked away towards Beekman Avenue.

"Hey, hold it, Rattigan," Mousey shouted, running after her. "This is a sport, right?"

"What?" said Maureen, turning to face him. "What did you say?"

"I said, it's a sport," Mousey answered. "You know, skipping rope is a sport."

"Of course it's not a sport, stupid," Maureen replied, looking down her nose at Mousey, who at fourteen could still get into the movies for under 12. It's rope jumping. It's not a friggin sport."

"Well, it's rope jumping when girls do it," said Mousey, calmly. "But when guys do it it's a sport."

Maureen Rattigan's wheels stopped turning and then suddenly the anger sort of rose from her feet all the way up to the crown of her head so that her wiry red hair looked as if it had caught fire.

"You're trying to trick me, Mousey O'Hara," she said, fighting for control.

"No, I'm not," said Mousey apologetically, knowing he had her.

But Maureen wouldn't buy it. Right there in the middle of 141st Street she started yelling.

"Mrs. O'Hara, Mrs. O'Hara, your son, Francis, was down on Willis Avenue with . . . "

"For crying out loud," said Mousey. "Shut up. You did it again."

Maureen stopped yelling and a look of cold fear came over her freckled face.

"I did what?" she said.

"You broke off the agreement," Mousey said. "You broke the contract."

"What agreement? What friggin contract?"

"Not to speak to my mother."

"Mother of God," said Maureen and almost dropped to her knees in front of the Emerald Store.

"It's off, Rattigan," Mousey said calmly, playing his last ace. "It's off. No double-dutch. I'll see you around."

Maureen grabbed his arm and spun him around.

"Hold it, O'Hara," she said. "Not so fast. It's not off. Nobody heard it."

"Whatta ya mean nobody heard it," said Mousey, turning his anger on her with full knowledge that whatever you could say about Maureen Rattigan, she was an honest Catholic girl.

"Nobody heard me, O'Hara," she said. "Your mother went to the butcher and she's not back yet."

"So what," snapped Mousey. "You broke the agreement. Halligan's sitting right up there in his fire escape right now, copying everything down. He's been scouting you since yesterday. It's off. See ya."

Maureen looked up and there was Kevin Halligan sitting on the second floor escape, peering down at them through his thick glasses and writing furiously in a notebook. Kevin was a bookworm. He studied everything and for this reason was feared by everyone on the block. He also had a couple of uncles that had fought in the IRA. Although Kevin couldn't throw a Spaldeen from one sewer to the next without hitting a building, he was respected by the Rebels for his great memory and the accuracy of his reports. He was so smart that one time, when Greenberg, the kosher butcher, hit Timmy Henry on the head with a bag of chicken guts for calling him a kike, Kevin made one of his Bazooka bombs and blew out Greenberg's window.

When a bunch of the Rebels went and told Kevin about it, he peered at them, nodded and said he'd take care of it. Nobody saw him for the rest of the day but later they found out he'd gone to the other side of St. Mary's Park to see Orsino, who provided the neighborhood with firecrackers. He came back to the block after dark when Greenberg had closed his store and gone upstairs. Kevin had everyone chew bubble gum until all the sugar was gone and then collected it. The wad came to the size of a softball. He then went into a bag and brought out about a dozen packages of firecrackers. This was all in the yard of P.S. 65 under the light from the lamppost on Powers Avenue. He then put all the fuses on the packages together, flattened out the bubble gum, and keeping the whole mess warm under his arm, he told everyone to wait for him across the street from Greenberg's.

Johnny McGuire and Mikey Flynn volunteered to go with him, but Kevin shook his head and went through the hole in the fence at the end of the school yard and towards St. Mary's Park, away from Greenberg's. Matty Donovan, who was only twelve and had just started hanging around with the Rebels, made the mistake of yelling at Kevin that Greenberg's was the other way. For his breach of etiquette he got smacked on the back of the head about six times by Johnny McGuire, his cousin.

Everyone waited across the street from Greenberg's for about ten minutes and then here came Kevin Halligan down Cypress Avenue from the opposite direction. He had gone down Powers Avenue, turned at St. Mary's Street, to Jackson Avenue and back to Cypress Avenue. He went past Greenberg's shop, looked back up the street to make sure a squad car wasn't coming and ducked into the entrance to the store. Squatting down so you could hardly see him, he put the firecrackers up against a corner of the plate glass window and covered them with the warm wad of bubble gum. He waited until the bubble gum hardened in the cold, lit the fuse and then ran across the street to join the Rebels, huddled in a doorway. By the time he got inside, the fuse hit the powder and Cypress Avenue lit up like it was day. The explosion wasn't like that of firecrackers, one exploding after the other but one loud bang as if someone had dropped a bomb from above. All the glass blew in, slicing salamis and beheading bled chickens where it hit. The cops showed up about ten minutes later but by that time the Rebels were scattered all over the neighborhood. No one had seen anything and Greenberg blamed it on the Puerto Ricans, of whom there were none for blocks around.

So Kevin Halligan was not only smart but he had guts and was therefore respected by the Rebels. With Maureen Rattigan shaking her head, Mousey O'Hara yelled up at Kevin and asked him if he'd gotten everything. Kevin nodded professionally from his perch and went on writing. Among his duties as an administrative member of the Rebels, it was his responsibility to make detailed reports on any opponent the team was to encounter.

Nobody asked him to do it. He just took it on himself one day when the Rebels were playing football against the Knights, a team from the other side of the park. Kevin climbed up a tree and figured out from the way the Knights' quarterback was planting his feet who he was going to hand off to. He came down and told Charlie O'Brien, the Rebels' coach. The Rebels were losing at the time, but after half-time, armed with Kevin's report, the Knights were stopped cold and the Rebels won.

When Maureen Rattigan realized what had taken place she lost any reserve she had left and began screaming and pulling crazily at her red hair. They had done it again. She couldn't contain herself. They wouldn't let her play on their team because she was a girl. Even when she was little they made fun of her because she could roller skate faster than them and jump higher and run faster. She picked up an empty milk crate from the front of the Emerald Store and flung it at Mousey O'Hara. The milk crate struck Mousey on the shins, sending him down to the sidewalk writhing in apparent pain. In no time most of the Rebels were on the scene and Kevin Halligan, notebook in hand, was completing his report.

Jimmy O'Brien's brother, Charlie, their coach, was just coming into the block from his job with the railroad when he heard the commotion and rushed over. The whole matter became a disaster for Maureen since she now had to face Charlie, who was not only the Rebels' coach but her sister Peggy's husband.

"What's the trouble?" Charlie said. "Maureen, what are you doing here? Beat it."

"Hold it, Charlie," said Kevin Halligan, coming forward to lend an air of authority to the crowd of kids, which had now grown and included Maureen's sidekicks, Ann Gorman and Flora Burkheimer. "This has to do with Maureen. She threw a milk crate at O'Hara," Kevin said, pointing at Mousey, who was still lying on the sidewalk moaning and holding his ankle. Charlie O'Brien told Mousey to get up and try walking around. Mousey struggled to his feet, tried to take a couple of steps but stumbled and began groaning that it hurt too much. Some of the Rebels helped him to a stoop and Mousey sat there, rubbing his ankle and glaring at Maureen Rattigan who had become very nervous and pale.

After an hour of arguments and counter-arguments, the mess was finally untangled. Maureen had gone back on her word, but it wasn't serious enough to cancel Mousey's challenge. Of course Mousey had sustained an injury to his ankle and wouldn't be able to jump. It was now a matter of deciding who was going to do the jumping and when. As luck would have it, Belle Howitzer, who was studying engineering at City College, came down from her house to buy a half a pound of liverwurst from Klein's Deli on the corner of Beekman Avenue and joined the discussion. Well, she didn't join the discussion right away. She listened for about fifteen minutes. Belle was a natural arbitrator. At nineteen she was already a junior in college, held the chess championship of the school, and for a number of years had umpired or refereed most of the neighborhood's major sports events. She had the perfect temperament for settling disputes. But it wasn't her brains, her common sense or even her calm that impressed a person upon meeting Belle. It was her size. She was well over six feet tall and all muscle so that in the winter, when you saw her coming down the street dressed in dungarees and work shoes, wearing a Mackinaw, you could swear it was somebody coming to fix the plumbing.

When she finally spoke she explained that since the agreement had been violated, the Rebels could either have the contest postponed or make a decision about who was going to jump. Everyone already knew this but Belle's deep voice and seriousness made it sound like a new idea. Everyone nodded and said "good idea."

"Why not Mousey?" asked Ann Gorman, standing next to Maureen. "He's the one that challenged Maureen."

"Yeah, he's probably faking," said Flora Burkheimer.

"All right," said Belle. "Let's look at his ankle."

Everyone crowded around the stoop where Mousey was sitting.

"Lift up your pant leg, O'Hara," said Belle.

Mousey looked up at Charlie O'Brien.

"Do as she says," Charlie said.

Mousey rolled up his pant leg, wincing as he did so.

"Roll down your sock," Belle said.

Mousey did as he was told. The ankle looked fine, not a mark on it. When Belle touched it, however, Mousey stiffened in pain and named Jesus and his parents and then called on the Blessed Mother to save him from the pain.

"That's it," said Belle. "It's probably an internal fracture."

"He's faking," said Flora Burkheimer.

"Yeah," said Ann Gorman.

"Shh," said Maureen.

"The best thing," said Belle, "would be for the Rebels to name a designated jumper."

"A what?" said Flora Burkheimer.

"A designated jumper," Belle repeated. "Someone who can jump instead of O'Hara. How does that sound, Maureen?"

"Yeah, okay," Maureen said, in a little girl's voice. She had cooled off and was worried that Charlie would tell Peggy what'd happened and she'd tell their mother.

"Is that all right, O'Hara?" Belle asked.

"Yeah, sure," Mousey said.

Every one of the Rebels cheered and rushed up to Mousey to pat him on the back. He smiled sort of weakly but there was a glint of triumph in his eyes.

"You better have that ankle looked at," Belle said to Charlie O'Brien.

"Right," Charlie said. "You wait right here, O'Hara. I'm going up to get the car keys. McGuire, go tell O'Hara's mother that he twisted his ankle and I'm taking him to Lincoln Hospital for x-rays."

"Right, coach," said Johnny McGuire and went running up the street.

The crowd broke up, but that evening there was a meeting on the stoop of 598. After much bickering the nominations came down to Joey and Moose and Frankie Garboil. Next to Joey, Frankie was probably the best athlete in the group. Charlie O'Brien always said that Frankie had more potential than Joey, but that Frankie lacked desire. It wasn't that he didn't have heart but he was moody, like something was wrong and he didn't want anybody to know about it. About the only time Frankie came out of his private world and joined the others was when the subject was hockey. The rest of the time he was in a dream world. He performed adequately in the games but his mind was somewhere else.

The first time anybody on the block saw Frankie was when the Rebels were all about eleven and hadn't yet formed a team. They were throwing a football back and forth in the street and here came this kid on roller skates, pushing a roll of black tape with a worn hockey stick. He wasn't just skating leisurely, but coming full blast like he was on a breakaway, his dark eyes shining and his black curly hair flying in the autumn wind. All the other boys stopped playing and watched in sheer wonder. The only one who moved was Tommy Reardon, who was a hockey nut. He got down in front of a sewer in the middle of the street like he was Chuck Rayner playing goal for the New York Rangers. Frankie didn't even break stride. Right there, in the middle of Beekman Avenue, he made one of the most beautiful moves you ever saw. He faked to one side, gave Tommy Reardon the roll of tape for a fraction of a second, pulled it away, and by the time Tommy realized what happened Frankie had put the puck behind him.

Nobody moved as they watched the strange kid go by the sewer, his stick raised high, and make a turn, very low to the ground. He retrieved the roll of tape and stood tapping it back and forth with his stick. Tommy Reardon got up beaming as he dusted the rear of his pants. The other boys finally came over to

Frankie and pretty soon they were taking turns using his stick and shooting the puck.

Inside of a week the rest of the boys were playling roller hockey in the street. But as they grew older they got away from hockey and began concentrating on football.

In any case, on the stoop of 598 a vote was taken and Joey the Moose became a designated jumper. Not being chosen didn't bother Frankie Garboil. He took it like everything else, without any show of emotion.

When it came down to the final showdown in the case of Rattigan vs. O'Hara, or to put it more in perspective, the Rebels against poor Maureen Rattigan, it was no contest. Joey the Moose defeated Mauren 4-6, 6-2, 10-12, 6-0, 6-3. But the score doesn't reflect the strategy used by the Rebels. At the end of the third set, Kevin Halligan, nearsighted but ever on the alert, filed an official protest with the judges. You have to understand that in double-dutch one long rope is doubled so that the jumper is alternately jumping two ropes. The activity demands not only great physical stamina and agility but tremendous concentration. Any lapse in maintaining perfect rhythm and the rope is flicked, stopping it. At the end of the third set, which was a long and drawn out "jump," Kevin Halligan walked over to Belle Howitzer and Danny Moran, who was studying at Fordham Law School, the judges for the event, and pointed out to them that Maureen Rattigan was purposely distracting Joey the Moose and that she should make more of an effort to keep her skirt just above the knee. Belle Howitzer and Danny Moran ruled in the Rebels' favor and Joey the Moose won the match. Even with Ann Gorman and Flora Burkheimer, the best double-dutch rope handlers in the South Bronx, it was no contest. They tried to throw off Joey's timing. Nothing worked. At the end of the match Maureen shook hands with Joey the Moose, glared at Mousey O'Hara, who had made a remarkable recovery less than twenty-four hours after his injury, and together with Ann Gorman and

Flora Burkheimer went up to Flora's house to eat German potato salad and drink root beer.

Two weeks later, as Mousey O'Hara was walking past the synagogue on Beekman Avenue about nine in the evening, a brick fell on him, barely missing his head but bruising a bone in his right shoulder. This injury made him miss the Saint Mary's Park Recreation Center Indoor Shuffle Board Tournament in which he was a favorite. Mousey O'Hara blamed it on the Jews, but it was common knowledge that Maureen Rattigan had gotten her revenge. Kathleen Murphy, whom Mousey had spurned for Minerva Fuentes of Willis Avenue, did live next to the synagogue and was a friend of Maureen Rattigan. The neighborhood began coming apart right around that time. The Korean War was in full bloom and it seemed as if each week someone else was going into the service. Some of the Rebels tried to join but were too young. By 1954, at the end of the war, everyone had drifted away, their families moving further up into the Bronx or out to Queens to get away from Puerto Ricans, who appeared to be edging closer and closer. It was like they had come out of the river overnight and just kept moving into apartments vacated by the dead. At least that's the way Mr. Anderson, the janitor of P.S. 65 and the only black man anyone had ever seen in the neighborhood, explained it.

"They comes in ships down in Manhattan and they just swims up the river," he said. "Babies and all. Just like river rats. It's a disgrace."

Most of the Rebels eventually did go into the service, came back, got married, started working as cops and firemen or for the railroad. Some went to school on the G.I. Bill and were never heard from again. Others kept popping up from time to time. Francis X O'Hara (Mousey) married Minerva Fuentes, who became a social worker. He worked for the telephone company, went to school at night, got a degree in social work and became the director of a community center in Queens. Kevin Halligan became a public relations man for a soccer team in Portugal.

Maureen Rattigan ran away with a sailor and ended up in San Diego teaching tennis at a high school. And there were tragedies. Tommy Reardon became a cop, got married and was shot one night stopping a holdup a year later. Belle Howitzer graduated *Magna Cum Laude* from City College, couldn't find work in the States and went to Israel to live in a kibbutz. She helped build irrigation works in the Negev and died one night after single-handedly fighting off about two dozen Arabs. A monument was erected on the spot and it is called appropriately: the Howitzer Monument. It shows Belle holding a Sten gun, muscles rippling from her shorts and shirt and her jaw set in brave defiance.

Somehow or other all the desire and heart of the Rebels was put to use. Sports became something to watch or play at on Saturdays and Sundays, each year the weekend afternoons becoming shorter and less frequent. A few guys held on, playing regularly for softball or touch football teams in their new neighborhoods, betting two and three dollars a man and looking forward more to the time afterward at the saloon than the games. And even then, wherever they lived, the Rebels behaved with the same kind of poise they had when they played the big games back in the old neighborhood. If there were any errors, they were now mental lapses, due for the most part to worries about mortgages, car payments or tuition for the children at the parochial schools.

Once in a while guys would run into each other, have a few beers and recall the old days. They'd make tentative invitations to come to one another's neighborhood to play softball or touch but the excuses were always the same. Nobody had played for years. The truth was that they played once in a while, but were embarrassed to admit that the old fire was gone.

Joey the Moose tried a comeback. Sean Rafferty ran into him once at a Mets game. Joey had gained about fifty pounds, owned his own butcher shop and had married a fine Italian girl from Brooklyn. He had a couple of good looking boys with him and laughed a lot when Sean asked him to come up to Riverdale for a softball game. This was in 1969, and Joey was now thirty-two years old. He thought of Willie Mays almost forty and still going and decided to give it a try. He hadn't had a bat in his hands in almost three years, the business and the family taking up most of his time. His boys were still too young to play sports seriously so he had contented himself with going to Shea Stadium to watch the Mets play whenever he had a chance. But he still felt like competing. He showed up and even though it was obvious that he was badly out of shape he didn't embarrass himself.

On the way back to Brooklyn Joey recalled the brisk, fall days when he could outrun everyone on the football field. An accepting sadness enveloped him. That night after his wife had fallen asleep beside him he cried, knowing he could never again recapture those times. He had given it all he had then and missed the feeling. He made up his mind to lose weight and return to Riverdale and play on Rafferty's team. For the next couple of months he avoided second helpings, began jogging and played basketball every evening. Rafferty never called again but by the end of the summer Joey was in good physical shape and the talk of the neighborhood's sportsmen. He became the respected veteran, sought out by the younger athletes when money or honor were on the line.

But Joey's case was uncommon. Most guys make half-hearted attempts at comebacks but always fall short of their goals. They chalk up the failure to not having enough time or their legs giving out. Some are even honest enough to admit their fear of a heart attack. And yet if Joey's case was uncommon, Frankie Garboil's was extraordinary because with Frankie it wasn't a case of personal pride, but more like a battle with an unknown force, a demon which had invaded his being and fed on his hidden desires until it surfaced.

CHAPTER 5

In which we discover, if not already surmised, the true identity of John Chota, observe his superior's lack of chic, get a look into El Falcon's communication system designed to effect Armando Martinez' escape from Stuyvesant Hospital, but more importantly, learn why one should always be careful when more than one Puerto Rican is sitting at a restaurant table, apparently eating rice and beans.

After El Falcon finished speaking, young as well as old were dazzled by the brilliance of his strategy. They gathered around to bask in his aura. For more than an hour they lingered until he suggested they begin leaving. John Chota was one of the first to leave. By that time it was nearly midnight. As he came out into the street he was met by wind-driven snow. What earlier had been an annoying drizzle of wet snow had now turned into a powerful storm, the flakes thick and the strong wind driving them into high drifts. The temperature had dropped considerably, but John Chota walked with great determination, driven by his newly-found intelligence regarding El Falcon. He must contact Mullvaney immediately. He had them now. Right by the short hairs. Dead to rights. Let them pull their little stunt and he had them good. He had finally done it. When it was all over he'd be decorated. Gold shield for sure.

Detective John Chota was possibly the most unlikely New York City Police officer ever to don the blue. In fact he never did wear the uniform publicly since he went undercover as soon as he was on the payroll. Johnny grew up in the streets of the South Bronx, fighting and clawing with all of his five feet, one inch and one hundred and six pounds. He was fast, cunning and, for as long as he could recall, harbored a profound distaste for crime. From the time he was nine years old and dropped half a chimney on a drug addict's head, he had wanted to be a policeman.

One summer afternoon Johnny had been flying pigeons on the roof of his building when he heard a scuffle and looked out from behind his pigeon coop. A police officer was struggleing with a known neighborhood addict, someone named Pipo or Papo or perhaps Pupi, he couldn't recall which. Suddenly a knife appeared in the addict's hand and the policeman dropped, holding his stomach as the addict headed for the fire escape. Johnny rushed to the edge of the roof and watched the addict make his getaway, looking up once to see if the policeman was following him. When the addict got down to the first floor landing of the fire escape he leaped into the alley and stopped to hide the knife. Johnny was now standing next to a crumbling chimney five stories above him. He felt no anger. In its place he experienced a cold hatred against the addict. He pushed on the chimney, unloading five hundred pounds of bricks on the junkie's head. The bombardment did not kill the addict but was enough on target to fracture his skull and render him immobile. Johnny then rushed to the policeman, who was unconscious and growing pale from loss of blood. He hurried downstairs, ran out on Willis Avenue and stopped a patrol car cruising by.

The two patrolmen got to their fellow officer and rushed him to Lincoln Hospital in time to save his life. Before going upstairs the two officers radioed for help and within five minutes the area was crawling with police. Johnny told an officer what he had done. Sure enough, when they went into the alley they found the addict half buried under the bricks.

The next day Johnny appeared on the front page of *The Daily News,* standing next to Patrolman Charles Mullvaney, lying in a hospital bed. Johnny was wearing Mullvaney's hat. After that he would hang around the 41st Precinct and run errands for the cops. Everyone knew he was an informer for the police, but he had the knack of creating circumstances by which the information he obtained never reached the police from his own lips. As time went on, he was feared in the neighborhood.

When he graduated from high school he attempted to join the police force, but he was too young. He'd won the Flyweight Golden Gloves championship for the neighborhood PAL and had become an ambitious, civic-minded young man. His mode of operation was still the same, but with the constant influx of people into the neighborhood, no one really suspected him of being a police informer. Of course being too young to become a policeman did not deter John Chota.

He attended community college, worked as a bank clerk and helped out at the PAL club. Three years later he took the Police Department test, passed it, but failed the physical because of his height. His disappointment, however, did not last long. He conducted a small investigation and was able to track down the patrolman whose life he had saved twelve years previously. By this time Patrolman Charles Mullvaney had risen to Deputy Chief Inspector in charge of the Division of Special Investigations for the Borough of Manhattan. Mullvaney was able to obtain special dispensation for and training in all aspects of police work for Chota.

At Mullvaney's request he was assigned to the Division of Special Investigations. During the next two years he worked as an undercover man, impersonating addicts. He once received a citation for valor when, during a big arrest on the Lower East Side, he was caught and beaten up by the precinct narcotic squad. Chota never uttered a word in his defense. He spent three weeks in the hospital. After his discharge he was more determined than ever to combat crime.

For the past two years he had been attending Hunter College, combining the completion of his degree in abnormal psychology with some necessary undercover work at the school. He joined the discussions of the college's chapter of the United Front for Total Caribbean Independence and, during the disturbances of the spring of 1970 he distinguished himself by making smoke bombs from photographic film, planning the takeover of the cafeteria and hiding himself in one of the file cabinets in the president's office in order to tape a late night conversation she was having with the deans. Because of his zeal and apparent committment to the struggle he was asked to join the Young Barons, the more militant organization of the United Front. At first there was suspicion which still lingered, but it was always around the area of drug use. His lucky break and the one which completed his cover came when he was recognized by one of the addicts he had been arrested with on the Lower East Side. The young man was no longer using drugs and was an active member of the Young Barons. One evening John was challenged at a meeting and broke down and confessed to having skin popped a few years back, stressing that he had never been a heavy drug user. A couple of people were assigned to take him into the bathroom and check his arms and legs. When they found no track marks he was certified for membership in the Young Barons.

Since the summer of 1970, when he entered the organization, he had marched, worked on the organization's newspaper, helped families obtain medical treatment, picketed, talked endlessly about revolution and shared in smoking 1,438 joints. He kept an accurate record of the times and reported each case to Mullvaney. Other than smoking pot and receiving a few stolen television sets, nothing illegal had ever happened, at least nothing worth arresting anyone for and giving away the fact that he was working undercover.

Tonight was the first time anything spectacular was being planned and as he trudged through the heavy snow he couldn't contain his excitement. He found a phone booth, looked behind him to make sure he hadn't been followed, and dialed Mullvaney's number in Queens.

"Yeah, Chief," he said, after exchanging greetings with Mullvaney. "I think I got something on the Young Barons."

"How big, Johnny?" Mullvaney said.

"Real big, Chief. Just as you suspected. El Falcon's in on it."

There was a deadly silence on the line.

"Chief?" Chota said.

"I'm here, kid. Just thinking. El Falcon, right?"

"That's correct, Chief. You should've seen him. It was just like you said. All of a sudden, there he was. Not for nothing, Chief, it shook me up."

"Just maintain your integrity, kid. Everything's under control."

"Should I come over and give you a full report?"

"Where are you?"

"125th Street on the East Side."

"Not tonight, Johnny. Go home and get some sleep. We'll meet in the usual place tomorrow at eleven. I'm going to St. Pat's for the ten o'clock."

"Okay, Chief, eleven."

"Okay, see you in the morning."

After he hung up Chota jumped into a cab and headed for his apartment in the Bronx. Once there, he thought of getting into his car and driving to New Jersey to be with Lena Kojinsky, his Polish topless dancer, but changed his mind. He wanted to be fresh the next morning and be able to give Mullvaney an accurate report. He showered, had a bowl of Cheerios and was asleep by one in the morning. For Charles Mullvaney sleep did not come as easily. After he finished speaking with Chota he poured himself a glassful of bourbon and sat in his darkened living room, sipping the liquor and staring blankly at the silent picture on the television set. It had finally happened. After all these years another opportunity to tangle with the son of a bitch. How many times had he eluded him. The mere mention of his name sent a cold hatred racing through his veins. But he was glad he had escaped. It gave him an opportunity to challenge himself and put him away for good. The last time he'd had nothing to do with the arrest. Some nonsense about a heist in the jewelry district. He'd told the commissioner they were dealing with terrorists, but he hadn't listened. He's just a thief, the people in the commissioner's office had said, and the dumb mick had listened to them. A first class political agitator and terrorist. He'd show them this time that he'd been right all along. In spite of his resolve to capture El Falcon, Mullvaney felt apprehensive about the task. He could not identify the feeling, but knew he must be as cunning as his adversary. How did he do it? How did he just materialize in places and then disappear? Each time he'd been captured it had been relatively simple. It was as if he'd wanted to end up in jail in order to escape. Son of a bitch. Mullvaney took one long drink from the bourbon and shuddered. Around three in the morning he finally fell asleep on the couch.

John Chota woke up at 9:30 Sunday morning, dressed and headed for the Central Park Zoo. He arrived in front of the bear caves at the exact meeting time. Five minutes later, Mullvaney, dressed as an old lady, showed up. Now in his fifties, he was a large, beefy, no-nonsense cop. Dressed in a baggy coat, galoshes, kerchief over a gray wig and rouged up and lipsticked to beat the band, he looked no different than your average cleaning lady on her way back from ten o'clock mass on her day off. The snow was several inches deep and the sky bright blue, the air cold and crisp. Chota and Mullvaney nodded to each other and began walking out of the zoo and toward the Sheep Meadow, the wide expanse of ground near the southwest end of the park. To anyone watching the two figures, they looked like a mother and son out for a morning walk.

"What's up, kid?" Mullvaney said.

"They're gonna try and break that Martinez bastard outta Stuyvesant Hospital."

"Son of a bitch. What are they, crazy?"

"It's just like you suspected, Chief. Just like you said. He came out of nowhere."

"Just like that, right?" Mullvaney said, snapping his fingers.

"Right, Chief," Chota said. "One minute I was talking and the next minute he was there. You believe in spirits, Chief?"

"What?" said Mullvaney, his mind elsewhere.

"Spirits?"

"Not now, kid. I had a tough night with the stuff last night."

John Chota felt better all at once. Maybe he wasn't so crazy after all. Maybe El Falcon was a spirit. Maybe Mullvaney would come with him to see the spiritualist. As they walked Chota related to Mullvaney what had taken place the previous evening at the Young Baron's meeting. He went into great detail about the planned demonstration in front of the hospital on the day of the escape and how it was meant to create a diversion; how the group was enlisting help from other left wing organizations; how they were to pass information back and forth among each other.

"Let me get this straight, kid," Mullvaney said at this point. "They have a code right?"

"That's right, Chief."

Mullvaney nodded.

"And what they do is go in Portorican restaurants and sit down across from each other."

"Right," said Chota.

"And they pass the information to each other in hollowed out beans?"

"That's correct, Chief. All very subtle. The person passing the message puts the hollowed out bean on the other person's plate. In the process of eating the person receiving the message picks up the message bean with a forkful of food, puts it in his mouth and then he makes believe he's taking something out of his mouth and puts the hollowed out bean in his pocket."

"Son of a bitch," said Mullvaney. "Cooked or uncooked beans?"

"Uncooked, Chief."

"How many Portorican restaurants in the City, kid?"

Chota thought for a moment.

"Counting all the Cuban-Chink places, where they serve rice and beans, about five or six thousand."

"Son of a bitch," Mullvaney said, kicking at the snow as he walked. We haven't got enough men in the unit to cover a hundred restaurants. What's his plan?"

"That's just it, Chief," Chota said. "El Falcon didn't spell out the plan. All he said was that everyone should cut his hair short. No long hair, no Afros. No berets. Everyone look clean cut and normal."

"Son of a bitch," said Mullvaney once more. "Kid, you're just gonna have to go back in there and find out."

"Impossible, Chief," Chota replied. "That's why I called you. We got orders not to go back to the headquarters. I tried like hell to get in on the break, but El Falcon picked two of the old guys, two of the Young Barons and Martinez' girl. I'm useless unless somebody slips up and tells me what's going on and that's not gonna happen. There was a lot of talk about violence, but they cooled it right away. No weapons. A typical El Falcon operation, right?"

"Yep, that's his MO, all right. How much time do we have?"

"They're talking about the ninth of next month, Chief. About five weeks."

Chota and Mullvaney had crossed the Sheep Meadow and were now opposite Tavern on the Green. The cold had made Mullvaney's eyes water, making the rouge run in streaks over his fat cheeks.

"You okay, Chief?"

"Sure, kid," Mullvaney replied. "Listen, thanks a lot. Give me some time to think about this and I'll see you at the dentist tomorrow at four. Take care of yourself."

"Right, Chief," Chota said, and watched Mullvaney trudge through the snow on his way out of the park. He had mixed feelings about the meeting. On the one hand he felt like a failure since he hadn't been able to provide much valuable information on the breakout. He did, however, feel better that at least Mullvaney was also aware of spirits. He had to talk to someone soon. After walking south inside the park he emerged at Columbus Circle and disappeared into the subway.

The following day John Chota attended classes at Hunter College. At one o'clock he met with the school's chapter of the United Front and began discussing the upcoming demonstration, assigning tasks to the other members and urging them to devote themselves fully to the task of publicizing the plight of Armando Martinez. By the time he left school at three, there were large posters all over the school, demanding Armando Martinez' freedom. Leaflets were circulated and a collection table was set up for the "ARMANDO MARTINEZ DEFENSE FUND." When students began to find out that the person being detained was a student at New Amsterdam College, a sister school in the City University system, it caused quite a stir and issues of the slightest relevance began to be tied to the injustice of Armando Martinez' detention.

Within two days, word of the upcoming demonstration was on every campus in the City of New York. Even the Monarchist Club at one of the colleges had joined the cause. The group advocated the coronation of Richard Nixon as perpetual ruler of the country of "Columbia." Their motto and rallying cry was "Up Richard." To make their point clearer they wore large, six inch buttons on which there appeared a crown with the words "Richard the First" in a semi-circle on the top border, and a hand with an extended index finger, probing under the crown. Their rationale for joining the demonstration was an interesting one. Melvin Flank, self-appointed Duke of Rockaway, a mad genius majoring in Medieval European History, argued that if Richard Nixon was crowned and the country's name changed to Columbia, every man would be entitled to his own kind of madness without government interference. The detention of Armando Martinez was a case of government exercising too much power over an individual citizen while allowing its chief executive to display his own rampant insanity. "If he can be crazy, argued Flank, why can't the rest of us?"

While Frank's argument was a bit bizarre, most of the concern being felt on New York City campuses was genuine, sincere and motivated by nothing more than a deep sense of empathy with another young person caught up in a situation which he had not created, but into which he had been thrown by the insanity of the society. It was an emotion which only a few were able to articulate, but which was felt by all.

John Chota left Hunter College at three that afternoon, travelled to Queens and the dental clinic of Conrad Cameron, the place where he and Mullvaney met to discuss confidential matters at length. Several years before, Cameron had been caught receiving smuggled diamonds in patients' teeth and, rather than turning him over to the District Attorney for prosecution, Mullvaney now used him for various purposes, including particularly difficult dental work not covered by insurance. Mullvaney was proud that the men in his unit, as well as their families, had the best looking teeth in the department.

CHAPTER 6

From which we can draw a number of conclusions about the effects of a Protestant upbringing on the psyche of certain females reared in the United States, begin to examine a possible genetic relationship between human beings and pomegranates, observe how the Almighty employs hippopotami to do some of His dirty work, and get a brief glimpse of the main character's naked physique.

As Frank Garboil spoke, the two doctors, one moving up and down the glistening surface, the other standing in front of the goal at the far end of the room, listened as his words boomed out over the public address system. From time to time Dr. Kohonduro blew his whistle to remind the patient not to digress. At the end of the session the staff agreed that another breakthrough had taken place. Although Dr. Kopfeinlaufen had spent considerable time observing Nurse Konkruka through his goalie mask, imagining how an infant would feel nursing at her massive breasts, his keen, analytical mind was able to appreciate the significance of their patient's willingness to cooperate.

When the buzzer rang to signal the end of the session, there was cheering and horns piped over the public address system. Helen Christianpath, who had been on the verge of tears throughout the two hour session, rushed over from the scorer's table and shook Dr. Kohonduro's hand.

"That was brilliant, Doctor," she said, admiringly.

"Thank you, Miss Christianpath," said the doctor, humbly.

"Very nice, Armando," said Dr. Kopfeinlaufen, wobbling over to the bed. "But why do you want to tell us about Frank Garboil?"

"Because that's who I am. I'm married, I have two children and I'm thirty-four years old."

"You're joking again," replied Kopfeinlaufen. "Maybe you knew this fellow in Vietnam.

"I'm telling you the truth," Garboil shouted. "I've never been in Vietnam."

"Dr. Kohonduro intervened. "I think that's enough for this evening, Mr. Martinez. We have made considerable progress. I cannot overlook your crass remarks about members of my family but I must congratulate you on your openness."

"Nurse Konkruka."

"Yes, Dr. Kopfeinlaufen."

"Please remain with the patient until he is ready for bed. Make sure he showers, is rubbed down and has his evening snack."

"Yes, sir," said Nurse Konkruka, watching the rest of the staff leave.

As the door of the Armando Martinez Total Detraumatizing Environment closed, Frank Garboil got out of bed. Even though he is six feet in height, he barely comes to Ingrid Konkruka's nose. His eyes are constantly level with her mouth as he faced her.

"Let's go, Frank," she said, helping him remove his bathrobe.

"What did you call me?" he said, turning to face her.

"Frank," Ingrid said again. "That's who you are, aren't you?"

"Yeah, but they don't believe me."

"Well, I do."

"How come?"

"Go take your shower."

"Tell me first."

Ingrid Konkruka patted his bottom playfully and laughed.

"Don't be difficult, okay? Take your shower. I'll tell you while I'm giving you a rubdown."

Frank Garboil entered the bathroom, removed his pajamas and adjusted the water temperature before getting under the shower. His body was that of an athlete in his prime, the stomach flat and the muscles of his limbs, rather than bulging, long and sinewy. He soaped himself vigorously, got back under the shower and wished the room were warmer. Ingrid had reassured him that the temperature was just right, but it was taking him too long to get used to the cold after coming out of the warm water. When he finished, he reached for a towel, but had forgotten to bring one. Ingrid Konkruka, carrying a large New York Rangers towel, walked into the bathroom. Garboil immediately turned his back on her, faced the wall and with his outstretched hand reached for it.

"Turn around first," said Ingrid.

He protested, but she insisted and he turned around shyly, covering himself with the towel as soon as he had it.

"Why don't you wait outside," he said.

Ingrid shook her head and winked mischievously at him.

"You know something? You're not half bad. You should've seen those football players that came up to the clinic in Minnesota. Six-four, six-five and six-six with these little shrunken things. It's those pills they gave them. They grow all over except down there."

"Please wait outside," Garboil pleaded. "I'll be done in a minute."

Ingrid laughed again and went out of the bathroom. He dried quickly, wrapped the towel around his middle and came back out into the room. The cold air hit him and made him shiver. Ingrid covered his shoulders with the bathrobe and pounded his back vigorously. Her hands were large and strong. They reached into his bones and made his entire body tingle and vibrate. She continued to pound on him as she steered him to the bed.

"Tell me how you know that I'm Frank Garboil."

"Okay, but lie down. On your stomach," she said, turning on a heat lamp above her. She removed the bathrobe, left the towel across his buttocks and began kneading his back. "I saw the same thing happen to Hemingway," she said as she perched herself up on the bed. "He was up at the clinic for a while. What you did was smart. I mean, tonight. With him it was different. He was Roberto, Brett, Nick Adams, gunrunners, boxers and bullfighters. They finally convinced him he was really Ernest Hemingway, the famous writer. He went home and blew his brains out. He didn't want to be who he was so he chose someone else's identity."

"Right! That's what I did," Garboil said, turning his head to look at her. "How old are you, anyway?"

"Twenty-four," she said and pushed his head back down.

"That's what I figured. What the hell were you doing there? That was more than ten years ago. You had to be ten or eleven. Were you sick?"

Ingrid Konkruka laughed and pounded his back.

"Oh, that's a long story," she said. "You don't want to hear it."

"Sure I do."

"Well, I reached puberty at the age of six."

"What!"

"Sure. I was already five-four and quite busty so my mother took me to Rochester. They said I was a medical oddity and kept me there. I couldn't go to kindergarten because the principal was this flat-chested witch like Christianpath."

"You don't like Helen, I take it?"

"She's all right, I guess. Just a little too pious for me. Anyway, we lived in a small town called Otternose and things were rough as hell. My father was a lefthanded lumberjack and nobody would hire him. My mother had a little money stashed away so she bought a hundred pounds of flour and shortening and sugar and sent me out to collect berries, apples and whatever else I could scrounge up. We baked pies for three straight weeks and sold them. When we had enough money together we got our car fixed up and went up to the clinic."

"What happened?"

"When we got there and the doctors examined me, they decided I should live there for research purposes. They got a big grant from Washington. Very secret stuff. By the time I was ten I had graduated from high school and two years later I got my B.S. They couldn't figure that out either. One of their theories was that my accelerated growth had a direct relationship to my intelligence because I was the sum total of all the human beings that had ever been created. Do you know who Hera was?"

"Sure, queen of the gods in Greek mythology. Juno to the Romans."

"That's right, goddess of women and marriage, sister and wife to Zeus. I was the Earth Mother. The top scientists and doctors in the world were all ga-ga over a twelve-year-old girl with huge boobs. They examined me constantly so they had to justify their lechery with outlandish theories. I wanted to go to medical school, but I couldn't get in."

"How come? You're a genius."

"Well, when I was nine the director of surgery seduced me and had a heart attack right in the middle of the thing. They never forgave me. They made all kinds of excuses about my being too big and not being able to handle delicate surgical instruments. They let me get nurse's training, but only because I married Paolo Strettobuco, the famous Italian gynecologist. He was visiting from Milan at the time. Very gentle man. By this time they had altered all my birth records and I was functioning as a twenty-two-year old receptionist and college student. So I know a little bit about identity changes. After Paolo left they let me stay. They said I had wonderful therapeutic potential. For men only, though. I've seen women with a head cold develop leukemia under my care. So they suggested I only take care of men."

"Why didn't you go with your husband?

"That was sad. Paolo wanted children."

"So?"

"I couldn't have any so he had the marriage annulled."

"You were too young to have children."

"No, nothing like that. I told you, I reached puberty at six. No, I have built in contraceptive glands."

"You're kidding."

"No, really. I ovulate and everything, but I secrete something that wipes out the sperm as soon as it hits the uterus. There was this one nut up there with a theory that I was a throwback in evolution. He was a specialist in genetics. For a whole year he tried to get me pregnant. I don't mean the regular way, but artificially. He tried everything. First he started out with the different races. All the strains: Lapps, African pygmies, Navajos, Ainus, Watusis . . ."

"Puerto Ricans?"

"Yeah, they had a chart with all of them."

"That's amazing."

"It really was."

"No, I mean about Puerto Ricans. People say all they have to do is look at a woman and she gets pregnant. Nothing worked, huh?"

"Nothing at all. When they got through with the human race they tried apes and monkeys. Nothing. Then they tried polar bears and tigers and dogs. You know, other mammals. Nothing. Then birds, reptiles, fish, all the way down the evolutionary scale. Zero. Well, that's not true. No, it is true because it wasn't part of the animal kingdom. But one time something did stir. I aborted after about ten weeks."

"What the hell was it?"

"Don't laugh, all right?"

Frank Garboil turned around and covered himself.

"I won't laugh," he said, crossing his heart.

"It was a pomegranate."

A look of total disbelief came over Garboil's face.

"You're putting me on. A what?"

"A pomegranate. This madman isolated the pomegranate pollen and inseminated me with it. I missed my period, they ran tests and sure enough they came out positive. I felt great even though it was crazy. And then in the tenth week I lost it."

"That's too bad," said Garboil, sincerely. "I'm really sorry."

"Me too," said Ingrid. "After a while I really wanted a baby even if it was going to be half fruit."

"Sure, I can imagine how you felt."

"Yeah."

"So how did you know I was who I am?"

"I told you. You're starting to tell them who you really are. The way they figure it, you'll get it all out of your system and then you'll admit you are who you're not and everything will be fine. You'll be crazy as hell, but that's their standard for sanity. In this society, the crazier you are the more normal you're considered. Listen, I've got to go. I have a date with Engine Company 83 uptown."

"The whole company?"

"Yes, lover, the whole hosing company. Get your clean pajamas on and get your snack from the fridge. I have to run. I'll see you tomorrow. And stop insisting that you're Frank Garboil. The more you insist the less they'll believe you. That's the way they work. We're all crazy, you know. Some more than others. But the saner you are, the crazier you seem to crazy people like them."

With that, Ingrid Konruka said goodnight and moved across the glistening white floor like a walking snow covered alp. Garboil gazed after her more awed than ever. Unbelievable, he thought. Built-in contraceptive glands, puberty at the age of six, a genius brain and a body like he'd never seen. And she believed him. It was all crazy. He dressed, ate cookies and milk and turned on the television set near his bed.

The following morning, after breakfast, while he read the newspaper, Helen Christianpath entered the room. She was particularly serious this morning. Garboil had just finished reading the sports page. The Rangers were winning, the Knicks were winning, and Phil Esposito was heading for another one hundred plus point season with Boston. There was no mention of the upcoming New Amsterdam College hockey game against Brooklyn College. For a fraction of a second he wished he could lace up his skates. He shook his head as if to drive the thought away. He shouldn't have gone as far as he did. His thoughts turned to his wife Joan and his two boys, Joey and Peter. He wondered if they were playing ice hockey in California.

"Good morning, Mr. Martinez," said Helen Christianpath. "Did you sleep well last night?"

"Yes, thank you," he answered, putting the newspaper down and getting up from the couch.

"Please don't get up," she said, coming closer. "I just wanted to tell you that you were very honest last night. The doctors and I discussed the session in depth after we left. They've asked me to come back and talk with you this morning. I hope you don't mind."

"I don't mind."

"Good. This man, Frank Garboil, seems to be an interesting person. You seem to know him well."

Garboil began to explain that he was one and the same, but remembered Ingrid's advice.

"Sure, but I don't know where from." he said, sitting back down.

"That's all right," Helen said, tapping her notebook. "That doesn't matter right now, does it? What matters is that we get down to the bottom of why this person is such an important part of your life. Dr. Kopfeinlaufen seems to think that this other person, Frank Garboil, is someone whose identity you're trying to adopt. Let me reassure you, Armando. Can I call you Armando? Of course I can. Let me reassure you that you've made remarkable progress in the three weeks you've been with us. And now, finally, through God's Good Grace and the workings of the good doctors, you've begun to admit that you have a problem."

Garboil listened with veiled amusement. The leathery-skinned woman reminded him of a lizard, her eyes yellowish and tired. He wasn't sure, but in looking at the wrinkles of her face, there appeared to be dirt in them. There was an old, musty smell about her, much as if she had been recently in a closet. She sat down on the couch and patted his knee with her long, bony hand.

"Can I ask you something, Miss Christianpath?"

"Of course you can. But you must call me Helen. On my first mission the tribe I worked with couldn't pronounce my last name, so they called me Helen. They were strange people, the Coolobido. Almost like children. Easily hurt if their affection was rejected. And so affectionate. So you call me Helen and I'll call you Armando."

Armando fought off a wave of nausea at the fawning smile which had formed on her face when she looked at him.

"Sure, Helen," he said. "What I wanted to know was why I'd want to talk about someone I may not have even met. For all I know, I may be making this whole thing up."

Once again Helen Christianpath patted Armando's leg, this time halfway up his thigh. His nose wrinkled imperceptibly at the touch and he backed up on the couch.

"Precisely," said Christianpath. "Oh, Armando, you're such a bright young man. I feel like getting down on my knees and giving . . . "

"No, no, that's all right," Garboil said, bolting upright and taking two steps back while clutching at the band on his pajama tops. "I'm fine."

" . . . thanks to the Lord," said Christianpath, finishing her thought.

"Oh," Garboil said. "I'm sorry."

"Don't you see it?" she said, oblivious to his discomfort.

"No, I don't."

"It's all very simple. You're describing the person you wish to be. All young people should have dreams and aspirations. I think it's quite admirable that a person of your background should want to continue school and attain a doctorate. And in Economics! You may not be aware of this, but our technology has advanced too much as it is. We're going to need people to find uses for the surplus it has created. Your motives are humanitarian to say the least."

"Sure," Garboil said, playing along. "A lot of surplus."

"But I'm eager to hear more," said Christianpath. "That was fascinating to hear you talk about this person's childhood. You must have had a similar childhood, being looked on as different because you were Portorican, literally ostracized by other ethnic groups."

"Yeah, they ostracized me left and right."

"In any case, I want you to tell me more about this person that you wish to be. What happened to him? Was he a happy child at all? He must have had some happy moments. Who was he? You see, the more you tell us about Frank Garboil, the more you will be able to see who you want to be."

Christianpath patted the couch and asked Garboil to sit down. Garboil sat down, this time a cushion away from her.

"There's something I don't understand," he said. "Why would I want to make this guy thirty-four years old, with children and all that."

Christianpath smiled benevolently.

"I think it's wonderful. It's a sign of commitment."

"What is?"

"Wanting to project your life that far ahead. It shows that you have a genuine desire to fulfill your goals and help mankind. I was like that when I was your age and perhaps even younger. One day, back in my hometown of Ravena, Kansas, Reverend Ezra Fleischer came to our church and shared his missionary experiences with our congregation. I was left awestruck by his testimony and I knew there and then I would dedicate myself to the service of the Lord. Reverend Fleischer had given forty odd years of his life to working in the jungles of Africa. I was only ten at the time, but that afternoon at the church picnic he held my hand and I felt the calling.

"I had gone off by myself to the stream behind the church and he came there seeking solace. It was like a vision. I was listening to the gentle chattering of the birds when I heard a powerful streaming sound of liquid rushing rapidly and hitting the earth. I turned around and it was Reverend Fleischer relieving himself at a nearby tree. At first I though he was holding a child's arm in his hand. I was transfixed by the sight. A man of God performing a natural act, his pure, white, God-given maleness, huge to my child's eyes, held in his hand. His hand, Armando. The very hand with which he held the scriptures, with which he served communion and blessed us all. Up to that time I hadn't thought of such things. Ministers simply preached and shook hands. They were above such things. The enormity of the realization proved too much and I fainted. Fortunately, he didn't see me looking at him."

"But you saw him," Garboil interjected, not without salacious intent.

"Yes, vividly," answered Christianpath, two sighs away from a trance. "The memory has kept me alive many times since. In my deepest tribulations and perils I saw Reverend Fleischer time and time again that summer afternoon. I became more convinced that I, too, could dedicate myself to the working of the Lord. After he was finished, he came down to the stream to wash his hands. Let me add that Reverend Fleischer was a meticulously clean man. It was on his way back up the hill that he saw me. I must have rolled some when I fainted and ended up in a state of disarray. When I came to, Reverend Fleischer was rearranging my dress which had rolled up around my chest. 'Are you troubled, my child?' he said. He sat down near me and took my hand. 'I see,' he said. 'You were praying and the Spirit came to you. That was it, wasn't it?' I didn't know what to say, so I nodded. He told me about the miracle of prayer.

"Once, in Africa, while going from one village to another to conduct services, he was charged by a rhinoceros. He knelt, put his hands together and offered his life to our Maker. The animal came closer and closer, raising dust as he came so close that the air was dark. And then, when he was no more than twenty yards away, he tripped and broke his neck. A miracle. I was enraptured by his words, carried away by pure white angels. He had brought the message to the darkest part of that continent, probing deeply into the souls of ignorant people, unaware of the gospel of our Lord Jesus Christ."

Frank Garboil watched this strange woman as she spoke and began to understand his dilemma. There were times when he didn't know if he would be able to endure her fervor. But as she spoke he felt himself blushing at the intimacy of her words and the passion with which she spoke them. And then he wasn't sure if she was about to reach an orgasm or merely vanish in a thin vapor of goodness. He was conflicted and felt guilty about misleading her. Maybe Ingrid was right and they were crazier than he was. He wondered what kind of sex life Christianpath could have. The thought took him by surprise. It was the first time he'd thought about sex since ending up in the hospital. He now became aware that he was fully erect. If they were crazy this was a good a time to find out.

"Miss Christianpath? Helen?"

"Yes, Armando?"

"Would you like to fuck?"

"No, thank you."

She didn't even blink, her yellowish eyes gave no sign of shock. They were crazy. All of them, totally bananas.

"Are you celibate?" he said.

"What?"

"Celibate. I learned that in my English class."

"Why, yes I am."

"Are you a virgin?"

"Yes, I am. You see, Armando, young people who have genuine commitment to ideals are often tried by the Lord. I should add that I went through a long illness after my experience with Reverend Fleischer. No one, but no one, believed I saw angels.

But I did. I ate nothing but celery for a year. Only the memory of Reverend Fleischer standing by that tree sustained me during that period. I waited for years for him to return, but he never did. Years later I learned that he perished during a baptismal service in a river in the Congo. While he was performing the ceremony a hippopotamus family surfaced, was frightened by the natives shouting onshore, and in their haste to escape carried our dear Reverend Fleischer into the depths. The Lord works in mysterious ways His wonders to perform. So don't doubt or be afraid. You must tell me more and please don't mind too much if I write as you talk. What happened to that little boy? Where did he come from? Did he just skate in out of nowhere?"

Her attitude angered Frank Garboil and had made his erection vanish. He had put it straight to Christianpath and it was as if he'd brought up T.S. Eliot, geometric progressions, geological strata or friggin Australian wombats. She had been totally bored by his suggestion. Relieved as he was, he still experienced chagrin at the rejection. He imagined her vagina, as well as that part of the brain which corresponds to sexual desire, as smooth, harmless protoplasm, plastic and devoid of any sensation. The image made him laugh out loud and the laughter made him ache inside. It was as if he hadn't used part of his body in a long time. As he laughed, the image dissolved and in its place he saw a tiny, wrinkled, sexless, sixty-year-old Barbie doll, properly attired in granny clothes, sitting in a tiny pew in a tiny church, her head bowed in penitence for her celibacy. Bob was not there, most likely equally frustrated and either dead or drowning his sorrow in alcohol somewhere. Garboil had the strongest urge to lift up Barbie's dress and see the smoothness between her anile legs.

They were totally nuts. He'd give them all they wanted. He'd tell them everything, down to the last bizarre detail, even if it sounded like fiction. He knew they'd buy it all because they were crazy and it was what they wanted to hear. All at once he felt free and as if his body were soaring and he began talking about his life. Helen Christianpath smiled at him with her thin, lizard lips and began writing.

CHAPTER 7

In which we begin to examine the main character's search for identity, finally decipher the decades-old mystery concerning the disappearance of baseball's greatest hitter, scrutinize the genealogy of our hero, and understand, from a visceral perspective, his love for the game of ice hockey.

He spent only five years in the old neighborhood before moving on, hopping on a freight train after he graduated from high school and joining the Army when his adopted aunts suggested he study for the priesthood. But it was clear that his battle had started long before that. Somewhere along the way he had lost part of himself and, whether through his own doing or because of circumstances, he needed to find out how it had happened. Except that he wasn't aware of the battle back then and only admitted a gnawing suspicion that no matter where he stood, he did not belong. During one stage of his life he believed that everyone had a place in the world where he could stand and be at peace with himself. From this vantage point, one could see all that had transpired and all that was to occur. He had never found that magical place and each moment he lived he encountered greater complexity, defending himself from the turmoil by remaining aloof out of fear that, were he to give all of himself, he would be capitulating and would remain in the situation, molded and fixed forever.

He had come out of nowhere, skating, his hockey stick working miracles in the street, rarely smiling. There were memories of growing up in another part of the city and speaking another language, but he would not talk about it with his new friends. One time some of the boys went to his home and when they returned they told everyone that the apartment was spooked. There was no malice in the report. It had been, however, one of those things which get told over and over, and each time it is told grows because it is exciting or mysterious to the listener. It was Mickey Muldoon, perhaps the closest person to Frankie Garboil, subsequent to their fight in the middle of a football practice, who unwittingly started the rumor.

He, Buddy Kramer and Jimmy McGregor had gone to Frankie's house to ask him if he could come down and play. Kramer and McGregor had stayed outside on the stoop of the building while Muldoon went up to the fifth-floor flat.

"You should've seen his house," said Muldoon, upon returning to Mrs. Cohen's Candy Store on Cypress Avenue. "It was dark and it smelled like perfume. They had a lot of flowers and candles like at a funeral. His aunts were dressed in black dresses and had veils on like they was in church. They said the kid was doing his homework, so he couldn't come down. And they were speaking some strange kind of language. I couldn't tell what it was."

"Maybe it was Spanish," said Buddy Kramer.

"Naw," said Mousey O'Hara. "He ain't a spic."

"Yeah, you should know," said Kevin McCarthy.

"Shut up, okay, moron?" said Mousey.

"It sounded like Hungarian," said Muldoon.

"What do you know about Hungarians?" Mousey asked.

"More than you, jerk. My father was in the merchant marine and he told me all about it. They're gypsies and they go around in bright clothes, singing songs, playing violins and talking just like they was talking at the kid's house."

"You've never seen a gypsy," McGregor said.

"Yes, I have," countered Muldoon. "My father has pictures and I've seen them."

"Prove it," said Tommy O'Brien.

"I'll prove it," replied Muldoon. "Just wait and see. I'll run up to my house right now and get a picture."

And with that Mickey Muldoon ran out of the candy store and within ten minutes was back down with an old picture, somewhat faded and yellowed, but still clear enough to make out. It was a newspaper photo of a large, serious man in a baseball uniform, holding a violin under his chin. The man had a huge handlebar moustache and his hair was parted in the middle. On the front of the uniform the name MEMPHIS could barely be read. It was, of course, a picture of the legendary Butch Cornhorn, the famous first baseman of the Memphis Coonhounds of the old Appalachian Association, standing at home plate during a pregame fiddling contest. Mickey Muldoon had cut the explaining story from the bottom of the picture after removing it from his father's trunk. One year, during a one-hundred-fifty game season, Butch Cornhorn hit 78 homeruns and drove in 287 runs. The following year he had a tryout with the Saint Louis Browns, but they released him and blackballed him from professional baseball when they learned he was one sixty-fourth Black. He couldn't return to Memphis where he had married Cornelia Rittenauer, the red-headed daughter of Cory Rittenauer, U.S. Representative. When the story got out, Colonel Rittenauer vowed to send his people after Cornhorn and, in his words, "string the nigger up from the highest tree in Memphis." Cornelia, needless to say, was heartbroken. She took to drinking and psychic phenomena and ended up going west and living with the Hopi Indians, where she developed a reputation as a seer. Butch Cornhorn, embittered by the experience, became a Negro and joined the merchant marine where Muldoon's father met him. When Mickey showed the other boys the picture they laughed.

"That's just an old ballplayer," said Mousey O'Hara.

"Yeah," said Kevin McCarthy. "You don't know nothing about gypsies."

"Yeah? That's how much you know," said Mickey Muldoon.

"That's just an old ballplayer," said Mousey O'Hara.

"Where?" they asked in unison, advancing on Muldoon.

"In MemPiss," he said with confidence. "That's one of the towns in Hungary. Instead of bats they use violins."

"Oh sure," they all said, not at all swayed by the obvious and logical evidence being offered by Muldoon.

"Yeah, morons," Mickey said, calmly. "That's where the saying comes from."

"What saying?" asked Tommy O'Brien.

"You couldn't hit with a bass fiddle," Mickey said. "That's where it comes from. It's an old Hungarian baseball insult to someone who can't hit."

The candy store was silent for what seemed an eternity as mouths fell open and eyes widened to unbelievable proportions. Suddenly, there wasn't one skeptic in the crowd. Mickey Muldoon put the picture back in his pocket and walked triumphantly out of Mrs. Cohen's Candy Store.

From that day on everyone called Frankie Garboil the Gypsy. He didn't like the name, but accepted it, needing the companionship and approval of the other boys. Only once did he become angry at being called Gypsy. It was during the first football practice the Rebels held the year after he arrived in the neighborhood. He had been tackled rather forcefully by Mickey Muldoon, who was a mountain of a twelve-year old. Frankie lay on the ground somewhat stunned and it frightened Mickey.

"Com'on, get up, you punk Gypsy," Mickey screamed, in a characteristic New York form of concern. "Can't you take it, Gypsy!"

Frankie jumped up as if he had been kicked. He ripped off his helmet and began pummelling Mickey.

"Take it back," he kept saying. "Take it back, you mick bastard."

They swung at each other, missing for the most part, until they were exhausted and Charlie O'Brien broke them up. After that they were the best of friends. It was Mickey who, two years later, told Frankie how he had gotten his nickname. Frankie laughed but in some deep recess of his being he accepted part of the truth about himself. But it did not help because it was then that the quest began to manifest itself consciously. He was like a Gypsy, he thought.

He recalled moving from one place to the next after his mother died and then his father. At first staying with his father's closest friends, then with acquaintances and finally with people he hardly knew. His fondest memories came from the time when he had shared his life with his mother and father under one roof. But that had lasted too short a period of time. He recalled going to his father's store after school and helping him with the merchandise after his mother died. The store was narrow and protruded half out of an alley on Orchard Street in the Lower East Side of Manhattan. The establishment was more like a stall but his father proudly called it a store. From it his father bickered in Yiddish, Spanish, Polish and Italian with old ladies about the price of an apron or a pair of gloves.

His father was an old, dark man with thick, white hair, who urged him to speak English and told him stories about the places he had lived in and visited. One day, when his mother had been dead four years, Frankie asked his father what he was.

"Why do you want to know, Frankie?" his father said. "Does it matter? You are American. You were born here and that is what you are. Make the best of it."

"What about you and Mama?" he asked.

"That is a long story," his father said, and his voice trailed off as he recalled his youth. That night Frankie was allowed to stay up past midnight and did not attend school the following day.

The story of his mother and father was filled with adventure. It was a story of people seeking a home. Frankie's grandfather had been an Albanian merchant of French descent. He spent most of his time traveling back and forth to Greece and Turkey. His grandmother had been a Ukranian princess who had been captured early in life by the Turks. She grew up as a maid in the household of a very rich man. The man was a scoundrel and a thief. The authorities finally caught on to him, confiscated his property, dispersed his household and beheaded him. Hyacinth, which was the young girl's name, was thrown out into the street to fend for herself, for although she had been a princess, she was not as comely as princesses were wont to be. Nevertheless, she almost ended up in a harem. As luck would have it, Frankie's grandfather was passing through Izmir, Turkey, at the time and was taken by young Hyacinth. She was already in the hands of a merchant who was about to sell her into sexual slavery. His grandfather paid dearly to purchase her. In return for her freedom he gave up a fine Indian carpet, a pair of yellow Afghan hounds he was to deliver to the King of Greece, and a dozen good luck camel's ears from the Sudan.

Anton Garboil married Hyacinth and they remained in Turkey as the family began growing. In 1915 floods and plague hit their town and they left, setting off across Eastern Europe, settling in one place and then another. By this time Josep Garboil, Frankie's father, was thirty-five years old and wished to seek his own fortune. The family had settled in Poland where they had established a successful import business. It seemed that once again the family was to remain in one place for more than five years. It was 1920, the big war was over and times seemed prosperous again. But fate, fickle and cruel, rarely smiles when she points her finger. Josep fought a duel over his sister's honor, scarred the man horribly, was accused unjustly of killing a man, and had to flee. He escaped one night, hidden in a cabbage wagon bound for Warsaw. From there he made his way west, living in Germany, France, Spain and Portugal. He finally stowed away on a ship bound for Canada.

For the next ten years Josep Garboil traveled the breadth and length of Canada working at odd jobs: trapper's helper, caribou hunter, lumberjack, maple syrup thinner, sled repairman, and interpreter. And once, when his luck had all but run out, he became assistant stickboy for the Flin Flon Flying Fletchers of the Manitoba Hockey Association. But his wanderlust took him away each time. Around 1932, while he was in British Columbia, where he had gone to find a ship for the Orient, he found instead Frankie's mother.

One day, while wandering the streets of Vancouver, he ran across a band of Eskimos. They had with them a young woman, who, although dressed like them, looked quite different. She was a head taller than the men and her hair was lighter. Josep Garboil was stricken by her beauty and stately carriage. Up to this time he had thought of marriage only as an economic convenience, someone to cook and keep house. Being constantly on the move, he had foregone the arrangement. Suddenly, at the sight of the young woman, he found himself stirring inside as if some fierce animal had awakened from a winter's sleep.

He approached the Eskimos, with the help of a trader familiar with their language and, as luck would have it, was able to convince the band of his honorable intentions. They had brought the young woman to Vancouver for her return to white civilization after the death of her father the previous year. They were glad when, through the interpreter, Josep Garboil asked for her hand in marriage. The young woman's name was Summersun Magnussen and she was the daughter of a Norwegian polar explorer, the sole survivor of an expedition, presumed lost. The tribe of Eskimos had found him near death and nursed him back to health on a diet of polar bear liver and seal fat. In time he was strong enough and, convinced that he had come home to his ancestral dwelling place, remained among the tribe. He became a superb hunter and invented the split-level igloo. In time he took a wife and Summersun was born a year later.

Summersun had been well taught by her father in the sixteen years he had been with her. She could read the stars, make complex mathematical computations, play chess and speak languages. Although her English sometimes drifted into her Eskimo dialect and into Norwegian, she was able to speak with Josep. It mattered little because there was a deeper communication between the two. Instantly, they knew they belonged with each other. Gifts were exchanged, farewells expressed and the

Eskimos departed for their return journey north. Josep Garboil took his bride to a nearby chapel and there they were wed.

Again, as fate would have it, Josep's fortune seemed to turn against him. A salmon fisherman from Vancouver had heard about the band of Eskimos with the statuesque young woman, had seen them in town and gone back to his cabin to retrieve his savings and purchase Summersun. When the man learned that his future bride had already been given away to another, he set out to find Josep Garboil and kill him. Josep learned of the plot and spirited Summersun away from Vancouver and down across the border to the United States. For the next two years they wandered throughout the United States, meeting rejection everywhere they went; Josep for being a foreigner and Summersun for being his halfbreed wife. They trekked eastward, finally arriving in New York City in the winter of 1934, a time in the economic history of the country when skyscraper skydiving had become fashionable.

Here, in New York City, they found a small room above a Chinese laundry, where they set up housekeeping for the first time. The Lower East Side was the perfect place for them. For Josep it was a return to Europe and the bustle of the market place where different languages were spoken. For Summersun it was an opportunity to create a home for her beloved Josep, whom she had learned to love and admire, and to learn more about her father's world. Although Josep managed to earn enough money doing odd jobs to eventually move to more confortable quarters, open up a dry goods stall and purchase a small radio, Summersun found few people who spoke her father's language. To worsen matters, in over two years of marriage, the Great Seal Spirit had not yet answered her prayers. Had she offended her in some way? Was she being punished with barrenness? These questions plunged her into deep silence and resigned shame. Another year passed and winter came once more. With the cold weather a miracle visited Josep and Summersun.

For three months, since the first snow had fallen, Summersun had been rising in the middle of the night and leaving the apartment, returning in the early morning, happier than the previous day. Her nightly departures worried Josep, but he did not question Summersun, whom he loved and on whom he had placed deep respect and trust. And yet he was curious about his wife's new habit. One night, during a heavy snowfall, his curiosity at a peak, he followed her. She walked quickly through the snow. When she reached the East River, her mukaluks leaving deep tracks, she turned northward. At the end of two hours she had crossed into the Bronx and an hour later she reached the Bronx Zoo and was heading for the seal pond.

From a distance Josep Garboil saw his wife strip naked and dive into the water. He was certain she had decided to commit suicide and ran to save her, all the while calling her name. His voice muffled by the snow and the barking of the seals, she did not hear him. When he reached the railing of the pond, much to his amazement, rather than finding his wife's inert body floating in the water, she was frolicking with the seals, swimming and disappearing underwater and barking at them with equal zest. After a while she climbed out of the pool and rested near the entrance to their cave. Several seals climbed out after her, barking animatedly and nuzzling her affectionately. She rolled her body around in the snow and made small grunting sounds of pleasure. In the darkness it was nearly impossible to tell her apart from the animals. After an hour she stopped playing, climbed out of the enclosure and dressed once more.

Josep Garboil was dumbstruck by the experience. Grateful that no harm had come to Summersun, he hurried out of the park and rode the subway back to their home. He did not recall when she returned home for he fell asleep so soundly that he did not wake up until noon.

That evening Summersun was more cheerful than ever and did not leave the apartment. Instead she busied herself chewing on a new goatskin Josep had brought her.

"Are you well, Summersun?" asked Josep Garboil

"Yes, my husband," she answered, looking up at him with profound love. "I have found a birthing place for our son."

Josep Garboil did not question his wife further. He loved her deeply and had learned to accept her customs, much as he had learned to accept all that he had seen in his life.

That spring life stirred in Summersun Garboil and the following winter, in the middle of a snowstorm, carrying the tiny goatskin garments she had made, her old Eskimo parka swollen by the child she carried, she set out at midnight.

"Shall I accompany you, Summersun?" Josep asked, dutifully.

"No, my husband," she said. "It is a long journey to the birthing place. I have communed with the Great Seal Spirit and it is best I go alone."

Josep obeyed his wife's wishes and early the following morning, he awoke to the cries of an infant. He found Summersun sitting by the gas stove, nursing the baby. The boy was red and fat, his hair coal black. Josep's heart expanded with pride and tears of joy filled his eyes. They named the child Francois Enko-a-tuk Garboil. Francois for his great-grandfather and Enko-a-tuk, roughly translated, "glides over ice" in the dialect of Summersun's mother. The name was usually reserved for sleds, but Summersun's command of the language and customs of her people was not total and she liked the sound of the name.

And so it was that Frankie Garboil inherited his love of ice hockey. Before he was two years old Summersun had fitted him with a pair of skates, chewed by herself from beef bones. His interest in hockey enhanced by having served the Flin Flon Flying Fletchers, Josep Garboil began instructing his son. On Sunday afternoons during the winter, when the lake in Central Park was frozen, young Frankie, under his father's tutelage, began skating. By the end of the second winter, crowds would form around the edge of the lake to watch four-year-old Frankie, moving effortlessly up and down the ice surface while pushing an old bagle with the stick his father had fashioned for him.

But their happiness did not last. One summer evening when Frankie and his mother were strolling by the East River, Joey the Plumber's henchmen mistook Summersun for their archenemy, Sam the Chink, and shot her. It was an understandable misunderstanding since Summersun wore pants the year round. They thought young Frankie was Garbanzo, the Chink's bodyguard, who, because of his height, could easily spot machine guns protruding from car windows. Miraculously, Frankie escaped injury. The impact of his mother slamming against him sent him crashing to the sidewalk and knocked him out.

When he came to in the hospital his mother wasn't there. He never saw her alive again. All he could recall was that his mother was telling him about the Aurora Borealis when he heard three loud explosions. At the funeral Josep Garboil wept openly and finally looked like an old man. Years later, when the team Frankie was coaching, and on which his son Joey played, won the New York City Mite Hockey Championship, he recalled the funeral. Tears came to his eyes but he could not tell if they were caused by remembering his mother in her Eskimo parka, resting peacefully in the coffin, or by winning the championship.

CHAPTER 8

Through which we are given the opportunity of playing amateur psychiatrist by examining the conscious and unconscious fears of John Chota, observe his superior, Charles Mullvaney, begin to formulate a plan of feline cunning for the interception of the revolutionaries' communications, and, as an added challenge, consider the very possible relationship between divinity and orthodontia.

For John Chota the subway ride out to Queens to meet Mullvaney was usually a routine, sleep-inducing trip. That afternoon, however, although physically tired, he could not sleep. Not only were things becoming complicated at the college because of the upcoming demonstration, but on a personal level his love life had taken a turn for the worse. Making love to Lena Kojinsky had become an activity to which he looked forward. The previous night, however, he had failed miserably. No matter how much he'd tried to concentrate, his mind kept producing the image of an enormous bird which swooped down from the sky to sink its talons into his back each time he attempted to enter Lena. Even with her on top of him he'd failed. She had turned into a beaked figure, her arms like wings and her ample breasts feathered. In the dark room, rather than her usually strong perfume, all that he could smell was the overpowering stench of chicken excrement.

Lena had been understanding enough. He couldn't find fault with her although he was certain, had he told her about his fears, she would have thought him absolutely crazy. To top the entire episode off, when he finally fell asleep, frustrated and ashamed of his impotence, he dreamt of birds and saw El Falcon dressed in white pants and *guayabera,* his golden machete not in his hand but protruding from his unzippered pants and dripping with blood. He'd have to go and talk with the spiritualist soon. Birds always meant trouble. And how the hell had El Falcon popped up like that? How the hell did he do it? Did he actually fly? Was he a man or a hawk? Not used to doing much thinking, Chota's head ached terribly.

As he entered the dentist's office he heard the drill going off. It sounded like the fluttering wings of a large bird and he grimaced. Several patients were seated in the waiting room, each one attempting to convince him or herself that pain at Dr. Cameron's hands was their birthright. Chota went directly to the desk.

"Can I help you, sir?" asked the secretary, showing off her beautifully reconstructed teeth by way of advertisement.

"Yeah, I have an appointment to see Dr. Cameron," Chota said.

"What seems to be the problem?" smiled the secretary.

"It's my front wisdom teeth," Chota said, employing the password.

"I see," the young woman said. "I believe he's expecting you. Go right in."

Chota walked down the hall, passed several rooms where Cameron's associates were working, and entered the main operating room. Cameron was sitting in the operating chair, smoking a cigarette and reading the *Wall Street Journal.* He greeted Chota and then pressed a button near the sink. The far wall parted and Chota stepped through. Mullvaney was inside, pacing up and down the small room, which was small enough for just about two strides before having to turn back. Once Chota was inside, the wall closed again. The room was completely sound proof so that now the noise of the drill was inaudible.

"How you doing, Johnny?" Mullvaney said.

"I'm all right, Chief," answered Chota, sitting down on one of the chairs.

"Did you come up with anything?"

"Yeah, I think so."

"You want any coffee?"

"Sure, Chief. My nerves are shot. You should see the kids up at the school. They're going nuts with this Martinez thing. We even have the Geology Club hopped up about it. It seems this son of a bitch was a Geology major. I checked it out at New Amsterdam and that's what he's studying. Do you think there's a connection?"

"With what?" said Mullvaney, pouring coffee into two cups.

"You know, him studying Geology and the business with United Front."

"I don't know. I'll have Ramirez look into it. What else do you hear?"

"Nothing, Chief. Everything's in place as far as the demonstrators go."

"I think we're going to have to go in and wire the place up. I thought of trying to intercept some of the communications while they eat but it would take too much manpower. I had Pete Ramirez check on how many Spanish restaurants there are in the city, and not counting the Chinese joints up on the west side, there are over four hundred. So we're gonna have to go in and wire."

"I don't know, Chief. That's gonna be pretty hard. El Falcon's staying there. Nobody goes in. Only a couple of members."

"It's the only way, Johnny. We gotta find out what the hell they're up to. How about sending a couple of men in to check out the phone?"

"There isn't any."

"You sure he's staying there?"

"Yeah. And by Wednesday the girl and the three other guys. Why don't we wait till then and go in and bust them all?"

"We can't do that, Johnny. I mean we could, but we'd only have him on breaking out of jail."

"And conspiracy. I'd testify in a minute."

"No, Johnny. We have to get him in the act and then we can lay a dozen counts on him. We'll just have to go in and wire the place up, even if we have to start a fire next door and send one of the boys in as a fireman."

"What about the people in the building?"

"That's the only problem," Mullvaney said, slumping down into the battered couch which Cameron had provided them when he'd been offered the deal. "It's always people. We're liable to burn down the whole building. By the time those chickenshit bastards in the Fire Department get there and the sickos stop throwing bottles at them, the neighborhood could be up in flames. Jesus Christ! We should've put the bug in there a long time ago. Son of a bitch."

Mullvaney got up and began pacing once more. He removed his jacket and loosened his tie.

"What are we gonna do, Chief?"

"I don't know, kid," said Mullvaney, showing the strain being exacted on him by the case. "Do you know what this means? If we bust El Falcon, we'll put him away for life and we'll break the U.F. wide open once and for all. We're starting to get to the core of all this bombing and disorder in this country."

Mullvaney was working himself up into a frothing, commie-eating lather. His face was flushed with anger and as he paced he pounded his forehead with the palm of his right hand as if to force an idea out. By the end of the hour he was cursing and screaming.

"Goddamn radicals. Stinking, fucking pinko bastards. Weatherman sonsabitches. Fuck them all. If I had my way I'd line them up along with the junkies, pimps, whores, Mafia, Protestants, Jews, Muslims, Wasps and shoot them all and dump them in the river. SDS, Young Lords, Black Panthers, ACLU, communists, all of them. Sonsabitches."

And then he stopped in his tracks, threw his head back and began laughing.

"That's it," he said, pounding his fist into his head one last time. "That's it, Johnny. The cat."

"What cat, Chief?" asked Chota, afraid that his boss had lost his mind.

Mullvaney sat down. Gone were the lines of worry in his face, the reddened face and bulging veins in his neck.

"The black cat at the United Front headquarters," he said. "We'll bug him."

Chota was confused

"Bug him, Chief? I wouldn't mess around with that cat. Bugging him'll just piss him off more."

"What?"

"I don't see how bothering a cat is gonna get us anything. Like what are we gonna do, call him names? Not that he won't understand, because that cat is smart. But it'll just piss him off. You should see him. He's the biggest fucking cat I've ever seen."

Mullvaney was shaking his head.

"Johnny, calm down," he said. "What the hell are you talking about? All I wanna do is get a hold of the cat and wire him up. When he goes in we can listen in on their plans."

Chota's face took on a very curious look, much as if someone had caught him fondling himself.

"Oh," he said. "That kind of bugging."

"Yeah," said Mullvaney. "Tell me about the cat again. Jesus, why the hell didn't we think of this before. Go on, tell me about the cat."

"Well, he's a black tom cat. Big as hell, like I said. The group calls him *Pantera.*"

"Panther in Puerto Rican, right?"

"Right, Chief. In Spanish."

"Whatever. Go on."

"So they keep him around because of the mice. The thing is he doesn't eat them. He breaks their neck, carries them outside to the front of the building and puts them in the garbage can. He won't eat cat food, either. I went to see a spiritualist about it one time and she told me that the cat was probably some bad ass *moreno* in a previous life. You believe in reincarnation, Chief?"

Mullvaney looked at Chota suspiciously. The kid was losing it. He should've never put him on a case where he had to go to college as part of his cover. It never failed. But he should've learned from experience. He'd lost his share of men on school cases. Mulligan, Alfiero, Ryan, Patterson. All of them good cops until they started going to school. Once the colleges got a hold of them they were useless. Everything that came up, even parking tickets, became multiple choice questions.

"Just tell me about the cat, Johnny," he said. "I don't know anything about that other stuff. I mean, what the hell can you believe these days. I'm not even a practicing Catholic. I believe in God and everything, but between finding out that Jesus had a Jewish mother and the Pope being Italian, I don't know what the hell to believe anymore. Just go on with the cat."

"Anyway, he won't even eat cat food," Chota said. "He eats *cuchifritos.*"

"The what?"

"*Cuchifritos.* You know, fried blood sausage, pig ears, stomachs and all that."

Mullvaney made a face and lit a cigarette.

"Jesus, Mary and Joseph, Johnny. Who the hell cooks up the stuff for him?"

"They don't, Chief. They buy it already cooked at a *cuchifritos* place."

"Private operation, right?"

"No, they got stores in the neighborhood that specialize in the food."

"Food?" I thought it was for cats and dogs."

Chota laughed.

"No, Chief. They eat the stuff themselves."

The anger was returning to Mullvaney.

"Sonsabitches," he said. "The U.F., right?"

"No, people in the neighborhood. It's Spanish food. I've never tasted it," Chota lied. "But they say it's pretty good. Especially for sack work."

"What do you mean?"

"You know, when you're with a woman," Chota said. "You just fill up on some pig uterus and go at it," he added, but felt ashamed of himself because it hadn't helped him the previous night with Lena Kojinsky.

Mullvaney was now a mass of confused emotions. On the one hand he was nauseous thinking about someone eating the insides of a pig. His mother had been a swineherd in the old country and the stories she told weren't pretty ones. They had once found her baby brother half eaten by pigs. But he was fascinated by the idea that the food gave one sexual powers. The mixture of the two ideas produced greater anger in him.

"They're sex maniacs on top of their leftist tendencies," he said to himself.

"What?" Chota said.

"Nothing, kid. Go on."

"That's about it, Chief."

Mullvaney thought for a moment.

"That settles it," he said, wiping his brow. He was sweating profusely. "What we'll do is lure the cat out with some of those koochihoochies, whatever you call them, and grab the son of a bitch. We'll take him over to the police vet at the armory and get him to plant a bug in him."

"You think it'll work, Chief?"

"Sure, kid. How do you think they busted that big dope ring in Chicago two years ago? They grabbed this big hood's girlfriend's poodle, bugged it and listened in. Oh, you shoulda heard the tapes. Last year when I went to Denver for that big undercover policeman's convention they'd listen to the tapes day and night. This poodle used to sleep in the same bed with the broad, and most of what was picked up was the bastard plowing his old lady. But they finally got some pretty good intelligence on a shipment and busted them all. The fucking poodle's still carrying the bug around with him, but the Chicago people don't monitor it anymore. Once in a while you get some barking over the police radio. It drives the regular cops crazy trying to figure out what the hell's going on. I guess the transmitter's wearing out and the frequency's drifting. What do you think, Johnny?"

"Sounds good, Chief. We'll just get a nice bag of the stuff and grab him."

"That's it. Neat, efficient police work."

"Anything else, Chief?"

Mullvaney stood up, put his hands in his pockets, took them out, lit a cigarette and then looked at John Chota, unsure as to how to phrase the next question.

"Kid, let me ask you something," he said.

"Sure, Chief."

"This stuff . . . "

"The *cuchifritos*?"

"Yeah, does it really work for . . . well, you know . . . "

With his right fist turned knuckles up at his solar plexus Mullvaney made an outward stabbing motion.

"With the women?" Chota said.

"Yeah," Mullvaney said, blushing just the slightest bit.

"I guess so," Chota said, shrugging his shoulders.

"It figures, given the way they breed."

Chota laughed. He liked the Chief. Here he was talking about Puerto Ricans and it was like he didn't even consider him one. The feeling, rather than angering him, made him feel accepted by Mullvaney.

"Anything else, Chief?"

"No, that's it. You go out first. And tell Cameron I wanna see him in here."

"Right, Chief."

Mullvaney pressed a button and a moment later the wall parted and Chota stepped through the opening. The wall closed and Mullvaney sat down. He felt unusually warm and images of his youth flashed across his mind. Even back then it hadn't been a big deal. You went in, moved in and out a couple of times and it was over. What the hell was the big deal with birth control? He couldn't imagine subjecting himself to the indignity every day. A couple or three times a day to hear some of the young guys. Once every couple of weeks to keep the old lady from going nuts and to keep the plumbing in order. And it wasn't even that often now that he had turned fifty. What the hell was it with the Kennedy's? McMahon, who had done some work for them in Boston, said they were maniacs when it came to that stuff. You could see it with Bobby and all his kids, but McMahon said that JFK was the worst. What the hell did they eat? It sure as hell wasn't corned beef and cabbage and boiled potatoes.

At that moment the wall parted and Conrad Cameron stepped through. As usual he reeked of cologne, except that it didn't take away the foul smell coming out of his mouth. It was so bad that he didn't even work on patients anymore without first having his technicians turn up the gas to the maximum. Mullvaney lit a cigarette, stood up and went to the other side of the small room.

"Sit down, Connie," he said. "How've you been?"

"Pretty good, Charlie," Cameron said. "No complaints. Everything's in place. Investments earning up the kazoo. How about yourself?"

"Can't complain. How's the work going on Mary Margaret?"

"Great, Charlie. Your daughter's going to have the straightest teeth in the convent when she goes in."

"Good, good," Mullvaney said. "How's the family?"

"Everyone's okay, Charlie."

"Wife?"

"Yeah, sure."

"I gotta ask you something, Connie."

"How about . . . ?" Mullvaney said, and again made the stabbing motion from his solar plexus outward with his fist. "The old lady."

A look of panic came over Cameron's face.

"Ellen?" he said.

"Yeah," Mullvaney replied.

"Wait a minute, Charlie," Cameron said, squirming in his seat. "She's my wife, Charlie. Gimme a break. I appreciate what you've done and I don't mind working on your men and their families for nothing. And the work I'm doing on Mary Margaret I would've done anyway as a personal favor. But what you're asking now is too much. Don't get me wrong, Charlie. I owe you for that business with the diamonds and I don't mind being out forty or fifty thousand dollars a year. As far as Ellen is concerned the answer is no."

Mullvaney was puzzled.

"Not even once a month?"

"Not even once a year, Charlie. I'd kill myself first."

A smile of pleasure came over Mullvaney's face. At least he wasn't alone. Cameron was barely forty and he'd packed it in also. He crossed the room and battling Cameron's foul breath, extended his hand.

"You're a good guy, Connie," he said. "I'll see you around."

"Sure, Charlie," Cameron said. "I'll see you."

Mullvaney hit the button on the wall and the panel parted. He stepped through, leaving Conrad Cameron badly shaken and nearly in tears.

CHAPTER 9

In which we catch a fleeting glimpse of El Falcon in action, recognize him, in spite of his disguise, because of his accent, may or may not appreciate his ingenuity in delivering his message, learn a new use for jello as a party treat, are subjected to a sophomoric, but necessary, linguistic exercise, and fantasize a bit more, if given to that type of literary indulgence, about a possible romantic liason between Ingrid Konkruka and the protagonist.

After the story was featured on TV, staff working on the Martinez-Garboil case became more diligent. For the next three weeks they continued to probe, spending longer periods of time questioning Garboil and examining his life. Weekday evenings settled into a routine. The sessions were now taped. Once in a while Helen Christianpath returned in the morning to help him fill in details of what they felt was his fantasy life, but which under analysis they felt he had avoided. He looked forward to the human contact but he was growing weary of their questions and a deepening regret about his life was beginning to set in.

"That was wonderful, Armando," said Helen Christianpath, breaking into his thoughts. "I'm sure the doctors will be pleased."

"Helen, when do you think I'll be able to leave the hospital?" Garboil asked.

"That's not for me to say, dear," replied Helen, rising from her seat and tapping her notebook with a pencil. "Your recovery depends on so many things. I'm sure God's will shall prevail. Have faith. Do you pray?"

Garboil shook his head.

"I'm an agnostic," he said.

Helen Christianpath smiled benevolently.

That's absolutely charming," she said. "Another sign of your need to reject your strict Catholic upbringing as a Puerto Rican and be accepted into an elite group of American society."

Garboil began to protest, but remembered Ingrid's warning.

"I'm sorry," he said. "Just a word in the last vocabulary test."

"I understand, dear," said Christianpath. "I know we're not of the same religious persuasion, but we're all God's children. He listens to us all. I must go now. These notes have to be typed. Be patient. Everything will work out."

She turned and with her prim, crane-like walk, left the large room. Garboil got up from the couch and walked over to the windows. He looked out over the city and a feeling of absolute despair came over him. Things would not work out. He was trapped and there was no way out. In time his mind would dissolve and nothing but a blank would remain. At that point they could do whatever they wanted with him. They had refined their techniques so much that they no longer needed to do lobotomies. But their questions achieved the same results. He fixed his eyes on a tugboat making its way upriver. It sounded its horn and the cry was lost in the cold winter grayness. It was like his voice screaming for help, only no one would listen, and if they did, wouldn't care. He imagined being on the boat, braving the icy wind and feeling the deck roll beneath his feet. Freedom, he thought. That's all he wanted. It wasn't much to ask for. To be able to come and go without fear, to know that he wasn't being controlled by some force outside himself. At that moment he felt a hand on his shoulder and turned to find a man holding a tray of food.

"Powell to the peeples," said the man in a whisper.

He was a medium sized man about forty years of age and although he wore the uniform of a hospital attendant, his carriage was not that of an ordinary helper. His eyes burned with a passionate determination, and his mouth was set in a thin line beneath a full, black moustache. He looked as if he were accustomed to issuing orders rather than receiving them. He set the lunch tray down on the table and spoke in Spanish and then in English.

"Tine is ob de essen," he said. "Jew fine de infolmayson in de yellow."

"What?"

"Nebel mine. It yul lonch an don folget de yellow."

"Who are you?" Garboil demanded, annoyed by the man's directness. "Where's Lester?"

"Shh! Kip qwhyeh," whispered the man, bringing a finger to his lips. "I an El Falcon."

"Holy shit," said Garboil.

"Kip yul boys down. Al jew crasy?"

"I'm sorry," Garboil said. "What are you doing here? You're supposed to be in jail."

"Is a lone story. I go now. Don folget to it de yellow."

"Yeah, sure,"

"Juan more tin."

"Right," Garboil said, although he understood less and less of what El Falcon was saying to him."

"Maritza say don wory. I go now. Powell to de peeples."

El Falcon retreated from the room, looked both ways when he got to the corridor and then was gone. Frank Garboil looked at the tray of food, his eyes going directly to the dish of raspberry jello and fruit. He dug at the red gelatin and began eating it and then changed his mind. Perhaps it was poisoned. He examined it more closely and found, among the pieces of fruit, a small hard object. It was a white jelly bean. He wiped it clean, looked at it for a couple of minutes, turning it in his fingers until he realized that it had been hollowed out. With the end of his ball point pen he pried it open. Inside the jellybean there was a message. LIBERTAD 2/9 8 P.M. F.U. What the hell did it mean? *Libertad.* That meant freedom. 2/9 was the date and 8 P.M. the time. F.U.? The only thing that came to mind was fuck you. Was this some kind of joke? It could't be. F.U.? Frick University. Perhaps some of the radical students were planning something on his behalf. But how had they found out? It couldn't be them. They were harmless. Mostly rhetoric. He turned the tiny message over and he was hypnotized by what he saw. On that tiny piece of paper which had come inside of a jelly bean, there was a diminutive color drawing of the Puerto Rican coat-of-arms given to the island of San Juan in 1511 by the Catholic Spanish kings. Maritza had shown it to him in one of her books. Except that it wasn't quite the same seal. There was no longer a helpless lamb in repose holding some ancient and forgotten royal flag, but a powerful charging ram holding the Lares flag. And atop the coat-of-arms no longer a crown but the castle of El Morro. Instead of the crowned letters F and Y for Fernando and Ysabela were the letters F and U crowned by thatched Indian roofs. Replacing the flags of the Catholic Kings around the placid lamb, there were now the flags of Puerto Rico, the Dominican Republic, Haiti and Cuba. But what was most striking about the coat of arms was the bannered legend beneath it. On one side there was a rifle and on the other a hoe. Instead of the legend JOANNES EST NOMEN EIUS on the banner the word FUCIT had been lettered in the same type of calligraphy.

He studied the word closely, trying to decipher its significance. His Latin studies in high school had been a failure. All he could recall that came close to any meaning was *tempus fugit*. Time flies. Perhaps the artist had made a mistake and misspelled the word. Flies. Flying. Fleeing. It made no sense. FUCIT. Fewcit. Fuse it. It was the Spanish creeping in again. The different flags meant some sort of unity. Fusion. No, that could be it, but it wasn't. It was crazy. What did it mean? Dammit, dammit, dammit he said, frustrated by his ignorance. And then he slammed his fist down on the table and said out loud. "I give up. Fuck it, fuck it, fuck it." And then a curious look came over his face and he began laughing. FUCIT. F.U. of course. *Frente Unido.* FUCIT was the acronym for *Frente Unido Caribeño de Independencia Total.*

His elation in having deciphered the acronym was short lived because he had immediately understood the significance of El Falcon's visit. Maritza was a member of the real United Front, not some silly student organization, just as he had suspected. A cold shiver of fear ran through him. They were getting ready to come into the hospital and free him. *Libertad*. Freedom. It could be an armed assault, a series of bombings to divert attention and he'd be away, living underground for the rest of his life, part of the revolution without even asking to join. He wanted no part of it and yet was touched by their courage and their concern for him. But he was once again caught in the circumstances of someone else's doing. There was no way he'd tell anyone, not even Ingrid about El Falcon or about the planned escape. But perhaps it wasn't anything like that. Perhaps it was a trick, some malevolent scheme the doctors had concocted to test him. But why had El Falcon come himself? Perhaps he was not really El Falcon. It had to be his imagination working overtime. There was no way El Falcon would come on such a risky mission. Kopfeinlaufen, Kohonduro and Christianpath were trying to trick him into something. He quickly destroyed the message by rolling it between his fingers and then dropping it into the toilet and flushing it.

He spent the next two hours thinking about Maritza, El Falcon and the United Front while he stared out at the river, wishing desperately to be away from it all. He next tried reading the newspapers and magazines which were brought to him each day, but found it difficult to concentrate. All he could think about was his freedom. Not the escape on February 9th, but his freedom from the oppression of his life. He then remembered that he hadn't eaten his lunch. The food was cold and suddenly he wasn't hungry. He lay down and closed his eyes but couldn't sleep. By the time the sun began setting he was exhausted.

Around six o'clock that evening, Lester, the regular attendant, came in with his supper. As he ate he thought about Maritza, her warm smile and seriousness. She was the first one to really believe in him. And he had not been able to tell her the truth about himself, about his mascarade as a Puerto Rican. How could he explain how it had all happened?

When he finished eating he tried watching television but fell asleep. When he woke up it was completely dark outside and the hospital seemed unusually quiet. For a moment he thought it was February 9. It was still the middle of January. He rose and went to the desk they had installed the previous week in his living area behind the boards of the simulated hockey rink. He found paper and pen and began writing. He had written a couple of paragraphs when Ingrid Konkruka walked in. She was in uniform and as usual, stunning.

"Good evening, Mr. Garboil," she said, smiling at him. "Are you writing an essay on economics or a love letter to an admirer?"

She was the only one who called him by his right name. Hearing it always surprised him these days. Was part of the treatment brain washing? That was impossible. No, it had been more than eight months since anyone had called him Mr. Garboil.

"Hi, Ingrid," he said.

"Well, which is it?"

"Which is what? Oh, right. I'm writing to my wife."

"You think she'll answer?"

"It doesn't matter. I just want to let her know where I am in case one of the boys wants to know."

"What happened to her?"

"What do you mean? Nothing happened to her."

"I mean, did she split or what?"

He began to explain and hesitated.

"Listen, it's Friday night," he said. "Helen says that the doctors have an emergency meeting about the Ponchartrain people. They're not coming."

"I know." she said.

"Well, you must have things to do. I don't want to take up your time with my problems."

"I don't mind," she said. "I don't go out that much."

Garboil didn't believe her.

"Why are you looking at me that way?" she said.

"What way?"

"Like you don't believe me. C'mon now. No secrets, Frank."

"Okay, okay," he said. "It's that you usually go up and see the firemen."

Ingrid laughed and sat down on the couch.

"Oh that. If you're interested, the only thing I can tell you is that it's pretty innocent stuff. I met one of them when he helped bring in a patient and we got to talking about one thing and another. It turned out that his grandfather was Scandinavian. He asked me about rya rugs, which I do for relaxation. The chief of his company is dying of cancer and he thought it'd be nice if they gave him something special before he died. I've been teaching them how to hook ryas. We're hooking a twelve by ten rug of the firehouse. We finished last Friday."

"You're joking," Garboil said, shaking his head. "I thought you were up there to . . . "

"Yeah, I know. That's what old Kopfeinlaufen thinks. I'm sorry if I gave you that impression. I mean, don't get me wrong. I've been known to throw a leg over someone, and I even had a fantasy about sleeping with the whole Minnesota Viking football team. But it's all latent. Your're right, though. It's weird. The firehouse, I mean. The hoses and poles and a hole to slide down into. The thing is I like being around real men. They enjoy what they're doing and aren't phony like these doctors. Tell me about your wife and kids. Do you want to see them again? I'll tape it and give it to Kopfeinlaufen and Kohonduro."

Garboil thought for a moment.

"Did they ask you to come and pump me?" he said.

"Hell no," Ingrid said. "I wouldn't do it if they asked. It's just that they're more convinced than ever of their theory. It's the only way you'll get out of here, believe me. I hate to see people locked up. It's bad enough when they lock themselves in, but worse when somebody else does it for them."

"What would happen if I try walking out?"

"No way, sweetheart. They have this place locked tight. Electronic alarms, cameras and very sensitive equipment. After a certain hour the elevator doesn't even come up to this floor unless you have a special key. The only way out is to get them to certify that you are who they say you are. They know that I spend a lot of time with you and they think all we do is play house. I think that's one of the reasons they have me here."

"I don't follow."

"You know."

"Oh, I see," Garboil said, catching on. The notion made him laugh with embarrassment. He had been so preoccupied with himself that he hadn't given the idea of making love to Ingrid much thought. "Is that why Kopfeinlaufen always pinches your cheek and tells you to have fun?"

"Right, plus the fact that he's got it into his head that he has to make one last breakthrough in his own self-analysis. He wants to regress to his first feeding and he thinks I'd be the perfect subject."

"Boy, he's really a nut case," Garboil said.

"You got it, Professor. So let's tape. The more convinced they are that you're getting better, the sooner you'll be out of here."

"I guess so," Garboil said.

He wasn't quite sure how much he should trust Ingrid. He liked her, but she was no dummy. With her brains there was no telling what she was up to. He watched her turn on the tape recorder and began talking.

CHAPTER 10

Out of which one may, if not suffering from the ailment, derive pleasure in watching the protagonist wrestle with the demon of early mid-life crisis, meet Joan Worthington Alcott, get some insight into the word *honey* as a term of endearment, ponder the possible application of hubris as the main character exposes his innermost feelings (wherein is posed a further question regarding the value of philosophical analysis as it pertains to sports), meet the protagonist's sons, watch them play ice hockey, interact with their father and bid them a fond adieu since they are only incidental to the main action.

Frank Garboil began thinking seriously about playing ice hockey competitively one morning late in April 1970 while riding the Long Island Railroad to his job at Frick University. He was correcting the examinations given two days previously on which he'd asked for one-word descriptions of the economic systems of a dozen countries, and a short essay on a relatively simple subject. Using his briefcase as a writing surface, he concentrated on recalling the student's face as he corrected the test, attempting at the same time to fathom why some of the answers appeared so far removed from what had been discussed in class.

The essay question: "The role of capital in a socialist economic system," was a fairly basic one. He finished correcting the last of the exams, that of McKinely Robinson, and reread the second, and last line. "In conclusion, the role of capital in a socialist economic system is to corrupt the mothafucka," Robinson had written. Garboil thought for a moment, his red ballpoint posed above the paper.

"Interesting analysis, but much too brief!" he wrote above the student's name. He generously gave Robinson half of the 40 essay points, added up the other answers, wrote 48 atop his comment, circled the grade and shook his head disappointedly.

Where did the anger of the blacks come from? He couldn't understand them. Everything was a battle, a matter of life and death it seemed. Perhaps their paranoia about cultural genocide was justified, but he couldn't see it. The blacks that he knew professionally, the ones on his same level of accomplishment, did not suffer as acutely, so it had to be a matter of education. For someone to maintain his guard up at all times there had to be a threat. But what was it? His thoughts turned away from a psychological analysis to an economic one, but there was even less substance there. Everyone, including most whites, was faced with the same difficulties. Hadn't he had to struggle to pull himself out of poverty? Other than the color of the skin, the problems were the same, so why so much anger? Nothing made much sense anymore. He gave up thinking about it and closed his eyes, recalling his oldest son's game the previous evening.

Peter had scored three goals. The first one had been on a breakaway halfway through the second period. The next on a slapshot from the top of the left circle, and the third on a beautiful give-and-go with one of the other boys on his line. A hat-trick and the championship for the team. But that had been Peter's accomplishment and not his. The parental pride had been there but simultaneously there had emerged a profound feeling of regret. On the way back to their Manhattan apartment, as they drove in a steady drizzle, Garboil had finally understood something which had eluded him for as long as he could remember.

He had always thought it was winning when the stakes were high that made the difference in an athlete, but it wasn't that at all. It was a quality which he imagined all great men possessed. A quality which never manifested itself in other fields of endeavor as clearly as it did in sports. He imagined it must happen as well in war and for a moment felt a loss in having been too young for Korea and too old for Vietnam. Recognizing the feeling as a death wish, not of himself but of some deeply buried dream, he shuddered and concentrated on the rain-slick highway. Peter had fallen asleep and Garboil was thankful that he didn't have to make conversation with the boy.

But the recurring thought emerged once more and with it an unusual anger, one which he had thought himself incapable of experiencing. Why hadn't he been able to truly excel at sports? Everyone had always lauded his potential, but he had never truly lived up to their expectations, or his own. Only three instances stood out in his mind which he could equate with that certain quality which so much obsessed him. The one which appeared as most significant was so intimately connected to his wife that it shamed him to think about it now that their marriage was in such a state of disarray.

In his third year of college he had singled to drive in two runs in the bottom of the ninth inning to win the game. The count was three and two and the pitcher had already struck him out twice. His other time at bat he had grounded weakly to second. Joan had been in the stands, watching him, he'd thought. They hardly knew each other at the time. An Art History class the previous year and a few passing greetings in the corridors of the school. He'd kept himself busy with the girls who gravitated naturally to the atmosphere which college athletes created, establishing a casual rotating society which allowed for interchangeable partners. All of it fun and games with never a thought of permanency. But Joan was different. Unconsciously he had been pursuing her since he became aware from motion pictures and novels that such girls existed. Blonde shining hair always in place; clear blue eyes, innocent and trusting and yet intelligent; a reserve and propriety which was at once casual and haughty. Joan Worthington Alcott, whose family, though not Mayflower stock, had arrived soon after and claimed the distinction of being the first broom makers in America, so that even now, more than twelve years after meeting her, he wasn't sure if he had loved her or whether she represented some obscure need which set him apart from other men.

When the game began he had wondered why she was there. Sports didn't seem to interest her as such, he'd learned from the passing inquiries he'd made. One of the cheerleaders had been with her in high school and said that Joan rode horses, swam and loved being outdoors, but that she never attended athletic events. But there she was, sitting in the stands behind their dugout. In his mind she'd come to watch him play and he concentrated on not being distracted by her presence. Fortunately, playing left field kept him at enough of a distance and when the team came in to bat he was in the dugout. With a left hander pitching he'd had to bat right-handed so that his back was to her. But he'd been flattered that she was there and had witnessed his heroics. Later he was disappointed to learn that she was simply doing research for a sociology paper on participation in civic organizations. Part of the research was a poll. The best place to find people sitting for long periods of time was at a baseball game.

When he came to bat in the bottom of the ninth, the score was 4-3 in favor of Loyola, against whom they were playing that afternoon. There were men on second and third and the most he'd hoped for was a walk. But once he stepped in, something happened which he had never experienced. He knew there would be one pitch to hit and all he'd have to do was recognize it. In his mind's eye he saw the pitch and saw himself hitting it perfectly. When the count went to 2 and 2 and his pitch hadn't come, he stepped calmly out, knocked the dirt out of his spikes and stepped back in. He could hear nothing and his entire concentration was on the pitcher, watching him as would an animal stalking its prey. The next pitch was way outside, a sweeping curve which the pitcher had hoped he would swing at. Once again he stepped back in and looked directly at the pitcher's eyes and, for the briefest of seconds, saw an edge of fear in them. He knew it was a fastball even before the pitcher went into his stretch. When the ball was released he saw it so well that even now, in memory, it appeared clearly, the rotation quite even. He was outside of himself watching the entire brief episode and the pitch seemed to take longer than usual to get to the hitting area, a small eight inch square on the inside part of the plate, barely above his knees but undoubtedly a strike. It was almost as if the ball had been pitched underhand with no other purpose than to be driven.

He had swung at the pitch evenly, confidently, watching it all the way as the bat struck the ball and exploded into a rising line drive a foot over the shortstop's outstretched glove and deep into the left-center gap. As he dropped his bat and began running to first, he heard his teammates' voices from the dugout. He turned first base and was halfway to second when he was intercepted by them. They leaped on him and pounded his back and then he felt himself lifted up on their shoulders and looked for Joan in the stands. She'd already left and with her the feeling of triumph.

But the feeling had been there ever so fleetingly, so that he connected the victory over the circumstances of the base hit to Joan Alcott. More than ever he gave himself to winning her, to breaking into that aloofness and propriety which set her aside from the others, to capturing that elusive secret which he felt she possessed. A month later, after devising ways of being in places where she was bound to be because of her schedule and talking to her briefly about social anthropology, her major, she finally agreed to go out with him. That evening they ate at a small Mexican restaurant frequented by the athletes. During dinner they talked about school and the upcoming exams and their common desire to pursue graduate work and eventual careers in teaching. Halfway through the meal they found themselves opening up and talking about childhood disappointments. When he spoke about his mother's death she stopped eating and her eyes slowly filled with tears. They finished eating and then drove up the coast past Malibu where they walked on the beach and watched the waning moon and the stars and listened to the surf, not yet holding hands but feeling the tension of their attraction for each other. When they finally said goodnight in front of her parents' Bel Air home, he'd felt as if his entire body had been shot through with some wonderful intoxicating drug which gave him power over everything that would ever come his way. They kissed ever so lightly, but driving back to his small apartment near the college, he could see her face clearly and smell the fragrance of her hair and feel the smoothness of her skin.

They did not see each other again for a couple of days, cramming desperately as each prepared for the upcoming final exams and prepared term papers. On Tuesday morning he saw her as he left his Micro Economics final. Needing to be near her, he ran down the sloping lawn, hurdled a low hedge and caught up to her as she was crossing the main quadrangle of the school. They said hello and stood looking at each other dumbly until he asked her if she'd like to see a movie that evening. "Not until after exams are over," she said. She wrote out her phone number, he nodded and she went off towards the library.

The following Saturday they went to the movies and held hands and kissed and afterwards he asked where she'd like to go and she said, "Someplace where we can be alone." "My apartment?" he said. And she nodded and once there they made love almost immediately and she'd cried afterwards just like all girls did in those days, explaining how happy she was, and he held her and caressed her body, exploring as would a blind man new objects, feeling his heart expand with greater passion as he considered his luck in being with her.

That summer he worked as a laborer in a construction company owned by the father of one of his friends, played baseball for a Hughes Aircraft Company team on weekends, ran and lifted weights in preparation for the upcoming football season and saw Joan on a regular basis. Their initial attraction quickly turned into a passionate need for each other, a love which neither of them understood clearly but which they relished and accepted as necessary. During that summer she discovered a sensuality which she had thought impossible before meeting him, becoming remarkably uninhibited in bed and even more secure in her propriety out of it. He in turn was insatiable in his need for her. She reciprocated his ardor by becoming uncanny in her instinctive awareness as a lover, finding new ways of varying and prolonging their lovemaking, never fearing to be thought wanton, a favorite word in her mother's vocabulary.

Towards the end of the summer, when the football team had begun its practice, but school was not yet in session, she called him early in the morning, reminded him that her parents were leaving that afternoon for a two week vacation in Hawaii and that she wanted him to come over with the condition that, once he got into the house, he had to find her. Yes, the door would be open, but he should ring the bell three times in quick succession to let her know it was him. He said he had practice until two that afternoon, but he'd be there as soon as he was finished. During the drills that day he could not keep from thinking of her and was yelled at several times by one of the coaches. During the lulls he found himself fully erect, the swelling uncomfortable inside the protective cup of his jock strap. During the final laps he felt so much energy that the head coach pulled him aside and asked him to ease up, warning him about possible injuries that early in the training camp. He nodded and the coach smacked him on the helmet.

He drove recklessly on his way to her house, not knowing what to expect but wishing more desperately to be with her, touching her body, kissing her and listening to her voice. When he got to the house, he parked the car in the driveway and walked up the winding walk, landscaped and manicured so delicately that it appeared to be sculpted, the edges of the lawn so cleanly cut, the hedges clipped precisely and trees perfectly shaped. He had never seen the house in the daytime, usually picking Joan up in the evening outside the house. Unlike many of the houses in the area which featured Spanish architecture or ultra modern design, this house was a colonial type structure, exuding an odd New England elegance in the middle of the bright California sun. It was a huge three story house and, as he rang the doorbell, his heart beat more rapidly with the anticipation of seeing her. Once inside, he closed the door and stood admiring the opulence within. Some of his friends at the school were wealthy and it was quite obvious when he visited them. This house, however, had a different quality, a dignity and staidness which made him instantly ashamed of his New York background, the tenements and streets and crassness which he had known and from which he thought up to that moment he had managed to escape. The paneled wood, the winding staircase, the chandeliers, the carpets, the furniture, the paintings on the walls, the wall paper itself, seemed to make a statement about propriety and tradition, a warning that one had trespassed onto hallowed ground.

Awed, reduced to childhood emotions of inadequacy, he began searching for her, feeling foolish and betrayed by his naivete, entering each room as if into a sanctuary. By the time he reached the third floor and had not found her, he began to feel a profound loneliness. Nothing existed outside the house. It had swallowed him up and destroyed all his illusions about a better life. There was no way that he could compete on this level. As he came out of a bedroom and back again into the hall, he saw the metal ladder attached to the wall. He looked up and saw that it led to a trap door. He climbed up, pushed the trap door open and there she was. When his eyes became accustomed to the semi-darkness, he could not believe what he saw. Joan was streched out on a double mattress, completely naked, and the front of her body slick and shiny as if she had poured a quart of suntan oil on herself. There was a sweet odor mixed with the mustiness of the storage in the attic, and he shook his head and smiled at her. He sat on the edge of the mattress, afraid to touch her, confused and still injured by the house. "You're crazy," he finally said. "About you," she replied, mouthing the words and opening her legs. Without removing his clothes he began lapping at her, his head spinning from the taste of the honey and his desire for her. He had eventually removed his clothes, entered her and held back a scream as he released whatever pent up feeling the experience had loosed.

Afterwards they had thrown their clothes down from the attic and descended and then had walked around the house naked while she spoke of her family and explained the difference between a sitting room and a living room, poking fun at the house and its pretentiousness until he felt quite at ease and as if he belonged there. They had showered and made love standing under the water. Later that evening, they had made love once again in front of a fire in the library, lying, he could not believe the scene, on a bear rug, shot, she explained, by her grandfather, James Worthington, an explorer and bosom buddy, comrade in arms during the Spanish-American war and presidential confidant to Theodore Roosevelt; making love slowly, methodically, painfully now so that when it was over they fell asleep joined, and he woke up later with the fire out and the room dark and cold, and they made love again quickly, and then ran shivering up the stairs to her bedroom and got into bed without another word, holding each other like small children lost in a dream.

They never spoke about the incident, but whenever she felt as if their lovemaking was being threatened by routine, she thought of ways of shocking him, of changing whatever had become expected. She lured him into making love to her in the most ludicrous places: under beds, in closets, atop tables, in swimming pools when everyone had fallen asleep at parties. And when he thought she'd run out of ideas, she showed up one day at his apartment and simply said: "licorice or peppermint?" He was puzzled, but knowing her, didn't give it much thought. "Licorice," he said. She went into the bathroom, showered and came out dressed in a black negligee, very short and pantiless. He was already in bed naked when she came into the room. She climbed into bed, straddled his chest and took his face in her hands. He immediately smelled the licorice and began laughing. They did not make love and instead talked about marriage and graduate school and letting her parents know how seriously they were in love. He had been to their home on a number of occasions, got along quite well with both of them and was no longer as frightened by the house.

During that last year in college he continued to study as hard as he always had, rose in status as an athlete but did not recapture that feeling of giving himself totally in a crucial situation, except for the second instance which stood out in his mind. As he drove over the Manhattan Bridge, the rain falling more heavily now, he recalled with bittersweetness that crisp fall night in 1961. She was pregnant with Peter, not yet showing, but more beautiful than ever. It was the first game of the football season. Their opponent was the University of California at Burbank, quarterbacked at the time by the great All-American, Bob Littlejohn, who after graduation was drafted number one in both the National Football League and the Canadian Football League but instead chose to join the Peace Corps. Later through a misunderstanding on the sale of rugs from a cooperative he had organized in a village in the Andes, he had to flee. Officially that is the story put out by Washington. Unofficially, the truth turned out to be more tragic. Littlejohn was a haunted young man. He had turned down professional football offers in the hope that his true inclinations would not be discovered, only to go into the Andes and fall in love with a young man of similar proclivities. The other young man, Juan Valdez, turned out to be the son of the mayor of the village. After they were discovered in amorous embrace in Littlejohn's rented house by the police, Juan committed suicide and Littlejohn, alerted by friends that the mayor wanted him killed, escaped higher into the mountains, more out of shame than out of fear. He was found nine months later near the statue of the Christ of the Andes, frozen in what appeared to be a passing stance. The Peace Corps surmised that Littlejohn had been attempting to wave to a rescue airplane rather than making a supposed last sportsmanship gesture. Neither assumption was correct. Bob Littlejohn instead had gone mad. Existing on nothing but coca leaves for two weeks he had begun an extensive remonstration with nature for his misfortune. Nature, impersonal, austere, unconcerned with the rantings and ravings of a gay, All-American quarterback, quieted him forever.

But Littlejohn in his days as a college quarterback was feared by opposing coaches and players. A game against his school sent shivers of fear through opposing secondaries and even the most courageous of players shook when Littlejohn got down under center and began calling signals. That evening, with a slight ocean breeze in the air, Frank Garboil had read a pass play so clearly that he had been able to come from his left cornerback position, step in front of the receiver and intercept one of Bob Littlejohn's passes. UCB had been marching steadily downfield against them, taking the opening kickoff from their own 25 yard line deep into enemy territory. And then, on second down and one yard to go, it happened again and Garboil saw exactly what was to happen. It was uncanny. Everything went very still all around him and he only felt himself speeding ahead and everything else slowing down. When the ball was snapped, he saw the receiver cut over the middle and then make a cut to the outside. Garboil was watching Littlejohn's eyes as he moved. Littlejohn was looking to the other side of the field, but Garboil knew the pass was coming into his area. Without any further thought, he raced directly to the spot where he knew the reception would be made, stepped inside the receiver and was gone. He caught the ball on the run, faked once to the inside against a back who had come out of the backfield and was racing down the sideline for sixty-seven yards and the only touchdown the school was to score that game. The play occurred three minutes into the game and made Littlejohn furious. Coming off the field at half time, after Littlejohn had made shambles of their defense, hitting for four touchdowns, Garboil caught Littlejohn's eye. The quarterback looked around him to make sure no one was watching and then narrowing his eyes, his unhelmeted head resting on his shoulder, he mouthed the word "bitch" at him. Garboil had never seen such hostility in any human being and it made him laugh nervously. This angered Littlejohn more and he came back in the second half and threw for another four touchdowns, picking on Garboil's zone practically every down. Little flares, square outs, deep sideline patterns, posts; so that by the time the game was over, Garboil swore he'd never play football again. The final score was 63-7, but even throughout the embarrassment, Garboil held on to that glorious moment when he had read the pass play, had seen everything before it happened and triumphed.

The other time he had experienced the feeling had almost faded from memory, but it was clearly the most significant. Once in a roller hockey game, he had been able to sustain the feeling for the entire game. When the boys in the old neighborhood began concentrating on football, he would go into Manhattan's Hell's Kitchen to play for the Tenth Avenue Red Wings. On that day the Red Wings were playing against the Bay Ridge Rangers from Brooklyn. There was big money on the game and Bay Ridge had Otto Dusselhofferhaus playing goal. Otto was the best goalie in the history of New York City roller hockey. In practice back in Brooklyn, Otto's teammates would fire four-ounce ball bearings at him, not with a hockey stick but thrown by hand. Once in a while the steel balls got by him, but it was great practice. In actual competition, Otto had recorded 403 shutouts over a period of twenty years. He was once offered a tryout by the New York Rovers, but he had a mental block about playing indoors. A better than average skater outdoors on ice ponds, he became totally incapable of concentrating in an enclosed space. He was convinced that during the game the entire structure would collapse. He went out on the ice, heard a puck slam against the boards in Madison Square Garden and fainted.

Before the game against Bay Ridge, the tension was immense and Frank Garboil had felt absolutely calm. He went on to score one goal that day, but he'd felt totally in command and completely free, skating on the smooth asphalt as if it were ice, the electrical tape puck seemingly attached to the blade of his stick by an invisible string. He made one dazzling move after the other, weaving in and out of players as if a sixth sense were operating somewhere within him. He was only fifteen then, but the older boys had dubbed him Gordie, not daring to award him the last name of the great Howe because then it would've been a joke and they respected this strange kid that came all the way from the Bronx to play hockey for them. He was an unknown quantity, a mystery. No one would ever know what he would've been like on ice. He was big, fast and strong. And he had a reserve, a shield of untold emotions, so that he appeared to be older and more mature than others around him.

As the train moved on in the early spring morning, Garboil regretted once more not having had the opportunity to play ice hockey. But there had been little chance to play then. If he were sixteen now, in 1970, he would be playing Junior A Hockey in Canada, and in a few years he might be drafted by the National Hockey League. But could he really have played? Could he have gone that far? Did he have all that it took? The doubts bothered him and he wished he hadn't thought about them.

There had always been doubts. And yet he loved the feeling his body gave him when he ran, the strength of his legs as cleats or spikes cut into the fresh grass. He loved the smell of autumn, the cold of winter in his face, the freshness of spring when every aroma from the earth was rich and new. He'd loved playing sports: racing after a line drive, knowing that it seemed impossible to catch, but going beyond himself and catching up to it, feeling the ball strike the glove and remain there as he tumbled over, his heart pounding and the sweet smell of his perspiration on his face; the hitting of football and the strategy that went into each play; the bonds that were created between men during games and the comraderie of the locker room, that special constant bantering of athletes, the jokes about ability and that special courage which once in a while was displayed by the athlete. There was about athletics a freedom which he now missed. But he'd never known what it was to feel that freedom, that camaraderie on ice. And even in the other sports he felt as if he didn't have that special quality which separated the true athlete from the one who simply plays, a purity which set him apart.

At the age of thirty-three, Garboil had finally understood the meaning of the saying, "It's not whether you win or lose, but how you play the game." So many of the people he knew—the liberals, the Marxists, the revolutionaries, the intellectuals, the artists, the frisbee-playing hippies, stoned and programmed and not coordinated enough to throw a football back and forth without looking like a troop of Girl Scouts—criticized him because he enjoyed sports, liked competition and did not deny it.

The ones on the left had something to say about sports which left him angry and frustrated. They either turned up their noses in analytical derision or fawned over the people in sports, calling their heroes by their first names. They were like potbellied, asthmatic groupies. But they seldom played and when they did they didn't take the games seriously. Not do-or-die seriously but with integrity and enthusiasm. And the conservatives were no better with their VFW, American Legion, bomb-the-hell-out-of-them rhetoric: the policemen, the firemen, the civil service workers or maybe a sanitation worker and you want a nice air conditioner to keep cool in the summer hardhat jerks, who were just as afraid but instead screamed their guts out and dropped dead with the same regularity as the liberals. All of them were unfulfilled, having killed their dreams early on out of fear. But with the hardhats winning was everything and losing equated with personal dishonor, something akin to treason when the situation was political and wifely infidelity when social, punishing themselves, pushing their beings to the point of fanaticism.

Both sides, however, left and right, were involved in winning or losing without any knowledge of their impact on each other. And even in war, the ultimate game, both held on to the same attitudes. One side calling for bombing without regard for the lives of those they bombed; the other side ready to bomb the opposite if given the opportunity, using a rationale which left them violated and empty; each one accepting the role of winner or loser solely on the basis of superficial reality, having separated the self from participation. And, yet it was how the game was played, after all, that counted. Not the rules but the attitude one brought to every aspect of the game, the challenge of knowing that the odds could not be computed accurately, since the two elements necessary for victory, luck and the human spirit, were not predictable. And more importantly, one was connected to the other. For no matter how much luck was thrown one's way, one still had to have the vision, the anticipation, to see it coming a micro-second or even a year before the event took place.

One had to see, not simply look. And one had to see and learn to see what was apparently not there, making of the self a microscope one second and a telescope the next. And to what end? The trophy? The congratulations? Or simply the knowledge that one had triumphed against the unknown, the absurd, the seemingly incomprehensible, tagged fear for want of a better word. For if one were to know, one had to choose to be a winner and that alone stopped the process, since awareness stopped and attention shifted to the telescope, looking ahead and focusing on the dais, the presentation, the awards ceremony, the print in the newspaper, the manufactured humility of the acceptance speech. And in that micro-second of indulgence, luck presented a break which required immediate recognition and instantaneous reaction. Ice hockey more than any other sport required that type of selflessness and concentration.

The knowledge stunned him and yet his discovery had come vicariously, analytically, through observation rather than prolonged experience. The train came to a stop at the Jamaica station. He watched the people from Brooklyn and Queens enter the train. The exmuters, he thought. They lived in the city and worked in Long Island like himself. Except that his job was a joke. Three classes to be taught three times a week, some faculty committee work, four hours of time spent in his office in consultation with students for a fairly substantial sum of money. The people on the train were mostly black women going to clean other people's homes.

After the train began moving again Garboil returned to his musings. He was now certain that those who won consistently did so by being so in command of themselves that they saw every break, every turn of the action. But it wasn't control over emotions or releasing of them through intimidation, but an energy which was constantly being released and taken in, a psychoemotional symphony in which the true athlete was both conductor and orchestra, his or her presence constantly in play even when seemingly static.

He had seen them, felt them, heard their vibrations in ball parks, stadia, ice rinks, boxing rings, tennis courts, golf courses, card games, cocktail parties and meetings and he envied their ease. And he had played against them, experiencing the fear and the awe at their madness, their magic and power, at times frozen by imagining what was to happen and therefore capitulating before it happened. Littlejohn had been superhuman that way, so it had nothing to do with what people thought of as traditional male roles.

The fear was ancestral, he had thought lately, some historicogenetic occurrence which took place in the developmental stages of the human race. He'd asked Joan and she'd looked at him curiously. She had finished her dissertation in Cultural Anthropology, and whether he had phrased the questions incorrectly or she was aware of the phenomenon and would not let on, she chose to be confused. But she was one of them. Her cool demeanor and indomitable spirit and will had always pointed to it. How could he have ever thought that she wasn't a competitor? She simply competed at a higher level and he had never been aware of it. Where did that leave him? It was as if his type of person belonged to an inferior species and she to a father race which now inhabited the Earth, crossing color lines, transcending ethnic groups, surmounting cultural barriers to establish supremacy over the weak. The joke was too brutal. Three million years of development culminated by a master race.

As the train moved through the Long Island countryside he felt a deep hatred for those supermen and the paralysis they caused him. The paralysis was always fatal. It was like walking in a jungle knowing there were carnivores all about and never knowing when they would strike. And always the gnawing guilt that it could've been different, aware that in some way he could have closed the gap because the talent was there. Forever having to accept in disgust the "Hey, shake it off, kid. You missed it by inches. A little more and you'da had it." Substituting the missed fly ball, basket, touchdown, or goal with the rationalization that the opponent had been lucky or just great.

Joan and Peter belonged to that master race and he and Joey were the outcasts, the second bests. But it wasn't that simple. He had triumphed with Joey's team. Poor out-of-it Joey, so sensitive and confused by everything about him. He had chosen to coach out of a need to see Joey develop some self-respect and not compare himself to his older brother. He hadn't been aware of everything he'd learned in the past twenty-four hours and simply wanted to be with Joey, guiding him, sensing that he was more like himself than Peter. Peter was so different. He was a superb athlete, a fierce animal-like creature whose hunger and drive reminded him of those others. Joey on the other hand, although technically as good a skater, lacked that special quality and would resent the shortcoming later in life.

The league had given Garboil the Crusaders, a group of six- to eight-year-olds in what was called the house league of the Mite Division. The house division, as opposed to the all-star team, was for beginning players and those who were developing or lacked the necessary skills to play at the all-star level. Of the boys on the team, Joey was by far the best skater, having played the year before. As the train sped on, Garboil recalled the day in October of the previous year when he was handed the gold and black jerseys. He gave them out to the boys, reserving number 9 for Joey, because nine is a special number in hockey, given out to players of great promise. But even with their jerseys on, the boys did not resemble a team. They were awkward and uncomfortable on skates, hardly able to skate across the rink without falling. It gave him pleasure to see Joey outskate them. The pleasure was short lived. They lost their first game ll-l. That was in early November. The boys had chased the puck wherever it went, falling down every couple of steps, at times even crawling after it, drawn to the black rubber disk out of some ancient and primal instinct to hunt down prey.

In spite of the disappointment, a couple of boys showed promise. They lost another game and then another. Eventually they managed to win one. By this time their skating had improved. One of the boys, a quick, seven-year-old blossomed from one week to the next. Whether because of his father's incredible pushiness or because the boy had an innate knack for the game, he began showing flashes of talent. Inspired by the change in some of the boys, Garboil purchased bright gold letters and named a captain and three co-captains. The big gold C went on the Klein boy's shirt. As he had hoped, the letter became a talisman. The same was true of the three other boys he had chosen, including Joey.

Garboil began explaining the game to them on the ice and off, reminding them of their responsibilities and outlining for them each position separately. By the time Christmas came, the Crusaders had a 4 and 8 record. And then it happened. There was a two week hiatus for the holidays and, whether or not it was the plateau necessary before they peaked, they came back with a totally new spirit and approach to the game. It was as if all the information that he had given them had finally been internalized.

The two week period gave Garboil a chance to rest and spend some time away from the college. He skated regularly, going off early in the morning and returning just as Joan was getting up. Although he felt unsure of himself on ice skates at the beginning of the season, in time he was able to skate as well as many of the parents who skated with their sons. The only exceptions were the few fathers who had grown up with ice hockey and had played on varsity or intramural teams. And even then some of them did not seem to have his drive.

He wished he had started playing as early as Peter and Joey, with someone trying to teach him. His father had been good before he died, but he never had much time and then they always had to wait until the lakes froze. The memory of his childhood was so hazy that at times he wasn't sure if many of the things that he recalled had taken place or he simply had made them up to fill up a blank in his recollection.

But Garboil loved ice hockey. For him the game was a metaphor of life, full of times which could not be recaptured, each occurrence distinct from the next and even in the little boys' games, the quality of the unexpected set the sport apart from all others. The time was filled with constant motion with only minor pauses. Often the action resembled a game of pool with bodies bouncing off each other and the sideboards. Other times it was like some badly staged representation of a jousting match, each small helmeted warrior wielding his stick at dangerously high levels. And yet in the middle of the madness, all at once and as if by magic, the grace and beauty of the game shone through brightly and the interaction between one team and another reminded one of a fine and well choreographed ballet. And the comparison to dance was not far-fetched. The grace and beauty of movement required both strength and grace.

By the end of January each of the boys was skating with greater confidence, kept their sticks on the ice and passed with surprising accuracy. Most of all they respected his insistence that the puck belonged to all of them and that it didn't matter who scored the goals as long as the team won. They won their first game after the holidays. It was a tension-filled game in which they fought back three times and won 4-3. The parents were ecstatic. Garboil examined each boy's face for a sign of elation, but they were impassive, a cold glint in their eyes, but none of the wild enthusiasm of their parents. The thought crossed his mind that they had not truly understood the significance of the win. The goalie, in particular, had been spectacular. As he came off the ice after taking a couple of laps around the rink, Garboil was greeted by the goalie's father, a big, red-faced man who had been less than cordial in the past.

"Great game, coach," the man said.

"Thanks," Garboil replied. "Your son kept us in the game."

"Well, he better. That's his job. I had him out every day over Christmas. I put weights on his skates and told him, if he wasn't going to skate, he'd have to give up the game. He cried and complained, but after a while he started huffing and puffing."

"That's good. Let's see what happens next game."

He sat down next to Joey and began to unlace his own skates and then Joey's. He looked at his son and tried to decipher Joey's lack of enthusiasm. Joey had played better than he thought was possible, but he looked absolutely withdrawn, morose in fact. Parents were now coming over to congratulate Garboil. Norman Klein, his captain's father, couldn't stop talking about the game.

"Did you see those passes, Frank? What did you tell them before the game?"

"The same thing I always tell them. They just caught on. It happens. A team just goes along at the same level and then all of a sudden starts playing together and zooms up."

He wanted to explain about plateaus and growth and learning, but thought better of it. Why take the enjoyment out of the victory. It was still a mystery why one group of people became a team and another with equal talent did not. But that wasn't it. Something had happened which he couldn't explain. When he was finished putting his skates and gloves away, he helped Joey with his own equipment. The boy was as serious as ever but something had changed.

"You played a fine game, Joey," he said.

"Thank you, Daddy," said the boy, dutifully. "What place are we in now?"

"Oh, we're still in last place. But if we keep playing like that, there's no telling where we'll end up. After a while we'll have our name right above the bulletin board and up on the wall we'll be so high."

Joey laughed and waved his hand at him.

"You're just joking," he said.

"Oh, yeah? Wait and see. Com'on, let's go and pick up Peter and get some pancakes."

"Okay," Joey said. "Let's go."

The words, their ring, startled him momentarily. He looked at Joey and knew immediately that he was one of the others. His heart ached at the thought that Joey would also become one of them. He should've been happy, but he wasn't, and his fears were confirmed on the way to pick up Peter. Outside, the sky was low and gray and the air bitter cold. He waited some five minutes for the car to warm up and then drove through the light traffic of early Sunday morning, speeding moderately to catch the last period of Peter's game at the Coney Island rink. Halfway there, Joey asked him if Peter was a better hockey player than him. Garboil hesitated before answering.

"I can score goals just like him," Joey said.

"Can you?"

"Sure. You want me to?"

"That's up to you, Joey," Garboil said, pleased by the boy's confidence.

"I'm going to be on the All-Star team. You watch."

"All right, but remember that you can't hog the puck."

"I won't. I can pass."

"I know you can."

When they arrived at the rink, Peter's game was tied 2-2 with ten minutes to go in the twelve-minute last period. The Squirt Division All-Star team on which Peter played was the top nine- and ten-year-old team in the entire Metropolitan New York area.

Rather than a group of regular nine and ten-year olds, they resembled a pro team. Their skating, passing, hitting, defense and knowledge of the game was spectacular. They were playing a similar team from Massachusetts. As father and son sat down in the stands behind the benches, Peter's line came on the ice. Garboil watched his older son stride effortlessly onto the ice, his shoulders bobbing defiantly as he approached the faceoff circle to the left of his team's goal.

He was a strong looking, fast skating kid with what seemed to Garboil to be ice water running in his veins and yet an explosiveness which sometimes left him amazed that he had sired such a specimen. There was no way Joey could ever be like him. As soon as the puck was dropped Peter drew it back to his defenseman, wheeled behind his net, came out in front and took a pass effortlessly on his forehand. He rushed out over the blue line, looked up ice to the left, saw that his left wing was covered, looked to his right, caught his right wing a step ahead of the back-checking opposing wing and hit him perfectly with a pass. He then broke furiously ahead. He skated quickly and with a flashiness that was breathtaking even to Garboil. In a few long strides he reached the opposing blue line and took a return pass from his wing and he and the other boy were in two-on-one on a lone defenseman, who was backing up as they came. Peter faked, faked again, his head moving rapidly from one side to the other, the puck dancing on his stick and in another second he was around the defenseman and streaking in on goal. At the last moment he caught sight of his left wing and fed him a perfect feathery pass which the boy tucked up high over the goalie's shoulder. The sticks went up and Garboil found himself staring at the ice in blank amazement. Usually he would jump out of his seat flying, his hands up in the air as if he were on the ice and raising his own stick. Instead he felt a coldness akin to the anger which he imagined came over people when they were about to kill without ensuing regret.

"I'm going to do it just like that," Joey said, and Garboil knew he meant it.

Peter went on to score another goal, giving him two goals and two assists for the game. The final score was 5-2, and as they skated off the ice at the end of the game, Garboil watched Peter and had no doubt the boy would be at least a better-than-average college player. He was still not sure how much Joey had.

During the week, Garboil pretty much forgot about Joey's resolve. As they drove out to the rink the following Sunday morning, Joey seemed no different than before. He seemed as quietly sad as ever. They were playing the first place team and Garboil concentrated on the road while he thought of the upcoming strategy. All they needed to do was play defense and wait for a break. The other team could score at will, so it was important to stay close to their players.

When the game started, Garboil hoped for the best but wasn't quite sure if the Crusaders had a chance. The Klein line, his first line, went out and nothing much happened. Each side had a shot on goal but beyond that it was as he had expected. The first line would play their first line evenly. It was the second and third lines which worried him. He called out for the second line to go out on the ice.

"Let's go. O'Brien, Garboil and Bova. Patterson and Russell on defense."

What happened next gave him goose bumps and a feeling of nausea. Joey completely dominated the action. In one sequence he picked the puck up behind his own net and skated the length of the ice, weaving in and out of players and finally letting go a shot that totally took the goalie by surprise. On that first shift, he scored a goal and had two assists. The rest of the game was the same. No contest. Joey had five goals and three assists and the final score was 16-2. After the game everyone came over to Joey and congratulated him. His expression didn't change. He nodded and thanked each parent or teammate. More than Peter, he was reminded of Joan and his heart ached more than ever. He felt totally alone and the victory felt ashy in his mouth. Later that day while he was preparing a lesson for the following day, he received a call from the Mite All-Star coach. He'd seen the game and was wondering if Joey could come to the next All-Star practice.

"I think he's ready, Frank," the coach said.

"I guess so," Garboil said, emptily.

"Listen, I know it's a lot of driving with Peter on an All-Star team, but it'll be worth it. Joey deserves it. He's as good as Peter, if you don't mind my saying so."

"I don't mind and I agree."

"Good. Wednesday evening at six."

He told Joey about it and the boy nodded and went back to watching television. That Wednesday he'd gone out on the ice and blended right in with the other boys. He was put on the third line because one of the boys had been hurt. That Saturday he'd played in his first game out in New Hyde Park and scored a goal and an assist in a 5-3 win. In subsequent weeks he continued to improve and was moved up to the first line and he and Peter began palling around, talking hockey all the time and exchanging looks of confidentiality which left him feeling like a stranger.

When Garboil returned to teaching the following week, he couldn't keep his mind on his work. Even as he lectured, scenes of Peter and Joey playing flashed across his mind. By Wednesday he stopped lecturing and began talking about hockey in the Soviet Union, as an example of the drive of socialist nations and the dedication of the athlete within that economic system. Of course their system was different and their top players might as well be professional, but nonetheless we had to respect them as players. As he looked out over the class no one seemed impressed by the subject. He asked the students if they had any comments on the subject but was again met by silence. Most of them were not interested in sports. The ones who were divided their interest between football and basketball. He tried again by asking if any of them had ever seen a hockey game. A couple of students shook their heads. McKinley Robinson was glaring at him.

"What is it, Robinson?" Garboil said.

"It's a honky sport," Robinson said.

Garboil smiled uncomfortably at Robinson, agreed that for the most part it was. He wanted to tell Robinson about Billy Barnes, the goalie on Peter's team, and about Jeff Thomas, who the previous year had received a scholarhip to play for Brown University, but knew that it wouldn't change Robinson's mind. He felt annoyed and dismissed the class ten minutes early. The loneliness enveloped him once again and he sat down at his desk, pondering what it all meant. He was totally alone. Joan and Peter and now Joey were not part of him anymore.

That had taken place at the beginning of February and there it was April and the feeling of loss and despair had not left him. Now as the train pulled into the station and Garboil stood up, he knew he'd have to find a way to play the game on a more serious level than simply getting on skates and carrying a puck around the rink during practices of little boys' teams. He owed it to himself. He knew now what had been missing all those years. His sons had that quality and it hadn't been inherited solely from their mother. No matter what it cost, he had to play.

CHAPTER 11

In which we pause briefly in order to advance the plot, observe Inspector Mullvaney put into operation the vast law enforcement machinery at his disposal in order to foil FUCIT's plan to rescue the protagonist from psychiatric incarceration, become acquainted with the police department's veterinarian, and decide for oneself whether Johann Reich was correct in stating: "A Saint Bernard is better than nothing."

The day after his meeting with John Chota in Conrad Cameron's dental clinic, Deputy Chief Inspector Charles Mullvaney moved into high gear. Needless to say, Charles Mullvaney had not risen to his present status through sitting by idly while crime ran rampant in the streets. Charles Mullvaney was a modern officer of the law, totally versed in the latest intelligence techniques and the most advanced methods of electronic detection. He walked into his office early Tuesday morning and set into motion a plan which only a genius of police work or the writers of Mission Impossible could have conceived.

His initial move was to phone the police veterinarian. The veterinarian's duties were primarily the medical well-being of police horses and dogs. Once in a while he had to detoxify one of the pot-smelling dogs, but outside of that, there was nothing much to the job. Beyond his official duties he sometimes gave advice to officers on their pets and on occasion treated the pets for a small fee. His salary was unimportant, since he also had a private practice catering to the affluent residents of the Upper East Side of Manhattan. In reality he had no need for the extra money which the department paid him. The son of a Lutheran minister from Iowa, Wellington Kincaid had come to New York after completing his training at the end of World War II and remained to make his fortune. He was instantly captivated by the pace of the city, ever in wonder at its capacity to go on year after year, viewing the great urban center as a giant, lovable, but very sick Cocker Spaniel.

A moderate man in taste and habit, he was at times given to flights of fancy in which he saw himself performing difficult medical feats in order to save the city from disaster: a rampaging herd of circus elephants in Central Park, a poisonous and deadly snake loose at the Metropolitan Opera, a man-eating tiger at the City Council or a bear at the Fifth Avenue library. But nothing of consequence ever happened. Whenever the occasion arose for him to display his heroism and civic spirit, the ASPCA was called in and it was they who rescued kittens in sewers or coaxed raccoons down from liquor store signs. He was still quite upset that Elissa Paddleford, living no more than a few blocks from his office, and a dear friend for years, had not called on him when that crazed goat had invaded her property.

He yearned for adventure and even took to riding patrol with the mounted police in Central Park. His only notable piece of police work had occurred several years ago while riding with Sergeant Kassimir Michailovitch, a giant of a Police Department cossack, who spent most of his time on patrol humming Russian ballads and feeding squirrels. On that day late in a spring afternoon, Dr. Wellington Kinkaid, riding the bay mare Linseed, spotted movement in some bushes near the eastern end of Castle Lake. He patted the mare's neck and approached slowly. He dismounted a few yards away from the movement and signaled Sergeant Michailovitch to cover him.

Kinkaid squatted and peered through the dense foliage. What he uncovered was one of the most distasteful and distressing sights he had ever encountered in more than thirty years of working with animals. There, under a clump of bushes, was a young woman necking with a Saint Bernard. Sergeant Michailovitch, who had followed Kinkaid, got down from his horse and made the arrest at Kinkaid's insistence.

"This is the most disgusting sight I've ever seen," he said. "Arrest this woman, Sergeant."

"What's the charge, Doc?"

"Corrupting the morals of an animal," said the outraged Kincaid.

"You got it, Doc," said Michailovitch. "Let's go, lady. You *and* the dog. You're both under arrest and make sure you keep him on a leash or I'll have to charge you with that too."

The young woman, a Madison Avenue advertising company graphic artist, at the time undergoing Reichian sexual therapy, began barking, baring her teeth menacingly, and exposing herself to the two men. The young woman's behavior excited the Saint Bernard into joining her in barking and baring his teeth and the young woman's ample breasts excited Michailovitch, who didn't know whether to draw his gun or drop his pants, such was his confusion. Kincaid reacted to the situation calmly and efficiently. He went to his horse, removed his medical bag from the pommel, and returned with a small tranquilizer pistol with which he shot the Saint Bernard. The large dog was at first startled by the pop and then slowly his eyes became glassy, his legs rubbery, and finally he collapsed in a heap. At this point the young woman went berserk and attacked Kincaid. Michailovitch sprang into action and subdued the woman but not before she had bitten the inside of his thigh and had an orgasm in the process.

It should be pointed out that the reference to Reichian therapy has nothing to do with Wilhelm Reich, the famed psychotherapist, but with his self-proclaimed third cousin, Johann Reich. A charlatan and contemporary of Wilhelm, the latter Reich, jealous of the former's prominence, sought to revolutionize sexual therapy by insisting that certain cases of female hysteria were caused by poor integration with members of the opposite sex, whom the women considered worse than dogs. These women needed the companionship of men, but in ninety-eight percent of the cases, they were highly sexed but unable to be in their company without wishing to bite off the men's sexual organs. Johann Reich suggested in his now infamous paper "A Saint Bernard is Better than Nothing," delivered in Vienna in 1934, that in order to cure these women of their androphobia, they had to develop full sexual relationships with dogs, preferably large, woolly ones. Johann Reich was of course laughed at and scorned by the medical community of his day. He went into hiding in Bavaria to continue his research and experimentation. His papers, thought to have been lost when his paramour, assistant and one-time patient, Marlene Fleischman, later known during Hitler's reign as the Dog of Deggenmdorf, chewed them up, were discovered in the basement of a West Berlin pet shop by a British Intelligence officer. Eventually the papers came into the hands of an American medical school dropout who saw their possibility as a money-making scheme, set up shop in an apartment in New York's East Village and advertised in *The Village Voice*, claiming a new cure for this specific sexual dysfunction in women.

Of course, from Wellington Kincaids's point of view, the matter of the young woman and the Saint Bernard came to naught. The case came to trial, but as in so many cases in which alleged sexual abuse has taken place, the defense lawyer was quite explicit in eliciting testimony from the witnesses. Kincaid, a deeply moral man, was further outraged by the questions. At one point in the proceedings, the judge himself burst out laughing when the lawyer asked Kincaid to describe the degree of sexual excitation being experienced by the Saint Bernard when Kincaid first saw the young woman and her dog in pre-coital embrace. Kincaid was struck dumb. Unable to utter the simplest of explanations, he sat staring out at the courtroom. The defense attorney called for a dismissal and the judge had no alternative but to grant the motion, agreeing with the attorney that there was insufficient evidence to charge the young woman. Of greater chagrin to Kincaid was Michailovitch's part in the case. In attacking the sergeant, the young woman had finally broken through and, as Johann Reich had predicted in his paper, the young woman fell madly in love with the handsome cossack. Michailovitch, lonely, sexually starved and unable to drive the image of the young woman's orgasm from his mind, reciprocated her interest in him and chose to fabricate a story which totally contradicted Kincaid's account.

It was with unqualified pleasure then, that Kincaid received Inspector Mullvaney's telephone call. Although the two men didn't know each other, it was sufficient that they worked for the police department to create an atmosphere of mutual trust. That trust, however, proved to be a disappointment.

"Yes, Chief Mullvaney," Kincaid said, cordially when he picked up the phone.

"Doc, I need your help."

"I'm at your service, Chief," Kincaid replied. "Do you have a pet in need of medical attention?"

"No, nothing like that," Mullvaney said. "I have to do a little job and need your expertise."

Kincaid's heart skipped a beat and he found it difficult to speak.

"Does this concern business within your area of responsibility in the Department?" he stammered.

"Yes, it does, Doc," Mullvaney said. "The job has to be done in a hurry or else all hell's gonna break loose in this city."

It was the opportunity Kincaid had yearned for.

"Can you be more specific, Inspector?"

"Not right now, Doc. This line's probably unsafe. We run a check on it every day, but this guy at Gracie Mansion doesn't miss a trick, if you know what I mean."

"Yes, he's quite a precocious young man. I understand your concern perfectly."

"Good. Now here's the story. Meet me in the Central Park Children's Zoo at noon. Over in front of the Rabbit Hole. You got that?"

"Yes, Children's Zoo, Rabbit Hole. How will I know you?"

"Right. I'll be carrying a New York Mets banner. Just ask me who's winning. Wear a white rose on your coat. You got that? Twelve noon."

"Very well, Inspector. I'll be there."

At ten minutes to twelve Mullvaney entered the Central Park Children's Zoo. A few children were running back and forth over the bridge which crosses the duck pond. Mothers and nannies chatted pleasantly in the brisk February air. Huddled at one end of the enclosure as they sought the warmth of the sun, they took little notice of Mullvaney as he came in. Only one person, a nine-year-old with long hair, came over to him. He wore gray slacks, a blue school blazer with a crest and a blue tie.

"You lost, mister?" he said.

"No, I ain't lost, sonny," Mullvaney replied, ignoring the boy.

"So what are you doing here?"

"I'm looking at the animals," Mullvaney said, growing annoyed. "Now go on and beat it. Go ahead."

"Oh yeah? Looking at the animals, huh?," the boy sneered as he stood his ground. Mullvaney walked away and the boy followed. "You should be looking for the seven train. That's the one that takes you to Shea Stadium for the Mets games. Anyway, you have plenty of time. Two months at least. Bye."

Mullvaney became immediately self-conscious about the Mets banner.

"Smart ass, liberal schmuck kid," he muttered as the boy ran back across the bridge.

At exactly twelve noon Wellington Kincaid walked into the Children's Zoo. He was a short, plump man whose close association with domesticated animals had given him a rather docile appearance. He wore a white rose on the lapel of his expensive camel hair coat. When he saw the man with the Mets banner at the other end of the miniature zoo, he waved his hand and then shouted in a rather shrill Pekingese bark of a voice.

"What's the score, Chief?"

The nine-year-old had gathered a few of his playmates together and told them about the lost man. When they heard another adult obviously assess the situation as they had, they burst out laughing and ran laughing over to Mullvaney. In their semi-long haircuts and school blazers and ties, they represented to Mullvaney another generation of the upcoming liberal, Wall Street types who had ruined the city. He was livid with rage and glared menacingly at the kids. They glared back defiantly, daring him, he imagined, to make a mistake so that they could run to their fathers, who would in turn run to the mayor or the *New York Times*. Bastards.

He stomped off in Kincaid's direction, took his arm and led him forcefully out of the Children's Zoo. When they were outside the gate and out of hearing range of a pretzel vendor, Mullvaney broke the Mets banner over his knee and threw it into a garbage can.

"What the hell are you doing, Kincaid?" he said, through his teeth.

"I was just following orders, Inspector Mullvaney," replied Kincaid, totally intimidated by the bigger man.

"What in the hell do you think I'm running, an advertising agency? You could've blown the whole operation. Those little liberal s.o.b. kids are probably plants for the mayor. He's dying for us to screw up so he can get on television and collect more votes from the scum of this city."

"I'm sorry, Inspector," said a contrite Kincaid. "It won't happen again."

"I hope not," said Mullvaney, having overcome the worst of the embarrassment. "For all our sakes, I hope not."

"That serious?" asked Kincaid, growing anxious to be let in on the plan.

"More than you can imagine, Doc. Let's take a walk over to the Bird House. No one'll hear us in there."

Inside the Bird House, among the racket of three hundred cackling, whistling, cawing and clucking birds, Mullvaney outlined his plan. Kincaid listened to the shouting Mullvaney, who was convinced that one of the mynah birds was saying, "Fuzz, fuzz, fuzz."

"What you have to make clear to me," Mullvaney said, "is if you have any reservations about putting the device in the cat."

"None at all," said Kincaid.

"What?" shouted Mullvaney. "Speak up."

Kincaid moved closer to Mullvaney.

"I said I don't have any reservations about my part in the operation. Animals have been used before to do police work and I have a good deal of experience in this type of thing."

"How long do you think it'll take once we get the cat to you?"

"Not long at all. It's a relatively simple operation, provided the device is not too large."

"It's just a little thing, smaller than a dime and thinner."

"Then there's really no problem. A small incision on the abdominal epidermis, implantation, suturing and it's done. Of course we'll have to sedate the animal, but he'll be up and around within the hour. By the time we get him back to his destination, he'll be ready to go to work."

"Good. We're all set then."

"Inspector?"

"Yeah, Doc."

"May I ask you a confidential question?"

"Shoot, Doc."

"I was curious. Is this one of your new trained animals?"

"Right, Doc. Straight out of the academy."

"You have a cat training program at the academy?"

"Brand new. Nobody knows about it. Not even the commissioner. So, mum's the word. Okay, Doc?"

"My lips are sealed, Inspector."

"Right. We'll bring him by the armory about midnight."

"One suggestion, Inspector."

"Go ahead."

"I think we might be better off at my clinic. Better facilities and all that. You don't want to subject the animal to unnecessary stress before the assignment. Do you have my address?"

"No problem, Doc. We know where you are. Thanks for the help."

"My pleasure, Inspector. Always glad to be of service."

The two men exited the Bird House, one to relish his role in the exciting undercover operation, the other to make further plans for carrying it out. They parted company by the seal pond, shaking hands as would any two business associates after consummating a deal. When Mullvaney returned to his office, he called in one of his assistants.

Joe Cahill was a rotund, cherub-faced lieutenant who was more of Mullvaney's gopher than a police officer. He was completely loyal to Mullvaney, took his abuse and considered himself lucky to be working for what he considered a brilliant law enforcement mind. A one time member of the bow and arrow squad because of his drinking, Cahill had managed to give up his habit and divided his time between his job, which often entailed twelve hours a day, and counseling services for other cops whose guns had been taken away because of their drinking and irrational behavior.

"Yeah, Chief?" Cahill said, standing in front of Mullvaney's desk.

"Joe, who's our best man on the bum detail?"

"We're not doing bums any more, Chief. We're doing little old ladies from the Lower East Side."

"Well, who was the best one when we *had* the bum detail?"

"Paterno, but he's transferred to Safes and Lofts."

"Who's running that?"

"McBride, Chief."

"Kevin or Francis?"

"Francis, Chief."

"Good. Call him up, tell him I need Paterno over here. On the double. Top priority stuff. Extremely sensitive. When Paterno gets here, tell him to get into his bum outfit. Explain to him how sensitive a thing it is."

"That bad, huh?"

"The whole city could go up any minute, Cahill. Get on it right away."

"Right, Chief. On the double."

By this time, the entire floor housing the Special Undercover Squad was buzzing with excitement. Something big was in the making. The ones already assigned to the operation went around in a state of professional resignation, as soldiers preparing for battle. The others, resentful at not being included, looked on in envy. By four o'clock that afternoon, Cookie Paterno, the most decorated detective in the short history of the Bum Squad, was in Inspector Mullvaney's office.

"Cahill said you had something for me, Chief," said Paterno, saluting Mullvaney informally. "What's up?"

"Here's the story, Cookie," said Mullvaney, standing up. "There's a bunch of Porto Rican radicals planning a guy's escape from Stuyvesant Hospital. We know where their headquarters is located, but we don't have any intelligence on how they're gonna perpetrate. We had Chota on the case, but we didn't get a listening device in on time before they hit on the plan. They've split up into teams and the only thing we can do is hope we can listen in on the people left at the headquarters. El Falcon's in on this thing."

"Holy shit, Chief," said Paterno. "That's bad news."

"That's right. When that sonofabitch gets into something, we have to move fast. It could be worse than the Harlem riots."

"Right, Chief. The way I heard it, the whole thing started when this colored guy spit on this other colored guy's spare ribs."

"That's what happened. So you know how these things can snowball. Here's the plan. The only way to get a listening device in there is to kidnap this black cat."

"That's a pretty rough assignment, Chief. You're gonna need more than me going in there. I can't handle one of those big spooks by myself. Suppose he's got a couple of friends. Even if they're not armed I couldn't handle it by myself. I figure myself and two other guys to go in and a team of four as backup."

Mullvaney pounded his desk with his fist.

"Goddammit, Paterno. It's a cat. A four-legged cat."

"Oh, I see. Okay, Chief. That's different. One of those cats."

"Right, Paterno. A black tom cat that hangs around their headquarters. Now, here's the story. He likes Spanish food. You buy some when you get up there, lure him out and grab him. The cat doesn't eat anything else but this greasy Spanish food. You got that?"

"Right, Chief. Spanish food."

"Right. So you get the Spanish food, lure the cat, grab him and there'll be a car waiting for you on the corner. After that your're free to go back to Safes and Lofts. I'll make sure McBride gets a full report and it goes on your record. You got your gear with you?"

"It's downstairs soaking in some Gypsy Rose. You still got the dryer?"

"Yeah, it's there in the basement."

"You know something?"

"What?"

"I'm glad to be back. If I'd a known about the operation earlier, I'd a let my beard grow a couple days. This way I'll have to use charcoal. It's not the same, you know. I feel like a phony when I do that. What time do we start out?"

"As soon as it gets dark."

"Right, Chief. I'll snooze in the basement and be ready to go when you give the word. I always feel like hell when I get up."

Detective Anthony "Cookie" Paterno exited from the room, practicing his stagger as he went. Mullvaney returned to his seat and nodded with satisfaction. By the following morning they'd have the goods on El Falcon and the rest of the sneaky red bastards.

CHAPTER 12

From which one, if not well schooled in lingustic prestidigitation, may receive entirely the wrong impression concerning the actions of Ingrid Konkruka, if not broad minded enough about life's true purpose, that is, that it should be enjoyed, may grow annoyed about supposed political implications, if not secure enough about ethnic identity may be offended, and if not given to silliness as a way of life, may groan in earnest instead of simply groaning in appreciation of the harmlessly bizarre.

On Saturday morning following her tape session with Frank Garboil, Ingrid Konkruka woke up about eleven o'clock. She climbed out of bed, donned a yellow sweat suit and began her daily routine of calisthenics and stretching exercises. When she finished her fifteen minute warm up she pulled on a pair of sweat socks, laced up her running shoes, put a head band around her forehead and let herself out of the apartment for her customary two mile run. When she returned a half hour later she showered, got dressed and fixed herself a breakfast of pickled herring, raw onions and celery juice. As she ate she found herself thinking more and more about Garboil. He was nearly ready and she wasn't sure how aware Kopfeinlaufen was of this fact. More disturbingly, listening to him talk so intimately about himself had touched something quite dangerous in her. When she was finished eating she went directly to the phone and dialed Kopfeinlaufen at home. The phone rang several times before the doctor answered.

"Good afternoon, Doctor," she said pleasantly. "It's Miss Konkruka."

"Ah, Miss Konkruka. How are you? To what do I owe this pleasure. How is our patient?"

"Well, Doctor, that's why I called you."

"Aha! Don't tell me he insisted on watching the hockey game after calling Doctor Kohonduro a rag head?"

"No, Doctor, nothing like that. On the contrary. Mr. Martinez was very cooperative."

"Is that right?"

"Yes, we had a chance to talk last night. He did most of the talking and I don't know if I've overstepped my responsibilities in encouraging him to reveal himself. I did record everything and I think you ought to listen to the four cassettes as soon as possible."

"That's wonderful, Miss Konkruka. No, I don't think you overstepped your responsibilities at all. I knew your influence on him would pay off. Has he admitted he is not this Frank Garboil character?"

"No, sir. But it seems like his fantasy about this person is quite extensive. Family background, job, children, sexual fantasies about women. In my estimation he's spent considerable time fabricating his story and possibly living it out in some corner of his mind."

"Exactly, Miss Konkruka. That is exactly the conclusion I have come to. It's a pleasure to work with competent people. My theory is that when he rids himself of this defense he will realize his true identity and find himself suitable employment in the garment industry or something which will not demand too much in terms of his intellect."

"He seems quite bright."

"Yes, yes, that's how it seems." Kopfeinlaufen said and paused for a moment as if measuring his words. "Miss Konkruka," he said, when he resumed speaking. "I hope you're not offended, but what appears to a lay person to be intelligence is in most cases an elaborate defense mechanism composed of bits and pieces picked up randomly from television, films and orally transmitted societal myths. What we have here is a sophisticated but nontheless classical case of the *idiot savant*."

"I don't know, Doctor."

"Miss Konkruka, please do not concern yourself with this aspect of the young man's therapy. There's nothing to worry about. My diagnoses are never wrong."

Ingrid Konkruka sighed deeply as if to resign herself to the doctor's assessment of Garboil. He was ready and this moronic psychiatrist was delaying the process. She had never been on a case with such a madman. How did he stay on the payroll?

"You may be right, Doctor," she said.

"Between you and me," Kopfeinlaufen said, lowering his voice to a conspiratorial tone. "The entire matter is very simple. This young man does not want to identify with Puerto Ricans. The boy is going to be fine. Please do not worry."

"I'll try."

"Of course we must be very careful that in admitting his true identity he does not confront the reality too directly. It's fine that he admit that he is Puerto Rican, but in effect this may prove too much for him to handle. I have worked out a plan."

"A plan for what? His release?"

"That depends. What we're talking about is basically a very sophisticated test. I have spoken to the TV reporter who did the original story, remember?"

"Nevera. Reynaldo Nevera."

"Yes, that's him. As you know he's Puerto Rican. He's assured me that the problem of identity is a common one and that he himself went through a rather trying period in which he went through several ethnic incarnations, including that of a young British rugby player by the name of Reginald Coldstorage. He's come up with a brilliant idea. We are going to have a television sports special on Armando. Howland Gosell, the sportcaster, has agreed to interview Armando in depth, or up close and personal, as they say in the trade."

"Doctor, don't you think it's a mistake to expose the patient that way?"

"That's just it, Miss Konkruka. It's an extremely sensitive situation. We are at a crucial point in his recovery. Of course I'll have to listen to the latest tapes, but the idea is that we must put his recovery to a test. Armando must be made to confront his reality. You see, television is the ultimate test of a person's ego. A well integrated ego can handle the exposure. The opposite is also true."

"The opposite?"

"Yes, a scattered ego, an immature ego, requiring infantile reenforcements. You've seen common people become a bundle of nerves and act childishly when confronted by a television camera. Even people who function capably in every aspect of their lives are affected adversely by appearing on television. The tiniest flaws and maladjustments surface immediately and are amplified. This is normal behavior."

"I still don't follow," Ingrid said, wishing to learn more about the plan.

"It's very simple, Miss Konkruka. If our patient, faced with cameras and the imposing figure of Howland Gosell, can handle the situation, then we're dealing with an advanced case of delusion and our work has been a failure. If on the other hand the patient disintegrates, then we have triumphed and accomplished the normalization of the patient."

"I'm more confused than ever, Doctor. I'm sorry."

"Let me see if I can put it another way, Miss Konkruka."

"Yes, please do."

"What you must always keep in mind is that we're dealing with a Puerto Rican."

"Yes."

"And that a Puerto Rican by definition suffers from a disintegrated ego, caused by an inversion of id and superego. In every other ethnic group the superego serves as a deterrent to the baser inclinations of the id. In the Puerto Rican, particularly the male, the superego encourages anti-social behavior. Instead of the superego saying: 'That's a married woman, don't approach her sexually,' the superego insists that not approaching her is unmanly. I have done considerable research on the subject, Miss Konkruka. Every male child is brought up to believe that his sexual organ has magical power. It is not uncommon for mothers to hold up their male child and kiss his phallus, often referring to it as a flower. Since we are dealing with a matriarchical society it is no wonder that males behave as they do. All they are doing in insisting on conquering every woman is adhering to the wishes of the mother. Not to do so would be a breach of their highly complex superego. Every male child is suffering from an inflated ego. And it is no wonder, since from early infancy he is made to feel as if he is special."

"But Doctor, I'm really sorry to interrupt."

"Not at all, my dear."

"Doesn't every parent convey that same feeling of uniqueness to his child?"

"Very true."

"Then?"

"In the case of the Puerto Rican the assessment is totally without substance."

"But why?"

"It's very simple and it has nothing to do with the merits of the ethnic group, its intelligence or creativity. What we have here is a profound maladjustment at the most basic level. Do you know what Puerto Rico means."

"Sure, Rich Port."

"Aha, there you have it! Rich Port. At the most basic level of language a glaring contradiction. The country is the only one in the world which reflects the opposite of its actual reality. The country is poor and yet it sports the appellation 'rich.' A most glaring contradiction leading to an inflated ego."

"If you say so."

"I see that you do not agree with my analysis."

"No, but I haven't had your training."

"Yes, that is true."

"One more thing, Doctor. When is the program planned for?"

Kopfeinlaufen laughed.

"Ah, that is a secret, my dear," he said, chuckling, and once again the endearing master of psychiatric intrigue. "I will let you know in plenty of time."

"Oh, that's not fair, Doctor Kopfeinlaufen."

The tone of Ingrid's voice was that of a child left out of something important. Kopfeinlaufen could almost see the pout and immediately relented.

"Well, I guess you are right," he said. "I will give you a hint. It is going to be a live show on National Television and very, very soon. We must work fast because I think he is reaching the point when he could go one way or the other. Did I ask you if he went into a description of his fantasy mother?"

"Yes, he did."

"Well, what was it?"

"It was a vague remark about the place where he worked and how someone found out that his mother was part Eskimo."

"Aha, and part Norwegian, correct?"

"No, he didn't say anything to me. But he did tell Miss Christianpath, because she told me about it."

"Exactly," said Kopfeinlaufen, his voice rising to a high pitch of excitement. "He recounted his family tree to Miss Christianpath and made specific comments about his birth. Very unusual fantasy. Most Puerto Ricans are satisfied with saying that they are Spanish. There is tremendous confusion in this young man. Also his feelings of hostility towards his mother are extremely convoluted. Her death puzzles me. Not that wishing to have his mother dead as a symbol of the end of her dominance is not common, but the way in which he represented her death is most unusual. You see, in this fantasy of being Frank Garboil she was shot by gangsters. Obviously the gangsters are a recognition of his anti-social behavior. But the part about her being Eskimo is even more unusual. The human mind is truly remarkable."

"What do you mean?"

"You see, not only does it justify his playing hockey, but at the same time gives us an indication of how atypical his mother was as a Puerto Rican. Had she been your typical doting, over protective, indulgent Puerto Rican mother, he would not mind being Puerto Rican. But she was obviously cold and inscrutable."

"I see," said Ingrid, dubiously.

"Ah, Miss Konkruka. You are still young and untrained in these matters. We are now getting into profound symbolic material. It is very likely that if our patient were suffering from a basketball related delusion his mother might have been represented by a Watusi."

"Yes, of course," said Ingrid. "Why didn't I see that?"

"It takes years of practice, my dear. Well, thank you for calling. Are you going to the hospital today?"

"No, but I can if you want me to."

"It's not important but if you're going by, please leave the tapes on my desk. I'm going there later in the day and I can bring them home and listen to them in preparation for Monday's staff meeting."

"All right. They're in the file cabinet in my office but I can have them on your desk this afternoon."

Good, Miss Konkruka. And thank you again. I must go now. My wife thinks we are having some sort of affair. She is very jealous. Terrible German temper. You understand."

"Yes, of course, Doctor. Goodbye."

After hanging up the phone Ingrid laughed, but the laughter was tainted by a an overriding concern that something had gone wrong with the case. She put on her coat, tied a scarf around her head and was out the door immediately. As she sat in the cab on her way to the hospital she wondered if her size made Frank Garboil uncomfortable. She was nearly two inches taller than he. As the cab pulled into the hospital driveway she realized she had been thinking about him ever since she'd stopped talking to Kopfeinlaufen. At that point she resolved to drive all thoughts of him out of her mind. To continue to think about him other than as her charge would only damage her chances of carrying out the mission.

She rushed into the hospital, showed her identification and got into the elevator. Dressed as she was in bellbottom corduroy pants, a bulky sweater, running shoes and a pea coat made her appear less imposing than she did in her nurse's uniform. At the entrance to the solarium wing she again showed her identification to the two guards and went directly to her office. She removed the four tapes from a file cabinet, locked the door once more and let herself into Kopfeinlaufen's office where she placed the tapes on his desk. Out in the corridor once again she took a deep breath and proceeded down the corridor to Garboil's hockey rink-like room. Garboil was eating lunch, but as soon as he saw her, he stood up and came across the gleaming white floor.

"Hey, what brings you around today," he said. "You should have at least one day off. I mean, not that I'm not glad to see you."

She took his hand and pulled him over to the couch.

"I have to talk to you," she said. "Sit down."

"You look great without your uniform," he said, as he sat down. "Less official."

She thanked him without allowing herself to feel the import of his comment.

"Look, Frank," she said. "We have to talk and we have to talk fast. I just finished speaking with Kopfeinlaufen and told him about the tapes. He's convinced it's a good sign that you opened up to me. He hasn't heard them yet, but I'm sure once he does he'll be more convinced than ever of his theory. They even have a TV program planned for you."

"You're joking. What the hell are they trying to do to me? I'll never get out.

"Don't say that," said Ingrid, turning and kneeling on the couch. "You have to stay calm. If you don't, we'll give the whole thing away."

Garboil jumped up off the couch.

"Well, what am I supposed to do? Why a television program? If this thing gets out, I'll never be able to get another job."

"Sit down, please. Relax. It's exactly the way I told you. The only way to get out is to play their game. If you want to leave, you won't even mention your previous identity seriously. Did you have a moustache when you taught? No, right? Nobody's going to recognize you. What Kopfeinlaufen is planning is a very elaborate test. If you handle being in front of a camera, it means that you're still suffering from the delusion of being Frank Garboil. If you fall apart and start staring at the camera and saying really dumb things, you know, stuttering and being nervous, it proves you're Puerto Rican."

"But I'm not. I don't know exactly what I am right now, but I'm not Puerto Rican. That was just an expediency. It was the only thing open at the time."

"What do you mean?"

"Well, it was the only identity available. It was the only way I could get into school again. I know it was stupid, but I wanted to prove I could play hockey. You don't want to hear about it."

"I do, but I think you ought to save it for the doctors themselves. Don't worry about it. I believe you. Whatever happens, in front of that camera you have to appear totally incompetent. A bumbling idiot. Is your wife pretty?"

"What? Sure. I told you she was pretty, but that wore off after a while. Not that she was dumb or anything. Far from it. On top of that she was a little driven. Take the business with the book she wanted me to write. It was only a theory. Christ! Not even a theory, but more of a joke. Something I amused myself with to pass the time. She took the whole thing seriously."

"What was it about?"

"What?"

"The book."

"Oh, it was a study of pornography as it relates to Economics. She thought it was great and it'd make thousands of dollars and be a household name. Guest appearances on talk shows."

"You're kidding!"

"You see?"

"What?"

"Well, when I first told her about it, she said: 'Oh, Frank, I think that's a wonderful idea.' I mean, she couldn't have a normal reaction, right? Everyone else thought it was crazy like you did. Nobody took it seriously. They knew I meant it as a joke. It's abnormal, even though the relationship exists. Why do you think pornography's such a big issue in the United States?"

"I don't know. Why?"

"You see, you're starting to laugh."

"Okay, I won't laugh."

"No, go ahead and laugh. The whole thing is hilarious when you think about it. You see, economics is dull to most people, but that's because we're a society that is basically sexually repressive. What I was toying with was making economics, well, not dirty, but at least sexy, interesting."

"Sure," Ingrid said, trying to remain serious.

"It seemed the only way to get the greatest number of people interested in the subject. If I could establish a relationship between economics and pornography, I would be able to show people how they were getting screwed by the system."

Ingrid couldn't help laughing this time.

"Go ahead and laugh. As long as people are sexually repressed, all they'll have on their minds is sex, and naturally, as long as pornography is forbidden, they'll be drawn to it and won't have the clarity of mind necessary to understand how economics affects their lives."

"Makes perfect sense," Ingrid said, between fits of laughter. She looked at him incredulously. "You really believe all this, don't you?"

"Of course I believe it, but not enough to want to write a book about it. It was just something to amuse myself with. I had great titles for the chapters: 'The Promiscuous Market Place,' 'The Theory of the Sinful Class,' 'Penetrating the Stable Equilibrium Model,' 'The Erect Average Revenue' and 'The Reluctant Output Curve.' And all kinds of spicy terms like: Gross National Passion for Gross National Product. You know, the GNP."

"I understand."

"I was even thinking of sexy illustrations and graphs superimposed on couples making love. You know, nothing explicit, but there for the subconscious to chew on while the person is studying. Joan badgered me and badgered me so I began working on it for real. She even got a hold of some of her snooty contacts and got me an editor and a huge advance. The publisher thought it was a great idea and already had an advertising campaign planned out. Anyway, Joan was like that. I guess once the passion wore off, she had to justify having married me by helping me to become famous. I never knew what the hell was going on with her. Very complex libido or something. Why did you ask me if she was pretty?"

"I don't know. I just wondered if after you got out, you'd look her up again."

"I don't know. I really don't. I'll probably go see the kids, but I don't think I'd want to live with her again after all this. Even though I don't like what's happened and my being stuck here, I'm starting to feel different about myself."

"Listen, I have to go soon," Ingrid said, standing up. "I just wanted to let you know what was going on. Play along with them and I think they'll let you go. They're pretty crazy and unless you understand their insanity, they think you're the one who's crazy. It's the whole Catch 22 thing. Try and tell them as much as you can. All right?"

"Yeah, sure. I just don't know who the hell I'm kidding anymore. I'm tired of being who I'm not. I don't know how much it'll help to talk about myself. Even before the whole hockey thing, I felt like I was someone else anyway."

"I thought you were feeling better."

"I am. I just don't know if I should or not."

"You should. You're doing fine. Just keep telling them what they want to hear. Tell them the truth and don't insist that it is the truth. To them it's a fantasy. That's their fantasy and to destroy it for them, makes them crazier. Do you understand that?"

"Yeah, sure."

"Listen, thanks."

Ingrid Konkruka smiled at him. She had a strong urge to go to him and kiss him, but she turned and went quickly out of the room. She went straight home, watched a television movie, had a light supper, wrote to her mother and went to bed early. Before falling asleep she thought about the last tape. She was jealous of Angela Piscatelli and of Joan Alcott Garboil. She was even jealous of Jo Ellen Chestnut Bacon because they had shared his life. But she had no right to feel that way. She was a professional with a job to do.

CHAPTER 13

In which Mullvaney's feline strategy is put into operation with rather surprising results, a belle has a ball in spite of being treated with disdain, first by nature and then by *la creme de la creme* of society, it is learned that almost anyone may be suspected of being Puerto Rican, P.M. Ramirez is met and all feel totally inadequate in his presence because of his impeccable manners, speech, dress and remarkable ability to analyze information, and as an academic treat a refresher course in genetics and natural selection is offered.

At the offices of Special Undercover Investigations developments were taking place at a rapid pace. Everything was proceeding as scheduled. Receiving equipment had been hooked up, a new telephone line installed and a team of electronics experts assembled. Meanwhile, up in El Barrio, at ten minutes after eight on that night of February 2, 1971, Detective Anthony "Cookie" Paterno purchased two dollars worth of cuchifritos at *La Manita de Oro*, a landmark emporium for the cognoscenti of Caribbean fried food. After leaving the store, Paterno stuck the paper bag into a pocket of his ragged wine-soaked overcoat, staggered up Lexington Avenue, along the James Weldon Johnson housing project, until he reached 116th Street, where he turned east towards the East River.

The temperature was well below freezing and the streets nearly deserted. Even with few people taking notice, Paterno concentrated on his role. By the time he arrived on the block where the United Front had its headquarters, he had developed the swaying grace of the professional New York City bum who maintains his precarious equilibrium whether waiting at the edge of a subway platform or crossing an icy sidewalk.

Paterno descended the stairs to the basement of the building, walked past the door of the headquarters and was in the backyard without incident. Once there, he scattered several pieces of food on the ground and in no time a large black cat was nibbling on a piece of cow uterus. He grabbed the cat by the scruff of the neck, held him up to the light of a flashlight to make sure he was black, and in one motion dropped him into the laundry bag he'd brought for that purpose. As quickly, he was back out on the street and swaying. On the corner of Pleasant Avenue and 120th Street an unmarked police car picked up Paterno and his catch and drove him to Wellington Kincaid's office where Mullvaney was waiting.

"Here's your cat, Chief," said Paterno, smiling proudly through the charcoal and grime on his face. "I have to go home to the Bronx. You think one of your boys could get me back up there? I have to report for work tomorrow morning and I'd hate to get arrested on the subway."

"No problem, Cookie," said Mullvaney, and turned to a Black plainclothesman. "Get him up to his house, Patterson. On the double. And no stopping off at chicken and rib joints. We have to turn this cat loose in an hour."

"You got it, Chief," Patterson said, and went off muttering something that sounded remarkably like: no lip, honky faggot.

The operation on the cat went quite smoothly and an hour and a half later the animal, slightly dazed but no worse for wear, was released in front of the United Front's building.

But all does not always go well in police work. There are times when jobs are fouled up, not through ineptitude on the part of the technicians but because of circumstances. By one o'clock that night signals were starting to arrive at Mullvaney's office. At first only faint stomach noises and a steady heart beat were heard by the technicians monitoring the tiny transmitter sewn into the cat. An hour later there were a couple of goodnights, the theme for the Late, Late Show and nothing more.

At seven o'clock the next morning Mullvaney, who had remained at the office to examine the information as it came in, was awakened by Cahill with a report that they were receiving a stronger signal. Mullvaney was instantly awake and listening. After a few minutes, however, Mullvaney screwed up his face with worry and shook his head.

"There's something funny going on," he said to Cahill. "These people are talking English. The girl sounds like a teenager. She's complaining that she doesn't know what to wear to school."

"That's probably the girl Chota was talking about," Cahill said. "Maritza something. She goes to New Amsterdam College, right?"

"Right," said Mullvaney, satisfied for the moment with Cahill's explanation.

Nothing else came over the receiver during the day except some street sounds which Mullvaney analyzed as the result of the cat's roaming outside the headquarters. It was not until five o'clock on Wednesday afternoon, after Mullvaney had gone home, that his finely honed police instinct told him something had gone wrong. He tried to eat supper, couldn't and finally returned to the office. Cahill had little to report. The technicians were drinking coffee and smoking, each one involved in his own thoughts. It was eerie, thought Mullvaney. They were out there plotting to destroy the system, there was a bug in their headquarters and the place was like a tomb. Mullvaney sat down and tried to relax by reading a James Bond novel. The Bond adventures were so unlike anything he'd ever experienced that it was laughable. But he enjoyed the escape from the tensions of the job. This time, however, he found it impossible to relax. His mind felt scattered as it searched for whatever it was that didn't feel right about the operation. About twenty minutes later the speakers on the other side of the room were alive with an incredible din.

"Christ Almighty, Cahill," he said, jumping up from his seat. "Listen to all that racket. There must be a dozen broads in that place and they're all talking Portorican at the same time. What the fuck are those terrorist bastards doing, celebrating already? that goddammed El Falcon! On top of being a commie he's a whoremonger. Cahill, get Ramirez in here. He talks Portorican."

"Spanish, Chief," Cahill said. "He gets kind of annoyed if you mix up the two. He's Spanish Spanish."

"Yeah, yeah, whatever. Get his ass in here."

A few moments later Detective Lieutenant Peter Minuit Ramirez—Harvard '66, B.A., Political Science; Columbia Law School '69; admitted New York State Bar '70—walked into Mullvaney's office. Tall, handsome, trim and suave in his Brooks Brothers three-piece suit and wingtip shoes, refreshed after squash and a massage at the New York Athletic Club, Ramirez not only looked great but knew it. A confidant to the mayor and a favorite of the police commissioner because of his political contacts, Ramirez was despised and feared by everyone in the Office of Special Undercover Invetigations. As the head of the intelligence division, it was his responsibility to analyze all relevant information pertaining to SUI. After less than a year on the job, he had gotten rid of six staff positions and now did the work alone with the aid of a computer, coming in a few hours each day and accomplishing what had previously taken seven men to do. Mullvaney didn't care. He disliked Ramirez and his white jaguar and mink-draped society girls. But as long as he did his job and Mullvaney didn't get any flack from the commissioner, everything would work out. However, the minute there was any noise out of the commissioner's office, there were ways to put Ramirez out of commission permanently.

As Ramirez came into the room, the technicians almost jumped up and stood at attention, so imposing was his appearance. To his society friends he was the son of Winifred Bronck Gansevoort, a descendant of the original Dutch settlers, and a nobleman, the Count Francisco Ramirez y Menudo of Valladolid, Spain. Although Ramirez was unaware of the fact, only half of his pedigree was accurate. He was indeed the son of Winnie Gansevoort, possibly the ugliest girl ever to graduate from Vassar. So ugly was Winifred Gansevoort that the year she was to come out, the Debutante Ball committee suggested to her mother, through their lawyers, that Winnie be sent to Switzerland, improve her French, learn German and Italian and make her debut somewhere in Europe where requirements were not as stringent. The lawyers intimated, in rather convoluted language, that if the Gansevoorts chose to challenge the committee's request, the Ball would not be held that year and the family sued and ostracized from New York society. Winifred's mother had no choice. She investigated the European situation and received negative responses in each case. Because of the language difference, the French were unintentionally cruel in their response, stating that an "apparition by Mlle. Gansevoort was an impossibility."

A flighty child, unaware of the importance of good looks, and a hopeless romantic interested in science fiction, folk art and botany, Winifred was unscathed by the rejection. She informed her mother that she had decided to travel to the Caribbean and pursue her interests. She immediately packed her bags and sailed for Puerto Rico to study mountain music and collect botanical specimens. In the mountains surrounding the town of Cacimar she met Elpidio Ramirez, better known as *El Ciego*, a young guitarist and the foremost exponent of traditional mountain music at the time. Owner of the finest, most talented hands ever to play the guitar, but blind as a bat, Elpidio was immediately captivated by the lisping and nervous *americana*. After a week they learned that they shared a love of music, rainfall, bananas and sex. By the time Winifred returned to New York she was five months pregnant.

Upon informing her mother of her state and her intention to carry the pregnancy to term, her mother immediately contacted acquaintances in Spain, informed them of her predicament, and stressed that financial considerations should not deter the hunt for a suitable partner for her daughter. Although a strenuous effort was made on behalf of the Gansevoorsts, the best they came up with was a marriage by proxy to the Count Francisco Ramirez y Menudo, dead the previous year at the age of 78. In order to carry out the deception, a young Sevillian bullfighter was used as a model. Dressed in fine clothes, posed at dinner parties and places of business, with thoroughbred horses, vintage automobiles, airplanes and sailboats, photographs of Winifred were superimposed next to the handsome *torero* and a family album created. The announcement of the wedding appeared in the *New York Times* along with the particulars of the union. Although it produced a few laughs, Winifred's mother was satisfied that she had done everything she could on her child's behalf. Winifred was unimpressed by her mother's efforts.

When the child was born, Winifred's mother was ecstatic. He looked nothing like Winifred. In fact he was a beautiful child. Winifred treated the birth with characteristic detachment as an understandable cosmic phenomenon in which she had been used as the vessel for the seed of some interplanetary traveler. She went on cultivating her interests in folk art, botany and blind guitarists. When Peter was three years old, Winifred left the Gansevoort town house one morning, announcing that she was going to the Bronx Botanical Gardens. It was the last time anyone ever saw her. Along with Judge Crater, she ranks among the greatest mysteries of the Missing Persons Bureau of the City of New York. Rumors exist, however, that *El Ciego*, her first lover, had come to New York around the time of her disappearance and that they now lived in the area of Longwood Avenue in the Bronx, he continuing to compose his music, and she, in spite of her flightiness, using her heritage as descended from shrewd merchant stock, dyeing her hair black, acquiring a Spanish accent, and becoming a supplier of herbs and medicinal plants for *botánicas* in the New York City area.

Peter grew from a beautiful child into a handsome, intelligent young man. He attended the finest schools and from an early age understood his social position. Like his mother, however, he developed a romantic predilection for the exotic. In his case this was mirror writing, police work and Polynesian dances, which he performed quite ably in a grass skirt. From his father he inherited an uncanny ear for music and sound in general. Although an accomplished pianist, he rarely performed publicly, but he had the rare capacity of recalling the particulars of any music he'd ever heard.

"Good evening, gentlemen," he said, affably as he took a seat in front of Charles Mullvaney. "What can I do for you, Chief?"

Mullvaney glared at Ramirez and explained the entire operation. P.M. Ramirez listened intently to the shrill voices coming over the receiver. With great style he coughed once, crossed his legs and lit a Virginia Slims cigarette.

"What do you think, Pete?" Mullvaney said.

"Somebody goofed, Chief," Ramirez said.

Mullvaney was shocked.

"What do you mean 'somebody goofed?' " he said, standing up and coming over to Ramirez's side of the desk.

"That's not the people we're after," Ramirez said, letting the smoke drift out of his finely shaped nostrils.

"Why's that?" Mullvaney said.

Ramirez ground out his cigarette on an ashtray and smiled smugly.

"That's *merengue* music playing on a Sylvania combination TV-record player, diamond needle," he said. "It's an extinct Tico vintage, re-recorded from a Dominican Republic label by the name of Quisqueyana. From the accents of the people I can tell they're not Puerto Rican women. There are nine Dominicans, three Cubans and one Panamanian and they're having a Tupperware party. In any case there's only one Dominican in the U.F. and he's a very eccentric man. He doesn't even listen to weather reports on the radio for fear that it's propaganda.

There's no way that could be the place unless they've moved someplace else in the meantime. Your man probably caught the wrong cat."

"Goddamit," said Mullvaney. "Are you sure, Pete?"

Ramirez ignored the question and lit another Virginia Slims. Mullvaney was coming totally unhinged. He began pacing up and down the floor, kicking at trash cans and empty chairs.

"Of all the rotten, radical, left wing, commie tricks, he said. "How the hell did it happen?"

"Simple, Chief," Ramirez said. "Elementary as a matter of fact. Figure it this way. You have a big tomcat such as the one your man Chota mentioned in his report. He's got expensive taste in food, does his mouse catching efficiently and professionally. No messes, no sadism, nice and clean. He even disposes of the catch in order not to inconvenience the humans who feed him. Not simply carrying the defunct rodents outside but placing them into garbage cans. What we have then is an exceptional kind of animal, one of uncommon intelligence. Do you agree?"

"Sounds right," Mullvaney said. "Go on."

"Natural selection," Ramirez said.

"What?"

Ramirez stood up and paused momentarily for effect before delivering his bombshell in the midst of what he considered cretinous laborers.

"It's the way nature has of weeding out imperfections and improving on its stock. You've seen litters of dogs in which there is a runt, right?"

"Yeah."

"Well, for every runt there is a stronger specimen at the other end of the spectrum, one which will ensure that the best qualities of the species carries on its genetic strengths. Once in a while an adaptation is necessary, one which will guarantee the survival of the race or breed under particular circumstances. Because of this adaptation and strength, an animal such as that is going to be in great demand with members of the opposite sex. Survival of the fittest and all that jazz. In this case we have a prime case of urban adaptation. A genetic mutation, which cognizant that the people among whom it lives do not generally keep cats as pets because of the expense, has adapted to eating the food which they consume."

"Holy smokes, Pete," said Mullvaney. "You mean there could be two or three more like him around there?"

"Not quite, Chief," said Ramirez. "It's not as simple as that. The gestation period of a cat is a little more than eight weeks. From all intelligence that we have received, the cat in question is at least three years old. He has been mature over two years. Even with a conservative estimate of one sexual contact per week, you have a possible 104 litters during that two-year period. It's quite likely that the entire neighborhood is now infested by this type of black cat."

"Son of a bitch," said Mullvaney, philosophically. "We'll have to bring the whole bunch in and fit them with the transmitters."

"It looks that way," Ramirez said, keeping his opinion to himself. It was obvious the entire operation should be cancelled immediately, but this was exactly the type of departmental waste of manpower and funds which the commissioner suspected and wanted to prove existed.

"We'll have to put them on different frequencies," said Mullvaney.

"That's also true, Chief," Ramirez agreed.

"And get more technicians to monitor the operation."

"Right."

"Cahill," yelled Mullvaney, turning away from Ramirez.

"Yes, sir," said Cahill, coming forward.

"Get me the Con Edison people and tell them we'll be down to pick up a cable truck inside of an hour. Tell them to strip the insides out of the truck. After you do that, get a hold of Kincaid and tell him to get ready to move by midnight. I want him to mount an operating room inside of the van. Contact Frankewicz and tell him to get, let's see, how many do you figure, Pete?" he said, turning to Ramirez. "You know, transmitters."

"At least fifty, Chief," said Ramirez, quickly computing Punnett squares in his head.

"Right. Tell Frankewicz to bring seventy-five of those extra sensitive, dime-sized transmitters, each tuned to a different frequency."

"Anything else, Chief?" said Cahill.

"Yeah, tell the doc what happened, but try not to shake him up.

"Right, Chief."

When Cahill had left the room Mullvaney looked at Ramirez and shook his head.

"Crazy business, isn't it, Peter?"

"Not really, Chief," Ramirez said. "You run a clean, efficient, heads up shop."

This pleased Mullvaney.

"Listen, Pete," he said. "How'd you like to go on this thing?" We'll get you a blue hard hat and some overalls. You never get a chance to go out in the field. It must be boring as hell analyzing intelligence all the time."

Ramirez smiled at Mullvaney and shook his head in regret.

"I'm sorry, Chief. I would love to join you and the men, but it would be a heavy price to pay at such a critical juncture in the operation. I just can't. If I go up there, inside of an hour I'd be broken out and indisposed for at least a month."

Mullvaney looked puzzled.

"Are you allergic to cats?" he said.

"Garbage," said Ramirez. "I never go beyond 86th Street except in an air tight automobile."

"I'm sorry to hear that, Pete," Mullvaney said. "You would've had the time of your life seeing the way we conduct this type of undercover operation. Some other time."

"Sure, Chief," said Ramirez. "Thanks for asking. Do you need anything else?"

"No, not right now. But as soon as everything is operational be ready to start working on the data."

"Of course, Chief," said Ramirez, getting up to leave. "You can count on me for that."

When Ramirez was gone Mullvaney sat back down at his desk. His thoughts turned to this new development in the operation and centered about the skewering, quartering and sodomizing with antique night sticks, every pinko who made his life miserable, including the damned, genetically mutant supercats who, he was convinced, had been imported from Russia. Later on, as the operation went into full swing, he realized that the most likely place for the cats to have originated was Cuba. "That was it. They had been selected and trained for urban guerilla work in Cuba. We had our dogs, but they had to go one better and start using cats. Sneaky, red spic bastards.

CHAPTER 14

In which one may be forced to make severe moral judgments on issues such as avant-garde architecture, the value of a Poison Ivy League education, faculty extra-marital affairs, drugs, student participation in faculty matters, the idea that the university is a laboratory for the exploration of democratic principles, the more intriguing idea of the university as a living organism with emotions and desires, but mostly desire, and as a bonus see the protagonist struggle to find a way out of the jungle of academia.

Frick University was an odd conglomeration of several noble ideals gone awry. The school proper, that is, the physical establishment, was situated on the old Frick Fuller estate, deeded to the trustees of the university in order that they found an institution dedicated to "the examination of the urban experience in a rural setting." In certain academic circles this gave rise to the criticism that four years at a place such as Frick left the individual itching for knowledge. Along with several other colleges founded in the early '60's, Frick became part of the Poison Ivy League. It is important to emphasize that physically Frick University was on the Frick Fuller estate because, in terms of its fundamental philosophy, student body and faculty, it could well have been at the other end of the galaxy.

Take, as an example, its architecture. Designed by the firm of Hoffstader, Mazzini & Kashimoto, it appeared to the layman as a diabolic plan to produce insanity rather than promote education. Keeping in mind that the school was to have a 30-30-30-10 ratio of ethnic representation, the architectural firm did a commendable job. Thirty percent of Black, Puerto Rican and White and ten percent of Other certainly presented seemingly insurmountable architectural problems. The firm, however, produced a solution which should have satisfied all four groups.

Upon arrival at Frick, anyone with half the sensitivity of a moribund brussels sprout was stricken with fear of impending doom, extreme paranoia and free-floating anxiety, a condition common to denizens of urban centers. The road from the Long Island Expressway to the site on which Frick University had erected its first buildings was a well maintained, winding macadam ribbon, rising and falling and turning gently through thick woods and open fields. In the spring wild flowers were in full bloom and birds filled the air with song. In the fields horses and cows grazed peacefully in the warm sunshine. The scenery had the appearance of quiet, unassuming Long Island decadence, perfect for a fox hunt. The serenity and propriety of the land, its apparent passivity, conspired to make one wish to own it, to daydream about the big killing.

But the drive was a ruse, a sinister and yet unintentional occurrence which titillated pastoral longings only to shock one back into the harsh reality of twentieth-century America. As one emerged from a well forested stretch of road and into full sunlight again, there it was. Six acres of pure lawn, rising and falling like so many green breasts. Atop each of these mounds sat a round concrete and glass structure about the size of a Volkswagen. Where the lawn was flat there rose in symmetrical spacing ten thirty-foot, polished granite obelisks, topped in precarious balance by squat, octagonal structures which resembled the top of a lighthouse. Confronted by the unusual landscape, some visitors screeched to a halt, wheeled their cars about and fled, convinced they had been tricked by extraterrestrials into a trap.

The architects had reasoned, perhaps correctly, that most of the students that would attend the school were either initiated into radical politics in high school or other colleges, or were raised in the ghetto, or as Rudolph Mazzini described it, "the metropolitan viscera." Their reasoning was good, but in executing the design they had gone too far. Dormitories, classrooms, offices, cafeterias, library, art studios, gymnasium, stadium and recreational areas had all been constructed underground.

The obelisks, designed by Shunzo Kashimoto in a disgorgement of misguided brilliance, served as periscopes which refracted sunlight down to the different areas of the school and duplicated sky conditions outside for the ten tropical gardens below. Kashimoto, the son of a Japanese submarine commander who perished during the latter stages of WWII, was chastized severely by a number of architectural publications for creating "an environment with schizophrenic atmospheric conditions which caused one to observe snow and rain falling and never reaching the ground." Kashimoto's response was typical of a Zen practitioner, which he had been for twenty years. In a letter to one of the magazines he asked four basic questions: What is snow? What is rain? What is reaching? and signed his name.

As for the round structures atop the mounds of the expanse of lawn, they were the brainchild of Heinrich Hoffstadter. Publicly called modules, but referred to by Hoffstadter as bunkers, they served as entrances and exits to the underground complex which housed the university. Each one contained a ten person cylindrical elevator.

There were no personal cars allowed near Complex A, the name given by the president of Frick University to the first of six planned "educational environments." The rule concerning cars was adopted at the wish of the "Students for Ecological Sanity," who were also the biggest supporters of the architectural design, arguing that the plan as executed did not tamper with the natural beauty of the surroundings by creating artificial man-made dwellings. To them, the bunkers and obelisks were rocks and trees, bare, simple: an artistic and symbolic representation of human disregard for the environment. Their logic was curiously circular, but one day somebody was going to come along and gas the entire student body and faculty. To that end the detractors of the architectural design, with absolute justification for their fears, had begun tunneling out alternate exits on the sides of the hill. No matter how hard the landscaping staff worked, at least one human gopher hole was discovered each week.

But as vociferous as supporters and detractors of the architecture were, they comprised a small percentage of the student body. Nearly 90% of the students did not voice their opinion, exercising their inalienable right to remain uninvolved. And as bizarre as some may have considered the architecture, it was inconsequential when compared to what went on within it. In the three years that Frank Garboil spent at Frick there had been 77 recorded suicide attempts, two of which were successful. Of these attempts, none was more dramatic than that of Sinclair Grenko, an anthropology major, who assembled twelve speakers in his room, turned the volume on his stereo to ten and played a tape of the sound track from the film *2001: A Space Oddysey* for 39 hours straight before security guards finally broke down his door and pulled him out screaming that he was Pithecanthropus Erectus.

As if to create greater tension in an already difficult situation, the school had a stringent set of rules against drug use. Coupled with that most hallowed of democratic principles, that what one did behind closed doors was sacrosanct, within six months of the inauguration of Frick the campus was rife with drugs. A year later there were three rival factions vying for control of the drug traffic. To insure a balance of power there was one independent assassination squad which hired itself out for jobs outside the school, but which for a fee could dispose of any student on or off campus. Whether through their own intellectual efforts or through more primitive means, the members of the hit squad were all straight A students.

And then there was Marshall "Rabbit" Lachien, a high-yellow Black, who along with his partner, Juan "the man" Sanchez, perhaps the handsomest male on campus, operated what they called a social club, which in reality was the only known sporting house operating in a North American college under the auspices of the Psychology Department.

Experiences, especially those that counter one's expectations, often harden the human spirit. After three years at Frick University, Frank Garboil had become used to irrational arguments, fist fights in the middle of seminars on economic growth in the Third World, stabbings, racial slurs, threats, manipulations, bribes and general all out hustling.

The hustling game became so intense that anyone was suspect if he didn't have at least a cover of being on the make. The atmosphere at the school became so corrupt that the only arrest for drugs came about because an undercover man for the local police, through contact with the students, became seduced by the apparent freedom they enjoyed and began identifying with them. He attended consciousness raising sessions about oppression. In one of them he confessed to working for the police. The militants in the school thought that the policeman had suffered a nervous breakdown, felt sorry for him and took him into their fold. At one Radical People's meeting it was decided that they would rehabilitate their fellow student.

"Man, he has totally identified with the man out of his fear of the establishment. He's a brother like you and me. We got to help the dude out."

The policeman tried to present proof that he was working undercover, but they wouldn't believe him. Eventually he got to know everyone who was dealing drugs in the school, began smoking with other students and had the best possible cover ever devised. But his feelings of guilt became so pronounced that he began to ingest large quantities of pills and then acid. As expressed in the vernacular, he went a little too far and freaked out. The local police couldn't admit that he was an undercover man because it would cause a panic in the school and there was no telling what the situation would produce. The president of the school, who abhorred violence, having worked in the civil rights and peace movements for a number of years, allowed the police to take their man away without further incident. Some of the radical students attempted to make an issue of the situation.

They threatened to strike, held impromptu political education. In the end, they were asked to tone down their activities or face a confrontation with the three drug-dealing factions. The radicals were reduced to posting communiques on bulletin boards, plastering walls with posters asking for the release of the undercover man, whom they still belived was a bona fide student, and meeting clandestinely to discuss the issue. Eventually the movement died down and things went back to the frenetic normality of bizarre campus life.

But one had to have a hustle or at least appear to have one. It was the only way one gained respect. Frank Garboil, from the beginning, maintained that all he wanted to do was to teach economics as a key to understanding the system. He was laughed at. When students saw that he meant to teach, that he was fair and staunchly committed to what he saw as his mission, they began to suspect him.

"He's just one of those smooth talking dudes the government plants in Third World schools, man. Don't let him fool you. Sure, he knows what he's talking about. How else is he gonna pull off his shit?"

"What shit, man?" asked Rahman El Hashish, leader of the Black Intellectual Teaching Communications Haven.

"You must be blind, brother," said Rip Truex, the leading white radical. "What better way is there to get poeple into the system than by having them understand it? Once the brothers and sisters understand it, they start manipulating it and there's no way they're gonna get free, you dig? I mean, do you dig?"

"Sheet," said El Hashish.

"Let me put it to you this way, brother," said Truex. "Garboil's hustle is better than most. Take it from me, bro. I know where he's coming from. He may fool some of the black and Puerto Rican brothers and sisters because all you have to mistrust is that he's white. But I don't have that problem. I can see right through him. He's one of mine. Sure, take his courses. Learn about Marx and Engels, about banking and microeconomics, but don't forget that there's an underlying message behind the whole thing. A gut message. The more stuff that gets into your head, the more it's going to reach your gut and then you've had it."

"Dit it," said El Hashish.

"Right on," said the other radicals in the meeting.

"The man is a hustler like anybody else," added Truex. "Maybe a little smoother and a whole lot more articulate, but a hustler. Your best defense is to get your own shit together. Make him believe you understand what he's talking about, but don't understand it, because as soon as you've understood it, you've become the Man."

"And how you gonna pass his courses?" someone asked.

"Don't worry about that, brother," said Truex. "We've got ways."

After word got around as to Frank Garboil's hustle he became respected and even acquired a following. More significantly, he was accepted into the Third World Faculty Caucus because of what other faculty members perceived as a rapport with the students. When the issue of segregating classes arose because of the supposed advantage which whites had in previous educational opportunities and the intimidation and threat they presented to Third World students by their presence, Garboil stood up and asked to be heard. He was shouted down and a number of the faculty members moved to have him expelled from the body permanently. Not wishing to create further strife in an atmosphere which he perceived as a virtual powder keg, Garboil agreed to withdraw his participation in the group. Before leaving, however, he informed those present that his mother had been half Eskimo and therefore he could indeed speak on the subject. He was told to shut up and hurry up and leave. Humiliated and openly condemned as not only a liar but a "northern cracker pig," interested only in disrupting the growth of the Third World community at Frick University, Garboil left the meeting dazed and hurt by the confrontation.

The only person who came publicly to his rescue was Ariadne Yin Chen, the editor of the Frick University radical newspaper, *The Electric Mole*, who managed, two weeks later, to produce a photo of Garboil's birth certificate and printed it in the newspaper. Front page. "Mother — Summersun Tek-o-muk Magnussen; Birthplace — Aklavik, Northwest Territory, Canada; color — Eskimo". It was the scoop of the year. The discovery of the birth certificate, thought by him to be lost or non-existent, gave Garboil the run of the school. Blacks and Puerto Ricans still found it difficult to accept his reticence, his lack of emotional affect, but no longer attributed it to the belief that he was white and therefore genetically turned off. Instead, they adopted the explanation set down by Ariadne Yin Chen, leading advocate Other, outlined in her editorial the day Garboil's birth certificate was printed in the paper. "Professor Garboil," wrote Ariadne, "is basically an Asian person with all the cultural implications *that* may carry. What is sometimes humorous to some brothers and sisters may not necessarily be so to persons of Asian descent. If Professor Garboil does not seem as gregarious to some as they would wish him to be, it is because he has been taught from birth to be reserved and allow for the natural flow of events. We must respect each other's cultural differences if we are to create a peaceful, loving and understanding intellectual community."

With the exception of the first six months at the school and this latest struggle with an unfulfilled athletic career, Garboil's life at Frick University was a relatively smooth one. Once he became used to and saw through the many disguises of the people around him, he was able to understand and even care, in his own way, for students as well as faculty. He soon became a professional with a capital P. No matter how difficult the task, how mistrusting the student or how boring the committee assignment, he was able to attack the problem and produce satisfactory results. That he never seemed to gain absolute emotional satisfaction from his work was another matter and something he was now beginning to face.

As he got off the shuttle bus and headed for bunker A-9, which would bring him down to his office, he felt an overpowering desire to find himself alone in the elevator and urinate in it. As he got into the elevator along with two coeds dazed from some pill or other, he tried to understand his urge. When the elevator stopped at the first underground level he got out quickly and headed for his office. The office was the one place in the entire underground campus where he found absolute solace. If anything of value could be said for the architects, it was that they had spared nothing in providing faculty members with spacious comfortable offices. Each faculty member had a two room suite. In one of the rooms, Garboil had his desk, typewriter and files. In the other, there were comfortable chairs, a couch, some potted plants, pictures of his sons in hockey uniforms and three original paintings a student had given him. This room had a window with a view of one of the tropical gardens below. As he entered the reception area he was greeted by the secretary of the Economics Department.

"Good morning, Professor Garboil," she said, cheerfully.

"Good morning, Mita," he said, absentmindedly as he began going through the mail on Mita's desk. Mita Ritter Rade was a jolly, widowed English war bride, whose nine-fingered typing technique had once been the subject of a doctoral thesis in Typing Education. Although she had no choice in developing the technique, having lost half of the index finger of her right hand while opening a tin can during a Liverpool blackout, she was quite proud of her handicap and subsequent fame. She was punctual, precise, tidy and consistent, never varying from her routine to the point that at least twice a month for the past three years she had inquired about Garboil's attire and complimented him on his taste in clothes.

"Oh, you look just ducky this morning, Professor," she said as he finished going through the mail. "Is that a new suit you're wearing?"

"No, Mita," Garboil said, tearing an envelope with a pencil. "Same old suit, but you look just as lovely as usual."

"Thank you, love."

"Mita, could you please call the president's office and try to get me an appointment to see him."

Mita wrote the request on a pad, said she would take care of it right away, and resumed typing. Garboil thanked her, turned away and disappeared into his office, closing the door behind him. He sat down and tried to prepare himself for his morning class, but it was no use. The walls of the room appeared to be closing in on him and his heart was beating more rapidly than usual. He glanced nervously at his watch several times as he scribbled in a notebook. His mind wandered away from the tasks he had set for himself and seemed to be going in a dozen directions. When everything he tried doing began to annoy him, he tried breathing deeply while laying on the couch. All that this attempt accomplished was to make him feel as if what he was about to do was wrong. What was the use of having figured out how to be a winner if new doubts were going to creep in to paralyze him. He recalled how he had been able to will his team of seven-and eight-year-olds to regain their composure during one of the playoff games. He hadn't even spoken to them, but deep within him a surge of energy had appeared and with it the will to triumph. But where had that energy gone? How did he recapture it? In that situation it had been for them, so that they could learn to win. Now that the problem was his own he appeared incapable of producing that same motivation.

He managed to get through his class that morning, prattling on about preparing well for final examinations, deadlines for term papers and reassuring his students that the final wouldn't be as hard as they imagined. At twelve o'clock he headed for the cafeteria. If he was going through with his plan to play hockey he had to begin eating the right foods. He picked out a bowl of chicken soup, some cottage cheese and a small dish of canned peaches. More than ever he wished to be alone. In the din of the cafeteria, solitude seemed impossible. He did find a table at the far end of the large chrome and steel room. It was a cozy nook which looked out onto one of the tropical gardens. Below, through a tangle of trees and jungle vegetation, small alligators basked near a miniature swamp. Illuminated beautifully by the light from the obelisk above, it was possible to lose oneself in the scene. Colorful tropical birds flitted back and forth, their calls piped into the cafeteria.

Before he could settle in and begin eating, a striking looking woman came to his table. She resembled a gypsy in looks and attire and had large mysterious eyes. In her ears she wore large hoops and her skin was tanned the color of well worn leather. Her name was Angela Piscatelli and she taught Spanish, French, Italian, Portuguese, Rumanian, Romansch, Provencal, Gallego, Catalan, Basque, Arabic and Swahili. Along with Jan Kubichinski and Greta Nuddlefudden, they comprised the Language Department at Frick University. Between them they spoke and taught 61 languages. It was not unusual to see them sitting together, each speaking a different language and laughing at some fine point of wit. The curriculum at Frick allowed for a good deal of independent study and conferences. The enrollment for a class might be limited, but the course was given anyway. The class roster printed at the beginning of the semester sometimes read: "Hernandez, Ralph, Basque I, M-Th, 2-3, R230, Instructor — Piscatelli."

"Hello, Frank," said Angela Piscatelli, sitting down and taking his hand. Her voice was husky and mysterious. "How are you?"

"Oh, I've been all right," Garboil answered, wavering a bit and attempting to retrieve his hand.

Their romance was common knowledge in the informal conversations of both faculty and students. Officially, however, they were merely colleagues relating to each other on a number of important human levels. This had been the pronouncement by the president of the university when confronted with the issue of their affair by "The New Sons and Daughters of Christ the Savior," and "Puritans for Pot," religious groups on campus. In spite of the official neutrality and consent of the president, Garboil was always taken aback by Angela's public displays of affection. It was not uncommon for her to kiss him passionately at faculty functions and informal gatherings. "*Ah, caro mio*," she'd say, and sort of crawl up his chest to kiss him.

Right then Garboil wanted to be left alone, but he knew that was impossible. Angela wasn't the type of woman easily discouraged. Not because she didn't understand his discomfort or lacked respect for his wishes, but because she was animal in her desire and, when she wanted to display her affection and have it returned, it didn't matter where it took place. She had once threatened to walk out of his office naked unless he made love to her on his desk.

"Trouble at home, Frank?" she asked, dipping her long index finger into his soup and tasking it. "Oh, that's awful soup, Francesco. "Aspetta," she said, and bending down, brought up a large cloth bag from which she produced a bottle of chablis and two glasses. She poured the wine and offered him a glass. "Go on, drink. *Buvez, mon cher*. Drink up and tell me what ails you. Is it that awful, pretentious wasp wife of yours?" Frank shook his head and drank half the glass of wine.

"She's just hurt since she found out about us. You never should've sneaked into our house, Angela."

"I just wanted to see where you lived," she said, her large eyes, suddenly heavy-lidded and her thin nostrils flaring as if she were in heat.

"On top of that," Garboil said. "You could've killed yourself, dangling from the roof sixteen stories up. What would've happened if the rope came loose? I respect your stand as a woman, but that was a bit much."

"It was nothing," she said, tossing her long black hair back. "If you felt in your heart the vitality I feel, you'd have done the same thing. Life is for living, and desires are part of it. I wanted to see you that night. Men have been known to do things like that and they're accepted and even applauded. Look at Giovanni Giacomo de Seingalt, 1725-98. Now, women can get in on the fun too, *mi amor*. Anyway, tell me what's wrong. If it's not Joan of Arc, who is it?"

"It's not anybody else, Angela. It's me."

"Well, sure, I know it's you. But what's the trouble?"

Frank chuckled nervously and drank the rest of the wine. Angela poured him another glass.

"You're not going to believe this," he said. "I've got an appointment with John Friday afternoon. I'm resigning."

Angela Piscatelli applauded and whooped it up at the news.

"That's great, Frank," she said. "Really beautiful. You'll knock J.D. right on his ass. There's nothing that gets his nose more out of joint than having one of his people up and split from his plantation. It makes him feel guilty as hell. Like he didn't do enough. Let me ask you something. Do you have another job?"

"No, nothing like that."

"Listen then. I know this great place in Colorado. Little experimental college. A cousin of mine is a dean there. We could go and teach and do some snow and fresh mountain air."

"No, I just have to take off. My life's sort of getting ground up in all this crap. I have to stop and look at it and find out what's wrong."

"You're gonna hit the road?"

"Yeah," Garboil answered, glad that she'd offered an answer which would suit her sense of freedom. "I'm gonna take off." He was glad she hadn't pressed him because he didn't want to tell her that he was going to train and play hockey. "You understand, don't you? I have to split."

"Beautiful. Of course I understand. Like if it's stirring around in your gut, do it. If you don't, you'll regret it later on. I guess you'll let your hair grow and have a moustache and everything else."

"Yeah, sure."

"I'm really glad for you, baby," Angela said. She shifted to the chair closest to him, grabbed his face in her hands and kissed him, forcing his lips open with her tongue, embracing him so forcefully that they almost toppled to the floor.

The taste of wine, mingled with a trace of garlic, produced a strange sweetness in her mouth. It contrasted greatly with the cottage cheese he had been nibbling at while they talked. When he finally let go of him his head felt light and the wine buzzed around his system making him giddy. She was the first person to whom he'd confessed his wish to drop out of the rat race.

"Thanks, Angela," he said, touching her face. "Maybe I'll come back and see you sometime."

"Whatever turns you on, Paco," she said, using her nickname for him. "Just live out your thing. You know where to write. If you ever need me, just call or write and I'll drop in, with or without a rope."

"Right," Garboil said, smiling fully for the first time since he'd decided to resign.

"And let me know how old John takes the news," Angela said, as she got up.

"Sure. I'll do that."

"Okay, so let's get together sometime and celebrate. I have to go and meet some students at one in my office. I'll give you a call. *Ciao*."

"*Ciao*," he said.

He watched her moving in and out of the crowded cafeteria and when she was gone he wiped his mouth, got up and took his tray to the disposal area. His next class wasn't until three o'clock that afternoon, more than two hours away. The small amount of food he had consumed and the two glasses of wine he'd drunk made him fell drunker than he had imagined while he was sitting down. He returned to his office, locked the door and lay on the couch. He couldn't imagine how he was going to break the news of his resignation to Joan.

As he lay on the couch, his mind drifting lazily in the wine, he thought about the first time he'd walked up the wooded path leading to the president's house. It was the fall of 1967 and in a few months he was to be thirty years old. He had two years of teaching experience under his belt and felt quite proud that he had been accepted to teach at Frick University, a place which in the two years since its founding had acquired quite a reputation in progressive academic circles. Word of the new job had reached him at his job with the Economics Department of San Tiburcio Junior College in California. Upon seeing the posted announcement, he had written immediately, sending his curriculum vitae and a long letter, stating how eager he was to return to New York and teach. The response had been immediate and positive.

Joan had remained in California until he was able to rent a house near the school. That fall he spent the first two months of the academic year living alone in an apartment a few miles from the campus. By December he had rented a house in Syosset, a twenty minute drive from the campus. A year later they had to move again. Joan couldn't adjust to the steady stream of typical New York students—brash, loud and ill mannered—who invaded her house under the school's policy of faculty open houses three nights out of the week. At least twice a month they had to attend a celebration of some sort at a faculty member's house. Everyone talked a mile a minute and each one knew everything about everything.

They had eventually rented an apartment in a cooperative in Greenwich Village. Surprisingly, the bustle of the city awoke something in Joan and she became involved in several community activities and enrolled in New York University in order to obtain her own Ph.D. The challenging scene, the quaint shops and people, the narrow streets and landmark buildings, the natural aristocracy of an artistic community were a much needed balm. In her new apartment, high above Washington Square Park, she was once again mistress of her destiny. People called before they visited and, although fun loving, they were reserved and respectful in their manners. She once again resumed her exotic seductions of her husband, leaving him notes at strategic places in the apartment on those days when he came home early from the college and the boys had been taken for a walk by their sitter. They once again made love under beds and in closets, among rose petals and jelly beans.

Garboil recalled the new faculty reception in October of that first year when he had been accosted by the president's wife, Jo Ellen, who, after the introductions had been properly completed and people had split up into small groups, drove him to a corner of the large living room and held him there for the next two hours. Jo Ellen Chestnut Bacon was one of those women, not necessarily a product of the South, who hold onto their innocence forever. With crow's feet begining to etch themselves around her eyes, she retained the startled expression and delight she must have experienced the first time her husband had known her. What had made him think of Jo Ellen? He thought a moment, feeling the wine still, his body relaxing as his mind drifted back to those days. It was Angela, of course.

After the family had moved to the city and Joan was settled into a routine, Garboil found himself spending longer periods of time on the campus. Sometimes he drove back to the city near midnight only to return the next day. Once they had visited all the museums, taken in Broadway plays, eaten at quaint restaurants, seen a half dozen foreign films and Joan learned to travel on her own, the city became hers. For him the return to New York City stirred up memories of his childhood and the deprivation he had endured. He appreciated Frick University and the opportunity that he had to get away from New York City each day.

In the winter of his second year at Frick, after an all-evening battle with the Personnel and Budget Committee of the school over obtaining another line for the Economics Department, some of the students and faculty members invited him to go and listen to Charles Kinney, the jazz saxophonist, instrumentalist, composer and head of the Music Department, play at one of the local clubs. Garboil had heard Kinney's records in his years in college and had been impressed upon meeting him at the new faculty reception the previous year. He called Joan and told her he would be late and went along to listen to Kinney.

The club was crowded and before he knew it he found himself stuffed into a booth and sitting next to Angela Piscatelli, who along with Greta Nuddlefudden, was clapping and shouting encouragement to Kinney as he wailed away on one of his West Indian influenced tunes. He didn't know Angela well, having talked to her only a few times at faculty meetings. He'd been intrigued by her and had been immediately sexually aroused. She was dark and sultry and exuded a sexual confidence which reminded him of Joan as she was privately. Squeezed into the booth as they were, he felt Angela react to him instantly. She shifted her ample hips, nudged him and when he turned she looked at him with such abandon that he had the overpowering urge to enter her immediately. She laughed and then kissed his cheek. He was had even before he had decided whether he wanted to get involved or not. After the set was over she nudged his leg again, he slipped out of the booth and she followed him, hooking her arm through his. Without either of them uttering one word they walked out of the club, she to her car and he to his. He followed her for about ten minutes before she turned into the driveway of an apartment building and parked her car. He did the same and then followed her into her apartment. Their lovemaking was quick and desperate and afterwards he felt almost as if he had been violated. She was easily aroused and had a voracious sexual appetite, coaxing him and chiding him into greater and greater sexual prowess. The relationship became something which he was familiar with: athletic competition. She was easy to talk to, bawdy and unbridled in her opinions about life, so that he often felt as if he were back in the locker room. Although he went home that night, he began spending some nights at her apartment, calling Joan and explaining that he had too much work and would sleep on the couch in his office. Joan had no reason to mistrust him. There had never been the slightest infidelity on his part since that first date when they had walked on the beach and he'd known that he would someday marry her.

A month after his affair with Angela Piscatelli had taken root, he experienced a cold fit of jealousy. Inspired by her openness, Garboil asked her point blank if she were also sleeping with the president of the school, John David Bacon.

"You have got to be kidding, honey," she said, laughing at his seriousness. "The closest thing I came to that scene was my first year at good old Frick U. His old lady thought the same thing. She told me all about her thing with the massa. Oh, man, Paco. Not in a million years. And you know why she told me? J.D. had hot pants and she thought I was going to oblige him. She asked me up to the house and we had tea and all kinds of yummy things to munch on. She asked me about my family and I told her about growing up in San Francisco and how my grandfather made his own wine and raised his own vegetables and the big family dinners we had. And then she took me out into the rose garden and, as she trimmed and cut, she told me all about it. It was incredible. 'Professor Piscatelli,' she says. 'Call me Angela,' I says to her. 'Yes, of course,' she says. 'You're aware that I'm deeply in love with my husband.' I told her that I knew that. 'Why we have,' she says, 'what can only be described as a spiritual relationship based on deep respect for one another. You see, I know he wanders from time to time and I know it's my fault.' So like a fool I asked her why she thought it was her fault. You know, I was actually concerned for this poor demented belle like what's her name in Ibsen's *A Doll House*."

"I don't know," Garboil said. "Hedda Gabler?"

"No, no. That's another play. So anyway she goes into this long, weird description of her wedding night. I couldn't believe it. 'There I was, Professor Piscatelli,' she says. 'Twenty-one years old, frightened and innocent, laying back waiting for the worst to happen. Not daring to open my eyes for fear that my suspicions about the enormity of his parts were true. I could feel him stalking me like he was a wild animal in search of prey and I a helpless lamb, trembling. He knelt between my thighs, just barely touching me, Professor Piscatelli. And before God Almighty I swear this to you. He began praying. The Lord is my Shepherd, I shall not want. He maketh me to lie down in green pastures; He leadeth me besides still waters. He restoreth my soul: He leadeth me in the paths of righteousness for his name's sake. Yea, though I walk through the valley of the shadow of death, I will fear no evil: for thou art with me; thy rod and thy staff they comfort me.' "

"She recited the whole thing?"

"Yeah, sure. And ended it with an Amen. She stood there with a bunch of red roses in one hand and the scissors in the other, her head thrown back so that I thought she was gonna reach the all-time cosmic climax and recited the whole thing. And then she said, 'Professor Piscatelli, you can well imagine what my state must have been.' I told her I couldn't. 'Well, I nearly fainted and the phrases kept spinning in my head...thy rod...thy staff...in the valley of the shadow...comfort me...a-nointest my head...my cup runneth over. Mercy! And then I felt it, Professor Piscatelli. It was like falling down and bonking your head as a child. There was a burst of stars and my body went limp. I could feel him within me, but he was disembodied, weightless. It was like I was being ravaged, invaded, torn apart by love itself. Did you ever feel that way?"

"Wow!" Garboil said.

"Yeah, right. I was going to tell her I had once eaten a peyote button ground up in lime jello with some friends and then had gone to the Guggenheim and felt like I was being raped by a Calder mobile, but decided to keep it to myself. Instead, I told her that I once felt the same way playing leapfrog with my cousin

Dante when I was eleven. She looked at me like I was a toad. 'In any case, Professor Piscatelli,' she says. 'I just wanted you to know that I realize that you are a very attractive and seductive young woman, but that there is no chance that anything quite like what happened between President Bacon and myself will happen with you.' I told her I was glad that she had warned me, but that I liked getting my head anointed to Bach or the Modern Jazz Quartet and that in any case I was the product of a strict Catholic upbringing, still a virgin and had no plans to change my status."

"Was that true?" Garboil said, naively.

Angela laughed and kissed him as they lay naked on her bed.

"Of course not. I've been balling my butt off since I was fourteen and Dante's friend, Vito Palumbo, and I got caught in a rain storm and we ran into my grandfather's tool shed and I dared him to do it. We were both in junior high and he was the same age as me and had a big reputation with the girls. I was very competitive, still am."

"So what happened?"

"Oh, Vito was all talk. I had to show him everything even though I didn't know anything either. You know, from reading hygiene books and *Playboy*."

"No, I mean, with Bacon's old lady."

"Oh, that. Right. When I told her I was a virgin she was relieved. 'Oh, you poor darling,' she says. 'I'm sure I've embarrassed you no end. I'm glad you told me,' she says. 'You remain chaste and I'm sure in time you'll be rewarded as I was. There are good men left in the world. Let me reassure you. If J.D. becomes too aggressive, you just let me know and I'll tell the cook to stop making hush puppies, you heah?"

"I couldn't believe it, Frank. The woman is a nut, a throwback in time. Wow! And you know what I found out from Dora Phillips in Bio? She only balls him on their wedding anniversary to relive the experience. The rest of the time J.D. picks and chooses. Faculty, students, student's mothers, trustees' wives. It doesn't matter. Dora had a thing with him and she says he's insatiable and so grotesque that it feels like your insides are being pushed up into your lungs. Forget it! Not me, daddy. I'm not into elephant banging. No way. I like you, my little zucchini."

Jo Ellen Chestnut Bacon was indeed a rarity among women. For if her husband was a sexual giant, literally as well as figuratively, she was by no means a midget. Her own desires, although deeply repressed, surfaced in rather unusual ways, never overtly with men, but always lurking beneath the surface like some legendary monster fish everyone talks about but never manages to catch. She was a small, pretty woman who, although well educated and articulate, chose to speak in soft undulating phrases which teased and excited the men around her. Her accent was upper class, Deep South, correct and yet hinting of magnolias and mint juleps.

"Oh, Professor Garboil," she'd said once she had isolated him from the rest of her guests at the new faculty reception. "You just can't imagine how glad we all are that we've finally captured a real life-size economist at Frick. I hear countless arguments about the relevance of education, but no one talks about the real issues. Why economics is the lining which holds and sustains a student while he's in this four-year-long gestation period called a university education. Don't you agree?"

"Absolutely," Garboil had replied, disguising his perplexity and trying to find room to back away from Jo Ellen Bacon's aggressive bosom. "I think the study of economics in a capitalist society is possibly the most important political education a student can receive."

"Precisely," said Jo Ellen, fluttering her eyelashes ever so lightly. In the dimness of the spacious living room, her lashes, moving against the background of her brown eyes, appeared as so many tiny moths dancing about a flickering candle. An intense passion seemed to burn in her eyes. "From the moment a student becomes aroused by an idea, begins to practice the delights of intellectual intercourse and reaches a climax in the form of insight, it is the responsibility of the educator to create a safe, warm and fertile environment for his seed to grow. If the university is to be the womb where this precious intellectual fetus is nurtured, then economics is the lining of that womb. Don't you agree?"

Garboil nodded, wishing for all he was worth that he had caught a cold and could have excused himself from coming to the president's house that night. It had been more than six weeks since he had left Joan in California and he ached for a woman. And then out of the wish to escape, he endeared himself forever with Jo Ellen Bacon.

"Of course," he said, "your're aware that mathematics is a major part of economics. It's through mathematics that we really can begin to provide some of the answers facing us."

"That's brilliant," she said, cutting in on him. "Oh, do excuse me. But you do understand, don't you?"

"Yes, I think so," he replied, stunned by what she could have understood from his comment.

"Mathematics," she went on, "is simply the mitotic process of cell multiplication. But you knew that, didn't you?"

"Yes, I did. For a number of years, as a matter of fact."

She moved closer to him and placed a hand on his arm.

"Oh, I'm so happy you've come to Frick. May I call you Frank?"

"Yes, of course."

"And you call me Jo Ellen."

"All right."

"You have two children, don't you?"

"Yes."

"You'll have to bring them to the house when they get here. And of course, your wife," she added as a well timed afterthought. "John and I have none of our own, but I'm sure we will. There's no hurry."

The next two hours were filled with every conceivable subject, always analyzed by Jo Ellen Bacon in the same manner.

Garboil attempted to talk to her about sports, a subject he was certain she would feel uncomfortable with. Without the slightest hesitation she launched into an explanation of the line of scrimmage in football as the sacred and divine place at which the ovum and spermatozoa collided.

It all made perfect sense to her. During his three years at Frick University, Garboil was to see each aspect of the university as a corresponding phase in the process of reproduction or as some part of human sexual anatomy. The humanities were one ovary and the social sciences another. Sports were the vaginal canal, a fact which not only infuriated but embarrassed Hummer Williams, the Athletic Director, a devout Black Baptist. Art and Music were the labia, and through some strange, logical progression, writing was the clitoris. Of course reading was the maidenhead and once that was ruptured only the delight of education awaited. She was quite frank in employing the metaphor and not one male faculty member had escaped a quasi-sexual encounter with Jo Ellen Bacon.

When Garboil left the reception that evening, he wrote to his wife. It was a long, rambling account of the event. She wrote back, stating that he sounded as if he'd been psychologically raped and was simply reacting hysterically. She was sure Jo Ellen couldn't be as bad as he made her out. The letter disturbed him, but by the time she arrived three weeks later he had forgotten about it. He was so glad to see Joan and that first night, after the boys were asleep, they had made love for hours, unable to fall asleep, wanting each other more and more with each union. And now everything was so different, so distant. She had found out about Angela the previous winter and had avenged herself with a passing romance, the lawyer to whom she had gone for counsel concerning a possible divorce.

The experience had embittered her. Immediately after, he had explained to Angela that he had to stop seeing her. Angela took it well. No tears, no recriminations. But as hard as he and Joan had tried, something had been lost and their lovemaking was now infrequent.

As he rose from the couch, looked at his watch and made ready to teach his three o'clock class, he felt a deep longing to be back in California, relatively free of adult pressures, walking with Joan along the beach, wanting her and loving her. He recalled her pregnancies and the pride he felt in being her husband, the one who had made her wondrous body swell with life. And it would all be gone soon. He knew it. It was all over and the knowledge tore at him, making him wish to be dead. But he had to go through with it. He had to find out if he would have been any good at ice hockey.

He let himself out of the office and, in a trance, walked down the corridor, oblivious to anything but his inner self marching forward into the unknown.

CHAPTER 15

Wherein we examine abnormal animal behavior, get a preview of the upcoming demonstration against the injustice being perpetrated on the protagonist in his guise as a Vietnam veteran, visit the spirit world, learn that gentrification occurs there as well, and hopefully develop new appreciation for Puerto Rican food since it is evident that in the spirit world there are no Puerto Rican restaurants or, for that matter, designer clothes to wear to them.

Mental illness and anti-social behavior are not phenomena exhibited solely by human beings. There are chemicals in living organisms which can be triggered, either by stress or diet, to produce bizarre behavior in almost any member of the animal kingdom. Any animal, wild or domesticated, can depart from what is considered normal behavior for its species and act erratically if its chemical system is not in balance. Horses, cattle, dogs, cats, sheep, goats, pigs and zoo animals can suffer imbalance of this type. This can be the result of pre-natal influences, conditioning or genetic traits. Personality plays a very small role in animals, since there is little variance within species. Those that occur are generally magnified by the anthropomorphizing of the observer. Upon closer examination, one may conclude safely that what was thought to be a personality trait falls within the normal range of that species. However, when a cat, for example, butts everything that gets in its way, or a cow follows the farmer around, wagging its tail and attempting to lick his face, then we may be dealing with a chemical imbalance and aberrant animal behavior, rather than personality traits of that particular animal. As we work down the evolutionary scale from mammals, we can find the phenomenon of animal insanity in birds. Pigeons, for instance, are not exempt from bizarre and lunatic behavior.

In Vinnie's Pet Shop on 116th Street there was such a pigeon. Pepe, as the employees of the shop called the bird, was a remarkable physical specimen. A large male with resplendent white plumage and an elegant carriage, Pepe had been sold by its owner, Mr. Alejandro Santiago, one of the most famous pigeon flyers of El Barrio, because of its aggressive behavior.

Hatched in one of Mr. Santiago's coops, Pepe exhibited signs of aggression a week or so after emerging from its shell. During a feeding, Pepe reached up and pecked out its mother's left eye, blinding her instantly. The mother abandoned the nest and Mr. Santiago was forced to feed the chick by hand. Pepe refused to eat pigeon feed and Mr. Santiago, unable to find worms, fed small bits of hamburger to the young fledgling. As it grew Pepe's eyes took on the look of a bird of prey and as soon as he was released from the coop he took to the air and soared further and higher than some of the more mature pigeons. With each passing day Pepe grew stronger and developed the habit of flying alone, circling above the two hundred or so pigeons which took to the air daily under Mr. Santiago's supervision. At first Mr. Santiago thought that his magnificent specimen flew above his other birds in order to serve as a lookout against hawks, which, while small in number, do nest in some of New York City's higher skyscrapers. How noble for a bird to risk his life to protect the others, thought Mr. Santiago. But such was not the case, as Mr. Santiago found out one morning. All that Pepe had been doing was using the flight of pigeons to camouflage his attacks.

Mr. Santiago had just opened his two coops and watched the pigeons fly out. They formed up quickly above the roof of his building, constructing beautifully symmetrical echelons, turning and sweeping the sky as one. As usual, Pepe climbed higher than the rest of the flock. He flew wide circles for some five minutes and then, as Mr. Santiago watched in rapture at the clean white lines of his pigeon against the cloudless sky, Pepe dove straight down through the V of the flight, his speed increasing as it hurtled to the sidewalk below. When he lost sight of Pepe, Mr. Santiago leaned out over the edge of the roof just in time to see Pepe swoop in on the shopping bag of a woman walking away from the A&P Supermarket. Pepe swooped down and removed something from the bag and climbed rapidly aloft, the package suspended from his talons. Effortlessly, it climbed, circled and landed atop one of the coops. Mr. Santiago scrambled up the ladder to the roof of the coop and watched as Pepe ripped apart a package of breakfast sausage and began eating. Mr. Santiago shook his head and clucked his tongue in chagrin at what he had witnessed. Aware of Mr. Santiago's disapproval, Pepe stopped eating and fixed him with a wild, murderous look from his red eye. Mr. Santiago immediately caught the defiant act and waved his hands, but Pepe, rather than being startled, flared his wings, puffed up his chest arrogantly and even took a couple of steps towards him. Two weeks later Mr. Santiago sold Pepe to the pet shop.

Because Pepe hadn't stopped with the theft of the breakfast sausage. The top of the pigeon coop became the repository for small packages of hamburger, pork chops, chicken wings, chitterlings, fish, shrimp and lamb. One time Pepe even brought a newborn kitten, which Mr. Santiago rescued before Pepe had a chance to disembowel it. But the rapine didn't stop there. Rather than just satisfying his voracious appetite for meat, the pigeon's facility for pilfering turned to sport. His hunger satisfied, Pepe would often swoop down on innocent persons walking leisurely on a sidewalk and steal their hats, scarves or small pocketbooks if carried too loosely. Worse yet, Pepe began to recruit other young pigeons to join him in committing these crimes. The outcome was clear to Mr. Santiago. In time he would have a gang of teenage pigeons dedicated to mugging his neighbors.

Convinced that Pepe and his cohorts would eventually graduate to greater and greater crimes, Mr. Santiago waited until the pigeons were asleep one evening, went into the coop with a pillow case and threw it over Pepe. In the morning he walked over to the pet shop and traded Pepe in for two dollars worth of pigeon feed. He explained the problem to the people at the pet shop. They had all heard about the pigeon's exploits and immediately named him Mugging Pepe or *Pepe El Pillo* and placed him in a special cage by himself. Mr. Santiago also explained about Pepe's dislike of pigeon feed and his appetite for meat. Benjamin Pardo, the manager of the pet shop, listened attentively enough, but did not believe Pepe would eat anything but meat. He ordered the other members of his staff to give Pepe pigeon feed. Once in while they would give him a few scraps from a hot dog or a Big Mac, but Pepe shunned the supposed treats. He hated mustard and just the smell of the McDonald's sauce made him sick. He was then forced to eat pigeon feed which was dry and tasteless. Their disregard made Pepe angrier each day and one would imagine, given his diet, created a greater imbalance in his system.

Pepe also took to making sounds very much unlike a pigeon. The sounds were more like coughs, but harsh and menacing. If anyone came near the cage Pepe batted his wings rapidly and surged forward to peck at the person., Initially, the staff at the pet shop joked and teased Pepe, but after a week of his awful noises and menacing gestures they grew to dislike him immensely. Alfredo, whose responsibility was to clean out the cages where dogs, cats, guinea pigs, hamsters, gerbils, rats and other assorted mammals were kept, suggested they strangle Pepe. The others agreed, but no one volunteered to perform the execution. "Well, it was your idea," they said to Alfredo. One evening, after taking care of the last customer and closing the store, Alfredo opened the cage, determined to break Pepe's neck and be done with the unruly pigeon. He stuck his hand inside and immediately let out a yelp and began hopping up and down and cursing. The manager of the store, Benjamin, came running over and closed the cage just as Pepe was about to make his escape. He looked at the gash on Alfredo's hand where Pepe had pecked him and shook his head.

That settled it. Tomorrow morning they would take the cage up to the roof, open it and let Pepe go. Let the police handle him. It would serve him right if they shot him down. The following morning, before they could carry out their plan, John Chota walked into the pet shop. He had spent another sleepless night fighting with Lena Kojinsky. Incapable of making love to her without the fear of a large hawk sinking its talons into his back, he was unable to reveal the problem to Lena. She was now convinced that he had another girlfriend. He denied the accusation, but the denial only served to further anger the now irascible topless dancer. For Chota, the thought of El Falcon appearing and disappearing at will became an obsession. A malevolent shadow of paranoia stalked him wherever he went.

His assignment by the United Front to coordinate the upcoming demonstration had gotten out of hand. Once the different groups at the college had been aligned, he'd lost track of the role each one was to play. Each group following its own philosophy and agenda, it now appeared as if the sum total of their disparate expressions would cause a chaotic and possibly explosive situation. One group had purchased a large pig which they planned to slaughter in front of the hospital in order to smear themselves with the blood and, thus, dramatize the injustice being enacted against Armando Martinez, a Vietnam veteran. One ecology-minded group had rented picks and shovels and was going to dig up the sidewalk in front of the hospital and plant a vegetable and flower garden. The pressure and stress in the school became so great that a large majority of the milder students began staying away, making classes resemble a leftists' convention. For Chota the experience had begun to take its toll. He now felt as if his mind were slowly unraveling. Like a ball of yarn which someone had untied and dragged by one of its ends, his mind was being bounced along, growing smaller and smaller as it rolled to the end of the string. Having no other source of security, Chota called Mullvaney with the only ray of hope he'd found in an otherwise bleak situation.

"Chief, I think I figured out a way to trap El Falcon," he whispered when Mullvaney came to the phone.

"Sure, Johnny," said Mullvaney, humoring Chota and making a mental note to inform the Department's psychiatric counseling staff of his condition. "What is it?"

"I went to see the spiritualist," Chota said, his voice dropping further in volume.

"What?" said Mullvaney. "I can't hear you."

"The spiritualist," Chota said, a little more loudly. "I went to see her. She said it was possible."

"What was?"

"That he changes into a hawk and that's how he disappears."

"Sure, kid."

"We're gonna trap his spirit, Chief."

"Yeah?"

"Yeah, we're gonna do the ceremony. You see hawks eat pigeons. They hunt them down. The woman said the hawk is a messenger of the Devil. Not all hawks, but the ones that can change into men."

"I see, so what happens?"

"So to trap the hawk spirit, you gotta have a white pigeon. The white pigeon has to be a female."

"Right. Female caucasian. I got you so far."

"Yeah, so like the white pigeon is the spirit of a virgin. I know you don't believe in any of this stuff, but the Devil likes to see virgins raped. So when the medium starts calling on the spirits to help, the Devil listens in on the conversation and then the pigeon is brought out and put on the altar. When the Devil sees this, he gets all excited and sends the hawk spirit to rape the white pigeon. All along the woman is smoking a cigar because the hawk spirit, which is a macho spirit, feels at home with cigar smoke in the air. She also puts cigars, Bacardi rum and *chicharrones* on the altar."

"Chiwhat?"

"Sorry, Chief. You know, pork rinds. They come in little bags and cost a quarter. The macho hawk spirit likes to munch on them when he's drinking rum."

"Anything else?"

"Sure, Chief. The medium puts out nice pork chops and fried plantains and rice and beans and Schaeffer beer so that the spirit thinks everything's okay."

"No, no. I want to know if that's it with the hawk business."

"Right, I understand. There's more. When everything is set, the medium starts calling the spirits and then talks to them and they have this conversation, which is mostly about how things are over where the spirits are. You know, the weather and where they hang out. Then the hawk spirit tries to sneak in and rape the spirit of the virgin pigeon. The medium has this switch and she turns on this real bright light in the room and blinds the hawk spirit and that's it. The spirit of the hawk is caught and the man who was using it loses his power. El Falcon is as good as caught."

"No kidding?"

"No kidding, Chief. She told me. I'm on my way to buy a white pigeon right now. We're gonna do the ceremony this afternoon because this kind of spirit is easier to handle in the daytime. They spend the night out all the time, drinking and raising hell, but can't pass up the chance of raping a virgin. I'll let you know what happens."

"Right, kid. How's it going up at the school?"

"It's gonna be hell, Chief. We better have plenty of men out in front of that hospital. Every nut's gonna be there. They're gonna kill a pig, burn the American flag, dig up the sidewalk to plant a garden and screw in the street."

"What?"

"Yeah, one group has this girl who's gonna dress up as the Statue of Liberty and a guy in a three piece suit and a Richard Nixon mask is gonna screw her while she moans and says that thing about give me your people on welfare, who are tired of working. You know, the thing on the plaque."

"They're gonna take off their clothes in this cold?"

"Yeah, Chief."

"And screw in the street?"

"Yeah, they're nuts. The whole thing's totally out of control."

"Thanks for telling me, Johnny."

"That's okay, Chief. How's it going on your end?"

"Pretty good, kid. We're getting ready to hook up every black cat in that neighborhood. The furry kind, but don't think it wouldn't be a good idea to wire up the two-legged kind. We'll figure out El Falcon's plans in no time."

"Sounds good, Chief. But it's not gonna matter once we capture his spirit. It'll weaken his power."

"Right, kid."

"Okay, Chief. I gotta go."

Chota hung up the phone and headed for Manhattan and Vinnie's Pet Shop. Being inside his apartment and talking to Mullvaney had calmed him down considerably. As soon as he was out in the street, however, he again became nervous and filled with a sense of doom about his life. By the time he reached the pet shop the tick in his eye was so pronounced that it had traveled down his face and the entire left side from eyebrow to chin was twitching spasmodically. The staff of the pet shop saw him come in and knew they had trouble on their hands. The owner of the pet shop loved animals and the worst thing they could do was to sell one to someone who was going to mistreat it. Pepe, however, was an exception. They had already gotten the okay to dump him any way possible. If they could make a profit on it, better yet.

Benjamin, the manager, came over to where Chota was standing and asked him what he wanted.

"I need a pigeon," Chota said, his voice squeakier than usual and his face twisted as he tried to control the tic. "A white female. You got one?"

Benjamin thought for a moment as if he were going over his inventory.

"What's it for?" he said, returning to his post behind the counter.

Chota looked nervously around and then leaned over the counter.

"It's for capuring a spirit," he whispered.

Benjamin nodded knowingly. His grandmother often talked about spirits and how people sometimes sacrificed animals in their ceremonies. He looked at Alfredo's bandaged hand and bit his lip as if he were making a decision.

"Get me the gloves, Alfredo," he said.

Alfredo reached under the counter and brought out a thick pair of workmen's gloves. Benjamin put them on and headed for Pepe's cage. Chota followed and watched Benjamin open the cage, reach in and grab Pepe, who put up a fight but was quickly subdued by Benjamin's strong hands. He lay still, hoping the grip on his body would lessen so he could escape. The fire in Pepe's eyes was so intense that Chota looked away.

"Here you go, *panita*," Benjamin said. "One white pigeon."

"Is it a female?" Chota said.

"Yeah," said Benjamin. "She layed a couple of eggs last week."

Chota hesitated before asking the next question.

"Is she a virgin?"

"I haven't touched her," Benjamin said, looking around to the other employees. They all shook their heads and laughed nervously. "Just kidding," Benjamin said. "You don't have to worry about that. She was hatched right here and no other bird has gotten to her."

"How did she lay eggs?" Chota said.

"All female birds lay eggs, but they won't hatch unless the *macho* gets to the female. No *macho* has had his way with Pepita yet."

"Is that her name, Pepita?"

"Yeah," Benjamin said. "Pepita."

"Okay," Chota said. "How much?"

Benjamin shrugged his shoulders.

"For you, five bucks," he said.

Chota went into his pocket, brought out a billfold and extracted a five dollar bill. Benjamin went back behind the counter, asked Alfredo to bring him a box with a top and, holding Pepe with one hand, rang up the sale. Once the box was brought he put Pepe inside and in one deft move withdrew his hand and put the lid back on the box. He tied string around the box, cut a couple of air holes on the top and pushed the box towards Chota.

"There you go, my friend," he said. "One virgin white female pigeon. Anything else. A hamster maybe?"

Chota shook his head, took the box off the counter and headed for the door. Before the door closed, Benjamin, Alfredo and the other two clerks were roaring with laughter and holding out their palms for slapping. Chota opened the door to his car and placed the box in the back seat. The drive back to the Bronx was interminably long. He was shaking badly and was afraid of going too fast. Once in his apartment he placed the box with Pepe in it in a corner of the kitchen. He looked at his watch and then went into the bathroom and began filling the tub. As the tub filled he added the ingredients which doña Ursula, the spiritualist, had prescribed and which he had purchased at the *botánica*. There was a blue powder for courage, a green one for luck, a yellow one for his nerves and a red powder to increase his sexual potency. To the brown, foaming concoction he added Oil of Holy Prayer, Oil of Forgetfulness and Oil of Peaceful Loving, the latter to recuperate his potency as a lover. He topped the bath with an assortment of green leaves and dry twigs. When the tub was full and the water resembled that of a swamp and was as fetid, he lit four sticks of incense and placed them in the four corners of the bathroom. That accomplished he lit a large red candle in a glass, turned off the lights, stripped and got into the tub. For the next hour Chota sat in the tub smelling the awful fumes until he thought he would vomit. But he endured the treatment, following the woman's instructions to purify himself in order to be able to communicate with the spirit of his grandfather, which, although quite faint, was the strongest of the spirits which she had contacted.

And there was no doubt that it had been his grandfather two nights before. That afternoon he'd have a chance to talk to him again, to explain the problem he was having with Lena. While they talked, the Devil would listen and send the hawk spirit to rape the virgin pigeon. The incense burned and the fumes filled his lungs, making him feel tired and sleepy. But he musn't fall asleep. Doña Ursula had specified that he must sit in the tub only one hour and then he must rinse, dry himself thoroughly and dress all in white.

Meanwhile, in the home of doña Ursula Porrata, final preparations were being made for the afternoon ceremony to capture the hawk spirit. She had cooked rice and beans, pork chops and fried plantains. The aroma of the food filled the entire apartment, obliterating for the moment the thick smell of incense which usually permeated her home. In the consultation room she had covered the larger of the two tables with a red tablecloth and set it for three: her client, herself, and the spirit which was to be their guest. Off to the side, at a smaller table, covered in white, she lit two white candles in glass, spead a bed of aromatic leaves in the middle and burned powdered incense in a small brass receptacle. Behind the leaves she set out a fifth of Bacardi rum, several packages of pork rinds and two cigars, still in their cellophane packages.

All around the dimly lit apartment, statues of saints and other brightly painted plaster figures stood in readiness, seemingly eager to assist doña Ursula to capture the spirit. African warriors, Indian archers, Arab swordsmen, and virgins of all sorts, some of them as large as children, made the room a cluttered sanctuary in which wayward saints had taken refuge. Doña

Ursula felt badly for the young man for whom she was to perform the ceremony. She had seen several evil spirits struggling inside of him and it would take more than her powers to help him. But Suncha Yunqué's grandson had called and said she should go ahead and do her best. He'd said Paquito was in trouble and she must help him. Poor little boy. How she wished he'd come and see her once in a while. Serena had died and he probably didn't know it. Suncha's grandson said Paquito was a professor. Sol would've been so proud of him. What a tragedy that was. She'd do as she was asked and do everything possible to throw this Pancho Miranda off. Oh, he was an evil one, this rodent-looking man. So small and yet so mean. It served him right having to pay two hundred dollars for the ceremony. Usually she charged ten or fifteen dollars to make people feel better. The more they paid the better they felt. They believed in spirits and what could she do. She couldn't tell them that whatever they suffered from they had brought on themselves. She truly believed that. Whatever happened to a person, even great tragedies, were their own doing. There was no one to blame. It was all destiny. If a man was poor in this lifetime, he had to have been a thief in his previous one. All he could hope for was to have better luck in the next. Anything not to accept full and total responsibility. Poor God. If He existed, and Heaven forgive her because after seventy-five years she had come to realize that it didn't matter, then He was quite weak. But she had a gift and could see pain and illness in people. She always had seen clearly into people. If they chose to believe in spirits and wished to speak to them and felt better afterwards, so be it. It was a living and less degrading than taking a handout from the government. But this Pancho Miranda worried her. He had serious mental problems and was dangerous. Why did he explain that his grandfather called him Johnny, if his name was Pancho? Whatever she did, she must protect Paquito. Suncha Yunqué's grandson was right. Nothing mattered except fighting evil and protecting the innocent, keeping their dreams alive.

At exactly two o'clock there was a knock on Ursula Porrata's door. Using her cane to help her move her small, wizened body across the room, she answered the door. John Chota, dressed entirely in white and carrying the box with Pepe the pigeon in it, entered the apartment. He felt much better after his purification bath.

"Here's the pigeon," he said. "Where do you want it?"

"Put it on the altar," said Ursula, pointing to the small table.

Chota walked over to the table and put the box atop the bed of leaves.

"What about the money?" he said. "Two hundred, right?"

"Yes, it will please your grandfather if that is taken care of now," said Ursula.

Chota handed her four fifty-dollar bills. She took the bills, counted them and disappeared into the room, where she took a large tin can of Sultana Soda Crackers from a closet, pried the can open and placed her fee inside. She replaced the can in the closet, returned to the consultation room and stood behind the chair next to the altar.

"Please sit down," she said. "Across from me. Leave the end place for your grandfather's spirit. I'll get the food."

John Chota sat down in the dimly lit room with the candles burning and the more than fifty statues staring down at him and felt protected from the hawk spirit which had haunted him since seeing El Falcon at the United Front headquarters. He watched eagerly as Ursula Porrata went back and forth from the room to the kitchen, returning each time with pots of food. Once the rice and beans, pork chops and fried plantains were on the table, she uncovered them and sat down. She closed her eyes and immediately began mumbling as if she were going into a trance. When she next spoke, her voice had a wavering quality, much as if the words were being carried by the wind. It reminded Chota of ghost movies and he felt chilled.

"Close your eyes," she said. "Concentrate on the image of your grandfather. Ask him to come and help you in this hour of great need."

Chota did as he was told. His mind traveled back in time to his childhood. Somewhere inside of him he heard a humming and then he heard his grandfather respond. The voice was faint yet audible.

"I can't hear him very well," Chota said.

"Shh, he's weak from hunger and still very far away. When he smells the food, he'll get closer. Call him to come and eat."

Chota concentrated harder.

"Abuelo, it's me, Johnny. Come and eat."

"Hello, Johnny," the voice said. This time it was closer. He felt goose bumps form along his arms. "How are you?"

"I'm in a lot of trouble, grandfather," Chota said.

"What kind of trouble? Money or women?"

"Women, grandfather. I can't help them anymore."

"Yes, yes," he said. "I know how you feel. That happened to me once, but I was past sixty and your grandmother looked like an old sack by then. I had to get myself a girlfriend. She was nice and fat and worked in a belt factory in Brooklyn. Her name was Magdalena and her skin was brown and soft. She mooed like a cow when we were in bed. But you're a young man. Are you eating all right?"

"Yes, grandfather."

"You're not sleeping well."

"No, grandfather. I have terrible dreams."

"Oh, that's too bad," his grandfather said and then paused. Chota could hear him sniffing. "Is that pork chops I smell?"

"Yes, grandfather," Chota replied. "And *tostones* and rice and beans and Schaeffer beer. Please come and sit down. I need to talk to you."

"Thank you, Johnny."

Chota wanted desperately to open his eyes, but kept them closed, just as doña Ursula had asked. To open his eyes would break the spell and his grandfather's spirit would fade. He heard bumping in the room and then the chair at the head of the table moved back on the floor and then forward again. When his grandfather spoke again he seemed closer than ever.

"The pork chops look wonderful," he said. "We don't get anything like that up here. Everything's changed so much. Our section used to be all Puerto Ricans, but each day we're getting all kinds of different people. Mostly high class people. Bankers, lawyers, doctors and teachers, but none of them Puerto Ricans. I heard that Guillermo Lebron died."

"That's true, grandfather. Last year."

"You're not gonna believe this, Johnny. I haven't seen him yet. When I got up here the place was a real dump, but it's getting kind of nice. Less of our people. I don't know where they're sending them. And the food is terrible. No fried food, no sugar, no salt, no Valencia cakes. Nothing. Mostly cottage cheese and yogurt and health food. No Puerto Rican food anywhere. My friends complain, but I don't mind because of the women and the dancing. Once in a while I remember your grandmother's cooking and then I feel homesick. How is she?"

"She's fine, grandfather. Doesn't remember too much anymore."

"That's too bad. Do me a favor, Johnny."

"Anything."

"Don't tell her about the women up here. I'm seeing this American woman and I don't want her to get jealous."

"Sure, don't worry. I won't say anything."

Chota could hear Ursula Porrata dishing up the food to his left and then the silverware clattered against the china and his grandfather was making chewing sounds. He wanted to ask his grandfather what he ought to do about his problem with Lena, but suddenly he heard wings flapping and almost opened his eyes.

"That's it," said Ursula Porrata. "He's here."

"Who?" Chota said.

"The spirit," whispered Ursula. "The hawk spirit. Quickly. Open your eyes. Go to the altar, take out the pigeon and hold her. I'll tie her legs and wings with string so that the hawk spirit can have his way with her quickly."

Chota did as he was told and went to the altar. He quickly untied the string on the box, lifted the lid and reached in with his right hand. He had barely touched Pepe's feathers when he felt a sharp pain in the palm of his hand. He yowled and jumped back, holding his right hand with his left. At that moment Pepe flew out of the box with a great flapping of wings and a screech which even frightened Ursula Porrata. Pepe flew around the room a couple of times, barely missing a statue of Saint Lazarus and almost impaling himself on an African spear carrier. On his second pass over the table, he spotted the pork chops and he snapped. All those days without meat had made him quite nervous. He wheeled rapidly around in the air, circled back, swept in on the table and took a pork chop from the dish. A moment later he was atop a china closet, tearing apart the pork chop among some smaller statues of Saint Bartholomew, Saint James and a virgin of unspecified origin and name.

The pain in Chota's hand was nothing compared to the fear he was experiencing. Had we been able to look into his mind at that moment, it would've resembled a pin ball machine with lights and bells going on and off in rapid succession.

"What happened?" he kept repeating. "What happened? It bit me. The pigeon bit me. What's going on? What does it mean?"

"Sit down, sit down," Ursula Porrata urged. "Remain calm."

Chota sat down.

"Close your eyes again," Ursula said. "Everything happened too quickly."

Chota closed his eyes. The fear was overpowering and he was shaking as if the temperature in the room had suddenly dropped to freezing.

"Tell me," said Ursula Porrata. "Did you put those slits in the box?"

"No, it was the people in the pet shop where I bought the pigeon."

"That's too bad because the hawk spirit went in through them and had his way with the virgin pigeon. He is now inside of her gorging himself on her purity. She's a lost soul."

"He's in her?"

"Yes, he was too quick for us."

"How can you tell he's in her?"

"Did you see how she behaved? Like a hawk. First attacking you and then stealing the pork chop. She's lost now. The hawk spirit's in her."

"What can we do?"

"We must wait until the hawk spirit satisfies his urges."

"Why did she take the pork chop?"

"To satisfy the hawk spirit. To please him. To show him that she accepts him and is at one with his spirit. Otherwise he would not only rape her but destroy her. Those are the ways of the macho hawk spirit. Remain calm. Soon he will be done. I will pour him some rum and light a cigar. He will smell the aroma, want to drink and smoke and then we will capture him. But please remain calm."

Chota nodded, waiting, trying to keep his heart from jumping out through his mouth. He was sweating and had an overpowering urge to empty his bladder. That bastard El Falcon. He screwed the pigeon even before we knew it. At that moment he once again heard the flapping of wings. This time he couln't help opening his eyes. Pepe was flying around the room again, measuring the angle at which he would attack the dish of pork chops. Chota's mind snapped. He drew the snub-nosed revolver he carried when he wasn't on duty and went after Pepe. Holding one hand over his head against a possible attack, he aimed the gun at the pigeon, following his flight among the statues. Having gauged the rhythm of the crazed Pepe, he fired three times in quick succession. The first shot shattered a large statue of the Virgin Mary, the next one tore into an Indian archer and the last one made a bloody, feathery mess out of Pepe's chest. The pigeon flipped once in the air from the impact of the shot and came tumbling down in the middle of the table and directly into the pot of red beans. "I got him, I got him," shouted Chota. "Right through the chest."

Ursula Porrata remained calm throughout the brief but bizarre occurrence. She had seen worse things. The possiblity of death never entered her mind.

"He's gone," she said.

"I know. I got him. He was inside the pigeon and I got him."

"Yes, you shot the pigeon but he escaped. As soon as you fired the gun he escaped."

"You saw him?"

"Yes, of course. Went back to the spirit world. Back to the Devil."

"But how did he do it? It was so fast."

"I don't know. Sit down and ask your grandfather. This time keep your eyes closed no matter what happens. The spirits don't enjoy being looked at. It's very difficult to look your best dressed in sheets."

"They really dress that way? All of them?"

"Yes, of course. It keeps them from being vain."

Chota replaced his gun back into the ankle holster and sat down. He felt calmer, more in control. It had felt good to fire his gun and kill the pigeon. He closed his eyes once more and concentrated on the image of his grandfather.

"Call him," said Ursula Porrata.

"Grandfather, come and finish your dinner. It's getting cold."

He waited, but there was no response.

"Call him again. Apologize to him. I'm sure he left because you opened your eyes. Try harder to contact him."

"Listen, *abuelo*," Chota said. "I'm sorry. You know I'm working on an important case. Please come back and help me."

He waited, and still no answer came.

"He's gone for good," he said.

"Shh, I hear him coming," said Ursula Porrata. "Listen."

Chota listened intently. Far away he could hear his grandfather's voice. It was shaking slightly but quite clear.

"That was very scary, Johnny," his grandfather said.

"It got away, grandfather."

"Yes, I know. That's too bad."

"What happened?"

"That spirit has many allies, Johnny. Here as well as there."

"Who are they? How do they help him turn from a man into a hawk?"

"Words, Johnny. There's a *brujo* involved. He gave him magic words. That's how he can turn into a hawk."

"What are they, grandfather. I have to know."

"I can't answer that, Johnny."

"What's the *brujo*'s name?"

"I don't know that either. But you must be very careful. Take care of your health. Get plenty of sleep and eat well."

"Yes, grandfather. Thank you."

"Don't mention it, Johnny. Listen, I have to go now. I promised some of the boys I'd play dominoes. Don't mention any of this to your grandmother."

"*Abuelo*, wait," Chota said, but received no further response.

"He's gone," said Ursula Porrata. "You can open your eyes."

Chota opened his eyes. He felt quite sleepy and warm.

"We have to find out the *brujo*'s name," he said. "You gotta help me."

"There's only one *brujo* I've heard of who does that kind of work," said Ursula Porrata. "And he's very hard to locate."

"What's his name?"

"Yunqué."

"Yunque?"

"No, Yunqué."

"That's it? Yunqué?"

"Yes."

"Where does he live?

"On the Upper West Side."

"What's he look like?"

"Like a bear."

"You mean he changes into a bear?"

"Sometimes, yes. He growls and waves his arms, smokes five cigarettes at the same time and sometimes he curses in Greek."

"And he's helping El Falcon out?"

"Yes, he's the one. But I've said too much. I'm doing you a special favor, but I could get into a lot of trouble for it."

"No, don't worry. I won't tell anyone. I don't want you to get in trouble. I'll go see this Yunqué, this *brujo*. I'll make him tell me the words that he gave El Falcon. I can learn too."

"Learn what?"

"To fly, and then I can follow El Falcon wherever he goes."

"It's very difficult to fly in the spirit world."

"I'll go see him. Thank you. And I'm sorry about the beans."

"That's all right. Be careful."

"Yes, thank you."

And with that Chota left the home of Ursula Porrata. He felt confident that he would be able to track El Falcon through the spirit world. They had almost trapped him, but he was too quick. He had his way with the virgin pigeon, ate a pork chop and was gone. Son of a bitch.

The first thing he did when he got outside was to call up Lena Kojinsky in Weehauken, New Jersey. She wasn't too happy to hear his voice, but agreed that he could come over and see her. He drove like a madman, eating up the miles on the Cross Bronx Expressway, the Westside Highway and the Lincoln Tunnel into Weehauken. He parked the car in front of Lena's apartment house and ran up the stairs to the third floor, his loins aching for the warm breasts and thighs of his near-sighted, topless dancer. When she opened the door he threw himself on her and violently ripped at her clothing. She giggled and made attempts to fight him off, but in the end she gave in. All he could think about was Lena as a white virgin pigeon and he as the spirit of the hawk.

When it was over, he lay in a stupor, spent, wiped out by the release. He slept for nearly eighteen hours. Lena had gone to her topless job twice in that period of time. When she once again got into bed Chota woke up and made love to her as violently as before. The sounds she made beneath him, which were mostly of displeasure at his force, sounded to him like the cooing of a pigeon. His release came almost immediately and as he lay there he thought of his luck in having found Ursula Porrata. He had gone to three others and they had all directed him to her. Everything about the spirit world was quite amazing. There was no doubt about it. He had frightened off El Falcon's hawk spirit. He had him on the run. Now he must track down this *brujo*, this Yunqué, and make him give up the words that would help him fly so that he could follow El Falcon wherever he went.

CHAPTER 16

In which we have the questionable pleasure of meeting the president of Frick University, learn the true meaning of the phrase "a wolf in sheep's clothing," and how such an individual solves problems; study the origins of liberality in the United States through the light perusal of the history of the Frick Fuller family; receive a smattering of political education; and watch the protagonist, in a battle with his conscience, resign his position and leave his family to pursue the American dream.

After four days of agonizing over his decision to resign his position at Frick University, Frank Garboil finally walked in to see President John David Bacon on Friday afternoon still filled with doubts. Was he doing the right thing? Perhaps it was all an indulgence on his part. He still hadn't told Joan his plans and with each day she grew more nervous around him, as if she already knew that everything was over between them. And how would he earn his living? Even if he were able to get into a college, there was no guarantee that he could make a college team. But he had to try. Each time he thought about not following through with his resolve, his chest tightened and he felt as if he couldn't breathe. No matter what happened, he had to accomplish this one thing.

"Good afternoon, Professor Garboil," said Mrs. Armstrong, as she came out of President Bacon's office. "He'll see you in a few minutes. Please take a seat."

"Thank you," Garboil said, sitting down in the neatly furnished reception area. He picked up a "Newsweek" magazine, turned a few pages and put it down immediately. He hadn't even thought out what he was going to tell Bacon. He'd make it hard on him and he'd feel guilty and maybe even end up being convinced by Bacon not to resign.

John David Bacon, President of Frick University, was a strange breed of man. In many ways he was the type of man who had haunted Garboil's life. He was a driven being who believed in himself above all others, paying homage to God only as an afterthought. For all his piousness, he always appeared to be mocking the Almighty, daring him to go against his will. A backwoods boy from Kentucky, raised on Baptist dogma and dirt-scratching survival, he had been quite a high-school athlete. Through the auspices of his minister, who saw both the athletic potential and the religious huckster in the young man, he obtained a football scholarship to Yale University for Bacon. Everything was neatly arranged by anonymous alumni, since scholarships for the purposes of beefing up the football team were frowned upon at institutions of its academic caliber.

His first year at Yale was pure hell for young Bacon. His speech, manner, religious zeal and body odor all served to make him the butt of numerous and cruel jokes. The only attribute he had, and the one which saved him from total ostracism, was his blocking and tackling ability. He was fearless, immune to pain and absolutely committed to winning at any cost. Many were the Ivy League linemen who were driven to drink dreading an autumnal confrontation against the Eli. As long as J.D. Bacon, as he was listed on football programs, kept his mouth shut, did not eat around them, and bathed regularly, he was allowed the company of gentlemen.

In spite of his shortcomings, by the end of his senior year he was a respected member of the college community, a scholar-jock. Not exactly Skull and Bones material or someone you'd introduce to your sister or invite to Newport, but okay. From the university, Bacon went to the Divinity School, where he distinguished himself as well. But after graduation, rather than dedicating himself to the ministry, he saw greener pastures and a larger flock in higher education and administration. For a number of years he was the bright young man at several schools, making the College Administration Hall of Fame by the time he was thirty-five. A born politician, he worked ceaselessly to correct his speech, improve his table manners and tone down his religious zeal. With the advent of roll-on deodorants, nothing human now stood in his way. However, one evening, when everything appeared to be going exactly as he had planned, John David Bacon had a crisis of conscience and decided to march against injustice. This, at least, is what he communicated to God. Privately, he saw the future and knew that blacks could not be held back much longer. If he were to ascend to the presidency of a college, it would not be Yale, Harvard, Princeton. This he knew and resented. But he would be president and the blacks were going to be there in droves. With this in mind, he asked for a leave of absence as vice-president of Hiram Closet College in Indiana. When the spring semester was over he was on a plane to Montgomery, Alabama.

The next day he was marching and singing spirituals and carrying on with the young, dedicated volunteers from Ivy League sister schools, keeping score of his kills in revenge for the many times he had been slighted by debs from Radcliffe, Bryn Mawr, Vassar, Sarah Lawrence and others. The young women had invaded the South like a plague of locusts with severe speech impediments. And like a man obsessed with stock market reports, part of his mind ticker-taped along each day, quoting his latest debauchery: Sarah Lawrence 28 down 2. Barnard 14 down 4. Radcliffe 20 down 14. Smith 1 down 1. Bacon 38 up 27, until in his mind he felt he owned and controlled the stock of up-and-coming Eastern Establishment womanhood.

In between his dabblings in carnalbroking he became confidant to the leaders of the Civil Rights Movement. To his credit, it must be said that he was instrumental in negotiating several delicate compromises with the white southern community. Using his now cultivated southern accent and suddenly turned-on religious fervor, he won the hearts of many a southern woman whose husband was reluctant to go along with the demands being placed on their institutions.

When his year was up and he had accumulated sufficient Civil Rights credentials, he returned to his position as vice-president of Hiram Closet. Two years had passed and the excitement of the marches, the songs and the young, spirited girls had worn off, leaving Bacon in need of more excitement. In the fall of that year he received a bulletin from a colleague regarding the founding of a new college in Long Island. Among the many positions open, the one of president immediately caught his eye. He wrote immediately and as quickly received a rather enthusiastic reply from the trustees of the Frick Fuller estate. In their letter they requested that he come east at his earliest convenience.

He replied by informing them that because of present duties and the opening of the school year, he would not be able to come to New York until the Thanksgiving holidays. The trustees replied graciously that they would be most interested in meeting him at that time. During that month and a half John David Bacon thoroughly researched the history of the Frick Fuller family. The fledgling university would prove to be the perfect place for Bacon.

Bacon learned that the Frick Fuller people had always been, as far back as the American Revolution, a God-fearing people, industrious and with strains of liberal thinking running through every generation since 1750. In fact, in 1761 Ebenezer Frick was the first known colonial to manufacture sheep-gut contraceptives, incurring for his daring enterprise the wrath of church elders and government officials. Banished and forbidden forever to set foot on Massachusetts soil, he traveled, along with the family, to New York. He cleared a stretch of forest, built a home and established himself in the state, manufacturing once more his contraceptives, clandestinely. An accomplished furniture-maker, but privately an advocate of family planning, he soon became a pillar of his new community.

Each succeeding generation of Fricks added to the family fortune and reputation by one means or another, but generally distinguishing itself for undertaking the most daring and difficult demands made by anyone with enough capital to justify the morality of the act. They became doctors, lawyers, teachers, brokers, ministers, shipbuilders, manufacturers, traders, soldiers, but never politicians, a profession which limited and constrained their actions. When John David Bacon presented himself to the trustees of Frick University, he was ready for them. Twenty minutes into the interview, the following issue came up. Needless to say Bacon handled it flawlessly.

"We want to create the sort of place which will allow young people from all walks of life to commune with each other and nature and feel free to exchange their experiences in an atmosphere of trust, conciliation and Judeo-Christian unity, Dr. Bacon."

"Yes, I understand fully, Mr. Biddleworth. I think my experience in religion, college administration, the Civil Rights Movement and my lifelong belief in the struggle of the underprivileged qualify me as your first president."

"Dr. Bacon, I'm sure I can speak for the other members of the board in saying that you are eminently qualified for the position. We have had nothing but excellent reports from our associates. Without question you have distinguished yourself in every endeavor undertaken. However, one thing is uppermost in our minds. How do you hope to establish a balanced ethnic community?"

John David Bacon, ever alert, had anticipated the question and recalled how Ebenezer Frick's son, Leland Chapman Frick, had convinced two warring Indian tribes to divide a long stretch of forest over which they had been fighting. The matter was settled when Leland suggested setting aside an area twelve miles long by ten miles wide as a neutral zone. This area would be held in trust by Leland until the two tribes settled their differences. The forest would be divided into thirds with the Patchogue taking the southern portion, the Massapequa the northern end and the Fricks the middle.

"Well, Mr. Biddleworth," said Bacon. "I believe the best way to resolve the situation would be to allow for equal ethnic representation. That is, for blacks to have thirty percent student enrollment, the whites thirty percent, the Spanish speaking thirty percent, and any others the remaining ten percent."

The eleven trustees nodded solemnly.

"And the faculty, Dr. Bacon?"

"I believe the same should hold true, sir," Bacon said.

"Excellent, Dr. Bacon," said Frampton J. Biddleworth.

"With all due respect, Mr. Biddleworth," Bacon said. "The idea is not a new one. Our republic functions in much the same manner in respect to the three branches of government and the checks and balances they exercise over each other. As you know the Judiciary has thirty percent of the power, the Congress another thirty percent, the Executive branch its thirty, and the rest of the power rests in the hands of the people."

They once again nodded solemnly. They liked the idea, the orderly parallel drawn by this daring young man on whom they placed complete trust to accomplish their mandate. It was this recognition by the Board of Trustees of Josiah Frick University which catapulted John David Bacon to the presidency of the school.

Bacon finished out the year at Hiram Closet College and in the summer of 1965 began setting up house in the old Frick Fuller mansion, a spacious fifty-room house, complete with ballroom, indoor tennis courts, swimming pool and an intricate series of tunnels leading to smaller houses and cabins on the estate. The mansion was built in the 1850's and became, during that time, one of the final destinations of the underground railroad. At the time of the Civil War there was a rumor among blacks working in the household of Chapman Fuller, architect and builder of the mansion, who had married Leland's daughter, Lisbeth Biddleworth Frick, that it was possible for a slave to dig himself a hole in the ground in Georgia and emerge two weeks later in the mansion's kitchen. Of course this rumor was never substantiated but, given the ingenuity of the Frick Fuller family, it was within the realm of possibility.

As he thought about these things Frank Garboil felt weaker and weaker in his resolve. How strange life was. Joan's ancestor Mary Alcott Farnsworth had been courted by Leland Frick before he married his wife, Abigail Pettiford Hammerstruck. And here he was related by marriage to the roots of American independence, sitting on land that had made history, ready to reject the entire thing, to act on a whim. But he had to do it.

"Professor Garboil?"

Mrs. Anderson's voice startled him and he stood up.

"I'm sorry," he said. "I was thinking."

"You may go in now," said Mrs. Anderson. "President Bacon will see you."

"Thank you."

He opened the door and walked into Bacon's office, his knees shaking and the palms of his hands sweating so badly that he felt as if the perspiration were dripping from his fingertips. The office was huge and nearly the size of a basketball court. Along one wall were at least fifty pictures of John David Bacon in football gear, a trophy case and off to the side a blocking sled which, it was rumored, Bacon used on occasion. The entire floor of the room was covered in thick green carpet, not disimilar in color and texture to a finely manicured football field. The desk as well was huge. A rectangle specially built for him, its surface was marked off in yard lines and numbered appropriately. On either end of the desk, at the goal lines, were miniature goal posts. Written in the left-hand end-zone, as you stood in front of the desk, was FRICK and in the other end-zone YALE. Behind the desk there was a picture window extending the length of the wall and looking out into a mountain forest, complete with log cabin and perpetual wood smoke coming from its chimney. Raccoons, possums and other Appalachian fauna inhabited the garden.

Garboil faced the athletic, fleshy-faced Bacon and nodded nervously. John David Bacon came out from behind the desk, shook his hand and patted him on the back. He was not quite as tall as Garboil but powerfully built. His hands and arms appeared simian to Garboil.

"How's the ole boy doing?" Bacon said. "I sure wish I had a dozen like you doing God's work in this place. You sure pushed that student participation resolution through the faculty senate, didn't you, fella? Well, that's what it's all about, ain't it? Yes sir! That's what I always say. Stick it to them. How's Joan?"

The apparent non-sequitur sent chills down Garboil's spine.

"Oh, she's fine, John. Fine."

"Great gal, Frank. And the boys? Still playing hockey, I bet. Great sport. Gosh Almighty, when I was in school I useta room with a fella played on the hockey team. Goalie he was. Good ole boy by the name of Pepsodent. Suffered from perennial halitosis. Put us together because in those days I had a perspiration problem. Just sweated and sweated. Rough sport that hockey. Now, what was it you wanted to see me about, Frank?"

"Well, John, it's kind of complicated."

"Shoot! You just sit yourself down. Nothing's too complicated for John Bacon."

Garboil sat down on one of the modern sofas at an angle from the picture window. He watched the simulated smoke rising from the log cabin. He turned and looked at Bacon, not quite sure how to tell him of his decision.

"I'm leaving, John," he finally said.

"You can't do that, Frank," said Bacon, laughing, not quite believing what he'd heard. "The term's not over yet."

"No, not right away. At the end of the spring semester. I won't be back next year."

"You don't mean that," said Bacon, coming over to sit at the other end of the couch.

"I do, John. I have to."

"That's bad news, boy. How am I going to replace you? I'm going to get good and mad if you don't tell me you're just joshing me."

"I'm not, John. I just have to sort things out."

"Well, what did we do?"

"You didn't do anything. I can't stay in education. I don't believe in the process anymore. Somehow, I've lost my sense of perspective."

"Hell, fella, that's no reason to just up and quit. How many people do you know that have a future like yours? You know something? I've looked into your background. You had to struggle just like me. And you got a good head on your shoulders. Why, I was just talking to the vice-president the other day and he tells me you have the highest faculty and student ratings. He thinks you have a bright future and definite administrative potential. In a couple of years you could be head of that department, tenured and who knows what all."

"Yes, I know, John. It's just that..."

"We're expanding, you know. Right now we have a thousand students. In a year we'll double and keep doubling for the next five years. Of course, I know how you feel about this facility. But I can assure you that everything will not be built underground. I just finished talking to Mazzini and he's completed the plans for our orbital unit. Completely mobile. It'll move from one part of the campus to the other on a monorail. The whole cotton picking thing. Think of it, Frank. One day you'll be teaching over by the brook and the next day by that big horse meadow in back of my house. I haven't told a soul about this, outside of the vice-president. In a couple of years, as head of the department, you'd be calling your own shots. After that the field is wide open. In five years, a deanship. In ten years, you know what. Shoot, I'm ready to nominate you to the College Administration Hall of Fame for your work on the Faculty Senate. How would you like that?"

"It wouldn't matter," Garboil said. "I appreciate the gesture but it wouldn't make that much difference in my decision."

"Think of the future, Frank. There's going to be colleges springing up left and right. If you go somewhere else now, you'll have to start all over."

"I can't, John, I just don't want to teach anymore."

"Research?"

"No nothing. I just have to get away and think."

"Is it the little woman? I heard she got wind of your thing with Piscatelli."

"That's right, John, but that's not it. I just have to reevaluate my life."

John David Bacon suddenly jumped up from the sofa. The move frightened Garboil and he drew further into his corner.

"What in God's green earth are you talking about?" Bacon said, waving his arms. "You were just reappointed for two years. After that you're eligible for tenure. What more do you want? You teach three classes, three days a week, work eight months out of the year and earn more than twenty thousand a year. On top of that, you've published in every major journal." Bacon stopped for a moment and then pounded his fist into an open palm. "That's it, isn't it? The book. It's not going the way you wanted."

Garboil wanted to tell him that he didn't want the book at all, but finding an escape in Bacon's reasoning, agreed.

"Well, yes," he said. "That's really the issue. I need time to finish it."

"Hot diggity!" said Bacon, coming back to the couch and mussing Garboil's hair as if he were a child. "Why didn't you say so, fella. You done scared the daylights out of ole John. We'll just give you two classes for next year."

"No, John. I have to get away."

"You can't do that, Garboil. The trustees will roast me. You leave and the line becomes open. What in heaven's name do you think's gonna happen? Next thing you know I have fifty resumes on my desk from Puerto Rican Student Alliance, Black Reformation and every other Third World group on campus. You know what will happen, don't you? One less white and there goes our racial balance. There's no way I'm gonna win. They'll accuse me of racism. You're just creating unnecessary problems here at Frick, Frank."

"I'm really sorry, John, but I have to do it. I'll write an official letter of resignation."

"You'll do nothing of the kind. You just hold on and let me think one cotton-weeding minute. You just hold your horses right there."

John David Bacon sat with his head in his hands for several minutes. At the end of that period of time he rose from the sofa and began pacing the spacious office. His breathing became labored and then he opened his mouth and roared like a lion. Wheeling rapidly about, he placed the blocking sled in the middle of the room and ordered Garboil to stand on the runners to add extra weight. Garboil got up gingerly and did as he was told. His heart was pounding and his palms sweating again. Bacon got down on a three point stance and began pounding at the pads on the sled. Five, six, seven times he drove his shoulders forward, each time driving the sled further until Garboil thought he'd be pinned to the wall. The next minute Bacon was running around the room, grunting and puffing as if he were psyching himself up to go against Harvard in the big game. After several laps around the room he got down on all fours and began bleating like a sheep. By this time Garboil was totally unhinged and seriously considered giving up the entire thing. He had never seen anything like it in his life. With each minute that passed John David Bacon seemed to be growing larger and larger, filling the cavernous office with his person, everything shrinking as if in fear. What took place next made Garboil ill and would cause him nightmares. He had finally understood how an Ivy League education truly made a difference. Bacon had crawled into a corner of the room, turned his back on him and began singing: "We're poor little lambs who've lost our way, Baa! Baa! Baa!" The performance distressed Garboil, but he fought to remain detached, lest the mournful quality of the song sway him into sympathizing with Bacon. He waited until the song was over, convinced more than ever that his life was being run for him. When Bacon finished singing, he let out one last bleat, stood up and returned to the couch. He was drenched in sweat and smelled like rancid ham.

"It's done, Frank," he said.

"What's done?" Garboil said.

"You don't have a problem anymore. You won't resign. It's impossible."

"I've made up my mind," Garboil said, his voice shaking.

"We'll put you on leave of absence. Take a year off and then come back. We'll talk about it at that time."

"I don't know, John. I really wasn't thinking of coming back."

Bacon closed his eyes and took the deepest breath Garboil had ever seen anyone take. His chest expanded to gorilla size and when he let out his breath, Garboil felt his hair move.

"Now look here, Garboil," Bacon said. "Gosh darn. You sure are a hard man to please. I've done gone and revealed myself and broken vows I took as an undergraduate never to let any person other than a fellow alumnus see how we problem solve and you're gonna sit there and tell me you don't know. You're as stubborn as any damn cracker I ever ran into. Take the cotton-cutting leave. It'll serve your purposes and I won't have to give any explanations to the board. I already have enough trouble. If Biddleworth, New Haven down to his undershorts, knew I was in here wiffenpoofing my ass off while you were in the room, he'd not only have my job, but I'd be excommunicated and probably wouldn't be able to set foot in the state of Connecticut for the rest of my life."

"I'm sorry, John. I won't tell anyone."

"Well, not as sorry as I am, I can tell you that. Don't you know what's at stake here? In two years the board wants me to have a major football power. You don't think they hired me only because of my credentials and ability in administration. Hell no! Football, boy! That's the name of the game. Two years. Do you know what that means? I have to get ole Hummer Williams to stop thinking the Klan's gonna come outta the woods and lynch his black ass if he starts thinking of going national. It's a cotton-ginning obsession with the man. I mean, they don't really lynch people anymore. They may scare them a little, but they sure as hen's eggs ain't gone come trooping in here and lynch him. So be sensible and do ole John Bacon a favor. Take the leave of absence, carry the wife off somewhere on a vacation, get her alone and romance her, boy. As far as anyone here is concerned, you're on leave of absence and we don't know where to reach you. That fair enough?"

"Sure, John. I guess it's better than staying here, but I don't think I'm coming back and then you'll have to face the same problem next year."

"You let me worry about that. A year from now we'll have twice as many students. The community out here's starting to rumble about ethnic balance. They're gonna try and push their sons and daughters in here by the hundreds. There won't be as much pressure to hire along ethnic lines and I'll have a freer rein after we start recruiting for the football team. I contacted my old high school coach, Coy McCallister, and he's sending me a pair of twin tackles from the hills. Both of them six-six, two-hundred-seventy-five pounds. They don't even speak English yet. Just shotgun."

"That's great, John," Garboil said, knowing he'd have to endure Bacon until he was spent and no longer saw a threat to his plans.

"It sure is, fella. We'll play some of the small colleges and beat the hell out of them. Now, if I can get ole Hummer Williams to stop thinking that some scrawny little cracker's gonna come up on him in a white sheet, we'll be in good shape. That's the trouble. The cotton-weaving rednecks don't have an ounce of power left, but they're still scaring the daylights out of a man as big as Hummer. Did you know that he holds all the football, basketball, baseball and track records at Southern Mississippi A.T.E.&I.? The first time they handed him a javelin he threw it 437 feet. Sailed right out of the stadium and over to the agricultural compound. Speared the prize porker. That's how he got that nickname. Put anything in his hands and ask him to throw it and it hums."

"Yeah, I heard something like that," Garboil said.

"It's a fact, Frank."

"Well, listen, John," Garboil said getting up. "I want to hear more about all this, but I know how busy you are and I have a four o'clock class."

Bacon came forward and pounded Frank's back.

"Then it's settled," he said. "You'll take the leave of absence. Let's shake on it. If anyone comes snooping around we'll just tell them you're off finishing your book. Let's hope it's not somebody from the Board."

"Thanks a lot, John," Garboil said as he went out the door.

"I'll see you around, son," Bacon said. "You just keep peckering away and don't worry about a thing, heah?"

Frank Garboil was dazed, his mind absolutely numb. The man went on like that twenty-four hours a day, except when he paused to entertain himself with a female. Rumor had it that he slept only two hours a night and that he dictated memos into a tape recorder while fast asleep. Once again at his office, Garboil began emptying his desk. Mita Ritter-Rade had gone to lunch. For the moment he wouldn't have to explain that he wasn't coming back after the summer break. He opened his briefcase and placed his sons' pictures inside. He thought better of it and put the pictures back up on his desk. The end of the term was still three weeks away and the missing pictures would prompt too many questions. He closed the briefcase and decided not to teach his four o'clock class. Half of the students wouldn't be there. The A's and B's would be studying in the library or in their rooms, the C's and D's would show up, hoping that attendance would count and that finally they'd be able to grasp concepts which had eluded them totally during the semester. The F's would stay away all together. They had given up two or three weeks into the course. It didn't matter. The briefcase seemed to weigh fifty pounds and he felt physically drained from his meeting with John Bacon.

In the hall several students said hello. He returned their greetings with a sliver of guilt slithering around inside of him like a worm. They were some of his better students and, although he regretted leaving them, it was ultimately for their own good. He entered the elevator and rode to the surface. Outside, the sun was shining, the sky cloudless and the air smelled of spring. He loosened his tie, removed his jacket and took a deep breath of the clean air. The air hurt his lungs and he felt a little dizziness. He had done it. He had quit. He was free, he thought, and smiled openly at no one. The shuttle out to the train was waiting at the bottom of one of the grassy slopes. He ran down the new spring lawn and got on, feeling some of the tension leave his body. A couple of sullen students were sitting in the back. He nodded to them but they didn't respond.

On the train ride home he slept so soundly that when he arrived at Pennsylvania Station his body felt sore and as if he had just gone through the first football scrimmage of the season. He took the subway downtown and was home. Joey and Peter had already left for their Friday hockey practice, picked up by one of the All Star coaches.

"I have to talk to you, Joan," he said, dropping his briefcase on the living room floor. He opened the terrace door, stepped out and looked out over the park at the Washington Square arch. Joan followed him out and stood near him, sensing that something had changed, but not knowing what.

"What is it?" she asked.

"I quit my job, Joan," he said, without turning around.

The unexpectedness of the remark made her laugh nervously. Her guard was back up immediately.

"You did what?" she said.

"I quit," he answered. "I'm not going back next year or the year after. You see that thing out there?" he said, pointing to the arch. "Well, that's what it's about. That's what I've been after."

She took a deep breath and let it back out.

"What are you talking about, Frank?" she said. "You're scaring me."

"The arch, Joan. The George Washington, cherry-picking arch. All these years I've tried to be like you, an American. Years wasted aping you and your manners and ways, hoping because your family's been here since the turkey-eating Pilgrims you knew what it was all about and I'd pick it up. But it hasn't helped. I don't even know who I am!" He pounded the raw concrete of the balcony with his fist. "Sure, I'm an American. I was born here, raised here, speak the language, can name all the state capitals, have a pretty good education and so what! The more I look at it, the less I know about it."

Joan listened to her husband ranting and felt a cold hatred developing in her. She was tired of his moodiness. He had been so seemingly deep, but now he appeared to be simply confused and more neurotic than ever.

"Let me fix you a drink, Frank," she said. "It'll help you relax. My God," she added, trying to humor him, but immediately recognizing a dark and deep desire within her. "You look like you're ready to jump off the terrace." How dare he upset her plans for him. "I'm sure you'll change your mind once you've thought things out. In any case, I don't think anyone's going to take this idea too seriously."

"I've already told Bacon. It's settled."

"Really?" she said. "Well, it doesn't matter. You can always go back and say you've changed your mind. Please come inside and sit down."

He followed her in and watched her fine legs as she walked away from him and towards the bar. He waited until she had fixed the drink and turned to give it to him. He took one long pull from the scotch and soda, wiping his mouth with the back of his hand.

"You know, you're exactly correct," he said. "That's the problem. Nobody takes me seriously. Not the people out there. Not the students. Not you or anybody. I'm just good old Frankie Garboil, the nice guy. Well, I quit. I don't really care what you think, or what your family thinks. I don't even care what the President of the United States thinks. What do you think about that?" He paused for a moment. "But what am I talking about? I don't care what you think. I'm quitting the whole thing. I'm turning in my Boy Scout badges and my degree and loyalties and my piece of the pie in the sky. I've never been anything I wanted to be in my whole life, except for the hockey."

"Well, you did win the championship," she said. "And Joey and Peter's team won theirs. That should mean something."

"So I won the championship of a mickey mouse kid's league," he said, and took another long swallow from the scotch. "That's supposed to keep me going? Well, it doesn't. If anything, all it's done is left me wondering what else I could've done."

"There's next year. I'm sure if you did it this year, you can do it again."

He stood up, drained his glass and began pacing.

"I don't want to do it again," he said, setting the glass down on the bar.

She immediately began fixing him a new drink. "I don't want to coach little kids. I want to play."

He heard the glass hit the floor and shatter.

"I'm sorry," she said. "Just sit down and try to relax. I mean, you do that now. You play."

"Sure I do," he said, sarcastically. He came over and sat on one of the stools and watched her make the drink. "Once every couple of weeks against a bunch of burned out, wheezing fathers like myself. And even then I embarrass myself because I haven't had enough practice. I'm just going to do it," he said, taking the drink and heading back out to the terrace. "I'm going to do it. That's all."

"You're going to play hockey," she said, following him back out.

"Right. I'm going to find out what I should've found out when I was eighteen and left home. I don't know why I have to." And then his face grew softer and he faced her. He reminded her of Joey and she steeled herself against crying. "Maybe if I do it, I can forgive America and maybe I won't feel so mixed up about you. It's like I feel cheated, like my whole life, growing up and chasing after an idea, has made me lose myself. Do you understand that? I have to do it. If I don't, I'll go on hating myself and you and resenting the kids. I mean that's what America does to people. I don't think it's done intentionally. I mean, I don't think there's a secret bureau set up to assign people roles and then pressure them into doing things they don't want do do. I mean maybe there is."

She was angry now, certain that he'd been talking to that madman writer.

"Have you been talking to Vega again," she said.

"No, I haven't seen him in nearly two years. He quit too."

"Is that why you're quitting?"

"Hell no!"

"Then what's all this stuff about a secret bureau? Isn't that one of the themes of that idiotic novel he's supposed to be writing about some planet?"

Garboil thought a moment, taken aback suddenly by his wife's passion.

"Yeah, as a matter of fact it is," he said. "But that's fiction and what I'm talking about is real. I'm sure there's not a bureau like that. It's more of a thing that happens because of the way things are set up. You know, the rewards, the incentives offered to them if they go into certain fields. And then they start thinking they can acquire possessions and positions and forget their true desires. Before they know it they've been programmed to act exactly as they want."

"All I've ever wanted was for you to be happy," she said.

"Happy at what?" he shouted at the top of his lungs, not directly at her but out over the terrace. "Jesus, Mary and Jospeh," he said, as he turned back to face her. "You talk about happiness as if it were something you bought. How can anyone be happy with doubts hammering away at him day and night. Could I have done it or not? Maybe I had it. Maybe I really had it and didn't believe it. Do you know what that's like? Well, I'm going to find out. I'm going to be totally ruthless and find out."

"I'm afraid that all that you will accomplish," she said, coldly, "is to give yourself a heart attack before you're thirty-five."

He looked at her and knew there was no way he'd make her understand.

"Don't try to scare me, Joan," he said. "I'd rather be dead than go on living like this. I don't know what I'm going to do. I haven't thought it all out."

"You must have some idea."

"Sure," he said, suddenly. "I'm going to enroll in a college and play hockey."

He said it and the words hung in the air, not drifting out over Washington Square Park, but hanging there like some specter of death in hockey skates and holding a stick instead of a scythe. He watched his wife finally give in, the mask of fright clouding her face. She ran back into the apartment, the hysteria beginning to enter her system, not fearful anymore, but convinced that her husband in a very small but real way had lost touch with reality.

He did not follow her inside. Instead, he sat down against the wall of the terrace and stared at the small clouds drifting slowly in the high, blue sky. He sat there until the sun began going down and the air turned colder. When he finally came back inside, Joan was cooking supper. She greeted him as if nothing had happened between them, convinced that it was over between them. Their life continued without incident for several weeks. By the middle of May, however, preparations were being made for her departure. The breakup was never discussed again and they agreed that the boys would go with her to California after she received her doctoral degree at the end of the month. The lawyers would take care of everything else and the boys could come back and visit him from time to time.

CHAPTER 17

From which we may draw certain inferences regarding Sigmund Freud's interpretation of the four-fold positive and negative division of the Oedipus complex, meet a mammary junkie, learn the true identity of the Bronx Werewolf, and observe how Dr. Kopfeinlaufen hopes to probe deeper into the protagonist's psyche in order to establish the identity of his alter ego.

F. William Kolodny, Private Investigator, was a troubled soul. He had been so for as long as he could remember. Guilt tore at his insides constantly as he fought a never-ending battle with his urges to squeeze women's breasts in public. He had seen a number of doctors, but none had been able to help him. Had he identified too strongly with his mother as an object cathexis, rejecting the father in a negative manifestation of the Oedipus complex, or had he identified with his father and retained an affectionate relationship with his mother? Or was it the other way around? Did F. William Kolodny have an eight-fold Oedipus complex? Were there two sets of parents involved?

Five years before, he had found a remedy, which by no means cured him of his strange affliction, but which at least sated his desires. In his years as a New York City policeman, Kolodny had come to know several prostitutes rather well. Many of them, now past their prime, contented themselves with two and five dollar tricks or had reluctantly opted for marriage and had settled down to the boring and thankless task of raising children and faking orgasms.

F. William Kolodny began contacting his old acquaintances and soon had several dozen who called him periodically to inform him where they would be on specific days.

"Kolodny here," he'd say, answering the phone in his office.

"Yeah, listen, Kolodny," the voice would say. "This is Dolores. I'm gonna be at Macy's about four on Tuesday. Housewares. And no funny business. I'm gonna have my fourteen-year-old daughter with me. Don't let your hands wander. This ain't no family deal."

"Okay, Dolores. Tuesday, four o'clock at Macy's housewares. No bra, right?"

"Right, no bra. And don't be late with the money. It don't collect no interest while you got it."

"Don't worry. You know I pay on time."

"By the way. I have a friend. She was never a pro, but her old man left her and she's in a bad way. They're giving her a hard time down at Welfare."

"How big is she?"

"Oh, don't worry about that. Thirty-eight, maybe forty with a C cup. But you gotta go easy on her, Kolodny. She might not even show up the first few times. I'll try to bring her on Tuesday so she can get used to you. Maybe we can work out some kind of group rate or something."

"Yeah, sure, Dolores."

Most of Kolodny's money these days went for his fixes and even though he had worked out five, ten and twenty-five dollar encounters with the women, there were weeks when he spent well over two hundred dollars on his habit. But when he thought of the release the encounters provided, he was more than grateful that he had found a solution to his problem. There was no greater thrill than following Tina Franklin, with her sprawling bosom, chocolate colored and as soft as ten dollars worth of mushed together Hershey bars, and eventually cornering her in a crowded Seventh-Avenue express as it rumbled through the middle of Manhattan. There was one place, coming out of the Chambers Street station going towards Brooklyn, when the train went around a sharp curve and the lights went out. Sometimes the lights were out for a full thirty seconds. That was the deal. Lights out, both hands. Ten dollars.

Although the fear of arrest had been removed, there remained still the insufferable guilt. He'd tried to rationalize the feeling by telling himself that his urges were normal, but he always came to the same point. If he were a man, he could control himself. Richard Nixon didn't have those urges. Not even towards his wife. And what about J. Edgar Hoover? Impossible. Now, there was a man! They were law abiding people. Great leaders. What about the mayor? Moviestar looks and high-class friends. He probably did it and got away with it.

To truly understand F. William Kolodny's life-long dilemma, we would need to know his entire story. In lieu of that, suffice it to say that he had an extremely competitive mother. Driven, aggressive, given to sudden departures from reality, she was, in addition, meagerly endowed in pectoral anatomy. She detested men and, upon the birth of her son, insisted that he be named Francine.

"It's a perfectly neutral name," she said, lying in her hospital bed, speaking with her husband. "It sounds French, doesn't it. It's no worse than Jean or Ives."

"His name's gonna be William like his grandfather," said Albert Kolodny, threatening to ground his cigar into his wife's face.

"But Francine has such a beautiful sound, Albert," she whimpered.

"William," insisted her husband.

"We could call him Fran, couldn't we?"

"Sure, call him Francis William Kolodny," he said, willing to strike a compromise.

"Francine," she said.

Albert Kolodny raised his umbrella.

"How'd ya like me to shove this up your nose?" he said.

"Well, you don't have to be so nasty about things," said Barbara Kolodny. "It'd be a terrible thing if your attitude and bad manners drove me to destruction and one day your son got his privates caught in the washing machine wringer."

Albert Kolodny was astounded by the threat. Shaking, he grabbed the umbrella in both hands and raised in a horizontal position aimed at his wife's face.

"Well?" she said, as he advanced on her. "It could happen, couldn't it?"

"All right, all right," he said, lowering the umbrella. "Name him whatever you want, but I won't be responsible when he turns into a fairy."

Poor F. William, as his father called him, grew up in a totally alienating environment. His father never forgave his mother. She, on the other hand, grew in power with each passing year. Needless to say that Albert Kolodny never went near his wife again, satisfying his sexual needs with a number of widows who frequented his butcher shop. But for the boy, the worst part of growing up was that he was forced to respond to his mother calling him Francine. If he did not, she would tie him up, make him wear dresses and would serve him cream of wheat, his favorite cereal, with laxatives in it. On his fourteenth birthday, however, F. William declared his independence.

"Francine, please cut the cake," his mother said, after he'd blown out the candles.

"I ain't gonna," said F. William, pimply-faced and petulant but almost grown to his eventual five feet, ten inches.

"Albert, tell him to cut the cake," said his mother.

His father relit his cigar and poked at his leftover meatloaf with the burnt out matchstick.

"Leave me outta this," he said.

Obtaining no support from her husband and not wishing to spoil the celebration, his mother tried appealing to her son's sense of filial devotion, which by this time had dwindled to practically nothing.

"Now, Francine, dear," said Barbara Kolodny. "I went to a lot of trouble to make this cake."

F. William stood up, folded his arms across his chest and looked directly at his mother for the first time in his life.

"I ain't gonna cut the cake," he said, shoving the lazy Susan on which the cake sat back to her side of the table. "I ain't gonna do it and if you call me Francine again, I'm gonna fucking punch you in the mouth."

Upon hearing his son express himself in such manly terms, Albert Kolodny let out his first laugh in fourteen years. He smashed his fist on the table, causing the cake to flip off the lazy Susan, make a tight arch over the edge of the table and land on his wife's lap. Attempting to salvage the cake Barbara Kolodny tumbled backwards out of her chair and knocked herself on the head.

"That'll show you," said Albert, in great spirits. "You can call him whatever you want, but he's still got balls."

"Well, I never," said his wife, wiping frosting from her face. "Of all the ungrateful things the two of you have done to me, this takes..." she added and stopped short of completing the sentence which she knew would give her husband further pleasure. "You bastards," she said, instead. "I know when I'm not wanted."

She got up from the floor and left the room. The next day Barbara Kolodny packed her clothes and left her husband and son never to be seen again. Albert Kolodny immediately divorced her and remarried, a very ugly, but very buxomy and agreeable young woman, the daughter of a bagel manufacturer. He later heard that his ex-wife had joined the Army, a fact which he never revealed to F. William, fearing that mention of his mother might rekindle any warmth he may have had for her.

And yet F. William Kolodny, in spite of his psychological peculiarities, was not a totally incapacitated human being. Upon graduation from high school, he joined the Marine Corps, became a reconnnaissance patrol expert, learned to speak pidgin Japanese and was instrumental in ferreting the enemy out of their bunkers at Iwo Jima. He almost made the now famous picture of the Marines raising the American flag, but just before the picture was snapped he'd gone behind a tree to relieve himself. After his discharge from the Marines he returned to New York, joined the police force and ascended to the rank of detective sergeant before his twenty years were up and he retired. Since that time he had established a private practice specializing in unusual cases, working closely with the Police Department and, in so doing, earning several civic awards. He owned half interest in a motel outside of Aurora, Kansas, a hunting cabin in the Adirondacks, a twenty-foot inboard motorboat and four champion-stock Chihuahuas. He drank moderately, did not smoke and, outside of needing to fondle women's breasts in public, led a clean, law-abiding life.

Now, as he splashed through the Monday morning gray slush familiar to New Yorkers the day after a snowfall, F. William was overjoyed. Here was a case that had promise, class. Usually the people he tracked down were confused nuts with no name, people on the edge of living, giving themselves one last try at notoriety in the big city. But this guy Martinez or Garboil, whoever he was, had to be a beaut. Maybe he was really a professor. He had to find out and, at one hundred dollars a day, it was going to be a pleasure.

By the time he arrived at Dr. Kopfeinlaufen's office, Kolodny had almost forgotten that he was to meet Rufina Malparao on top of the Empire State Building at three that afternoon. The weekly staff meeting was the place where the staff involved in the Martinez-Garboil case met to review the events of the previous week, make plans and devise a strategy for the next six days. The meeting was held in Kopfeinlaufen's office and usually lasted two hours, at which time the staff went to the cafeteria and continued its work informally.

Dr. Kopfeinlaufen's office was a large, carpeted room with a desk and chair, several file cabinets, a couch, some stuffed chairs and a water cooler. On the soft-yellow walls there were several enlarged photographs of the Bavarian Alps and the doctor's diplomas and medical awards. Ingrid Konkruka, sparkling in her white uniform, her yellow hair neatly combed and tucked away under her cap, was already seated when Dr. Kohonduro and Helen Christianpath entered the room. Helen, as usual, was dressed in a suit of late-forties vintage. She wore her hair pulled severely back in a bun.

"Good morning, Miss Konkruka," she said, icily, as was her manner toward Ingrid. She adjusted her glasses and skirt and sat down. "Congratulations on your excellent breakthrough with Armando."

Ingrid noted the jealousy in her voice; it was to be expected. She had intruded into Helen's area of responsibility and her pride had been injured. In spite of Helen's profession of love for humanity, she was given to subdued, controlled fits of passionate anger towards women whom she thought seductive. Ingrid thanked her.

"I don't think I could've done it without your preliminary work," she said.

"Yes, thank you," replied Helen, coldly. "We must do anything we can if we're to help this unfortunate young man."

"Truly remarkable work, Miss Konkruka. Really top rate," said Rapudiman Kohonduro, joining the conversation. "Dr. Kopfeinlaufen said you'd be instrumental in the patient's recovery, but I had no idea you could reach him so deeply."

Ingrid thanked him. Kohonduro was about to ask her about the method she had employed when Kopfeinlaufen walked in with a plumpish, florid-faced man dressed in a business suit. He carried a brief case and an overcoat and was about fifty years of age. He sat down in one of the chairs arranged in a small half-circle in front of Kopfeinlaufen's desk and placed the briefcase next to his chair. Kopfeinlaufen took the man's coat, hung it in the closet, returned to the circle and took his seat behind the desk.

"It is nine o'clock," he said, looking at his pocket watch. "Let me first introduce the gentleman I have brought with me this morning. He will be working with us from now on. This is Mr. F. William Kolodny. He is a private investigator."

Kolodny nodded and shook hands with the other members of the staff before Kopfeinlaufen went on speaking.

"You have all heard the tapes and I have explained to Mr. Kolodny the pertinent details of the case. There is one area in particular which I would like him to investigate. In order to finally confront Mr. Martinez with the reality of his psychic dilemma, we must get all the facts that contradict his fantasy. I want Mr. Kolodny to go to Frick University and do a thorough investigation to determine whether this man, Garboil, exists. It is quite possible Mr. Martinez could have seen his name or heard of the man. Please assist him in any way possible. Are there any questions you would like to ask Mr. Kolodny?"

Helen Christianpath was the first to speak.

"Mr. Kolodny, we are so glad you're going to assist us. I know that whatever you do will be appreciated by all of us. Does this seem like a difficult case to you?"

"No, lady, I've had stranger ones," Kolodny said, trying to evaluate Helen. "This guy sounds nutty as hell, but it was nothing like the case of the Bronx werewolf. He useta walk around in the subway tunnels and scare the hell outta the workmen. You'll never believe it, but it wasn't a werewolf at all. It wasn't even a guy. It was this old broad, a retired WAC sergeant. When she was in the service, she began getting a beard and made the mistake of shaving it. The more she shaved, the more it grew. She started getting hormone shots, but the medical people got mixed up and they gave her male hormones. Before they could figure out what was going on, she started getting hair all over her body. She flipped out and they had to give her a medical discharge. She went back for treatment at the VA hospital, but they couldn't help her. Her thing became mental. You know, whachamacallit."

"Psychosomatic," said Kohonduro.

"Yeah, like that," said Kolodny. "Pretty soon you couldn't even see her fingernails. One night she couldn't take living around people anymore and walked into the IND subway up near where the Polo Grounds useta be and began living underground. Once in a while she'd come up to scrounge around for food in garbage cans or sneak into the Bronx Terminal Market to steal chickens. She ate them raw. The doctors said her reaction had to do with not wanting to be a woman. That she could've built a fire down in the tunnels, found herself an old pot and made a nice chicken soup, maybe with a few matzoh balls and a little celery. But she was so bad off that just thinking about a kitchen made her worse. That's why she ate raw chicken. The regular cops knew about the werewolf, but wouldn't go after her. The Transit Authority hired me to flush her out. It was pretty bad. Smelled like rotten garbage. When I finally roped her and dragged her out into the light, she put her hands over her eyes. I thought it was the sunlight, but it wasn't. She kept saying: 'Oh, no. My own flesh and blood. My God, my own flesh and blood,' and tearing at the hair on her face. Crazy as a bedbug, if you'll pardon the expression. The doctors said she was, whatta you call it, paranoid. That she probably thought she was a rat and that the other rats down in the tunnels — some of them get as big as fox terriers — turned her in. So that was a weird case. But I've had weirder ones. This city's full of nuts. I specialize in them."

"That's good to hear," said Helen, "but we don't refer to our patients as nuts."

"Look, lady," said Kolodny. "You call 'em whatever you want. I don't know none of them fancy terms like pizzaphrenic or nothing like that. If a guy's doing crazy things, he's a nut. That's all I can tell you."

He surveyed Helen's bony structure with contempt and in his mind assigned her seventy-five-cents worth. Kopfeinlaufen stepped in as Helen was about to reply.

"Mr. Kolodny has one small request. I think you ought to hear him out."

"Well, I never seen this guy, so I don't know how to describe him. If I'm gonna go around and ask questions about him, I gotta see him. I have to get some pictures."

"Oh, Doctor, that would be terrible," said Helen. "It would traumatize the patient and possibly cause a serious relapse to have total strangers coming in to photograph him. It's such a critical period in his recovery."

"You're right, Miss Christianpath," Kopfeinlaufen said. "With the upcoming television program, it might prove too much for him. We will have to prepare him for that. But Mr. Kolodny has come prepared. Please show us the instrument. Mr. Kolodny."

Kolodny bent down, opened his briefcase and from it produced a stethoscope. He placed the instrument around his neck, inserted the end pieces into his ears and aimed the listening part at Ingrid's chest. He let the stethoscope down, looked at his watch and at the end of a minute removed the instrument from his ears. From the left ear piece he extracted a tiny protograph of Ingrid Konkruka's face and bust. The picture was the size of a postage stamp but quite clear. He handed it to Ingrid, who smiled and passed it around.

"Simply amazing," said Kohonduro. "May I keep it? Simply, simply amazing."

"Yes, isn't it, Doctor?" said Helen, sarcastically.

Fifty-cent broad, thought Kolodny, looking at Helen Christianpath.

"Miss Konkruka," said Kopfeinlaufen. "At twelve o'clock you will take Mr. Kolodny and find him a doctor's gown. Take him to Mr. Martinez' room and introduce him as Dr. Kramer from the cardiac section. Dr. Kramer wants to listen to the heart to determine whether the layoff from hockey has affected him in any way."

The rest of the meeting went on. Dr. Kopfeinlaufen explained his theory about the significance of the tapes. If all went well, they would tell Armando Martinez about the upcoming television program and begin preparing him for it.

"Do we wear hockey equipment?" asked Kohonduro.

"Absolutely, Doctor," Kopfeinlaufen replied. "It is imperative that we do not deviate from the process we're employing. The patient may not want to return to hockey, but he must be confronted with his psychic dilemma at all times. It is the only way we can produce a total breakthrough. When he finally sees he has been deluding himself, he will need something secure to fall back on. As you can see, even in his fantasy, this other person he has created, Frank Garboil, is involved in hockey. The game is the point of convergence of both personalities. We must do everything we can to destroy the fantasy while at the same time retain the integrity of the real person."

There was some further discussion of the subject, but nothing more of importance emerged. At noon Ingrid Konkruka brought Kolodny to Frank Garboil's room. Kolodny went about his business professionally. He nodded at the patient after he was introduced, coughed knowingly from time to time and was finished photographing Garboil inside of ten minutes.

CHAPTER 18

In which we see the protagonist make a fresh start by moving into a tenement, begin training in order to put his plan into operation, visit an old neighborhood acquaintance, enlist his assistance, obtain the necessary documents from a purveyor of stolen correspondence as a means to reentering college and begin to see the possible value of being Puerto Rican even as a fantasy.

Two weeks after his wife and sons left for California and he'd placed most of the family's furniture in storage, Frank Garboil moved into a small apartment on the Upper West Side of Manhattan. The move was made hurriedly, the motivation for taking the flat, its low rent. Once settled into his new living quarters he began resenting the three rooms. A railroad apartment, that is, with rooms one after the other, it had no windows, except in the kitchen. One window faced the brick wall of the adjacent building, the other, a garbage strewn backyard. The fire escape was outside the first window and led down into a bricked up alleyway. Day and night there was a constant din, the voices of the people distantly familiar.

One evening as he sat back in the reclining leather chair, one of the few items he'd kept from the old apartment, Garboil decided that he was now truly ready to begin working towards his objective. Reviewing his bank book he noted that after completing the move there was now four thousand dollars left from the original six thousand he'd kept. Joan had taken the rest of the savings, plus the stocks which her father had given her and which were rightfully hers. He decided that the four thousand couldn't last more than six months, but that would be enough time to fulfill his dream.

He got up from the chair and looked out into the backyard. Several dark, wiry boys were having a rock fight. He turned away, fearful that he'd witness the bloody consequence of the game. In a corner of the room his skates, gloves and hockey stick reminded him of the pick-up game that night. He looked at his watch. It was eight o'clock and Friday-evening Latin music had begun playing next door. He tried catching some of the phrases but the language was too fast. Maybe he should go to the rink and get in some light skating at the general skating session. It would give him a chance to warm up and, in any case, the more he skated the better his chances in the fall. The question still remained, however. How was he to enroll in college?

He had to contact Bones, but so far he'd had no success. He'd called all the Friedenberg's in Manhattan, the Bronx and Brooklyn. It was no reason to quit, he told himself. He picked up the phone and dialed Queens information. When the operator went through the usual questions: was it F as in Fred, and was it a residence or a business, did he have a first name or an address for the party. Yes, F as in Fred, and yes it was a residence, but he was sorry he did not have a first name or an address.

"Well, sir, I do have several Friedenbergs in the directory, but I can only give you three of them a time."

"That's fine."

"Well, I have a Charles Friedenberg, Sam Friedenberg and a Sandra Friedenberg. Which do you want? I also have a Seymour, Sydney, Sylvia and..."

"Just give me the first three, operator."

He copied the numbers and dialed the first one. He had no luck with that one, nor with the next. He waited until the phone had been replaced on the other end and slammed down his own in disgust. He dialed the next number without the least hope that it would produce different results. The phone rang several times and then an old woman answered the phone.

Garboil hesitated and then asked if Mr. Friedenberg was in.

"That's a good question," the old woman said. "If they've caught up with him, he's in, if they haven't he's out. Miami, Las Vegas, Monte Carlo, Churchill Downs and you'd think he'd call his mother. All I get is postcards telling me he's doing fine. David, I tell him, settle down. Find a nice girl, a doctor, a lawyer, a teacher or a social worker. Does he listen? He rattles those things in his pocket and says, 'Aw, ma, lay off, huh? I gotta go where the action is. I ain't getting married even if it's Barbara Streisand.' So what can I tell you about Mr. Smartpants? And who are you, may I ask, to be inquiring about where my David is? Are you one of his bum friends from the racetrack, or are you a cop from the district attorney's office? My David is a good boy. He never hurt anyone, my David."

"Mrs. Friedenberg, this is Frankie Garboil from the old neighborhood in the Bronx."

"Garboil? Are you a Jewish boy?"

"No, m'am, I'm sorry. I haven't seen David in a while. I'm in town and wanted to say hello. Maybe if he calls you could give him a message from me."

"Garboil? What was your mother's name? Did she shop at Morris Greenberg's butcher shop?"

"No, she didn't," he said, recalling the days back in the old neighborhood. "I lived with my aunts."

"Oh, wait a minute," Mrs. Friedenberg said. "You're the gypsy kid, ain't you?"

"That's right," he said.

"So you're a big college professor, I hear?"

"How did you find out?"

"*Meshuge* my David may be, but he keeps informed."

And then her voice dropped down to a whisper.

"Listen," she said. "We can't talk on this phone, it's bugged. Come by the house."

"What's the address?" he said, also in a whisper.

"It's in the phone book under Sandra."

"All right, Mrs. Friedenberg. Thanks."

"Don't mention it."

He hung up the phone and smiled to himself. Things were going to be okay. He felt it. Getting hold of Bones' mother was a lucky break. If anyone knew how to figure out this whole angle Bones Friedenberg was the one. He'd give him its chances of success in a minute. It was now eight-thirty. Too late to set out for Queens at that hour. He placed his gloves and skates into a bag, got his stick from the corner of the room and after locking the window gate, let himself out of the apartment and locked the door. On the subway downtown his mind was strictly on hockey.

The ice skating rink was in midtown Manhattan, some twenty blocks from the places where he had often played roller hockey. When he arrived there were a number of people lacing up their skates, the recorded organ music playing and the lights dimmed for the general skating session. He left his bag and stick with one of the older boys who knew him from the hockey league and who was now playing hockey for a college upstate, home for the summer and working in the skate shop. After answering questions about Joey and Peter, all of them reassuring as to their health and the fact that they'd be attending hockey camp in a couple of weeks, Garboil stepped out on the ice. He stretched his legs as he skated, feeling the smoothness and ease of his motions as he glided effortlessly around the turns, crossing his feet one over the other. For the past year he'd felt everything returning to him. In the games against the other fathers he'd experienced a tightness and inhibition, a fear that a fall would injure him and possibly lay him up for a while. Slowly the fear had ebbed away and now it seemed to have disappeared totally. As he turned the corner at the far end of the rink he took several running steps before breaking into long powerful strides. His speed was picking up with each time he skated. At the near end of the rink he braked, sending a spray of chips up into the glass above the dasher boards.

At a quarter to eleven the Zamboni machine which resurfaces the ice came on and Garboil came off, retrieved his gloves and stick and sat down to wait. He craved a cigarette but had made the resolution to stop smoking. Each day that went by he felt his lungs growing stronger. All around him older teenagers and men sat on benches or stood against the boards, dressed in their hockey outfits. Only a few, like himself, were dressed only in skates and gloves. He knew what drove all of them, but was certain none of them knew it better than he did. They were an odd mixture of ethnic variety. Most of them were from the old Hell's Kitchen and Chelsea areas. None of the faces were familiar. They were Irish, Italian, Puerto Rican and black. The neighborhood was mixed now. It never mattered in athletics. He was aware that there was racial prejudice in sports and that hockey had more than its share of it, but it was ultimately how one performed that counted. At a certain speed and tempo, boys as well as men transcended color and background and were celestial bodies caught in each other's orbit, instinctively aware of their relationship to the other bodies in space. He was positive that if a light were to be mounted on each player's helmet during a game and a movie camera turned on, it would record an intricate but logical pattern of intertwining ellipses.

At about eleven fifteen everyone went out on the ice. He stretched his legs once more, raised his stick above his head and stretched his arms and back muscles. He did this several times as he went slowly around the rink, helped place the nets in position and did some fast skating. There were several young men who were faster, but most of the men his own age could not keep up with him. There were now some thirty players on the ice. Sides were chosen and the game began. There were no periods in these games and the score was rarely kept accurately. More than an actual game the activity was a test of manhood and skill — manhood to see how daring one could be on skates. There was no hitting involved. He went out on the ice for the second shift and took up his position at left wing. The puck came to him off the faceoff and he skated it in over the blue line, handling the puck smoothly. He wished he could shoot a slapshot like Pete, but he hadn't yet mastered the technique. It would come in time as his timing improved. A defenseman was coming at him now, attempting to play him to the outside. He drew back his stick as if he were about to shoot, watched the defenseman stiffen, faked outside and went inside of him. In the slot area in front of the net he wristed a shot which beat the goalie and thudded loudly against the goalpost. The puck rebounded out and one of his linemates shoved it under the sliding goalie. The sticks went up and as he skated back up ice he felt the other players tapping lightly at his legs with their sticks. "Nice play," said a heavy-set man about forty years of age. "You young guys got it all over us." He thought of replying that he was no spring chicken himself but thought better of it. The more everyone thought he was younger than his thirty three-years the more his confidence would grow and the easier it would be to carry out the plan. His hair was beginning to grow and soon he would start a moustache, which, contrary to his own generation, appeared to make men look younger.

The next two hours went by quickly. He managed two goals out of the two dozen or so that his team scored but he'd set up numerous opportunities with his speed and passing. As he unlaced his skates he felt little aches and pains in his body. Next week he would begin running in the park to supplement his training. He took a deep breath and felt the dry feeling in his throat and remembered that he had shunned the water bottle during the game. In his days in college drinking water had been forbidden. Now players drank freely during the game and it was even encouraged. More than his thirst he felt quite hungry. He wouldn't eat much until morning, perhaps a grapefruit and some honey when he got home. He wondered if his weight was yet under 190 pounds. As he wiped his skates some of the players came by and congratulated him. He smiled openly at them, returning the praise, exhausted now and feeling the weariness invading his body.

When he arrived at his apartment, he shed his clothes, got under the shower and remained there for the next twenty minutes, feeling the hot water relax his muscles. He then turned on the cold water and shivered under it for more than a minute. His teeth chattering, he emerged from the shower and toweled himself vigorously. He admired his body in the full-length mirror he'd brought from the old apartment. He still had a bit of a pot and there was some fat around his hips but overall he liked what he saw. When he finished drying himself he put on a pair of shorts, brushed his hair back from his forehead and shaved every part of his face but the upper lip. Back in his kitchen he sliced a grapefruit in half, cored it and devoured the halves hungrily, chasing his "supper" with two teaspoons of honey from the health food store down the street. He added an assortment of vitamins which Angela Piscatelli had prescibed for him the previous year and which he had shunned but had begun taking religiously, hoping even if they did not affect his health at least their placebo effect would cause a positive psychological reaction. His meal complete, he brushed his teeth, turned off the lights and was asleep within five minutes.

He slept for the next ten hours straight, waking up around noon. As he shaved he listened to the news on the radio. His body felt sore, but nothing like those times when he'd played in games with the other hockey fathers. It had to be his improved physical condition and the sleep. After those games he had arrived home about two in the morning and had never been able to unwind until two or sometimes three hours later, and then only after drinking several beers. His sleep was invariably interrupted by fears that he wouldn't be able to wake up and make the train to school. By the time the alarm went off he was usually falling asleep and Joan had to shake him.

After he was finished shaving, he set about doing his exercises for the next hour. One hundred sit ups, one hundred pushups and two hundred hops on each leg. The strenuous exercise completed, he showered and sat down to a meal of wheat germ, fruit and yogurt, along with another dosage of vitamins chased with papaya juice. He read for the next two hours, alternating between *Play the Man* by Brad Park, a defenseman for the New York Rangers, the local professional hockey team, and the poetry of Federico Garcia Lorca in *Poet in New York*.

Two things gnawed at his mind as he read. One was that, although he'd done well the previous night, he still felt as if he weren't working as hard as he could, that he was holding back, watching himself, still concentrating on his skating rather than on the game. The other was the ever-increasing fear that what he was about to do had an unethical quality to it.

The first matter he resolved that same day by purchasing a full suit of equipment. The entire purchase came to more than one hundred and fifty dollars, but the investment was necessary if he was to prove himself before embarking fully on his project. The other matter was somewhat more difficult and the dilemma continued to plague him. And yet, as he walked out of the sporting goods store, he felt a sense of relief. With full protection he would now be able to risk more and consequently the idea of injury completely left his mind. In the process, however, he felt pangs of regret at not having been more considerate of Joey's feelings when he'd complain about not wanting to fall when he played. He'd thought it a fear of injury, but it hadn't been that. With him it was a matter of victory over his circumstances and was part of that special intensity developed or inherited by what he considered great athletes. As he rode the subway back uptown he was convinced that he would succeed.

That evening, after dressing in one of the two suits which he'd brought along from the old apartment, he visited Bones Friedenberg's mother out in Queens. She did not recognize him and insisted on questioning him extensively about the old neighborhood. Convinced of his authenticity, she gave him the address of a bar not far from her house and explained what he must do. Reliving those painful years of his life, he walked the dozen or so blocks to the bar. The place was an Irish tavern in a quiet neighborhood where a rather sedate, seemingly sober crowd was watching a Mets game.

When the bartender came over to him he asked for Bones.

"Nobody named Bones here, pal," the bartender said. "What'll it be?"

"Beer," Garboil said, a little dejectedly.

"What kind?"

"Any draft."

The bartender drew his beer and placed it in front of him on a coaster. Garboil put a five dollar bill on the bar and took a long pull from the beer mug and waited as he'd been instructed by Sandra Friedenberg. About five minutes later, halfway through his second beer, two well-dressed young men, both of whom could've been easily mistaken for businessmen, came over and sat on either side of him at the bar.

"Your name Garboil?" said the one on his left without looking at him.

"That's right," he answered.

"There's a black Caddy parked about a block down the street...we'll be waiting. Wait a few minutes after we leave and follow us. Just open the front door and get in."

He started to ask them if Bones Friedenberg was in the car, but the two men got up and left. He surveyed the bar, sweeping the length of the room, but no one had noticed the brief exchange. He was sure everyone had been aware of his presence and why he was there. Turning his attention to the game, he saw one of the Mets — he did not recognize his name — hit a long drive to dead centerfield. The outfielder on the opposing team went back as far as he could, jumped up and caught the ball just before it cleared the fence. The crowd in the bar let out a groan, echoed by the announcer and the crowd at the stadium. He wondered how anyone could become so involved in a baseball game. There was an inherent dullness to the game, as if it belonged back when people were not as concerned with their lives and the significance of their actions. Hockey was different. One had to know everything all at once and react instinctively. Pure motion and rhythm, everything constantly moving like life itself. He shook his head disapprovingly, left some change on the bar and walked out.

Outside there was a fresh breeze in the air, a welcome relief from the earlier heat of the day. Halfway down the block he spotted the Cadillac. He walked on, aware of the stillness of the neighborhood, the evenly spaced houses, lawns, driveways and hedges, and wondered, in a moment of panic, if anyone had ever walked to this particular car for their last time. He opened the front door of the vehicle, recognized the man who had spoken to him in the bar and got in. Once inside he asked again when he was going to see Friedenberg.

"Relax, pal," said the other man from the backseat. "You're gonna see the man. I hear you're from his old neighborhood in the Bronx."

"That's right," Garboil said, taken aback by the coldness in the man's voice. It was as if somehow he had been able to switch off all emotion and only a set of responses organized into words had replaced feeling. "We know each other a long time," he added, aping the street jargon he'd lost so long ago.

"Well, that's good cauze he wouldna seen you if it wasn't for that. Let's go, Petey."

The car started up, purring smoothly and then moving out powerfully as they hit the Grand Central Parkway. Going past Shea Stadium, Garboil wondered who was winning. His concern with the baseball game was the only indication of his anxiety about seeing Bones Freidenberg again. They drove on for nearly twenty minutes before exiting near Westbury on the Long Island Expressway. In a few moments they had entered a gate and were traveling slowly on a private road with large trees on either side of it. The road wound around bends several times and after a mile or so the car stopped.

Garboil got out and the two men escorted him to the front door of the columned mansion. The driver rang the doorbell and another man, dressed also in a business suit, greeted them. Like the men in the car, he too was reserved and showed little more interest than that of someone doing a boring job.

"How you doing, Carl?" said the one called Petey. "Tell the man we brought the professor."

"That's okay, Petey," Carl replied laconically. "I'll bring him up."

"Right," Petey said. "We'll see you around."

"This way, professor," Carl said, after closing the door.

Garboil followed the man accross the huge, carpeted living room, his eyes amazed by the opulence. It was difficult for him to absorb it all at once, but he was particularly struck by the size of the chandelier suspended thirty feet above the floor. He looked up the semi-circular staircase and the paintings hanging along the wall of the upstairs hall. They were large oils, mostly portraits of 17th century royalty. He followed the man named Carl up the stairs. Bones Friedenberg emerged from one of the rooms. He was a tall, elegant man, older-looking and more distinguished than his forty years and nothing like Garboil remembered him. When Friedenberg saw Garboil, his face broke into a crooked smile of pleasure and his eyes softened at the sight of one of his childhood memories grown up. He nodded approvingly as Garboil ascended the stairs and finally came forward to him.

"How do you like that?" Friedenberg said, sticking out his hand. "How's the kid?"

"How you doing, Bones?" Garboil said.

"Pretty good, kid, from what you can see," Friedenberg said, clapping Garboil on the back and then putting an arm around him. "You see that, Carl," he said, turning to the young man and then back to Garboil. "Carl here doesn't think it's a good idea for people to call me Bones. Bad for the image, he says. Even wanted me to change my name. He says it gives our people a bad name to have nice Jewish boys like us mixed up in the business." He squeezed Garboil to him. "Whatta you think of that, kid?.

Carl here graduated from law school, nice wasp background, passed the bar and two years later got busted and disbarred for withholding information on a bribery case. He's lucky he's not in the joint and he still wants to go around misrepresenting the facts. I mean, it's okay to do what you have to do, but you gotta be smart about it. Hey, Carl, you know what they useta call Frankie back in the old neighborhood?"

"No, sir," said the young man, still impassive after Friedenberg's revelation of his misfortune. "I haven't any idea."

"We useta call him Gypsy. He was a helluva ball player, but that's not why he had the nickname. I made my first big money betting on these kids. Nobody in the Bronx could beat them, so it didn't matter what odds I gave."

Carl remained impassive.

"Will that be all, Mr. Friedenberg?"

"Yeah, sure, Carl," Friedenberg said, and ushered Garboil into a large, softly lit room. "This is the library," he said, proudly. "I'm watching the game but we can turn it off. They're winning but it doesn't mean a hell of a lot. I don't even know how much money comes in from baseball games anymore. It's all handled by a team of accountants. Once in a while I have a private bet with a friend but it's all peanuts. The real money's in business. Hey, how about some pastrami and beer? It's imported from Katz' down on Houston Street. Maybe you want something else."

"No, that'll be fine," he said.

Friedenberg picked up a phone and asked someone named Wanda to bring up the food. The library, as Friedenberg had called it, still had the books which were in it when he acquired the estate. But rather than being a soft, quiet place where the master of the house sat down with his cronies to digest a meal, drink brandy and coffee and discuss business, the library had been turned into a game room. In the middle of the room there was a pool table, at one end a full-length mahogany bar, purchased from a West Side saloon, and at the other end the largest television screen Garboil had ever seen. As soon as they entered the room Garboil's attention was riveted on the set. The baseball players appeared life-size and it was possible for him to read the labels on the bats. Bones Friedenberg hung up the phone, laughed at the look on Garboil's face and explained.

"I took a trip to Japan about a year ago. I own half interest in a baseball team over there. Not directly, but through one thing or another. It comes down to the same thing. Well, while I was there I went over and visited the SONY people.

They make all kinds of sets, even little ones you can stick in your pocket. Everything experimental. I talked to them about it because I'd seen that big thing they have at the Felt Forum in the new Garden. I paid them in advance and they built that thing," he said pointing at the giant TV. "Inside of three months they had it here. You shoulda seen'em, kid. They sent four technicians and a sales rep. These guys are bowing every two seconds and talking funny like the Japs do, you know? Funny as hell. They're too much, the Japs. Bomb the hell outta them and twenty-five years later they come up smelling like roses."

"The thing must be at least five feet across," Garboil said, spreading his arms to measure it.

"That's right," Friedenberg said, proudly. "But listen, don't get too close. Sit over here," he added, directing Garboil away from the screen. He pointed to several overstuffed chairs, done in white and blue velveteen, which clashed violently with the dark, crafted wood of the paneling and bookcases.

"What's wrong?" Garboil asked, once he was seated.

"Well, that's the thing," Friedenberg said. "These Japs are smart as hell and vengeful. Here they make the best goddamned TV set in the world and flood the U.S. with it. And you know their angle, right?"

Garboil shook his head.

"Color television gives off radiation," Friedenberg said.

"Yeah, I read something about that," Garboil said.

"There you have it. They're getting their revenge. We drop the atomic bomb on them so that not too many more people will get killed, and they come back and try to stab us in the back again. They're playing it smart this time. They're gonna do it in small doses. It won't happen right away, but maybe in fifty, seventy-five years all kinds of freaks are gonna be born in the U.S. I went to the museum they had over there in Hiroshima. Pictures and everything. That's gonna happen over here. Two kids'll get married and boom, next thing you know a kid's born and he's got two heads or three arms or an eye in the middle of his forehead. I already got a bet down with a friend of mine. Fifty big ones that says it's gonna happen in the next seventy-five years."

"Yeah, Bones, but you won't be around to collect," Garboil said.

Friedenberg punched his arm.

"That's nothing. It's the spirit of the thing. The bet goes to charity anyhow. We're gonna need it if things keep going the way they are. Who knows? I might come back anyways. I belong to this body-freezing club. You pass away and they fill your body with this fluid and freeze you. When they figure out how to cure what went wrong and they can fix you up, you come back as good as new. I also got a bet on that. If by 2500 I'm not back, I lose. If I come back before that, I win. But you tell me the truth, kid. You know a little about money, don't you? I heard you wuz an economist. By that time a hundred dollars is gonna be worth about a nickel."

Garboil laughed.

"Might be," he said. "How much was the bet for?"

"You're not gonna believe it."

"Try me, you said I knew about money."

"A million bananas."

Garboil laughed again and whistled at the irony of his own dwindling bank account. Friedenberg was wrong. He knew nothing about money. Only theory.

"Who's the bet with?" he said.

"I can't tell you, kid. But I can tell you that his last name starts with an N and he's a politician. His friends put up the money."

Garboil thought a moment and then he understood.

"You're kidding," he said.

"About what?"

"It could only be the..."

Bones Friedenberg looked at Garboil directly. His face became that of the high stakes gambler and entrepreneur. Garboil backed down in embarrassment. In a few more seconds things were back to normal.

"So tell me what you've been doing," Friedenberg said, amicably. "You still a hockey nut?"

"And how," Garboil replied. "That's why I came to see you."

Friedenberg nodded.

"You need a backer or what. Tell me. Whatta you wanna do, buy a hockey team? I've been trying to buy a franchise for years, but I always run into trouble. It's these Wall Street, gentile bastards that control all the legit money. They're a pain in the ass, kid. And they talk about us. So tell me. If you got an angle on how to move and we can get a small franchise, we can talk about it. Money's no problem."

"Naw, it's nothing like that, Bones."

At that moment a tall long-haired brunette girl came into the room wheeling a cart replete with sandwiches, pickles, potato salad and beer. Garboil got up, but Friedenberg waved him back down.

"This is Wanda, kid," Friedenberg said. "Wanda, this is Frank Garboil. He's a college professor."

"How do you do?" Garboil said, moved by the young woman's sad beauty.

"I'm fine, thank you," she said emptily. "Do you want mustard on your sandwich?"

"Yes, please," Garboil said, and watched Wanda perform the task of putting together his sandwich as if she were a robot.

"Wanda lost her folks a couple of years back when she was about fourteen. I found her wandering around in Greenwich Village. She goes to college during the day and helps out over here at night. Isn't that right, Wanda?"

"That's right, Mr. Friedenberg," Wanda said, forcing a smile on her lips.

"What's your major?" Garboil said.

"Classics," Wanda said, her face lighting up momentarily.

"Yeah," Friedenberg said. "The two of youse oughta get along fine."

Wanda looked down at Garboil and handed him a plate with a pastrami sandwich on rye bread, some pickle slices and potato salad.

"Would you like me to pour your beer?" she said.

"No, that's all right, Wanda. Thank you."

She did the same thing for Friedenberg and poured him a beer.

"May I go now, Mr. Friedenberg?" she said, as the two men began eating.

"Yeah, sure," Friedenberg. "Me and Frank got a lot to talk about. No phone calls. I'll see you later."

"Good night, Professor Garboil. Nice to have met you."

Garboil watched her leave quietly, trailing an air of loneliness which disturbed him. She was like a bird that has broken a wing and has struggled to fly and failed so that it no longer flutters vainly on the ground, but has accepted its fate with resignation and lies as still as possible in order to prolong its survival. He took a bite from the sandwich and followed with a long draught of beer, forgetting for the moment his diet and enjoying the food. The Mets were coming off the field at the end of the game, the organ music playing in the background.

"She's a good kid," Friedenberg said, apologetically. "The story about her parents is what she gave me. I found her all drugged up and dirty. She had the clap and was nothing but skin and bones. That was six years ago. She's from the Midwest somewhere. Indiana, I think she said. A year of good medical care, three meals a day, plenty of sleep and no one hassling her and she was fine. I guess she was grateful. One thing led to another and that was it. You know how those things happen. One time I feel like she's my daughter and the next time, well, you know how it is with women. She doesn't complain about anything and is serious as hell about this Classics business. Once in a while she'll open up and talk about the country not having any myths, whatever the hell they are. And that's why it's getting destroyed. She sounds scary as hell and her mind is a million miles away when she talks. You know me, kid. I don't scare easy. I mean, when I was twenty I went to the man and told him I wanted work. 'I want a piece of the action, Uncle Meyer,' I said. He laughed in my face, but put me to work. So I've got balls, know what I mean? But she scares the hell out of me sometimes. Now, what's this stuff about hockey?"

Garboil spent the next fifteen minutes explaining his plan in elaborate detail. Bones Friedenberg listened carefully, figuring every possible angle.

"The only problem I see," Garboil said, concluding, "is doing it without getting caught. I just want to see what happens, but if I get found out, that's it. I'll never get hired by a school again. If I was a reporter or something, I could say I was doing a story."

"Keerist, kid," Friedenberg said. "You really think of them. What about your wife and kids?"

"You know about them?" Garboil said, puzzled.

Friedenberg smiled.

"Yeah, I know about them. I keep a book on everyone I gotta deal with."

"Well, they're in California. We split up. Finished."

"That's too bad. Listen, you're a smart kid, right? Why don't you forget this cockamamie scheme and come work for me? I could use somebody like you. I mean, you know the mechanics of how the system works. I'm doing all right, but I could do better. I'll pay you real money. It doesn't sound like you were too happy with the school business, right?"

"Well, sure. It was rough, but I don't know anything else."

"You know money, that's what you know."

"I don't know, Bones. This is something I gotta do."

"Com'on, kid. Forget all that stuff."

"I don't know."

"Com'on already. What am I asking you, to wear a yarmukle again? After a while we'll buy a hockey team and you could run it. How's that?"

"It's a great offer, Bones, but I can't take you up on it. I'm gonna be screwed up till I get this thing outta my system. It's like I got shafted on the deal and I have to get back."

"Com'on, kid," he said. "Everybody gets shafted in some way. That's the way things are set up. How do you think I feel? Sure I have a lot of influence in high places but it's all behind the scenes. You think I wouldn't like to see my picture in the papers with a good word once in a while? You don't know the money I've donated to charity. You wouldn't believe it if I told you. And not only here. In Israel."

At this point Bones Friedenberg's voice cracked with emotion. It was as if a deep pain had suddenly surfaced within him, a pain which he'd held a long time. He was silent for a moment and then he was back in control.

"You okay?"

"Yeah, sure. I was thinking aboout Belle."

Garboil thought a moment and then remembered.

"Belle Howitzer, right?"

"Yeah, she was my girl, kid. Only girl I ever loved. She got killed over there. I put up the money and they built a monument in her name. They made her look like a man. I mean, don't get me wrong. She was a big girl, remember?"

"Yeah, sure. She useta referee our games."

"Yeah, she liked sports. I don't know what the hell got into her. She started going to college and sort of flipped out. Went to live in a kibbutz and didn't wanna come back. You been over there?"

"No, not yet," Garboil said, and at that moment it dawned on him that Bones Friedenberg was convinced he was Jewish. Was he? He had no recollection of any religious instruction. "Maybe sometime," he said, suddenly self-conscious.

"Anyways she was guarding something or other one night and some Arab creeps tried to sneak up on the compound. It was out in the desert. The Negev. Ever hear of it?"

"Yeah, sure."

"She fought them single-handed. Killed about fifteen or twenty of them before they did her in. So her mother called me with the news and I felt like telling her to shove it since she didn't want Belle to have nothing to do with me because I was a bad element and dropped outta school when I was twelve. What did she want from my life, to be like her husband? A tailor, for crying out loud. A fucking tailor. No, thank you. Anyways, she's crying on and I said I'd go over there and make sure everything was okay. The people loved her. She was like some kind of heroine and they wanted to do something special, so I said I'd take care of it. They hired a sculptor and did this huge monument. She's holding a machine gun. So you know how I feel."

"Sure, I understand."

"Nothing. And when I'm gone, nothing. Not even a little plaque in a hospital. THE DAVID FRIEDENBERG MEMORIAL WING or THE FRIEDENBERG CANCER RESEARCH LABORATORY. Nothing. They'll take the money all right, but not one real word of thanks. So that's how it is, kid. Everybody gets shafted one way or the other. But tell me something, why hockey? If you told me that you wanted to change careers, that you wanted to go to medical school, I could understand it."

"Hell, I don't know, Bones. It's something I gotta do. I just need to know what my chances woulda been. I don't know."

Friedenberg shook his head.

"You don't know. I don't know. Looking at you I'd say you're in pretty good shape right now. What are you, thirty?"

"I'll be thirty-four in December."

"Well, I'll tell you something. You could be twenty-four, the way you look. And you could always play sports pretty good. You been playing hockey? Training?"

"Yeah, sure. I skate two or three times a week and play at least once a week. Nothing heavy yet. The only thing that worries me is having to use another name."

Friendberg thought a moment.

"Hey, that's no problem, kid. I'll send you to somebody'll fix you up right away. You tell him what your problem is and he'll take care of you. It's gonna cost you though."

Garboil's stomach tightened.

"How much?"

"Depends what you want. It can go as high as a couple of thousand if you wanted a passport, but I don't think you're gonna need nothing like that. The guy's name is Benny the Letter Thief. He contracts people out to get the stuff. You know, junkies and that kind of guy. They go into the mailboxes to steal welfare checks and come away with all kinds of things. He buys the stuff from them. He's got a collection of documents that'll pop your eyes out. Benny'll find something for you.

"Do the cops know about him?"

"Sure they know. What the hell don't they know. They don't give a shit. He's not murdering anyone or selling dope. It's petty stuff and any time they need a junk bust, they go to Benny and he'll give them a few hints, nothing specific, and they get their rocks off by putting a small-time pusher away.

It all balances out. The thing is you gotta go easy on Benny. He's an old man. As far as he's concerned, you need him and not the other way around. If you mention the law he won't even look at you. And he's a tough old bastard, so watch it. He's got a small newspaper stand over near the docks in Manhattan. Just go there and ask him if he's got the *Chicago Daily News* or the *Washington Post*. He'll probably send you to hell at first. Just tell him you thought he might be able to help you out. Benny's got a sense about people in trouble and if he decides you need help, he'll take it from there."

"That's it?"

"That's it, kid."

"Thanks, Bones."

"Don't mention it, kid. I thought you really needed help. Well, on second thought, maybe you do. I'll be honest with you. I wouldn't put good money on you pulling this thing off."

"You mean with Benny?"

"No, no. I mean that whole meshuganah business with hockey. What the hell's in it for you? Like I said, if it's hockey that's in your system, we can work something out."

"Thanks again, Bones. I appreciate the offer, but I have to go through with this thing. If I don't I'm gonna feel like I don't have any balls any more."

"I understand, kid. I don't like it, but that's life. It's like the kid, what's-his-name. The one that useta cross the Willis Avenue Bridge swinging from the railroad ties."

"Yeah, like that. Mickey Slavin."

"Yeah, Slavin."

"He almost fell in the river a couple of times."

"Right. Now that was balls. Didn't give a shit if a train was coming. He just had to do it to prove himself."

"Right, like that."

"Or like jumping from one roof to the other. I useta watch you kids and people wanted to bet me one of youse would fall off. I never bet on things like that. But I could understand why youse did it. Me, I never went in for that kinda thing. Whenever I'd get the urge to do something crazy, I'd start thinking of the odds of me winning and what angle I could use to make sure I won some money. And I mean win, because I wouldn't go into it otherwise. The cops and the papers call me a gambler. You know what? They're fulla shit. They're the ones who gamble and play the horses and bet on games. I just rake in their money. That's no gamble. That's just good business sense. For me there's gotta be money in something. Once in a while it's a gamble, but most of the time it's a sure thing."

Garboil took one last pull from the beer and got up.

"I better be going, Bones. Thanks a lot."

"Nothing to it, kid," Friedenberg said, rising. "Here, let me write down where you can get a hold of Benny. Carl'll drive you back to the city."

The rest of the weekend was peaceful and without event. On Sunday morning Garboil ran in Riverside Park. He was now up to three miles without much of a strain. When he was finished running he stopped off, drank some water and headed for the basketball courts. On Sundays there were usually a number of Columbia University students vying for playground honors with the blacks from the neighborhood, some of whom were college and high school players. The games were rough and quick and although he played passably, his heart was hardly ever in the games, playing only to improve his coordination, sharpen his reflexes and further build up his stamina and wind. He found the athletic camaraderie fulfilling, but after the games, people broke off and went their separate ways. No one talked to anyone else. The different groups, the blacks, the Columbia students, and the few older West Side men trying to keep in shape, reverted to their own rules and rituals and he was left to walk back to his apartment alone.

Thoughts of a woman had not occurred to him since Joan had left and he last saw Angela Piscatelli before she left for Tierra del Fuego to learn Indian languages. But now as he walked through the park he was aware of couples, and of solitary women, walking their dogs or riding bicycles. He was beginning to feel a new strength in his body and, with it, lust as he had once felt. And yet, for all the lust he'd felt there had always been a longing, a hurt that was now absent, as if in breaking away from his old life he had left it behind. There would be a woman again, but there was no rush. He walked up the stairs leading out of the park. There was so little strain in doing so that the feeling in his legs made him smile.

That night he treated himself to a pair of Bergman films at the Thalia. Sitting through the intellectual haze drifting up from the crowd and concentrating on the emotion of the actors, he decided that Bergman, if nothing else, made the films to keep busy, to somehow pass the time, building on one experience to fuel the next so that after a while memory blended into dream, and that into reality and back again into memory; never knowing or caring which was which, but treating it all as a whole; living it all out to its fullest so that death would perhaps come as a surprise and not as a sentence. And that is how he felt. The insight caused him neither joy nor concern. He was glad to be alone so that there would be no ensuing discussion.

On the way home he bought a newspaper and turned to the sports section. There was a story on the further expansion of the National Hockey League and the possibility of a new team in New York. He expected the story to fuel his imagination and push it further than his upcoming college adventure, but it did not. When he'd first thought of the scheme he'd carried it as far as the professional ranks, but the closer he came to actually playing, the more he realized what it took to play professionally. Sitting at home and watching the players skate on television or even watching them from a distance at the Garden gave one a false sense of the ease with which the players performed. It was the same with other sports. No matter how well one did, one had only to see professionals to feel inadequate. And yet that one haunting quality which had eluded him all of his life and which he'd finally captured came back time and again to urge him on. The trick was not to think too far ahead. The thought no longer occurred to him that he would not make the school team once admitted. If a doubt began to enter his mind it was quickly dispelled by the feeling of anger rising up in him. He did not know where the anger came from, what produced it, but it was enough to dissolve the doubt. He slept soundly that night and without dreams.

On Monday morning he dressed casually and went to the address Bones Friedenberg had given him. The news stand was on the corner of Eleventh Avenue and Forty-fifth Street. It was a small kiosk and within it was a very old man. He was thin and reminded Garboil of a wizard in a children's book, the skin of his face leathery and loose across the bones of his face, the eyes still surprisingly sharp and cunning.

"Good afternoon," Garboil said. "I was wondering if you had the *Chicago Daily News*?"

The old man looked into his eyes and shook his head with disdain.

"Does it look like I got the *Chicago Daily News*? What am I some fancy newspaper shop uptown?"

"I just thought you might be able to help me out." Garboil said, dutifully.

"Maybe I can and maybe I can't. The price of paper's gone up again. Everybody's got unions these days, including lumberjacks."

"Yeah, I guess so," he said. "You want something, you gotta pay for it."

The old man looked at him curiously for a moment before he spoke again.

"You sure got that right, buddy," he said, finally. "Was a time you could get a cuppa coffee for a nickel too."

"Sure, I remember when the *Daily News* useta be three cents."

"Sure, three cents. But listen, if it's the paper from Chicago you're looking for there's a place in Brooklyn you can get it. South Brooklyn to be exact, down by the docks."

Benny wrote down the address and set it on a stack of *New York Times*. Garboil took the piece of paper, folded it and put it in his pocket. He glanced at the newspapers for a moment. The Vietnam war casualties were going up with each day that passed.

"Any time of day all right?" he asked.

"It's gotta be in the evening, buddy. Papers don't get in from Chicago till late. The later the better."

"Okay, thanks," Garboil said, backing away from the kiosk and waving at the old man.

"Yeah," the old man said.

That evening Garboil set out for Brooklyn about ten o'clock. He was carrying two hundred dollars and it made him edgy. Gangs of kids were roaming the streets again and the addicts were always wise to someone carrying money. The train rumbled on, the people fanning themselves with newspapers and magazines. The train crossed the Manhattan Bridge and he watched the lights of Manhattan in the thick summer haze. The river looked dark and still. A lone tug was hauling a barge upstream. It let out a long, mournful hoot, the sound echoing in the night above the steady clacking of the wheels on the tracks.

One stop into Brooklyn, Garboil got off the train and walked out into the street. The area was deserted. As he neared the docks he heard water lapping against the hulls of the ships. After walking several blocks he found the address Benny the Letter Thief had written down. It was an old warehouse. He rang the doorbell and heard a dog bark upstairs. A few minutes later Benny opened the door and let him in. Within seconds, almost out of nowhere, the biggest Doberman pinscher he'd ever seen was at Garboil's side, eyeing him in that crazed suspicious way they have.

"Don't worry about Fritz," Benny said. "He only attacks on command. If you hear me start whistling anything from Brahms, just say your prayers and resign yourself to having your face be part of an Alpo commercial. Black son of a bitch comes in here about a month ago. Wanted a new social security number. While

I'm looking through a stack, he pulls out a gun and tells me it's a holdup. So I says: 'Why don't we work out a deal.' 'No,' he says. 'You don't hand over the bread, I'm gonna blow you *and* the fucking mutt away.' Fritz is standing right there not even growling, so I start whistling the lullabye and, before the spook could get off a shot, Fritz tore a hole in his throat. I just dumped the son-of-a-bitch down the stairs and called the precinct. The spook croaked the next morning. But Fritz won't bother you. Just don't raise your voice. He likes to sleep. Come upstairs."

Upstairs was a long loft with a small, cluttered living area with a dirty army cot at one end and a hot plate at the other. The rest of the loft was devoted to metal shelves, several rows of them, each one eight feet high. On them, boxes had been stacked in no apparent order. There were several aisles with a ladder in each aisle, so that Garboil was reminded of the library stacks of a college. Along the walls, there were large file cabinets, holding, Garboil assumed, more documents. Everything was dusty and smelled stale, the only light provided by a few bare light bulbs. Benny sat down at a roll-top desk cluttered with mounds of papers. He asked Garboil to sit in the chair next to the desk. When Garboil was seated Benny put on a green visor cap and turned on an old gooseneck lamp on the desk. Fritz lay down near the chair and closed his eyes.

"Now what is it that you need?" Benny said. "You don't have to tell me who sent you or what the papers are for."

"Well, I got a job to do and I need identification," Garboil said, unsure of himself. "That's about it."

Benny closed his eyes patiently.

"Look, sonny, I don't ask too many questions but that doesn't tell me a goddamn thing. Do you need credit cards, a driver's license, what?"

"No, just something that'll establish I'm someone else."

"You wanna start all over again?"

"Yeah, sort of. I wanna go to college."

Benny looked away and expelled a long breath.

"Jesus Fuckin' Christ! What am I supposed to be, a fucking enrolling officer? How old are you anyway?"

"Thirty-three."

"You think you can pass yourself off as younger?"

"How much younger?"

"I don't know. Christ! Twenty-three, four."

"Sure, I guess so."

Benny got up, followed by Fritz, and walked into one of the aisles. Garboil heard him moving the ladder and then rustling papers. When he returned to the desk he had a bunch of envelopes. He threw them down atop the already cluttered desk and sat back down. Fritz went back to sleep, his head resting on Benny's feet.

"I just got these in last week," Benny said. "Let me look through them. I think I saw something in them."

He extracted several pieces of mail from their envelopes and lay them out on the desk. When he had gone through a couple of dozen, he stopped and handed him a document. Garboil took it and read it. When he was finished he shook his head.

"Jesus," he said. "This is a notification that this guy was killed in Vietnam."

"So."

"What am I going to do with this?" Garboil said, more loudly than he wished.

Fritz lifted up his head, growled and went back to sleep.

"Go easy, sonny," Benny said. "Fritz is trying to sleep."

"Okay, okay," Garboil whispered. "But what's this nonsense?"

Benny handed him another document. Garboil read it, shook his head and gave the letter back to Benny.

"I don't know," he said. "I don't know what you expect me to do with this."

"That's up to you," Benny said. "You could wipe your ass with the fucking thing for all I care. I'm trying to help you and you got nothing but complaints. Whatta you want from life?"

"Yeah, but first you show me a letter telling some guy's family that he's dead and then another letter that some guy's been accepted into college. Suppose I show up and this other guy shows up too?"

"Jesus F. Christ," said Benny, annoyed with Garboil. "What the hell do you do for a living? Whoever sent you on this job's gonna have a lot of problems. I've seen junkies smarter than you. Did you read the names? The addresses?"

Garboil picked up the documents and looked at them again. The name was the same on both letters.

"It's the same person," he said.

"Right, bright eyes. You *better* go to college."

"What happened?"

"How the hell do I know! Who am I, the Postmaster General! The kid probably wanted to go to college after he got out of the army and got killed over in Vietnam. Both papers arrived in the same batch, the same day."

"That's quite a coincidence."

"Bullshit. It happens all the time. People get birth and death certificates for their kid the same day. Happens all the time."

"But this guy's Puerto Rican or something."

"So they're not entitled to die? Listen, sonny, you don't like the goods? Go to Abraham & Stauss. So he's Puerto Rican. Who gives a shit. It's a name. He could be Irish for all I care. I'm trying to help you out and you tell me the guy's Puerto Rican. Grow a moustache, buy a switchblade. Whatta you want from me!"

"Okay, okay. How much?"

"Fifty for the notification of death and twenty-five for the admissions letter. Seventy-five bucks in case you got trouble adding. With the notification you got no worries about the guy coming back. They'll probably follow it up with somebody coming to the house, which it should be the other way around but this government's full of assholes. So you got nothing to worry about."

Garboil nodded uncertainly.

"Armando Martinez, huh?"

"Yeah, yeah! Whatever his name is. It ain't gonna do him any good now, so you might as well use the name and enjoy it."

Garboil pulled the money out of his pocket and handed Benny eighty dollars. Benny counted the money, went into his pants' pocket and extended a five dollar bill out to Garboil.

"No, go ahead and keep it."

"Don't do me any favors, sonny," Benny said. "This is like Nedicks's. No tipping. You don't owe me nothing, I don't owe you nothing. From the look of things, you're gonna need it more than I do."

"Why do you keep saying that?"

Benny shook his head.

"Now he wants psychiatry," he said to no one. "Listen, with your brains, you'll be pushing a broom in the street if you don't watch out."

"Yeah, sure."

Fritz growled once more. Benny looked at Garboil and offered one last piece of advice.

"Just think things out with the papers. I don't wanna tell you what to do or nothing, but those are damn good papers. Maybe it was a coincidence and maybe it wasn't, but if you use them smart-like, you'll do all right."

Garboil got up, thanked Benny the Letter Thief and went down the stairs and back into the street. There was still a thick haze hanging over the city. It made the buildings seem to shimmer in the distance. The heat was now more oppressive and the river gave off a stench of putrefaction. He felt the two letters in his pocket and quickened his pace. What did he look like, this Armando Martinez? Had he been already buried and his soul at rest or was it still wandering the earth, troubled? Had he been in love? Was he big or small, dark or fair, quiet or outgoing?

On the subway back to Manhattan he had the urge to let the papers float out over the river as the train went over the bridge. It was foolish to back down now. What difference did it make, anyway? Tonight he'd got to bed as Frank Garboil and tomorrow he'd wake up as Armando Martinez.

The transformation did not take place overnight, but by Wednesday of the following week, Garboil had written out the name MARTINEZ in block letters on a small piece of paper and scotch-taped the paper to his mailbox in the lobby of the building.

CHAPTER 19

In which F. William Kolodny threatens to expose the President of Frick University, who, in a predicament, has a dialogue with the Almighty, out of which we consider the outside possibility that He, in all His omnipotence, may be just a good ole boy from Valdosta, Georgia, or Tuscaloosa, Alabama, and as an added treat, meets Dover Terry, an actor of superb temperament and skill.

Back in his office, F. William Kolodny moved into high gear. He let himself in, locked the door, checked the rooms for signs of burglary and set himself to the task of developing and enlarging Garboil's photographs. While he waited for the prints to dry, he wrote diligently in his journal. His personal shorthand was difficult even for himself to decipher from one day to the next, but he hoped some day to sit down and write his memoirs. Perhaps he would even write a few detective novels.

The character of the detective danced around in his head. Jack West: Private Eye. Even the music jumped forth. Hard, driving, frenetic sounds, screeching trumpets and crescendoes of insane timpani that would drive any criminal to instant surrender were he being pursued by a full studio orchestra such as Kolodny would hope was employed when his novels became films. Jack West: suave, knowledgeable and tough as nails. Women fell at his feet, panting for his caress. Criminals fled at the mere mention of his name.

When the prints were dry, Kolodny observed them carefully, noting each detail of the long-haired, full moustachioed young man staring back at him. Kolodny had managed to obtain several shots of Ingrid Kondruka's bustline, but they were deceiving.

No one could have breasts that luscious. He wondered what the nurse would be like dressed in a t-shirt, a wet one. He quickly drove the idea from his mind. Business was business and a professional did not fool around with his clients. In any case she looked like a two-hundred-dollar, one-hand-at-a-time broad.

Kolodny picked up the phone and obtained the number of Frick University. He dialed it and waited. After several rings a woman's voice announced that it was indeed Frick University.

"Yeah," Kolodny said. "Let me talk to the president of that there school."

"Yes, sir, I'll connect you with President Bacon's office immediately."

The phone clicked several times and another woman's voice came on the line.

"The President's office, Mrs. Armstrong speaking," said the pleasantly official voice. "How can I help you?"

"Is the President in?" Kolodny said.

"May I ask who's calling?"

"Sure, go ahead," Kolodny said. There was silence at the other end as Mrs. Armstrong waited for Kolodny to identify himself. After several seconds of his own waiting, Kolodny said, "Well, go ahead and ask."

"May I have your name, sir?" said Mrs. Armstrong coldly.

"Sure, sister," Kolodny said. "Why didn't you ask me in the first place. The name's Albert Wright and I work for the *Daily News*. We're doing a series on economics in colleges in New York. I'd like to know if I can talk with the president."

"Very well, sir. I'll see if he's available. Hang on, please."

John David Bacon had just returned from lunch and was in the process of pouring himself a small glass of sherry when the buzzer on his phone rang. He finished pouring, replaced the top on the decanter, put it back on a shelf and picked up the receiver.

"Yes, Mrs. Armstrong," he said.

"Sir, there's a man holding who says he's from one of the New York newspapers and would like to talk to you."

John Bacon thought for a moment. Things at the school were relatively calm. The spring semester had started without incident. And the fall semester, although chaotic at first, had turned out favorably. Perhaps they were interested in the progress of the football team. He asked his secreatry to connect him with the reporter and took another sip from the sherry. The phone clicked once more.

"Good afternoon," he said. "John Bacon here."

"Good afternoon, Mr. President," said Kolodny, affecting as official a voice as he could muster. "This here's about Economics. My name's Wright and I'm doing a piece of writing on the Economy. A lot of our readers want to know if the kids are getting taught any of this radical stuff. I was wondering if I could come up there and talk to you and maybe some of the professors."

John Bacon was mildly surprised at the request.

"Of course you can," he said, after a minor hesitation. "Always glad to talk to reporters," he added, letting himself drift into his folksy, cultured southern accent, his safest refuge in times of stress. "But let me put your mind at ease, Mr. Wright, that there's nothing radical going on at ole Frick U. We're just trying to educate the students to fundamental American values and trying to put together one of the finest football teams in this part of the U.S. of A."

"That's good, Mr. President," Kolodny said. "What I'm interested in is Economics. You have a guy out there name of Garboil. Frank Garboil. As we get it on this end, this here Garboil is the perpetrator of this here Economics, isn't he?"

John Bacon felt his mouth drying up. He suddenly had the urge to let out a long bleat. He knew Garboil would come back and haunt him. Son-of-a-cotton-pissing-bitch, he thought. It was the Board of Trustees checking up on him. If they found out Garboil's salary line was being used for recuiting players, they'd roast him for sure. It was just like the old skinflints to use a cheap private detective.

"Well, sure thing, Mr. Wright," he said. "As a matter of fact we do have a Professor Garboil and he does teach Economics."

"Good," said Kolodny, proud that he was on the right track.

"Mr. President, I'd like to come out there and interview that there Professor Garboil."

"Of course," Bacon said. "Let me take a look at my calendar. Yep, here we go. How about ll a.m. on Friday of next week? We can shoot the breeze, go to lunch and then meet with Professor Garboil."

"I'm gonna have to disappoint you, Mr. President," Kolodny said. "I have to fly upstate tomorrow night and won't be back till late Saturday night. My deadline is this weekend. Of course I could write that you refused to let me interview the professor. We have a lot of readers out in Long Island and I'm sure they wouldn't like that the president of Frick University's involved in a cover-up."

Hunker down, John David, Bacon thought to himself as he tried to control himself.

"Well, when would you like to come out, Mr. Wright?" he said, considering the possibility that the man was indeed a reporter. "How about tomorrow?"

"That sounds good, Mr. President. Tomorrow at eleven."

John David Bacon put the receiver back on its cradle and cursed. Beads of perspiration had broken out on his forehead and he felt dizzy. He reached down, opened one of the drawers on his desk and pulled out a half-empty bottle of Jack Daniels. His hands shaking, he opened the bottle and took a long pull. In spite of the relative security he had achieved in his 45 years, John David Bacon, president of Frick University, was plagued by the recurring premonition that all of it would one day vanish and that the Almighty, resplendent and vengeful, would rain destruction upon his life and strip him of all his gains.

"Oh, God," he said, and immediately regretted the utterance. He recapped the bottle, stuck it back in the drawer and ran into the private bathroom at the other end of his spacious office.

Inside the bathroom, he hurriedly washed out his mouth, sprayed his breath with freshener and ran back out. Made no sense to have the Lord pay him a visit and he with bourbon on his breath. Why had he called him? That's what came from taking the Lord's name in vain. Halfway to his desk there was a thunderous explosion, the lights flickered and then went completely out. And there He was again, only for the third time in Bacon's life. There He was, looking like a combination between his high school coach, Boone McCallister, John Wayne and the Marlborough man, except that He was wearing striped bib overalls, brogans and a straw hat and his skin was all chicken-like and leathery and like he'd been out in the sun forever, it was so tanned and red, like clay almost. He had steely blue eyes and was chewing on a blade of grass.

"Son, get up from there," He said, in a deep, resounding voice.

"I'm sorry, Lord," Bacon said. "I really am. I got shook up."

"John David," the Lord said. "I've had patience with you, son. And I've been good to you. I raised you from utter poverty in the backwoods of America. I gave you a strong body so you could run, tackle and block. I gave you a fine mind, agile but fair. I gave you a good speaking voice to move your flock and do my work. And damnit, boy. I never once told you nothing about what to do with your pecker. That's a man's business to do as he pleases. I don't mind you roaming free and straying from Jo Ellen. She's a good ole gal, but a mite strange. I know how difficult your job is. A man needs a little release once in a while."

"Lord, I, I..."

"Hush up and let me finish. Do you think I enjoy raining death and destruction down on people? Do you think I like to explode volcanoes and have molten rock cover whole villages so that five minutes later it looks like Hell after a Saturday night party? I don't like it one bit, son, but I have to get some release. I don't drink, don't smoke, don't take no kinda dope. That's right, not even a little weekend snort or nothing. Son, I don't even mess around with Mary anymore. I've just lost the ole urge, even though it puts me in a hell of a spot. She's starting to spread rumors about me being anti-semitic because of that whole thing over in Europe with that maniac, Hitler. What am I supposed to do? How are people going to learn any respect. A volcano here, a tidal wave there, an earthquake further on, a massacre, a pogrom, an assassination, a war and once in a while a miracle to give the people some hope. I'm running out of tricks, boy. It's hard work, let me tell you."

"I'm sorry, Lord, it's just that..."

"Hush, boy. Hot-diggity! Don't you have no manners? I think you're developing an attitude problem. I don't like it one bit, son. And I ain't going to kid you, John David. I don't like to see you cowering. You're a strong ole boy. You don't have to take any guff from them smartass Yankee peckerheads. You don't have to, heah? If you continue to be afraid of every little thing I place in your path so that I have to come down here every other day, I'm going to have to take the whole thing away. No Yale degrees, no honorable mention All-American, no college, no bourbon, and no hush puppies and black-eyed peas. And if that don't make you take notice, by gosh, I'll wither up your pecker quicker than you can say Jack Robinson."

John Bacon wanted to crawl into the carpeting. He wanted to cry, to pound his fist and wet his pants and scream like the time his mama had made him wear shoes for the first time. He controlled all those urges and knelt to ask forgiveness for his sins. He promised to do anything to reform his life. He'd walk barefoot across the desert and purge himself of evil. He closed his eyes and began praying.

"Dear God, Maker of the Universe," he began. That's all wrong, he thought. What was he to do? "Heavenly Father," he began anew and he could hear Him sort of tapping that big brogan of His. And then he recalled the exhortation of one of the students in the Jesus movement: "A just God is a hip God."

That was it, he had to talk to God sincerely.

"Look here, man," he said, his eyes still closed and his face raised. "I'm neck-deep in shit and there's somebody coming in a speedboat and you know that's gonna raise waves. These peckerheads on the Board are after my ass. They're spying on me and I can't let them get in the way of your work. Show me a sign that you're still with me, that you ain't taking them long executive lunches. I don't come sniveling up to you every time this place threatens to become a battlefield. All I'm asking for is a little hint about what I should do. I know maybe I shouldn't have used the money to recruit, but you know yourself there's some good ole boys out there with fine potential just like I had. They deserve a chance too. Just give me a little hint, Lord. You know I know you're the Man. Shoot! You're not only unanimous choice All-American, you're unanimous choice All-Universe. You're the best that ever came along at your position."

John David Bacon felt a strong gust of wind pass through the room and opened his eyes. He was alone once again. The lights were on and the only thing left behind to remind him of the visitation was a strong smell of Old Spice after-shave lotion. He stood up, smoothed out his pants, fixed his tie, pulled down his jacket and stuck out his chest confidently. He was a fine figure of a man. The crisis within had passed and his handsome face was once again determined and set into that pose of authority men of great purpose and responsibility possess. The words of his high school coach, Boone McCallister, echoed in his mind: "When the goin' gets tough, the tough get goin'." He sat back down at his desk and began to sign several of the letters Mrs. Armstrong had left on his desk while he'd been out.

No more than ten minutes later his phone buzzed.

"Yes, Mrs. Armstrong," he said.

"Sir, I have Dover Terry on hold. He's quite angry and says unless he can see you right away he's not responsible for what happens to Professor Lane."

"Tell him to come right up and see me, Mrs. Armstrong. Send him right in when he gets here."

Five minutes later Assistant Professor Dover Terry, co-chairman of the Theater Arts Department of Frick University, blew into Bacon's office like a tropical storm. He had shoulder length platinum blond hair and the large brown eyes of a doe in heat. He was dressed in an Indian sari, wore hoop earrings, a dozen bracelets on each wrist and tiny brass bells on his left ankle. He was barefoot and his toe nails were painted gold. Dover was a Garbo cultist and for effect gave long, exotic looks, mysterious and deep whenever he was pained.

He paused in front of Bacon's desk, turned his head so that it rested on his shoulder and sighed.

"Oh, John," he said, disconsolate. "That man is dreadful. He is pushing theater back to the Dark Ages. He wants to do 'Streetcar' in drag for the end of the term project."

"Well, Dover," said Bacon, soothingly. "I've always thought it was a damn fine play and these are modern times."

"I know, I know, Dear John," Terry said, tinkling across the room so that he now appeared to Bacon as if he were on stage. "But these students are too, *too* creative, darling. They want to improvise, to give of themselves, to do their own thing, so to speak. I've been teaching theater for twenty years and I have never encountered such an obviously sexual deviate. I don't begrudge the man his sexual habits, but he cannot keep his hands off those poor young girls. He accosts them wherever he finds them and they come crying to me, worried about their grades, about their training. How can artists progress under such pressure. John, he is running his part of the deaprtment as if he were a Hollywood mogul, complete with casting couch. Me, I'm like a breeze which comes to soothe. I cannot stand rejection, so my love is pure. If I feel love, I demonstrate it subtly. Openly but subtly, John. But Henry Lane is a pervert. You must get rid of him or else accept my resignation."

"Dover, Dover," Bacon said.

"No, John, I mean what I've said," Terry said, his eyes closed and his head turned to the side. "Unless he leaves, my days at Frick are over. Finito."

Dover Terry walked over to the large picture window which overlooked Bacon's private mountain scene and stood there with his arms crossed, whimpering, little sobs wracking his shoulders. He was hurt. John Bacon knew this, but didn't know by what.

"Now look here," Bacon said. "We need you around here, Dover. You can't go quitting like that. And furthermore, people love you at Frick. An artist of your magnitude is hard to come by these days. You put me in a very uncomfortable position. Why don't you come on over here and sit down on the couch. Let's talk this out. Would you like some sherry?"

"Oh, thank you, John," he said. "Perhaps a small glass of sherry would soothe my nerves." He turned from the window and in tiny little steps crossed the room once more and sat down on the sofa. "You're such a gentleman," he said, after Bacon handed him a glass of sherry. He crossed his legs, sipped the sherry and looked pleased.

"I'm such an emotional person," he said contritely. "I hurt so easily. I try to control myself, but some things are just wrong, arent't they, John. Lane is doing this drag 'Streetcar' just to mock gay life. Doesn't he know what kind of repercussions that can have on this campus. You have no idea how many people are homosexual, John. What a scandal if a member of the faculty publicly, through the vehicle of one of the departments, imposed his views on innocent people."

"Yes, of course, Dover," Bacon said. "That would be intolerable. Now, you know that Henry Lane is under contract, don't you? I just can't up and fire him. You'd have to bring charges against him and, unless some of the students were willing to back you up, they'd never stand up. Has he raped anyone?"

"No, of course not. Not physically anyway."

"Well, something like that can get messy. Why don't you let me speak to him?"

"I don't know, John. What am I to do? He's impossible to live with. I would do anything, turn myself into putty if he stopped being so rigid. Everything has to be his way. Puleeze!"

John David Bacon watched Dover Terry intently. What an act. Where had the search committee dug up these people. If he was less of a diplomat, he'd throw the old fruitcase out on his butt. But it was at that moment that John David Bacon knew that the Almighty had not deserted him. He stood up, walked over to the window, stood looking out at the little mountain cabin with the wisp of smoke rising from its chimney, turned around and came back to the couch. Standing in front of Dover Terry, he made him an offer which he knew would be impossible to refuse.

"Look here, Dover," he said. "You're coming up for tenure, aren't you?"

"That's right, John," Dover said, somewhat puzzled. "But don't think for a minute that such a triviality is going to sidetrack me from the courage of my convictions."

"Well, damn it, Dover. I know that. But all things being normal, you'd like to have it, wouldn't you?"

"I'd be more than a liar if I said no, John. I'd like to stay on and build on the work I've started. Frick University could become the cultural center of this barren wasteland."

"Well, good buddy, as far as I'm concerned you've got it, except that I need a favor from you. Now, I don't actually have the power to grant you tenure, but sure as God makes little green apples in the summertime, I can influence some people around here. I'll speak to Lane and get him to desist from this 'Streetcar' thing. But you got to do your part and not get so emotional."

"Oh, John, you're a darling," Dover said, getting up and kissing John Bacon on the cheek.

Bacon was used to Dover Terry's expression of affection and smiled appreciatively at him. What was the harm. He considered Terry one of his children, like Jo Ellen, perhaps a little strange, but nevertheless thrown into his path as a test of his strength.

"With tenure I'd be forced to name you head of the department and then we could transfer Lane back to Communication Skills."

"Oh, John, that's brilliant," Dover said, smiling like a child who's just been given a surprise. He jumped up and then down to one knee. "My liege, my lord, I am your humble vassal," he said, bowing his head.

"Get up, Dover," Bacon said. "It's all right. Do you remember Frank Garboil?"

Dover Terry got up, his affectations set aside for the moment.

"Oh yes, very serious chap, wasn't he? Economics, I believe. Very pleasant but quite closed. He was having a *flagrant* affair with that horrid Piscatelli person. A tart if I ever met one. I tried to communicate with him a dozen times, but I think he was afraid of my enthusiasm. And then what's her name, Angela Pisspotbelly, that Sicilian savage, told me that if I persisted on my seduction of Garboil, she'd pull out my hair. Some people, John. Those were her exact words, that peasant. But Garboil seemed unfulfilled, frightened. Don't get me wrong, I heard he was a very capable teacher. Where is he, anyway?"

"I don't know," Bacon said. "He left at the end of Spring semester last year. I switched his salary line in the budget and funneled the money into improving the old cultural ambiance at Frick."

Dover Terry fluttered his eyelashes, oohed, and tapped Bacon on the arm.

"Oh, you naughty boy. Tampering with the books, aren't you?"

"Well, now the Board's snooping around. There's this fella coming out here tomorrow to interview Garboil for a newspaper, but I know damn well he's from the Board. If they find out he's not here, they'll hit me with everything they've got. I don't think they like the way things are going, but they can't figure out how to remove me. Every couple of months I get a letter from one of them saying that some trustee from another university is interested in talking to me, but that he was told to stay away because I like Frick just fine. They're wise old birds and all they're trying to do is see if I'll nibble, take the offer and go someplace else. I don't want to go anywhere else. Frick University is my calling and I'm here to stay."

"I understand exactly how you feel, John. I threaten to resign every semester, but I'd be lost without a place like Frick, the freedom and love it offers an artist and academician. Do you want me to go over and see Garboil and tell him to come back? I don't think he'd let me in the door, but if you want me to, I'll go."

"No, Dover," Bacon said, patiently. "I don't know where he is. If I did, I'd call him myself or go see him."

"Oh, what then?"

"I want you to play Frank Garboil for this private detective," Bacon said.

"Oh, my goodness," Dover Terry said. "You do think highly of me. Do you think I can pull something like that off? I'd have to go out and find an old rumpled suit, some wingtip shoes, a black curly wig, get Ramon to do the makeup and take the paint off my nails."

"I think you can do it, Dover. You're a superb actor. One thing, though..."

"I know exactly what you're going to say, John."

"What?"

Dover Terry laughed.

"I must make sure I do not drop one bobby pin during the performance."

Bacon was puzzled.

"Bobby pin?"

"Oh, you know," Terry said. "I must be straight arrow, mucho macho, and all that."

It was Bacon's turn to laugh.

"Right."

"Oh, you straights are so weird, darling. Such a lot of pussy-footing."

"Well, can you do it?"

"With my eyes closed, darling," Dover Terry said, and then shook his shoulders coquettishly. "No, no, Dover," he said, admonishing himself. "Eyes open, no posturing, no fluttering of eyelashes. Pure masculinity." He steeled himself against the challenge and said: "Think Montgomery Clift, Dover."

"One last thing, Dover."

"What, John?"

"The earrings."

"No earrings?" Dover Terry said, putting Bacon on.

"No, Dover. Otherwise the dream of the free university will be a thing of the past. You understand, don't you."

"Of course, John. No earrings."

"Then you'll do it," Bacon said.

"Of course, John. I've played far more difficult roles than a turned-off Economics professor. When is this man coming?"

"Tomorrow at eleven. I'll talk with him for a while and then bring him down about twelve-thirty, one o'clock. Take one of those empty offices on the fourth level, next to the Physics labs. And not a word to anyone about this."

"You have my word, John," Dover Terry said, and tinkled out of the office.

John David Bacon sat down, closed his eyes and prayed again.

CHAPTER 20

In which we observe the protagonist start out his life as a Puerto Rican, continue his training, meet up with an Upper West-side liberal barracuda, who is taken in by his pose, and convince four neighborhood youths to take advantage of Open Admissions and attend college with him.

On Tuesday afternoon about two, Frank Garboil was deep into an article on grouse hunting in *Sports Illustrated* when Dr. Kopfeinlaufen and his staff entered the solarium. As usual the doctor was wearing his hockey outfit. This time, however, he had purchased a Ranger home jersey and appeared as ludicrous to Garboil as the first time he'd shown up in his room almost three months before.

"How do you like it?" Kopfeinlaufen said.

"I always felt better playing at home," Garboil answered.

"Good Armando," Kopfeinlaufen said. "We're playing at home then. The last session was great. Is this man Benny the Letter Thief still in operation?"

"I guess so," Garboil said.

"No matter. Let's begin. I will now go in the nets."

Kopfeinlaufen walked over to the net and stood in the crease, tapping his pads with the goalie stick. In the white Ranger jersey he looked like an overstuffed toy. He signalled Ingrid Konkruka to start the timer and tape recorder, told Helen Christianpath to take notes on Garboil's behavior and waved to Dr. Kohonduro to drop the puck. Garboil went on the describe how he'd gotten involved in going to school exactly as it had taken place.

He had continued his program of conditioning for the remainder of the summer, running in Riverside Park every morning and doing no less than an hour of stretching and isometric exercises. In the process he became acquainted with a number of dogs, getting to know which ones were vicious and which ones simply enjoyed loping along as he jogged. By the time August was halfway gone he was nut brown, his hair quite long and curling all about his head. His mustache had grown in beautifully and curled downward giving him a roguish, handsome look. His weight was down to 180 pounds and holding there and his body was full of new-found vitality. Once, after running in the park, he stopped to drink at a fountain and met a young woman, recently separated after ten years of marriage to a psychologist. She had just returned from an unfulfilling summer working on the California grape pickers' strike and could not stop talking about injustice and the system. Her two children were still up at the "Vineyard" with their father and that very same evening he found himself making love to the woman. There was no pressure to perform and he let himself be ravished by the young West End matron. The months of being alone and the doubts about his breakup with Joan left him and he released his desire in long spasms of pleasure which delighted Phyllis Abramowitz. They made love a few more times during the following week and then it was over as suddenly as it had begun.

"I don't know, Armando," she'd said. "It's like such a beautiful body thing, but like there's no communication between us. Like I really understand you being in Vietnam and all, but you have to talk about those things. There's a lot of anger and fear in you that's got to come out. I think it's probably better if we don't see each other again. It's like a beautiful thing, but I can't really get too involved." She laughed lightly and threw her long brown hair back, making her nipples stand out under her purple tie-dye tee shirt. "Like I'm going to be thirty-four in October and wow, I really dig you and wouldn't mind if you balled someone else once in a while, but I can't let myself get too hung up on a young guy like you and then you meet a nice Puerto Rican virgin."

"Oh, man," he said, imitating the accent of the group of young men he'd gotten to know at the 99th Street playground where he now played basketball. "I ain't into that jive with virgins and whatnot."

"Well, like, we can be friends because I really like you," she said. "We can talk whenever you feel like it, if I'm free."

"Sure, I understand."

"I think you ought to really think about going to school, like you said. If you need help the first few months, we can get together and I can tutor you. Anyway, I'm seeing this other person. I didn't want to tell you because I know where it's at with Latinos. Oh, wow, do I know. In California there was this dude that worked for Cesar and he couldn't even stand me talking to another man. He fainted on me one time, he got so angry. You know, like I really understand the whole cultural thing, but sometimes I have to be myself and have my own space and not be hung up on somebody else's trip. It's not like the whole thing with *machismo* or anything like that, but it gets very complicated and I usually split."

"I can dig it," Garboil said. He enjoyed talking like the others at the playground. It seemed freer and more to the point. "I know where you're coming from and it's cool."

"Yeah, well, good luck," she said, and walked down Broadway, her hips swaying beneath her long skirt.

The experience would've disappointed Garboil six months previously, but instead he shook his head and laughed at the absurdity of the conversation. The Latino thing. What the hell was she talking about? He shrugged his shoulders and was certain he didn't understand it anymore than Ray Cintron or Billy Perez, his new friends. When he told them about it, Billy Perez said: "Oh, man she's just one of those horny white bitches. Stick a dick in them and they don't even wanna talk to you in the street. In the dark they don't give a fuck what you look like, but in the street, you're just a spic." And the others would agree and say: "Ain't that the truth. Sheet! Who they be kiddin'! What they think, that their pussy don't smell like *bacalao*? Sheet." And there would be slapped fives and raucous laughter and a discussion of women and the pitfalls of getting too attached to a particular one. Was there a Latino thing? He didn't want to think about it.

But one thing was sure if there was a Latino thing, he had it. Phyllis Abramowitz had been convinced of his identity, and although he liked the way her body felt next to his, familiar like Joan's or Angela's, the fact that he'd been able to carry off his role as Armando Martinez was enough to get him over those times when he would long to be with her again.

By the time the first week in September rolled around, he was in high spirits. He had convinced Ray, Billy's one-eyed cousin, Pete, and Federico Pantoja — whom everyone called Big Papa and who was sure he could make the Jets or Giants if he received a tryout — that they ought to come up to the college and try to get in under the Open Admissions program.

"I mean, the thing's there," he explained to them. "If you wanna go in the Army or the Marines and get your butt shot at like I did, that's cool, but just because you're a spic don't mean you don't have brains."

"Yeah, but I was talking to Gloria's friend," said Ray, who was the most articulate of the four, "and she said it ain't nothing like high shcool. The thing is all serious and whatnot and nobody bothers you if you start messing up. She goes to Manhattan Community and if you start jiveassing, they let you slide and pretty soon you've slid out the door. They only give you like two or three tests a term and that's it. And a whole lot of reading. Man, she had like seventeen books for this one class. Sheet. But they don't even say nothing to you. That's some cold shit, man. At least in high school, the teachers would be bugging you and whatnot."

"Yeah," Garboil said, "but you didn't dig it, did you?"

"No," Ray said, "but you could tell they cared about what happened to you. Man, at Franklin there was this old guy, Mr.

Greenberg, and he started crying because we all failed this Algebra test. Everybody got an F, man. The highest mark was 16 and you could tell it hurt Mr. Greenberg. It wasn't no boo-hoo-hoo kinda thing, but he was crying. After that, all the guys studied and got good marks and there was no messing around and then the dude died and we got this young guy who was scared of everybody and we all went back to messing around."

"Yeah, but nobody's gonna care for you if you don't care for yourself," Garboil said. "That's the thing I learned in Nam, man. You look out for yourself, your piece and your main man, period."

"I don't know, man," Ray said. "It's a bitch cauze Gloria says all the dudes in college had academic programs in high school."

"No way," Garboil said. "If you graduated, then you can go to college. I graduated with a general diploma in high school. I already spoke to this counselor and he set me up with nice classes. I'm in this special program."

"SICK, right?" One-eyed Pete said.

"Not SICK, stupid," Ray said. "SEEK. Gloria's girlfriend told me about it. They pay you, right, Armando?"

"Yeah, they give you money for books and a little bread to live on. It's something like that."

"When you going up there again, Armando?" Big Papa asked.

"Monday," Garboil answered.

"Ama go up there with you," Big Papa said, lifting his 280 pounds off the stoop and flexing his enormous torso. "They got a football team?"

"They got club football," Garboil said.

"Ama go out for the mothafucka. Show them white boys where it's at."

"You gonna play hockey, Armando?" One-eyed Pete asked, squinting from behind his glasses.

"I'm gonna try out," Garboil said. "I don't know if I'll make it."

"Oh man, you'll make it," One-eyed Pete said. "I seen the way you play against those dudes at 33rd Street. Man, that's a bitch of a game. Can you dig Big Papa playing hockey. If he ever fell on a dude they'd give him a fifteen-minute penalty for squashing."

Big Papa grabbed Pete around the back of his neck and lifted him up in the air. Everyone laughed, including Big Papa, who loved the attention.

"Ama go out for basketball," said Billy Perez, a fair playground player, who had failed to make his high school team. "One of my boys from a hun-fifteen said New Amsterdam had a bad squad. He plays for Bronx Community."

So it was agreed. The following Monday they would all go up with their new friend, Armando, who had been to Vietnam and was together, and they wouuld fill out whatever papers they had to fill out and go to school, which all of them to a man hated. Billy Perez decided the issue when he finally admitted that: "The bitches don't even wanna talk to you unless you going to college. You make any scene and start rappin' to some biddy and the first thing she wants to know is if you're in college." Considering they were just hanging around with nothing to do and no prospects of employment, they had nothing to lose by going to college. The only one working was Big Papa, who helped his father at the *bodega*.

They said goodbye and agreed to meet later on that evening. It was Saturday and Ray's girlfriend, Gloria, had invited all of them to her house. Gloria's mother was having a birthday party for Gloria's sister, Miriam. Garboil said goodbye to his new friends, walked down the block and up to his apartment. He showered, read and napped for a couple of hours before he got up and changed. He wore bell-bottomed slacks, a light blue shirt with a flared collar and puffed out sleeves, which made him think of pirate movies, and his new pair of black platform shoes. He'd felt uneasy about buying and wearing the new clothes, but finally convinced himself they were necessary to complete the role he was about to play. It was no different than wearing hockey equipment for the first time. The shoes, at least. They gave him the same feeling as skates and made him taller than six feet.

At the party the girls eyed him with special interest. He found them unusual. They radiated sex and yet were poised, demure, each one aware of their sensuality, but conscious of how they must keep it in check. In their platform shoes, 1940's skirts and exaggerated dark lipstick and rouge, they looked like exotic tropical flowers. None of them was over twenty years of age and, although he was pleasant, he avoided them as much as possible.

He danced several times, talked to a few, but for the most part stayed away from the romantic aspect of the situation. One particular girl with long black hair and large eyes insisted on pursuing him. Her name was Marta and she had just turned sixteen. She tried isolating him, but her girlfriends always came over to join her. She finally quit chasing him when her boyfriend showed up.

A few minutes after eleven Garboil went to the hostess, who was in the kitchen talking to one of the other mothers, and excused himself.

"It was a nice party, Mrs. Quintana," he said. "Thank you."

"Ay, but don't go yet," said the woman. "It's early."

"*No puedo. Me tengo que levantar temprano*," he said, with a slight English accent which he'd found out was acceptable for first generation Puerto Ricans.

"That's right, mami," said Gloria, Ray's girlfriend. "He's in training and he's gotta get up early."

"Training?" said the woman. "¿Pa' qué?"

"Hockey," he said, with some embarrassment.

"Oh, hockey," said the woman, amazed. "Oh, sure, you get lots of rest."

When he was gone, Ray later told him, she had asked Gloria if he wasn't too big for the horses. "He's too big for hocky. But a nice boy. Very polite. Where's his family?"

"I told Gloria's mother they lived in the Bronx," Ray said.

"Actually, they're in P.R." Garboil said. "My father died and my mother went back to P.R. and bought a house. My sister's in Chicago. She married this dude. Some cowboy from out there."

"Yeah," Ray said. "I'd like to buy a house in P.R. after I get some bread. You know, for my moms and my pops."

"That's right," Garboil said. "I wish I could take care of my moms better. Maybe after I graduate I can get a good job and help her out. I useta send her bread when I was in the service."

"Maybe you'll be good enough to be a pro," Ray said. "Wouldn't that be something? A P.R. playing in the National Hockey League. That's all this city would need."

"I couldn't make the pros, man," Garboil said. "Them dudes are so good. There's this one dude who comes to the rink and he had a tryout. He's really outta sight and couldn't make it."

"Sure, but you can try, man," Ray said, admiringly. "That's what you told me about school, right?"

"Yeah, I guess you're right," Garboil said, and for the first time in more than two months began to realize part of the impact of his change in identity. He wanted to tell his friend Ray that everything going on in his life was a game, a thing that he had to do and that he wasn't being disrespectful to his people. He didn't say anything. There was too much trust in Ray's eyes. If he said anything, the trust, the hope that had developed in his life in the past couple of weeks, would be destroyed and the brightness replaced by pain.

"Ama go to all the games," Ray said. "Hey, that's really beautiful, all of us in school together."

"Yeah," Garboil said, halfheartedly. "Let's go see if the fellas are playing softball."

The entire weekend was a disaster. It rained and running in Riverside Park seemed totally useless. Only two days left and he'd be back in undergraduate school. As he ran, images of Joan kept recurring, conversations he'd had, their lovemaking, those first few days after the boys had been born, the love he once felt for her. One particular conversation disturbed him more than any other. As he walked back to his apartment in the rain, he tried deciphering its importance. It had taken place the day after he told her he had quit his job at Frick University and they'd fought and decided to split up. She'd been quite angry but then dissolved into long painful sobs.

"Please stop crying," he'd said, gently. "I'm sorry I've hurt you."

"Why did you want to get married in the first place?" she'd said, through her tears. "Was I some sort of trophy?"

"I don't know. I loved you, but in a way you were. I wanted to prove myself. You were the most beautiful girl on campus. The All-American beauty. I'd seen nothing but ugliness up to that time. Ugliness and harshness and I wanted you to take me in, to accept me. It happens to every immigrant."

"But you're not an immigrant."

He'd lit another cigarette and sipped his coffee, trying to find the words to explain the tangle of emotions in him.

"Listen to me, Joan," he'd said. "I've tried to explain it to you, but you don't seem to want to understand. I'm not the person you think I am and you're not who I thought you were. We've made each other into what we wanted to be and never were. I'm not some exotic creature, some wild Mongol or Eskimo, or whatever the hell I am, whatever hothouse hybrid. And if that's what I've been to you, I've hated it."

"I know," she'd said, bitterly. "You wanted to be an All-American boy, didn't you?"

"That's right. With parents and brothers and sisters and a home instead of bouncing from one place to the other, looking for I don't know what. And then I saw you and couldn't understand what I felt except the desire to have you."

"I was a thing, wasn't I? A little Barbie doll, a Playboy bunny. Maybe you're right. Maybe I represent America. But if I'm America, then we're in trouble," she'd said, sadly. "Really in trouble because I don't feel bountiful and clean and unfettered.

All I feel is a huge emptiness. I can't be what you think I am either.

"I know," he'd said. "And the saddest part is that I don't need it anymore. Something's happening to me. I can't explain it. It's like I'm someone else, like my feelings are not my own and there's somebody else inside of me."

And now he was somebody else and no further along in understanding himself. The rain now fell in a fine mist that had summer in it, except that in the air there was a threat of colder weather. He hurried on but the conversation with Joan would not leave him. They had continued to talk until Joey and Peter came home from school. After the boys arrived, she'd busied herself preparing their afternoon snack. Around five o'clock Garboil and the boys started out for the outdoor rink at the north end of Central Park. The boys were dressed in their practice outfits, all their protective equipment on, but instead of uniforms they wore street clothes.

He'd driven up the East River Drive, watching the river and talking about the boats to the boys. At 96th Street he came off the drive and headed uptown. Driving through the streets of East Harlem he recalled his days in the Lower East Side and his father's death. He read the signs, using his knowledge of college Spanish, but little of it made any sense. When he had to stop for a red light, he listened to the voices in the street and watched people's faces, looking for he knew not what.

His father's death had been sudden. He recalled being tucked in by him one night and waking up the next morning to find him lying on the kitchen floor, very pale and cold. Papa, papa wake up, please. Please wake up. There was a glass of tea and an evening copy of the *Daily Mirror* which Garboil had bought the previous night for his father. He was only ten years old and he tried to help his father get up, never once thinking that he was dead. And then it hit him and something very long and cold seemed to stab his heart and he froze for a moment before running out of the apartment.

He ran downstairs to the second floor and knocked on *mume* Lila's door. She was an old Jewish woman who lived alone and collected rags. When she came to the door, he couldn't speak and his chest hurt. He took her hand and pulled her out and she followed him upstairs where he pointed inside the apartment, but wouldn't go inside. The old woman went inside and then came out and held him to her.

"*Starben muz men*," she kept saying as she rocked him. We all must die, he later found out she'd been saying, although he wasn't sure how he'd remembered or whether he'd read the phrase and invented her and what she said.

He wouldn't go into the apartment and they came and carried his father away, but he couldn't look. He stayed with *mume* Lila for a few months until school was over and then went to live with Herman Krakauer's family, who knew his father and from whom he bought some of the damaged merchandise he sold at his stall. He felt like a beggar at their house and one day he never returned. He wandered the city, walking, stealing bread and hiding in hallways at night.

The two women had found him sleeping in their hallway. He was cold and sick and hadn't eaten anything for three days. They fed him, told him to take a bath and then showed him a bed. He slept a long time and, when he woke up, the house smelled sweet and he recalled the flowers at his mother's funeral. At first he thought he'd died and was in a coffin. He got up and looked around the apartment. There were small altars with statues in every room and candles and little dishes with coins and food on them. He wanted to run away from the strange house, but the women didn't ask any questions of him and they fed him and smiled their approval at everything he did, so he stayed.

They spoke Spanish, he thought now as he neared his apartment building. Then he'd spoken Spanish before he studied it in school and that's why it was so easy for him to pick it up now. All he was doing was recalling something he'd forgotten.

They'd urged him to call them *tia*. They were strange women. Spiritualists, and there were always people in the house to seek advice and prescriptions from *Tia*. Ursula and *Tia* Serena and the following year they'd moved up to the Bronx, to the old Irish neighborhood and he'd forgotten all of his Spanish, but it was now coming back. How strange that he should remember those things now. He ran up the stairs of his building, let himself into his apartment, showered, fixed himself some more of the stew which he'd cooked the day before and sat down to read. He spent the rest of the weekend indoors, reading and organizing his schedule for the school year, working desperately to budget every last cent so that he wouldn't have to worry about money in the middle of this mad thing which he must do.

CHAPTER 21

Wherein F. William Kolodny carries his investigative duties to Frick University in order to ascertain the veracity of the protagonist's claims, and in the process gets an eyeful regarding student life at that institution.

On Tuesday morning, February 2nd, F. William Kolodny drove out to see John David Bacon, president of Frick University, as they had agreed the previous day on the telephone. As he approached the grounds of the university, Kolodny stopped his car and stared in disbelief at the tall, ominous-looking structures rising out of the hill ahead. In the distance they resembled invaders from another planet. On this late winter morning, the sky lead-gray and the ground cold and desolate, he imagined himself on an expedition to a distant galaxy. He checked his directions once more, shook his head and drove on. Two hundred yards ahead, he saw the sign which welcomed visitors to Frick University.

Kolodny drove past the sign and up the paved driveway to the top of a small hill. Several young men and women in rather odd attire were waiting, huddled together as they smoked a marijuana cigarette. They made no attempt to hide their actions, even when Kolodny approached them to ask directions.

"Hey, Wayne," said a long-haired, bearded young man dressed in a Baltimore Orioles baseball uniform and an apron with Aunt Jemima embroidered on it. "This dude says he wants to see the president of Frick U. Tell him we do too."

They all laughed and Wayne — his head was shaved and had a tatoo target so that, should the North Vietnamese launch an aerial attack, they would have something to aim at — looked at Kolodny quite seriously.

"You see that flying saucer over there?" he said, pointing at the concrete bunker a hundred feet away. "That spaceship is due to depart in about two minutes. If you run real fast you can catch it. It's quite a trip."

Kolodny looked at the young man, hitched up his trousers and smiled malevolently.

"How would you like me to put my foot up your ass, wise guy?" he said.

"Oh, he's in the gay alliance, Wayney," said a young man with brown hair down to his buttocks and wearing a yellow bikini over a violet body stocking. "Don't be too hard on the poor dear, Wayney. He's probably one of those new New-Nazi professors John Porkchop is interviewing."

More laughter and pulling on the cigarette.

"Please don't listen to them, sir," said a young woman. She had on a Superman suit but seemed quite serious when she talked to Kolodny. "That thing's an elevator. Just press the button and when you get inside press M for the Main Level and it'll take you down."

Kolodny nodded, muttered an obscenity and walked away as the group broke into shrill laughter. He pushed the button and the metal doors opened. Half expecting a little green man to appear inside, he pressed M and with some anxiety awaited the results. The results were instantaneous and unexpected even for the now paranoid Kolodny. As soon as the doors closed, there was an explosion followed by a loud roaring noise like that of a jet engine. Above the noise a computer-like voice greeted him. GOOD — EVENING — LADIES — AND — GENTLEMEN — THIS — IS — YOUR — CAPTAIN — SPEAKING — WE — HAVE — JUST — DEPARTED — EARTH — ON — A — TOUR — OF — INTERGALACTIC — SPACE — WE — HOPE — YOU — ENJOY — YOUR — FLIGHT — OUR — DESTINATION —

— — INFINITEEEEEEEEEEEEEEEEEEE. The voice trailing down the decibel range to a bass hum. When the hum became more of a vibration than a sound, the lights in the elevator went out and the cylindrical structure was bathed in soft orange, purple and green lights which gyrated softly, synchronized to high-pitched electronic sounds and smells of burning wires.

Kolodny stiffened against the wall of the elevator, convinced that he had been kidnapped, if not by extraterrestrials, then by a cult of diabolical hippies who thrived on mind torture. In a few seconds, however, the lights, noise and smells had disappeared and the elevator had stopped. A soothing female voice announced his arrival on the Main Level and, with supermarket music in the background, the voice urged the passenger to purchase mind food at the nearest psychodeli. "A trip is only as good as its head," it said. "Nice day."

The doors opened and Kolodny found himself in the middle of a confusion of colors, sounds and smells once more. This time the stimuli attacking his senses were being produced by human beings. Along an immense corridor hundreds of students were involved in a variety of activities. The cement block walls had been garishly decorated with abstract murals and grafitti slogans of all sorts. The scene reminded Kolodny of a market place he'd once visited in Bangkok. The smell of burning incense was overpowering. One young man in a turban was playing a wooden recorder while sitting crosslegged on a bed of nails. In front of him there was a wicker picnic basket with a hole out of which there now protruded the head of a cobra. Off to the side five young men in the nude had formed a human pyramid. Further on a young woman dressed as a Volkswagen was trying to make her way through the crowd by beeping her horn, when she was stopped by a very large Black in a Cold Stream Guard uniform. The Cold Stream Guard began writing out a ticket, when all at once the young woman revved herself up and began speeding away. The Cold Stream Guard pulled out a pistol, took aim and shot the Volkswagen dead. Kolodny recoiled in horror at the sight. People rushed over to the scene and stood over the defunct car, saying in a chorus: "Oh no, oh no, oh no." And then they threw their heads back and said: "OH YES," and broke into singing "God Bless America" in whining voices so that they sounded like deranged Kate Smiths.

Kolodny walked quickly from the scene, making his way along the wall of the corridor. At the first open office, he stepped quickly inside and asked for the president of the college. He was directed further down the hall. As he continued walking, the crowd of students thinned out, but everywhere he looked he encountered something more shocking than before. Desperate to reach his destination, he nevertheless had to turn back and look into a classroom in which a couple was demonstrating the sexual act for a sex education class. What amazed him even more was the rather bored looks on the other students' faces. Further down the hall he encountered a thin coed walking an ocelot on a leash. The ocelot carried a sign around his neck which said: "My feminist friend may be skinny, but this feminist *loves* male chauvinist pigs." The girl looked at Kolodny with contempt and the ocelot made a growling noise. "Obsolete sexist," the girl said as she passed him. By the time he reached John Bacon's office, Kolodny was nauseous and his heart was beating in intermittent spasms.

He stepped into the outer office of the president's suite and closed the door. All the noise disappeared and he found himself in a comfortable, Madison-Avenue executive reception area.

"Good morning," said Mrs. Armstrong, the president's secretary. "You must be Mr. Wright of the *Daily News*. My name is Jacqueline Armstrong. President Bacon is waiting for you. Go right in, please."

Kolodny eyed Mrs. Armstrong's meager bosom, assigned her a price, thanked her and entered John Bacon's office. He felt no more at home in the wide, modernly furnished office, but at least it was something which he could hate with certainty.

Upon seeing Kolodny enter, John Bacon stood up from his desk and came forward to meet him.

"Good morning, Mr. Wright," he said. "Right on time. It's a pleasure to meet you. Always a pleasure, a real pleasure, to welcome a member of the press to ole Frick. Sit down and make yourself at home. I bet they keep you ole boys busy down there at the paper. How was your trip out here?"

Kolodny sat down and breathed a little more easily. John Bacon's voice reminded him of his old drill sergeant's. Its tones had down-to-earth honesty and at least the man wasn't a phony liberal, although he questioned his judgement in permitting the school to be turned into a human zoo.

"Mr. President," Kolodny said, opening his briefcase and pulling out several 8 x 10 photographs of Frank Garboil. "First off I'm going to ask you to identify this individual. The paper's interested in impostors, you know, people pretending to teach economics. We want to know whether this man has been here. He might've come to you looking for a job."

John Bacon took the photographs and looked through them. Kolodny watched him intently for signs that he knew the person in the picture. At first Bacon did not recognize Garboil. He then recalled hearing Angela Piscatelli telling another professor at the opening-of-the-year cocktail party about Garboil's plans. "It's the best thing that could've happened to him," she'd said. "He's going to let his hair and moustache grow and freak out in all kinds of beautiful ways." And then Bacon knew it was was Garboil in the photographs. He recognized the unmistakable confusion in his eyes and nodded several times to regain his composure.

"No, Mr. Wright," he said, quite seriously. "Afraid I've never seen the gentleman before, but that's sure a good lookin' hunk o' nurse you got there in the background. Is this man passing himself off as a professor?"

Kolodny ignored the remark about Ingrid Konkruka. All he needed was to start thinking about her and get an attack of the shakes by thinking about having a go at her breasts.

"Yeah, Mr. President, that's exactly what he was doing, but they finally caught up to him and got him locked up at an institution. You sure you've never seen him?"

"Sure as God made Kentucky-fried chicken, Mr. Wright," Bacon said.

Kolodny took the pictures back and returned them to the briefcase.

"Now, this here Professor Garboil," he said. "What approach does he use to teach this here Econonomics?"

"Oh, the traditional approach," Bacon said. "Very dramatic teacher but far from a radical economist. You'll get a chance to meet him as soon as we shoot down and grab a bite to eat. Why don't we do that now and then we'll go to his office. Ole Garboil feels his field's neglected and he's as happy as an ole hound who's treed a coon that you came all the way from the big city to interview him."

Kolodny dreaded going back out into the madness of the school, but steeled himself. He got up and followed John Bacon out of the office. Rather than going out the door Kolodny had entered, Bacon signaled Mrs. Armstrong, who pushed a button under her desk and a panel slid open behind her. Bacon invited Kolodny to step through and followed him. The panel closed behind them and a light came on. They were now in what appeared to be a tiny, rural railway station at which an equally small locomotive with several box cars was waiting. John Bacon sat atop the locomotive, pushed a switch and the engine made a whirring sound and started.

"Get on, Mr. Wright," Bacon said. "It's just a hoot and a holler to the finest southern kitchen north of the Mason-Dixon line."

Kolodny hesitated, but upon Bacon's further urging, sat atop one of the boxcars, found a place for his feet, and they began moving down the tracks and through a tunnel at about fifteen miles an hour. Every once in a while Bacon sounded the whistle on the engine and rang the bell. Three minutes later the locomotive came to a halt and Bacon was off and helping a rather amused F. William Kolodny up onto the platform of another small station atop which there was a sign announcing their arrival at BACONVILLE.

After Kolodny climbed up, Bacon pushed a button on the wall and the door of the station opened. They went through the door and were now in the vast kitchen of the Chapman Fuller mansion. A black woman in a red, polka-dotted kerchief dropped a pan when she head them enter.

"Doctor Bacon," she said. "Lawd God if you don't give us all a fright when yawl bust in here that way. Yawl should put a buzzer or a bell up somewhere to let folks know you comin'."

"I'm sorry, Philadelphia," Bacon said, smiling paternally at the woman. "That's a real fine suggestion. Is Miss Jo Ellen home yet?"

"Yassuh, she waitin' for you and the gentleman. Rufus be bringin' in the food in a minute. Yawl go in and leave a body tend to her chores."

John Bacon laughed and escorted Kolodny out of the kitchen. When they were gone, Philadelphia Morgan, mother to a nuclear physicist, two surgeons, three engineers and a bank president, muttered to herself: "Id-ridden, egomaniacal, sillyass cracker."

Bacon led Kolodny through a hall and into a large elegant dining room. Jo Ellen Bacon came forward to meet them.

"Jo Ellen," Bacon said, "this is Mr. Wright. He's a newspaperman from New York. Mr. Wright, this is my wife Jo Ellen Chestnut Bacon."

"Pleased to make your acquaintance, Mr. Wright," said Jo Ellen, extending her small, dainty hand.

Kolodny took Jo Ellen's hand an pumped it up and down several times.

"Likewise, Mrs. President," he said.

"Oh, that's sweet, Mr. Wright," squealed Jo Ellen. "Isn't that charming, John David?"

John David laughed and clapped Kolodny on the back.

Kolodny wanted to reach out and squeeze the perfect small breasts in front of him, president's wife or not.

"Did you say your name was Chestnuts?" Kolodny said when he was seated.

"Chestnut, Mr. Wright," said Jo Ellen. "From the Georgia Chestnuts. Why?"

"I was just curious," Kolodny said. "I useta know a guy in the service by the same name. He was a colored fella. I'm sure he wasn't related. He was from South Carolina."

"I see," said Jo Ellen, coldly. "My grandfather, Buford Lee Chestnut, lived in South Carolina for a time when he was a young man."

Kolodny nodded and listened to Jo Ellen go into her favorite topic.

"Now, Mr. Wright," she said, having forgiven Kolodny his faux pas. "You must tell my husband what a vital part jounalism plays in the education of a person. To this day there is no department of jounalism on the campus of Frick University. I think it's a perfect, intolerable disgrace. Why, a university without a jounalism department is like a young woman being courted by a young man without saying a word to her. Don't you agree, Mr. Wright?"

"That goes without saying, Mrs. President," said Kolodny, as he watched Jo Ellen's breasts rise and fall behind a possum pot pie.

"I'm glad you agree, Mr. Wright. You must convince John David of the need. Otherwise the educational experience, rather than a romance, can become a cheap, sordid and common affair."

When they were finished with lunch and were ready to leave, Jo Ellen looked at Kolodny with uncommon warmth, shook his hand, holding it for longer than usual before saying goodbye. Kolodny wanted to reach inside her dress and squeeze Jo Ellen until tears came into her eyes and she begged for more. His mind was adding up numbers. She could cost at least five hundred dollars. At the thought of the sum, Kolodny shuddered and shifted gears. No pleasure on the job.

They took the electric train back to Bacon's office and then his private elevator down several levels to the laboratories. There were a few students at this level. Most of them seemed to be actually working: measuring, mixing, boiling and looking through microscopes. John David Bacon smiled proudly at the activity. Although he would not even consider discussion of the issue, he was certain that most of the drugs on campus were manufactured or refined in these laboratories.

"Do you keep animals down here, Mr. President?" Kolodny asked.

"A few for experiments. Rabbits, guinea pigs and mice."

"No camels."

Bacon laughed.

"No, Mr. Wright. No camels," he said. "Why do you ask?"

"It smells like camel down here."

Bacon sniffed the air. Wright was right. There was a distinct dromedary aroma in the air. This confirmed the reports that "Rabbit" Lachien had finally gone into the drug business and was importing his own opium from the Near East and processing it in the Frick University labs. They continued walking and at the end of the corridor they came to a small office. John Bacon knocked and a voice invited them in.

Dover Terry was seated at a desk on which there was spread a large sheet of graph paper with small numbers written all over it. He was dressed in an ill-fitting three-piece suit, cordovan shoes and a black wig. He stood up, came forward, both hands extended and his blond lashes flickering. Kolodny thought he heard the tinkling of bells, but wrote it off as someone using beakers and test tubes in a lab.

"Dear, dear John Bacon, illustrious luminary of our educational community," Dover Terry said, taking both of Bacon's hands. "And this is, must be, Mr. Wright," he added, thinking to himself: If this is Mr. Right, I'm Greta Garbo or at least could be.

John Bacon introduced the two men to each other. Dover Terry extended his limp hand out to Kolodny, who took it and dropped it immediately. The hand was cold and clammy like that of a cadaver.

"Well, I guess I'll leave the two of you alone to get acquainted," Bacon said. "Mr. Wright most likely wants to do an in-depth interview, Professor Garboil. It doesn't serve any useful purpose for me to sit around and eavesdrop."

Kolodny was suddenly filled with fear at the suggestion that he be left alone with this flagrant homosexual. His mind was whirling and he felt dizzy. Somewhere, far away he kept hearing his mother calling to him: "Francine, Francine, you come in here right this minute and stop playing in that mud. Why, look at your hands and your new blouse." His mind felt like a large, pendulous breast growing heavier and heavier, threatening to come loose from its chest and fall, spilling into a thick mass of stickiness at his feet.

"Maybe you better hang around, Mr. President," Kolodny stammered. "This won't take very long."

"Well, as you wish, Mr. Wright," John Bacon said.

"Oh, dear," said Dover Terry. "I'm being so, so rude. Please sit down, John. Mr. Wright, you sit right here next to me so we can chat."

Terry pointed to a chair near the desk and Kolodny sat down. He took out a notebook from his briefcase and addressed the wall beyond Terry's flickering eye lashes.

"The thing I wanted to know," he said, "is if you think that teaching Economics leads students to thinking about riots and revolution."

Dover Terry laughed.

"Dear Mr. Wright," he said. "Nothing could be further from the truth. On the contrary. Economics is a rigid, musty discipline full of graphs, numbers and equations. By the time we're finished with a student, he's ready to enter our society as a full-fledged member. We try to desensitize the student, to strip him of all fantasy and help him deal with the reality of life in numerical terms. Everything must be measured, equated, weighed against reality."

"That's good," said Kolodny, although he understood little of what he heard. "That's what our readers want to know. Well, it's been nice meeting you, Professor Garboil."

Kolodny got up from his chair, put the notebook and pen away and then put his right hand in his pocket. John Bacon was puzzled by the man's actions, but quite pleased that he hadn't gone into more detail with Terry. Terry's knowledge of Economics was limited, to say the least, but then there was no telling when he would go rampaging into the wild on one of his monologues. Once during a faculty meeting, he had been asked to outline the curriculum of the Theater Arts Department for the coming semester and talked for the next hour and a half, part of which was a recitation of three of the *Canterbury Tales* in Old English. Fearing this, Bacon got up and escorted Kolodny out of the office.

"That was certainly a quick interview, Mr. Wright," he said, once they were out in the corridor.

"Well, he seems like a sincere man" Kolodny said, glad to have escaped he didn't know what. "Looks like he's got a lot of work in front of him and I didn't want to take up too much of his time. I have to visit twenty more colleges before the article is ready and that one quote is enough."

"Good then. I hope you'll come back and see us. You're always welcome here at Frick. Maybe one of these days you can come back and speak to our students about journalism. We have a newspaper on campus, but no one really has a grasp of some of the things which are probably like the back of your hand to a person of your experience. And if you think about it, put in a good word to your sports editor about our football team. We have no money right now, but maybe with a little publicity we can get started." It was so obvious Wright was a spy for the Board, and he hoped the information about the money reached them. If it didn't, then it was just as well, because it was very possible that the man was indeed from the newspaper and he might get someone else to come out and talk to him about the team and then he could go to the Board in earnest about the athletic budget. And then Bacon became apprehensive once more as Kolodny inquired about the things which he'd seen at the school.

"I never saw anything like it in my life," he said. "The Black guy shot the girl, and there was a girl walking around with a jaguar and these two kids were screwing in a classroom."

"It's all very harmless, Mr. Wright," Bacon said. "It's the new education. We figure once they get all of that infantile nonsense out of their system they'll become fine upstanding members of society. Most of what you saw is street theater, Mr. Wright. It's part of the required curriculum here at Frick. Every student must learn to act. It's therapeutic and comes in quite handy in the real world. All of us act in one way or the other."

Kolodny looked suspiciously at Bacon and thought for a moment. This son-of-a-bitch is a smart one. He sounds like a hillbilly, but he's a smart one, otherwise he wouldn't be president of the college. Maybe he's on to me. Better leave the whole thing alone. Obviously the guy at the hospital is not Garboil and that's that.

"Well, it looked pretty strange to me," he said, as they reached Bacon's office once more. "But you seem like an honest man, so I'll leave the running of the school to you. Mr. President, one more thing."

"Anything at all, Mr. Wright."

"Well, I was wondering if there was any other way out of here. I came down on one of your elevators and I have a feeling somebody's been tampering with it."

"Oh, that's right," Bacon said. "The electronic media people are conducting an experiment with the psychology department. You can use my private elevator."

"Thank you, Mr. President."

The two men shook hands and Kolodny left. Once outside, Kolodny got into his car, locked the door and sped back to the relative insanity of New York City. He drove to his apartment, went in, checked all the windows to make sure they were locked and without removing his clothes, got into bed, covered up his face and shivered with fright. It was the eyes. They were liquid, the blonde lashes enticing him to commit lewd acts. His head was pounding and, when he finally fell asleep, he dreamed he was making love to a dead fish with twelve breasts. He slept for the better part of the next sixteen hours, waking up only to check the door and the windows of his apartment.

The following day, Wednesday, he called Mike Christiansen at Special Investigations, and as a special favor, since he and Christiansen had once worked together, put in a request for a fingerprint check on Frank Garboil. He waited for the next two days, writing his report of the investigation and noting in his diary his impression of the castle of the evil East German spy, Baron Von Baconheim.

On Friday, February 5th, not having heard from Christiansen, he called him. "The prints are negative, Bill. The prints are not on record here or at the Bureau."

"It figures, Chris," Kolodny said. "I checked the guy out in person and he was there at the school, so the guy at the hospital's gotta be the spic kid, right?"

"It looks that way, Bill"

"Okay, Chris. Thanks a lot, buddy."

"Any time, Bill."

Kolodny hung up the phone, gathered up his information and headed for the hospital. He arrived just as Kopfeinlaufen was ordering his lunch. Kolodny dropped the file on the doctor's desk and gave a full account of the investigation.

"That's it, Doc," he said, summing up his findings. "It's all there. This professor Garboil works at Frick University. Teaches Economics. I had a long talk with him about his wife and kids and his work. The guy you got here is the real McCoy."

"Martinez," said Kopfeinlaufen, his mouth stuffed with cole slaw.

"What?"

"Martinez, not McCoy."

"Yeah, right," said Kolodny, cursing all foreigners under his breath.

"That's excellent, Mr. Kolodny," said Kopfeinlaufen, rubbing his hands together. "Excellent investigative work. Your money will be in the mail next week."

"One thing bothers me, Doc."

"Yes, Mr. Kolodny."

"This guy, Garboil, the professor. He's nuttier than a fruit cake. You understand, I know it's not part of my job and I didn't write it in the report, but I think he's a homo."

Kolodny whispered the last word and Kopfeinlaufen bolted from his seat.

"Aha," he said. "Of course, that explains the entire matter, Mr. Kolodny. If what you say is correct and every medical indication points to it, then our patient chose the identity of this person to punish himself for his lack of courage in combat. Please don't misunderstand me. There is absolutely no correlation between sexual preference and courage, but it appears that, in Puerto Rican culture and in Latin culture in general, this appears to be so. To be a homosexual is to be a coward, according to this young man's culture. I must congratulate you on your sensitivity, Mr. Kolodny. We do not want this information to get out. You were right not to include it in your report. Thank you very much."

"You're welcome, Doc," Kolodny said. "Any time you need me, be sure to call. I'm always available."

"I'll certainly keep you in mind, Mr. Kolodny. And if you're ever in need of help yourself, please feel free to contact me. I have very reasonable rates in my private practice."

"Nah, I'll be okay, doc. I'm not a nut case."

Kopfeinlaufen laughed. That's what you think, he thought.

F. William Kolodny breathed a sigh of relief. He headed out of the hospital, got into his car and drove north to the Cloisters where he was to meet Imogene Eberhardt dressed as a nun.

CHAPTER 22

In which the protagonist recounts the first days as college freshman Armando Martinez, his attempts to become a member of the college hockey team, and how he becomes involved with a young woman of true revolutionary spirit and strong hips.

The second Monday in September was a clear, late summer day. Frank Garboil met Ray Cintron, Billy Perez, One-eyed Pete and Big Papa on Columbus Avenue and they rode the bus up to New Amsterdam College for their first day of classes. The previous week had been a hectic one, scurrying back and forth up to the college, filling out forms, contacting the high schools to obtain records, walking about the campus and getting used to the new setting. For Garboil to get Armando Martinez' high school records proved to be a nightmare. He traveled to the South Bronx, contacted a friend by telling him he'd known Armando in Vietnam and found out where he'd gone to high school. At the high school he explained that Armando was coming home to go to college, showed them the acceptance letter and explained that he was Armando's cousin. He was able to obtain the transcript of Armando's high school work with relative ease. Armando had been an average student and had received a general diploma.

Garboil and his friends spent an entire day walking through every building on the campus. The excursion was as beneficial to Garboil as it was to them. Everywhere they went there was evidence that Puerto Ricans were part of the school. Signs in Spanish, faces, announcements left over from summer school inviting people to join the various clubs and societies. They even found Puerto Ricans working in some of the offices. This brought on a great deal of laughter from Big Papa, who was convinced that particular part of the university was doomed to failure. Ray and Billy didn't think that was so funny and it gave Garboil an opportunity to talk to them about self-worth, which made him feel twice as insincere as he already felt. The rest of the week was an unsettling experience for the four young men, as they had to discard pre-conceived notions about life on a college campus. Only Ray did not threaten to quit whenever a new problem came up. He remained introspective and reserved judgement, asking Garboil questions constantly.

For Garboil the problem of adjustment was different. He had to think of a strategy for conduct in his classes. He couldn't afford to be agressive, since the teacher would become suspicious. This would be especially true in the political economy class, a course he had taught. The course had been suggested by his counselor because it was being taught by "this heavy black brother from Harvard."

Most of the fears overcome, the group returned for its first day of class. They couldn't contain their enthusiasm as they rode the bus uptown and chattered about their dreams and future conquests. When they arrived on campus some fifteen minutes before nine, there was already a great deal of activity. Groups of students were talking animatedly and there appeared to be a constant stream of bodies moving up and down the walks and into the different buildings. Each of the friends eyed the groups suspiciously, looking for signs of friendship. By the time they reached their destination, they'd realized there weren't as many Puerto Ricans in attendance as they had originally thought. Garboil had enrolled in the same classes as the four and after each class tried to explain what was expected of them. Ray made some comments and asked further questions about the material they were to study. By the end of the first week he was participating fully in class discussions and, of the four, seemed to be adjusting the quickest to the fast pace of the school. The other three, however, although outwardly more sure of themselves, did not seem to understand the process and for the most part tried to conform to what they thought was good behavior, a requisite for acceptance at the school. Whenever a teacher made a joke which they did not understand and others laughed around them, they frowned disapprovingly and shook their heads.

For Garboil the first three weeks of school were truly uncomfortable. He couldn't get used to the idea of playing the role of the student. He resented being condescended to, sneered at, and snubbed by professors, lecturers and administrators. He wanted to break into a long, detailed lecture on economics systems, quoting massively from obscure works, analyzing difficult data, comparing, generalizing, theorizing to his heart's content until their mouths hung open and he had rendered them helpless and they begged his pardon and invited him to the faculty lounge for lunch. And yet there were rewards in being a student. He found himself enjoying simple things like 3.14 or the use and misuse of a comma. There were so many things one forgot which went into making up a teacher, small details which became part of a program and could be punched out in a microsecond, setting off millions of circuits and producing required answers.

By the end of his first month he was ready to actively begin dissenting in class, disrupting lectures with provocative questions, testing the teacher's knowledge much as he had done in his freshman year in college in California. But in questioning he also had to face a more important question. What had happened to him that had produced his eventual conformity? Had it been the intellectual discipline or simply a need to be accepted? At what point had it happened? Perhaps it had been Joan, her tanned body, athletic in a natural way, her mind made up, appearing flexible and yet convinced, righteous, driven by past generations of God-fearing people. No one had a right to force others to live in fear. The oppression only produced anger and then resentment and eventually the need for power and, in the case of Americans, a sublimation that produced a need to acquire property. He was certain that, had Joan been born a man, she would have been president of a large corporation by now. She would be no different than her brother, who never questioned anything but clung to his status and went ahead, using each difficulty as a challenge to his ascent to further success, power and further acquisition of property. He wondered, as he sat in his American History class at 2 p.m. on Wednesday, whether American presidents aspired simply to be remembered as the greatest president or if they ever imagined it as simply another step and entertained ideas about ruling the entire world. President of the galaxy, of the universe, of Time itself. "Get me the governor of Alpha Centauri, Mr. Haldeman."

The notion amused him. He smiled at his private joke while the lecturer prattled on about the Declaration of Independece. But the resentment of his role stayed with him. The day before his chagrin had been compounded by receiving a runaround from the Physical Education department when he inquired about the hockey team. No one knew when they were to have tryouts, who the coach was, where the team practiced, the number of games played or the names of the students on the team.

By Friday he had returned to the Physical Education offices several times without success. At noon, after attempting to find out once more about the hockey team, he sat down on a slope of lawn which overlooked the rest of the campus and beyond the Hudson River. The day was warm and cloudless with only a hint of fall in the air. His diet, the exercise, the weekly games during the summer and extra skating he'd done at great expense to his limited budget were being wasted. He felt himself winding up for a slap shot, which he had now mastered, and driving the puck straight into the mid-section of the president of the school. It was as if all the restrictions he had placed on himself to achieve his goal were being disregarded. But he didn't feel like quitting. Instead he felt the now familiar emotion roaring within him, as if his anger were flooding every part of his body with fight.

He had to stay with it; nothing would deter him. He recalled his previous lapses, his lack of concentration when he was younger and had the opportunity to excel and didn't know about that special something which drove the great. He knew of it now and there was no retreating from the knowledge. More than ever he had to maintain his pose as a student. He threw his head back, looked into the sky and let himself breathe deeply, relaxing, enjoying the Indian-summer weather and the smell of the grass. His eyes closed, he could hear the murmur of voices, the laughter, the steps on the concrete walks, not discerning any words, but allowing himself to absorb the atmosphere, the utter freedom of not having responsibility to anyone else except himself. He drifted off to sleep, dreaming of floating high above the city as a sky writing pilot: NOXZEMA, he wrote in his dream.

He hadn't been asleep for more than five minutes when he woke up suddenly. Sitting across from him was a young woman dressed in jeans, workman's boots, a blue pullover sweater and a green army field jacket. Her hair was jet black and it cascaded down her back like a gleaming ebony waterfall. He looked at her eyes, startled by their seriousness and intensity. She was smiling at him, but it wasn't an alluring, feminine smile, but more like one of deep understanding such as he had seen in Father McBride at Saint Luke's when Garboil had told the priest that he'd lost his mother when he was too young to recall. He bowed his head, as he had done then, taken aback by the silent openness.

"Hi, my name is Maritza Soto," the girl said. "I'm sorry if I woke you up. You're Armando Martinez, right?"

"That's okay," he said. "I was just resting."

"One of the brothers told me he was in your Political Economy class and you brought out some good points."

He sat up and shrugged his shoulders as she moved closer.

"I don't know, it was that the teacher was defending what the Russians did, and I had this friend when I was in Nam who went to college in Massachusetts. That's where he was from and he said that Stalin, to get some of his programs going, starved a whole bunch of people in the . . ." he stammered something, feigning embarrassment at not being able to pronounce the name correctly.

"The Ukraine," Maritza said, nodding.

"Right, that's the place. Maybe it was stupid of me, but I don't dig people not telling things where they're really at. What did you say your name was?"

"Maritza Soto."

"Right. How you doing, Maritza?"

"I'm okay," she said, and laughed. "That was a pretty heavy analysis. The reason I came over is because I'm the president of the college's chapter of United Front for Total Caribbean Independence. I mean, being president doesn't mean I tell people what to do. I just have more responsibility."

"I understand," he said. "But I'm not into political things. In Nam I almost got myself killed a couple of times, and for what? This government sent me over there and I still don't know why. Those people never did anything to me and, for all I know, if I had been walking down the street here in New York and met one of them, we would've maybe talked to each other. I don't mean talked, but maybe liked each other as friends. That happens sometimes even though you don't know the other person's language. I met some slopes over in Nam and liked them. They had funny ways like eating dogs and whatnot, but as people they were like anybody else. As a matter of fact, they reminded me of our people. You're Puerto Rican, right? I mean, I'm assuming."

"Yeah, I'm Puerto Rican through and through," she said. "And you?"

"Yeah, me too."

He had spoken the words exactly as he had heard them from one of his students at Frick, a bright Vietnam veteran who had been wounded badly. He bore no hatred for the Vietnamese and instead harbored deep resentment towards the United States for deceiving him. Recalling the gentleness of the young ex-soldier in describing his changed feelings toward the war made Garboil suddenly stop his pretense. It was a mockery of everything Jaime

Aragon had gone through. Worse yet, the price Armando Martinez, whoever he'd been, had paid. But he couldn't turn back. He'd always done so in the past, but not this time. The girl intrigued him. He was being recruited but there was something there which he recognized apart from the political. It was veiled in rhetoric and revolutionary sentiment, but it was there nevertheless. She nodded as she listened to him and when he was finished she'd made a point of using the name Puerto Rican and pronouncing it in Spanish.

"You were born here, right?" she said.

"Yeah, you?"

"Right. I didn't learn English until I went to kindergarten, though. But that was another trip altogether. Anyway, I thought, because you seemed interested, you might want to come to one of our meetings. It's mostly political education, but you'll get to meet some of the other brothers and sisters. There's a lot of issues you don't know about at New Amsterdam. A lot of racism, sexism and snobbism on the part of a whole lot of people on this campus. Mostly we rap about P.R."

"I'll come," he said, not knowing why, but drawn to Maritza. "I'm not too good in meetings so I don't promise you anything."

"That's cool. Most of us are still learning. Like nobody lectures. We just read, maybe from Marx or Lenin or Mao or Che and then discuss what it means in terms of Latin America and P.R. and the rest of the Caribbean. Once in a while we show a film from Cuba to raise funds. Nothing heavy. If there's some issue on campus we decide what our position is and try to figure out if there are any contradictions in our actions. Do you smoke?"

"You mean, *yelba*?"

She smiled at him and then laughed, showing small, white teeth.

"Yeah, grass."

"I use to, but I gave it up."

"That's good, because we try to discourage the brothers and sisters from using any drugs, even smoke. It's just another way for the man to distract us from our responsibilities. How come you gave it up?"

"Cauze of Nam. I saw people get so stoned they just went out and didn't care what happened. Most people were cool but once in a while somebody would flip out. I got scared it would happen to me on patrol. I use to smoke when I wasn't on duty. They had some heavy shit over there. Then when I got back over here, I saw little kids, ten and eleven years old, smoking and some of them even shooting dope and I got disgusted. Anyway I'm training."

"What for, football?"

Her eyes lit up and he was afraid that, like many of the radical women students he'd met, she would be rigidly against anyone who participated in sports, but her attitude appeared to be quite different.

"I play hockey," he said.

She let out a squeal and slapped her thigh.

"Oh, that's too much. That's really beautiful. Last year we had a lot of consciousness raising about this, because me and this brother, Orlando, ran track. I mean he ran track. I threw the javelin."

"Yeah?"

"Yeah, not too much distance but, good technique," she laughed. "Mostly it was to get the school to have more sports for women. There was a lot of criticism back and forth about what the F.U. stand should be. I kept telling them that all kinds of people were needed for the revolution. They kept telling me that sports were irrelevant to the revolution. The whole thing lasted about three months and some people even split over it. Like, finally, they gave in because Orlando brought out the things Cuba does around sports and how people who play sports have a role in teaching emulation rather than competition. That's really beautiful, but that's weird, because this place is funny about things like that. I mean, you skate and everything?"

"Yeah."

"Ice skates?"

"Yeah, ice skates," he laughed.

"Where did you learn?"

"Guess," he said.

"Wollman's?"

"Right. Did you ever go?"

"Yeah, when I was in junior high. Me and my girlfriend, Daisy, use to go and rent skates, but we never really got into it. It was mostly a goof, you know, to meet boys and get away from the house."

"Right."

"Maybe we even saw each other back then."

"Probably. Is Orlando your old man?"

She laughed and shook her head. She had moved closer to him and was now just another coed. Her demeanor as a revolutionary had dropped and she smiled more openly, throwing her head back and exposing her honey colored neck, smooth and rounded like the breast of a dove, he thought. He wanted to touch her, but it was too soon.

"Why do you ask?"

"I don't know," he said, and felt suddenly on the spot. "I guess it's the Latin thing to do. Make sure you're not stepping into somebody's else's turf."

She frowned and laughed uncomfortably.

"Do you think of women as turf?"

"Oh-oh, I did it," he said. "I take everything back. You're into Women's Lib and whatnot."

"Yeah, if you want to call it that. Does it bother you?"

"No way. You should've seen the slopes. . . I mean the Vietnamese women. They fought just as good as the men."

"Right," she said, excitedly. She appeared happy that she hadn't had to defend her position and returned to the easy, relaxed manner that attracted him to her. "Listen, that's a heavy sport," she said. "Are you going to play for the school?"

"I wanna try out but I can't get anything out of the people in the gym. It's like nobody knows anything about it."

"Yeah, I know," she said. "Last year was the first year and they say it's too expensive. I know this white brother who's into politics. I don't know his last name, but I think he's Irish. He played last year. He's a heavy dude. I mean, not heavy heavy, but considering all the hangups he grew up with, he understands what's happening. His parents wanted to send him to Holy Cross or Notre Dame, but he told them he wanted to go to New Amsterdam to become a teacher in the ghetto. He was starting to grow his hair long and wear raggedy clothes and they got shook up. He told them they should save their money and give part of it to the Church in the ghetto so that blacks and Puerto Ricans could have tutoring programs. They freaked out and he had to leave home. Anyway he plays hockey or at least played last year. If I see him, I'll tell him about you."

"Hey, thanks," he said.

"Listen, I have to go. I'm supposed to meet some people and start planning the first meeting. It's going to be next Friday about this time up on the fifth floor of the Klein Building. Room 517. Try to make it."

"I'll be there, but I don't promise anything."

"That's all right," she said, standing up. "I'll see you around."

She took two steps and then turned back around. She looked down at him and smiled.

"That was a nice rap, Armando," she said, a little embarrassed by what she considered her agressiveness. "Well, anyway, I'll see you around."

She had wanted to touch his face and take his fear away. There were no sexual feelings involved, but more of a wanting to soothe what she saw inside of him. She felt a sudden warmth low in her belly as she imagined fighting alongside of him, lying in the tall grass in the early morning, watching a column of soldiers as they approached their position somewhere in the mountains of the Island. It was to be their last day together and she could smell the grass and see the drops of moisture glistening like diamonds in the morning sun and could hear the birds at work and feel her breast pressing against the stock of an automatic weapon as she waited, wondering if she'd ever make love to him again or if she'd taken her pill or used deodorant and if it was anti-revolutionary to shop at Bloomingdale's or want to have a wedding dress whenever she got married.

Walking across the campus she knew he was her long-awaited companion, her mate, her friend. Destiny was no more than converging realities, thesis, antithesis, synthesis, one fading into the other until oneness occurred and maybe, if he was a pisces, that would help too. Why hadn't she asked him. Oh, he had to be a pisces. But she had to work slowly, gently like a mother caring for a young child, always tolerant and loving, without unrealistic demands on her part. She ran the rest of the way towards her destination, her hair flying behind her, as if she were being chased by a wide winged raven. Frank Garboil watched Maritza Soto until he lost sight of her. Only then did he realize how strongly she had affected him. He got up, picked up the bag containing his books and walked off campus and down the hill. The drabness of the neighborhood, the old buildings, the people sitting on their stoops, the garbage cans seemed to take on a new significance and he was torn once again by his loyalties.

He walked all the way to his apartment, nearly sixty blocks, observing people, thinking about Maritza Soto, her litheness and dedication, letting her play around in his mind, watching her make herself comfortable. She was more beautiful now that he was away from her and an unusual tenderness flowed from him. She reminded him of Joey. He didn't look like his mother, so blonde and Waspy. Joey was more like himself. There was something quite different about him. He tried recalling his own mother, but only saw Maritza's face and Joey's.

CHAPTER 23

In which we hear a recounting of the plan of feline cunning and its end result, observe the plot thicken as Inspector Mullvaney figures out the protagonist is a double agent and proceeds to set a trap for the United Front.

On Friday morning February 5th, at eleven o'clock, Deputy Chief Inspector Charles Mullvaney arrived at his office full of venom. The previous night had been a nightmare. He had to leave this type of detail to the younger men even if they did botch them up once in a while. He took off his suit jacket, draped it over the back of his chair and for the twentieth time since he'd gotten up that morning, smelled his hands to make sure the rancid smell of the fried food was gone. How could they touch the stuff, let alone eat it? You had to be starving to eat pig's entrails. It was probably gassed dog from the ASPCA and that was the reason the cats craved the stuff. Revenge. The word reverberated in the depths of Mullvaney's troubled soul.

Lieutenant Cahill walked into Mullvaney's office and greeted his beleaguered, hard-working boss.

"How did it go last night, Chief?" he asked, cheerfully.

"Beautiful, Cahill," answered Mullvaney, sarcastically. "Just beautiful." He slammed his fist down on the desk and roared. "How the hell do you think it went? Did you ever try to go into one of those greasy, hoochie-koochie places and ask for twenty-five dollars worth of the stuff? The bastards wanted to know if it was to go. When I told them it was, they got scared. They musta thought we were from the Health Department and wanted to analyze the stuff to see if it barked. He offered me ten dollars to give him a break. These people are not only stupid, they're cheap.

Who ever heard of trying to obtain a favor for ten dollars these days! I finally convinced him to sell me the garbage."

"How about the cats, Chief?" Cahill asked, sitting on the edge of the desk.

"Oh, the cats. I'm glad you asked. That's an altogether different story," Mullvaney said, getting up from his chair. "What's-his-name really distinguished himself. The Spanish kid. How long's he been with us?"

"You mean Ortiz?"

"Yeah, that's him. He should get a citation. You figure him growing up in that neighborhood, being that he's Spanish, he'd have enough brains in something as sensitive as this, right? Sure, he can gab a couple of junkies when he dresses up like an old lady. Junkies are dumb. These fucking cats were smart, Cahill."

"He's a good cop, Chief. He's been with us only six months and is still learning. A real go-getter."

"Sure he is," roared Mullvaney. "Bullshit. I get to the Con Edison truck with the three shopping bags of this filth and right away this Ortiz takes them from me. 'I got it, Chief,' he says. 'I'll do it. You got nothing to worry about.' Oh sure. A real go-getter. He went and got it all right. Went right into the back and pulled out this black thing. I asked him what the hell it was and he said the name and I asked him what the hell it was made out of and he told me it was pig's blood with rice stuffed into a pig's intestine. And then he started eating the filth. Oh God. It was enough to make a strong man throw up. And he's munching away and reassuring me that everything's under control."

"Yeah, he's like that," Cahill said, following Mullvaney to the window, where he stood contemplating a leap into eternity. "Ortiz always volunteers."

"Right! All we need is another hundred like him and the city would turn into a fucking zoo in a month. I want his ass transferred out of here. I don't care where you send him, but I don't want to see his face around here."

"What did he do, Chief?"

"The question should be, what didn't he do? For starters, he takes the three bags of this garbage, goes into the empty lot and empties the whole load in the middle. Here it is one in the morning, colder than a witch's tit and he dumps the crap out there. He couldn't pace himself, could he? No, not Speedy Gonzalez. We shoulda sold tickets, that's what we shoulda done. Sold tickets and announced it to the whole neighborhood. We could've probably gotten the Narco division to set up a heroin concession and busted half the junkies in Manhattan."

"What happened, Chief?"

"Some cop you are, Cahill! What the hell do you think happened! Inside of five minutes the place was crawling with those cats. It sounded like the Mormon Tabernacle Choir with a bad case of stomach cramps."

Cahill laughed and set his wide behind back up on the edge of the desk.

"Don't laugh, you dumb mick," Mullvaney said. "I'll have you waving at license plates again."

"I'm sorry, Chief," Cahill said, jumping up and standing at attention. "It's just that your sense of humor. . ."

"Sense of humor, my ass. I've heard some awful noises before, but this took it all. I've heard blood gurgling out of guy's throat when he's been shot, people screaming inside of burning buildings, whackos missing the net and splattering all over the sidewalk, but this was by far the most revolting single thing I have ever heard. And this Ortiz. All he can say is: 'Oh shit, I guess I blew it, huh?' That's all he can say."

"Did you leave then?" Cahill asked, sheepishly.

"Hell, no. How the hell are we gonna leave? The whole city's ready to explode. The Mayor wants to know when the next Mafia hit's gonna happen so he can be there to endear himself with the Eyetalian community and you want to know if we left? Hell, where the fuck would we go? Hell no, we didn't leave. We went inside the van and the vet is shaking and breathing hard like somebody's holding a gun to his head and he's about to have a heart attack and he wants to know if we have commissioner's approval or a court order."

"Did we?"

"Jesus, Mary and Joseph, Cahill, shut up for once."

"Well, what happened?"

"Okay, so I wait five minutes and then I step outside. Marconi and Fried are down in the manhole trying to keep from freezing, so I signal them with a flashlight, and Fried's the first one out, except that he's got his gun drawn. 'Sorry, Chief,' he says. 'Sorry, shit,' I says. 'Put that damned thing away and listen to me. You and Marconi get out here and get some of these gunny sacks and start grabbing these cats.' By now the fucking cats are roaring like lions in the zoo. You never heard anything like it. Deep roars down in their bellies. Marconi wants to know if he can shoot if he's forced to. I had to make him leave his gun in the van. We have about ten of these gunny sacks and the four of us, Ortiz, Marconi, Fried and yours truly go out into the yard in the middle of this roaring and yowling. There had to be a hundred of those goddamned cats out there."

"That many?"

"Maybe more, Cahill. Jesus it was awful. The doc, he stays in the truck and gives himself a shot of something. When we get to the yard the whole place smells like a leftover porkchop and all you can see is these little green eyes. The growlin's dying down but every once in a while one of the cats lets out one of those yowls and it's like death coming to get you."

"Did you get all of them?"

"How the hell do I know, dammit! Did you ever count black cats in the dark? We're just holding our own grabbing at the eyes and stuffing them in the bags. Five, six, seven of them to the bag and they're scratching and resisting like their fucking civil rights are being violated. The racket is unbelievable because every once in a while one of us would get bit or scratched so we're cursing and screaming and it's like a Chinese fire drill out there."

"Weren't you wearing gloves?"

"Of course we're wearing gloves, Cahill. You heard what Ramirez said, these are special kind of cats. They bit right through the gloves. Marconi got the worst of it. He was wearing a leather jacket and it looked like a bunch of Porto Ricans had gone at him with their knives. And in the middle of all this insanity, lights start coming on in the buildings around the empty lot and people begin screaming and throwing garbage and bottles to quiet the cats down. And not only bottles, but everything they could get their hands on. Fried got hit with one of those heavy wall crucifixes. It's a good thing he was wearing a hard hat or it woulda crushed his skull. The damned thing musta weighed ten pounds."

"What happened?"

"We finally managed to round up forty-two cats. All black. We had to keep them down in the sewer and bring them up one at a time. By this time they're so scared and wild that they're puking and pissing and crapping and full of grease. Jesus, Cahill, I thought I'd quit right there and then and the hell with the city. Let Lindsay deal with crime directly, if he's so fucking smart. The hell with it, know what I mean? Let the commies have the whole thing. Who cares. Kincaid, the vet, is operating a mile a minute. He knocks them out with a needle, cuts, puts the bug in under the skin, sews them up and out they go, except that it takes them about twenty minutes to come to and they're layed out all over the sidewalk. Some are stiff as a board, others are squirming and some are moaning like drunks after they've had too much Sterno. It was a fucking nightmare, Cahill."

"Didn't any of them freeze?" asked Cahill, whose hobby was taxidermy.

"No, none of them froze. After a while they just got up and wobbled away, meowing and carrying on like they'd lost their way home. That reminds me. Get me Kunkle up at the two-six. He's monitoring them."

Cahill left the office and the phone in Mullvaney's desk rang a few moments later.

"Mullvaney here," he growled into the phone. "What the hell's going on up there?"

Mullvaney listened for a few moments, nodded and then exploded.

"What the hell do you mean, you can only pick up thirty-seven cats and it's mostly street sounds." He listened some more, his brow wrinkled with worry and exploded again. "God-dammit, I don't give a fuck if one of them is hunting pigeons, Kunkle," he said, cutting into the report. "Locate the other five cats and get back to me with some positive intelligence or I'll have you out in the street making like a meter maid."

Mullvaney hung up the phone and shook his head, unable to contain his rage, but too exhausted from the ordeal to express it. He considered faking a heart attack but thought better of it. Why bother, the job was going to kill him soon. Cahill came back in sipping a Dr. Pepper.

"Chief, do you remember Kolodny?" he says.

"Who?" Mullvaney said, looking at his assistant, as if the younger man was kidding, and letting him know that he's in no mood for nonsense.

"Bill Kolodny, Chief. He retired a while back. He's working in the private sector now."

"Yeah, I remember. Are they collecting for his widow?"

"No, sir. He called up Christiansen and wanted a fingerprint check on somebody named Garboil. Says the whole thing's tied up with that Stuyvesant Hospital thing we've been workin' on. Chris wants to know what to tell him."

"When did Kolodny call?"

"Wednesday, Chief."

For the first time that morning Mullvaney forgot the previous night. He sensed an upcoming break and straightened up in his chair.

"Did Christiansen get the check back yet?"

"This morning, Chief. This guy in the hospital isn't Martinez. He's Garboil all right. The fingerprints check out. Army intelligence. He's a college professor. Kind of a jock in college. Taught at Frick University out on the island. No file at all on him. Clean as a whistle."

"And this guy in the hospital says he's not Martinez but Garboil, right?"

"That's what Kolodny told Christiansen."

Mullvaney thought for a moment and then the whole matter became crystal clear.

"Jesus, Mary and Joseph, Cahill. This guy's got a double cover. First he's a teacher in one place, then he's a student in another. I bet you a hundred to one he's with the Agency."

"Sure, Chief. He's with the Agency at the college in Long Island as a professor, right?"

"Right!"

"Then he takes on another cover as a student to get in with the United Front. He gets himself into the hospital, starts complaining that he's the other guy, which now gives him a triple cover, because nobody's gonna think he's working for the Agency and claiming he's someone else. He gets the Front involved, they make propaganda about his being held against his wishes and that he's being brainwashed and they try to score big in the media by trying to spring him."

"That's right, Cahill. You got it."

"Do you want me to call up the Agency and coordinate the operation from this end, Chief?"

Mullvaney laughed and shook his head.

"Cahill, Cahill," he said in a fatherly tone. "You manage two minutes of brilliant police work and in one question you revert back to your old self."

"What do you mean, Chief?" Cahill said, his feelings injured.

"What I mean is that the Central Intelligence Agency is not supposed to be working inside the U.S. If you call them up they'll disclaim the poor bastard and you've blown his cover. Somebody's managed to make him and he's just left there hanging."

"Yeah, Chief, you're right. I never thought of it like that."

"Now you see why I told you this was top priority. This is really big stuff if they got the Agency in on it, Cahill. The order probably came direct from the President."

"The thing I don't understand, Chief, is that if he's with the Agency, you'd think they'd stick up for him if he got into too much trouble."

"That's just the whole thing, Cahill. That's just how they work. Half of the trouble they're in is always part of the cover. The more trouble the deeper the cover. They do terrific work but half of those guys are nuts. Most of the time they don't even know who they're working for. They got more codes than Morse. One guy I heard about had his mother for a superior and never knew it until he retired."

"Hey, that's pretty good, Chief. Mother Superior."

"Leave the Church out of this, Cahill. We got enough trouble."

"What do we do?"

"We know for sure that the Front's gonna try and get this character out of Stuyvesant on the 9th. That's Tuesday. How they're gonna do this is the big question. For all we know what the Agency's trying to do is set them up for us. Have you heard anything from the Bureau?"

"Nothing, Chief."

"Then it's an Agency set up, otherwise they'd a called us by now. Who's in charge up at Stuyvesant? Whoever he is, he's gonna have a mess on his hands. I have to get a hold of him and let him know enough so that we can catch these creeps red-handed. Get Ramirez in here."

"What do I tell Christiansen?"

"About what?"

"Kolodny, Chief. The fingerprints Kolodny wanted Chris to check out."

"Right, Cahill. Good thinking. Tell Christiansen to tell Kolodny the fingerprints are negative. They're not Garboil's, so the guy in the hospital couldn't be Garboil. We can't have the private sector involved in this. It's too touchy. Tell Chris that and get Ramirez in here."

Cahill left Mullvaney's office and two minutes later Pete Ramirez walked in and sat down next to Mullvaney's desk. He lit one of his Virginia Slims and greeted Mullvaney in his clipped, polished accent. Mullvaney was reminded of Roger Moore playing The Saint.

"Long night last night, Chief?" Ramirez said, blowing smoke through his nostrils.

"I'm all right now, Pete," Mullvaney said, more in control now that the pieces in the puzzle were coming together. "Who's in charge of the Martinez case at Stuyvensant Hospital?"

Ramirez thought for a moment and then spoke.

"Kopfeinlaufen, Dieter. Age, sixty-two. Graduated Friedrich Wilhelm Medical School, Vienna, 1934. Psychiatry. London, 1938-1947. Member Royal Academy of Medicine. Arrived in the United States 1954. At Stuyvesant Hospital since 1962. Extensive private practice. Address Sutton Place. Homes in Palm Springs; Martha's Vineyard; Geneva, Switzerland; and Palma de Majorca. Detests J.S. Bach. Married to Uta Bilgehaus. No children. Freudian with Jungian and Reichian trimmings. Famous for isolating vulpophrenia disorder in middle-aged women."

"That's impressive, Pete. But what kind of guy is he?"

"Oh, he's a little eccentric. Works on the theory that his patients are affected by his diagnosis. Once he makes up his mind that a patient has an ailment, the patient, whether he's suffering from the ailment or not, has no choice but to get better. If the patient doesn't have the ailment, the doctor urges him or her to acquire the symptoms. Makes the patient much easier to cure. The ones who have real illnesses, he treats the same way. He ignores the real symptoms, gets them to acquire new ones and cures those. The patient becomes involved in combatting the bogus illness, sees progress and forgets the real ones. Seems to work from everything I've read."

"In other words," said Mullvaney. "A pretty reasonable guy."

"Yes, I imagine so."

"Good , I'm going up there this afternoon. You're welcome to come and get a personal check on him. First-hand intelligence."

"I'm afraid I can't do that, Chief," Ramirez said, putting out his cigarette and rising slowly from his chair. "Hospitals are one place I really have to stay away from. All I have to do is get a whiff of ether and I cry uncontrollably for weeks."

"I'm sorry to hear that, Pete."

"That's okay, Chief. Thanks anyway. Maybe next time."

Ramirez went out of the office and Mullvaney put on his jacket and prepared himself to go and see Dr. Kopfeinlaufen.

CHAPTER 24

In which we see the protagonist triumph in his quest to make his college hockey team and become involved with Maritza Soto, and we are treated to some obligatory love scenes.

During the month of October, Frank Garboil attended the weekly meetings of the United Front. Maritza Soto was all business at the meetings and he rarely saw her for more than a few minutes afterwards. Always involved in further planning or rushing off to another meeting, she did manage to introduce him to Kevin O'Brien, a slight, freckle-faced, long-haired redhead who sported a drooping moustache and spoke so slowly that Garboil at first thought he was an addict. Although bothered by Maritza's apparent avoidance of any further contact with him, Garboil was thankful that she had finally put him in contact with O'Brien. On their first meeting, O'Brien told him the schedule of tryouts, asked him what position he played, and the two agreed to meet and play at a late night game at the indoor rink at 33rd Street. Kevin O'Brien, despite his small size, was a superb skater and stick handler. He and Garboil played well together and their friendship was instantaneous.

"I'm sure the coach can use you," said O'Brien after the game. "He's a funny guy. Never coached hockey before. Used to coach football in Michigan somewhere and he's got a lot of funny ideas about the game. We got killed listening to him so we just nod our heads and go out and use what we learned from other coaches. As long as we win, he doesn't care. At the end of last season, we gave him a couple of books. One of them was by the coach of the Russian Olympic team. He said he wouldn't read anything written by a commie. But I bet you he read it and we'll be using some of the plays this year."

The tryouts for the team were held at the Bronx Ice Skating Place at eleven o'clock at night. Fifty aspirants plus eleven returning players showed up. Several of the students wore figure skates and Coach Malinowski cut them after the first tryout. The workouts were pure torture. As hard as Garboil had worked in preparation for the moment, he found himself aching after each skate. He managed to stay in contention down to the final cut. There was great competition for the remaining nine spots on the team, but it was a question of how hard he could drive himself. Several young men could skate quite well, but couldn't handle the vicious hitting in the scrimmages. Others could hit, but couldn't skate, and still others could hit and skate passably, but couldn't handle the puck. Most of the ones who would eventually make the team had some experience playing in the Greater New York City Ice Hockey League. Most of these had been skating since they were nine and ten and knew the fundamentals of the game well.

Of all the players still competing, he was the tallest. Among the eleven returning playhers, he ranked among the biggest, although not the heaviest, that distinction being reserved for Moose Martorelli, the star defenseman, a robust, baby-faced Italian with the checking instincts of a radar-equipped water buffalo. Typical dialogue between Moose and the coach would go something like this: "Good check, Moose," the coach would say as Martorelli came off the ice. "Aw, I had him lined up when he left the locker room, Coach." Moose was the captain of the team, the one who initiated and terminated disputes on the ice whenever opposing players became too aggressive. During the last few days of the tryouts, Frank Garboil was far ahead of the remaining aspirants. And yet doubts arose about what would take place if he indeed made the team. Should he simply disappear, having accomplished his goal? Or should he go a step further and find out how he'd do under actual game conditions?

When the final list of players who were to report to team practices appeared and his name was on it, Garboil had a feeling of elation like none he'd ever felt. After considering the implications of the supreme gamble he'd taken, he quietly assessed the situation and considered his mission accomplished, his wishes fulfilled. He had made the team and that was all he had been after. Five minutes later, however, the feeling of satisfaction had turned to numbness, somehow as if he'd been given a piece of bad news. His mind suddenly in a state of confusion, he walked out of the Physical Education building.

It was late October and a raw wind was blowing in from the Hudson River. He pulled his wool hat down over his ears, buttoned up his army parka, put his head down and began walking across the campus. It was his last time there and he would now forget the obsession. In a few days the madness of the past six months would drain from him and he could start thinking once again about what he was to do. Perhaps he would return to Frick University as John Bacon had suggested. His brief experience as a student had left him with a clearer notion of what a teacher's job truly entailed. Ray, Billy, One-eyed Pete and Big Papa, each in a different way, had become used to the idea of a fairly unstructured way of existence on the campus and each had found a different crowd of friends. Ray had learned to play chess and spent considerable time at the game. Billy had joined one of the intramural basketball teams, One-eyed Pete was captivated by a large-busted blonde girl with a similar affliction to her eyes and spent most of his time with her, and Big Papa had broken a tackle's ribs in a blocking drill and became the darling of the coach. He often saw them in the neighborhood, but each one had spun away from the other. Although they still got together to talk and play basketball in the playground, they were maturing in their own ways. Only Ray continued to seek him out, talking endlessly about the books he was reading and the new ideas to which he was constantly exposed. He seemed interested in thinking for the sake of thinking, his mind slowly acquiring a certain sharpness which, when well-honed, would serve him well in whatever he wanted to do.

As he walked, Frank Garboil began to feel the numbness disappear and the sense of satisfaction once again take its place. He had done more than make a hockey team. He had inspired four other people to excel and that was far more important. He couldn't leave now. At the gate to the school he heard someone calling him. He turned around and saw Maritza running to him. When she reached him she was out of breath and her cheeks rose-red beneath her honey-colored skin.

"I just saw Kevin," she gasped. "You made it."

"Yeah," he said, beaming, the muscles on his jaw hurting from the width of his smile. "I just came from the gym, but I didn't see him."

"He must've been there before you," she said. "Congratulations."

"Thanks," he said.

And then she threw her arms around him and kissed his cheek. He put his arms around her, holding her awkwardly at first and then feeling her yielding, adjusting the contours of her body to his. She rested her head on his chest and looked up at him for the briefest of moments before breaking away. She shook her head, not quite believing that she'd allowed herself the emotional outpouring. He wanted to touch the full lips, dry now from the cold.

"Let's celebrate," she said. "Let's have a real bourgeois celebration. You want to? It won't hurt. Once in a while you have to get away from the whole scene and go out and see the world for what it is."

"All right," he said. "Where shall we go?"

And while she was telling him that they'd go to the Santurce on 116th Street in El Barrio, he felt foolish once more. Where shall we go? he'd said. The correct words should've been: Where we gonna go? Something like that. What was he trying to do? Give it all away. If he was going to tell her the truth, he should do it in a straightforward manner rather than by hinting. But he had to do it. He had to tell her. But what about the others? Ray would be so disappointed. He couldn't.

"We'll order a real Puerto Rican dinner," Maritza was prattling happily on. "I'll even put on a dress and everything. I have a little bread and we'll split the check, okay?"

"Sure."

"I live about three blocks from there and you can come and get me at my house, or I'll meet you at the restaurant."

"No, I'll come and get you."

About eight that evening Frank Garboil traveled to the east side of Manhattan, to El Barrio, Spanish Harlem, East Harlem, the capital of the Puerto Rican community in the United States; he'd heard people call the place all those names and he'd driven through it a number of times on his way to the outdoor skating rink at the north end of Central Park and now didn't understand where the pride of the people lay; it was a rundown neighborhood, a ghetto full of abandoned buildings and empty lots and garish signs and storefront churches. Full of apprehension about going to the neighborhood and his date with Maritza Soto, he rode the crosstown bus, his mind playing tricks on him, deciding that he was somehow Puerto Rican and this was his destiny. On the elevator to the tenth floor of the housing project, he almost turned back and gave up on the entire charade. But he went on and knocked on the door of the apartment and an old woman answered it and smiled and said she had been expecting him.

"*Entra, entra, mi'jito*," she said, inviting him inside the apartment. "*Maritza está casi redi. Yo soy l'abuela de ella. Tú estáh en la escuela también, ¿beldá*?

"*Sí, primel año*," he said, avoiding the pronunciation of the r and substituting an l, which made the language sound so much softer, so much more musical, so that he couldn't understand all the disparaging remarks always made about the way Puerto Ricans spoke Spanish. "*Mi nombre eh Almando.*"

"Sí, yo sé como te llamas y que ereh veterano. Maritza me lo contó toíto," she said, and chuckled as she explained that Maritza had told her everything.

He had some difficulty following the Spanish, but managed to deduce that Maritza had painted a most impressive picture of him. She knew he was a veteran and played hockey, which she watched on television and liked. This made him laugh and she went on to say that in her youth she had been an excellent runner and wished she had been a man. He hoped Maritza hadn't told her grandmother that they had kissed and then wondered why he was considering something like that, as if he were a teenage kid out on his first date. She asked him if he wanted some coffee.

"No, gracias," he answered, desperately trying to aspirate the s. "*Vamos a la ciento diez y seis a comel. Maybe otro tiempo,*" he added, making a mistake intolerable even to himself, although he'd heard it made by students who had grown up in New York and were just beginning to learn their parents' language in college. So the old woman laughed at his translation of "some other time," but it wasn't derisive laughter, but rather filled with understanding and compassion.

She asked him what town his parents were from and the question stumped him. He tried to remember some of the towns on the island where his parents could have lived and couldn't, so he recalled his friend at Frick's, the novelist and short story writer who'd said all his characters were from a fictional town called Cacimar, so he said it, and she looked puzzled and said that wasn't a town, so it must be some kind of barrio of a town or maybe a mountain community. He stood there smiling and nodding his head as she explained, but didn't get too far, because Maritza came out of the bedroom and he couldn't think about anything else except how beautiful she looked.

She had on a long black dress and stockings and her platform shoes made her look a head taller. She wore no makeup that he could see, but her face had a softness and beauty he had not noticed before.

"How are you?" she said, touching his sleeve. "*Abuela, te presento a Armando Martinez*," she said, turning to her grandmother and pronouncing everything as she'd been taught in school. Her grandmother said she'd already met him and they had talked and then showed them out of the apartment, urging them to enjoy themselves. Out in the hall Garboil helped Maritza with her maxi-coat. In the elevator she took his hand and held it tight.

"I'm so happy," she said. "I haven't been out on a real date since I first went to college three years ago." He asked her if she'd really told her grandmother everything about him. "Sure," she said. "She's a groovy lady."

"You told her you kissed me?" he said.

"Yeah. What's wrong with that?"

"Isn't she worried?"

"Why should she be?" she seemed surprised by his question. "She knows I wouldn't have done it unless I meant it."

The response flattered him, although he didn't understand all of its significance.

"What do you mean?"

"Exactly what I said," she answered. "I don't do anything unless I feel it deeply and I felt like kissing you and hugging you. I'll tell you more in the restaurant."

They walked the three blocks to the Santurce and went in. As soon as they entered there was a waiter at their side suggesting several tables in the softly lit dining room. The restaurant had a quiet atmosphere and elegance which clashed with other Puerto Rican restaurants he'd visited in the city. He felt ill-at-ease, but didn't know why, only that here was a middle-class restaurant which probably sold the same food at higher prices, but, like all good restaurants, took more care in the preparation and the rituals attending the serving of the meal. They sat down and he watched the well-dressed people around them talking quietly. When the waiter came over with the menu, Garboil and Maritza studied it for several minutes before he decided she should pick out the meal.

"It was your idea and I've never been in a place like this," he said.

"Where did you grow up?" she said.

"The Lower East Side," he said.

"Listen, kid, I only came here once when my mother came to visit us and that was about six years ago. Let's order *arroz con jueyes*, a nice salad and some *tostones*."

"Sounds okay to me," he said, wondering about the *jueyes*. He'd never heard the word before. He pointed to the places on the menu and the waiter spoke to him in English, asking him if they wanted anything to drink. He looked at Maritza.

"Beer," she said.

"Two bottles of beer," he said.

"Miller, Bud, Shaeffer and Rheingold," the waiter said.

"*¿Y Corona, no hay*?" Maritza asked.

"*Sí, cómo no*," the waiter said, switching his demeanor. "*Dos Coronas*," he said and rushed away.

Garboil wanted to know why the waiter had seemed so cordial all of a sudden.

"Oh, he probably figured we were New York Ricans and didn't want to treat us like we were from the Island. They're very careful and polite in a place like this. The manager has an MBA from Brooklyn College or someplace. He's a reactionary pig. I don't want to get into that right now. I want to forget the struggle for one day and just be myself."

When the meal came, Garboil was overwhelmed by the large steaming plate of yellow rice, topped by strips of pimento and the four large crabs placed around the rice. The meal was superbly prepared and it took them the better part of two hours to finish. Maritza ate with great relish, attacking the crab legs with uninhibited ferocity. She shunned the nutcracker they'd brought to the table, used her small teeth and then licked her fingers. She laughed often and told stories about her mother, who had remarried and owned a string of beauty parlors on the Island.

"She pays for our apartment and for my education. I don't mean tuition, because that's free, but other things. Books, trips back to P.R. and clothes. She wanted me to go to Radcliffe or Sarah Lawrence and I applied and made it, but didn't want to go. She'd married a *yanqui* and it was his idea. He owns a company down there. She wanted me to live with her after she got married, but my father didn't approve so they reached a compromise and I stayed with grandma. I didn't want to go live with her anyway. She's super-conservative and it's a drag."

"Why doesn't your grandmother live in P.R.?" he asked.

"She doesn't like it."

"That's strange. All the old folks want to go back down there."

"That's not true. She doesn't. She says it doesn't make any difference. She says the *gringos* own the Island, so she would just as soon stay up here and take up space on their land. She's a very sharp woman. Very revolutionary. She remembers the invasion in 1898 when the U.S. landed at Guánica. She remembers the people opposing them. Her family knew Cesáreo Martínez, who was one of the leaders. Maybe you're related to him. He was a very brave dude."

"That's a pretty common name, Martínez," he said, but was struck by the coincidence and remembered his friend at Frick. He'd said his great-grandfather was Cesáreo Martínez. 'My grandmother, Suncha Yunqué's father,' he'd said. So he told her he had a friend, a writer, who was the great-grandson of Cesáreo Martínez.

"Oh, wow," she said. "That's really hip. Maybe you can introduce him to me sometimes."

"I don't know," he said. "I haven't seen him for quite a while and he's pretty strict about his privacy and hard to get along with sometimes."

"What's his name?"

"Vega."

"Never heard of him."

"I know, nobody has. He's really strange and he's got a book where all the people are not from P.R., but from another planet."

"Like Kurt Vonnegut?"

"Who?" he said, but knew that his friend didn't like his book compared to Vonnegut and had sworn that he'd written it before he'd read Vonnegut. "Is he a writer?"

"Never mind," she said, smiling at him, probably wishing she hadn't said anything, fearing that to talk about subjects he wasn't familiar with would make him ill at ease. "But that's pretty hip that you have the same last name because you're a pretty brave dude too. You went to war, didn't you?"

"Yeah," he said, sheepishly as he watched her face grow more serious. "That seems like a long time ago."

"Well, it's valuable experience and maybe some time you can use it for better purposes."

"I hope not," he said.

"You wouldn't fight to liberate P.R.?"

"That's different," he said, and watched her face soften.

She smiled and took his hand, seeing him by her side, marching through the rain forest, camouflaged in fatigues, weapons slung across their backs, but not holding hands or thinking about kissing and touching like she was now.

"In time," she said, softly. "And then we can be free and the children will be born free, something which has never happened in Puerto Rico."

The Christmas season was more than a month away, but the juke-box, hidden behind a potted plant, was already playing typical mountain music, the *tiples* and *cuatros* and *guiros* tripping complexly across a melody impossible to play unless one felt it in his heart. The singers sang the folk songs effortlessly, but with great emotion, one tune sassy and full of innuendo, the next mournful, and still the next like a prayer, relating the birth of the child Jesus.

"Do you like the music?" she asked. "I mean like it's what reactionaries call hick music, but it's really honest. That and the *plena* are the music of the people. Do you like it?"

He said he did and watched her and saw the same longing he'd seen in his writer friend, who couldn't teach anymore because he felt he had been bought off. His friend had played the music for him at his apartment on the Upper West Side and talked about his work. Maybe he ought to go and see him and talk this whole thing out. How would he feel that he was impersonating a Puerto Rican? The subject bothered him. Soon he'd have to tell Maritza the truth. If he told no one else, he'd have to tell her about his true identity.

"I'm glad you like it," she said, and then looked at him. "I like you so much, Armando," she said.

He had never seen anyone, man, woman or child, so open. He thought of Joey again, the sad eyes and the wanting of his small heart, not knowing either where he came from. But he was gone now, in more ways than one. He'd crossed over and would never again wonder. He wanted to tell her he felt the same way, that he thought she was the most beautiful woman he'd ever seen, but it wouldn't come out right with the lie between them.

"Do you know what I was dreaming about that first day? I was dreaming about writing in the sky, like those planes they have. And I was up there looping and writing Noxzema and when I got down to Earth, there would be this blonde who does the Joe Namath commercials waiting for me. And then you were there and you were the most beautiful woman I'd ever seen and I wanted to touch your throat when you laughed. It was like a small bird."

Tears formed at the corners of Maritza's eyes and hung there like crystal pendants growing larger and flickering with each movement of her long lashes. The evening was complete for her.

She sensed his love and was aware that he couldn't speak it. "I want to stay with you tonight," she said.

"All right," he answered, his voice thick with wanting her.

They ordered papaya, white cheese and black coffee and when they were finished, pooled their money together, paid the check and left.

The trip to his apartment was made in complete silence as they rode the bus across town. When they got off the bus at 106th Street and Broadway she took his arm and shivered against him.

"Are you cold?" he asked.

"No," she said, "just a little shook by the whole thing tonight."

"We can go back if you want."

"No, it'll happen eventually. Why not now while I'm feeling this way."

"Are you a . . ."

She understood immediately and shook her head.

"No, not really."

"What do you mean?"

"Only in my heart," she said. "Do you understand?"

"Yes, I think so."

Once in the apartment, they clung to each other, not bothering to remove their coats and he kissed her face softly, barely touching her lips. They seemed so unbelievably soft to his own. The spices from the meal were sweet in her mouth once he kissed her fully and her arms held him tight, making him feel smaller. Eventually they undressed each other and he let himself explore her body with his, enjoying every touch, feeling it without fear in his heart. There were no comparisons made. Instead, he was absorbed by her being, and she by his, not talking either one of them but breathing out of helplessness. When they finally found each other, there was no violent movement but an intensity which began in his heart and pulled sharply downward, flooding him with sadness. He did not feel the usual climax a man experiences, because he found himself crying uncontrollably.

Oh, my baby, my baby, he heard her whispering to him over and over from what seemed a great distance. My brave baby, my little soldier baby, my warrior baby up in the rain forest fighting with me, oh, oh, oh up in El Yunque, and in La Silla de Guillarte, and in la Represa de Comerío, and down in El Río Grande de Loíza, and in La Playa de Ponce, and in Guánica where it all began, and in the valleys and the sugar cane fields and the desert of the south, and oh, oh, oh, north to the capital, fighting in El Condado, and in the Parque Muñoz Rivera, and in the narrow streets of Old San Juan, the blood flowing on the five-hundred-year-old cobblestone, the great beast of imperialism bleeding ceaselessly from the wounds you have inflicted, my sweet baby, oh, oh, oh, oh . . .

And then it was over and they were laughing hysterically.

"You're really a brave dude, Armando," she'd said, snuggling closer to him after a while. "You're really too much. Wow!"

"Why do you say that?"

"Well, I always heard of women crying, but never men."

"That's the first time it ever happened," he said.

"Really?"

"Yeah, what do you think it means?"

"Maybe it was the first time for your heart too," she said.

"Why were you laughing?" he asked.

"I don't know. Why are you asking me? You were laughing too."

They both laughed again.

"Did you know that the Eskimos call the whole thing laughing with each other?"

"You're putting me on?" she said.

"Really, like people say going to bed. They say laughing with each other."

She suddenly looked at him suspiciously.

"How do you know? You sound like an authority. How old are you?"

He wanted to tell her that he was thirty-three and that he was sorry he had deceived her, but he couldn't.

"Twenty-four," he said. "And you?"

"Twenty-one," she said. "Are you experienced?"

"Not really."

"Can I sleep here tonight?"

"How about your grandmother? Won't she worry?"

"Naw, she's cool. I'll call her in a little while."

"All right, but I hope you don't have any big brothers."

"I have all kinds of brothers, big ones and little ones."

She made her phone call and she came back to bed and they made love again and fell asleep and did not get up in time for their morning classes. In the afternoon, after Maritza went to her apartment to change, they went to Central Park Zoo and later that evening they went to see "Love Story" and laughed a lot. Ryan O'Neal couldn't really skate and the scene at Wollman's was unreal. Usually the place was so crowded it was impossible to move. They ended up doing a class analysis of the film in which, as always, the capitalist does in the working class. The more the people in the theater cried, the funnier the picture seemed to them.

For the next month, until Frank Garboil was brought to Stuyvesant Hospital, they saw each other every day. On weekends, Maritza slept at his apartment and they made love often and sometimes she saw him wiping out hundreds of Marines and neither one ever mentioned the word love, although it was nothing else but that which they felt.

CHAPTER 25

In which we have an opportunity to observe the final stages of preparation in the plan to effect Armando Martinez' escape from Stuyvesant Hospital by FUCIT and their peerless leader, El Falcon.

On the evening of February 5, 1971, four days before the scheduled escape of Armando Martinez, the attack group of the United Front for Total Caribbean Independence held its final meeting in order to discuss their plan. The five members of the attack group, including El Falcon, were seated around a table studying a map of the hospital. The map showed every exit, elevator, corridor, staircase and window. From El Falcon's information acquired on his reconnaissance foray to the hospital the previous month, he had drawn the map. He had also carefully copied, on the back of a deck of cards which he had painted white, the layout of each area of the hospital vital to their success, including the eventual target of their plan, the converted solarium where Frank Garboil had been treated for the past three months. In the glare of the bare light bulbs of the basement headquarters, El Falcon now shuffled the cards and began facing them up to test the members of the group.

"The king of clubs," he said, directing himself to one of the members.

"The cafeteria, comrade," said the young man in the group.

"Good, comrade. You are well prepared."

While the four other members studied the cards, El Falcon was deep in thought, almost as in a trance. Something was causing him considerable preoccupation, but he had not yet figured out the source of his concern. The previous night had been an unpleasant one. The entire time he was in bed had been taken up with unsuccessful attempts to regain his sleep, only to be awakened time and again by the meowing of cats. At one point he thought he heard voices, but did not bother getting up.

And the dream. The one scene he recalled was enough of a puzzle to force him to ask one of the two old men in the group if dreams in reality foretold the future. That afternoon while they awaited the arrival of the young man and Maritza Soto, he had asked the question.

"I am not a man of superstitious beliefs, my commander," the old man siad. "But I have heard it told from people who are that some dreams have great significance."

"From what I can recall," El Falcon said, "I was back in the mountains of the Island as a young man. We were roasting a pig over a charcoal fire and there was much merriment. A birth, perhaps a marriage or a homecoming. I recall returning to my home after the war, but nothing like that comes to mind right now. I was a soldier with the imperialist army, but my homecoming was nothing spectacular. I woke up last night and I could smell the roast pig so clearly and it was as if I had not awakened at all, but was still in the dream, watching the pig turn on the spit and the skin crackling and the fine smells reaching me. Do you recall that fine smell, my friend?"

"Yes, I do, my commander," said Tomas Vizcarrondo, tugging at his greying moustache. "It is curious, but as I walked in here today, there was a smell, a very strong smell of roast pork. Did you have pork chops for lunch?"

"No, no, my friend. We ordered fish from *Del Pueblo* Restaurant there on Third Avenue."

"That is the strange thing about dreams, my commander. Or so people tell me. The people who believe in those things say that, when they are strong such as yours, they often leave a sign."

"Yes, I also have heard that. Do you believe my dream foretells the future?"

"Perhaps, my commander. Who is to say. A victory celebration. A war of liberation and then a great rejoicing. It must have been that way for the great Fidel and his comrades. Perhaps that is all that it means. After we help our compatriot escape, who knows what will happen. The people might rise up, their consciousness a total unit, their spirits uplifted and our island free."

"Yes, that is true, but I wish I recalled more of the dream. The infernal cats kept intruding."

"There were cats in your dreams, my commander?" Vizcarrondo asked, suddenly alarmed.

"No, no, man," El Falcon responded, laughing in one of his rare moments of mirth. "There were cats roaming the neighborhood. I had difficulty sleeping."

"Oh, I see. They were out serenading the ladies."

"Yes, yes, even with the cold as it was."

"They are worse than we ourselves were in our youth. Do you recall traveling four miles up and down the hills to serenade one of those country beauties?"

"Yes, my friend. I recall those times well."

The two men drifted into a reminiscence of their youth. It lasted well into the afternoon.

Now, as he watched the others memorizing their assignments for the operation, his mind was still troubled.

"Comrades," he said, intruding into their card game, which he had suggested they play. It was an unusual game, since they could see the backs of each others's cards and therefore, if they were able to recall the card, hold an advantage on how they were to play. "I would like your attention," he said.

The room became silent as he asked for a final report from all sectors. Maritza Soto began her report by stating that all the expected revolutionary groups would be there.

"As usual," she continued, "there will be groups there only to benefit themselves and their particular cause. The latest intelligence that we have, and it's pretty solid, is that there are no counter demonstrations of any significance planned."

"Please explain further," El Falcon said.

"My commander, I have an intelligence report that the Boy Scouts will be picketing to disclaim that our comrade, Armando Martinez, was ever a Cub Scout, but nothing of consequence."

"Was he?"

"Not to my knowledge, my commander."

"That is good," El Falcon said, approvingly. "I have never liked their uniforms and those short pants breed nothing but queerness. Are there any unusual developments? Anything out of the ordinary? Has anyone attempted to follow you?"

None of the members could think of anything and then Enrique Prado, the young man in the attack group, spoke.

"I do not want you to be alarmed," he said. "But last night when I came to bring your supper, there was a truck from the Con Edison company outside. The men had opened a manhole and were working. When I left here, the men were still working, but I did not notice anything out of the ordinary."

"Yes, thank you," said El Falcon, dismissing the information as irrelevant and turning to the other older man. "Comrade Ricardo, have you purchased all the rations we will need for our stay at the hospital?"

"Yes, my commander," said the old man. "Enough for eight days."

"Very well, have you figured out a safe route to the sanitary service for our comrade Maritza while we are in the hospital?"

"Yes, my commander, I have discussed it with her. She has been briefed. Everything is ready. We have bought all that is needed so that not even a piece of soap will be missing while we are there."

"Good. Comrade Tomas, the uniforms. Have you purchased them?"

"Yes, my commander. My nephew works in a hospital supply company as I told you and we have availed ourselves of a discount. I have obtained five white uniforms, name tags with three different names on each set of five, green operating gowns and also caps and face masks, all of the same color, and stethoscopes."

"Good, good," said El Falcon, quite pleased with the progress that had been made. "I assume," he said, "that we have ascertained the location of the ether."

"Yes," young Enrique Prado said. "It will be no problem to obtain plenty of the gas."

"Good, I have been able to obtain gas masks by gaining entrance into the police station two nights ago. In the event that it becomes necessary to use the gas, I will open the valve and at the first sign of the smell, you will put on your masks. All of you have smelled ether before, have you not? Everything must go according to schedule. Let me review what is to take place.

"Five of our people will be at the hospital for minor ailments. Do not be concerned. It is nothing serious and all of them have Blue Cross or other types of hospitalization plans, so that they will incur no added expense. Each one of you has the person's name you will visit on Sunday evening during visiting hours. You will all sign in as relatives. Each one of the patients is on a different floor, so make the visit a good one and familiarize yourself with the location, so that in case of an emergency, we will be able to bring our liberated comrade to the most propitious locale and replace the patient from his bed onto the operating table and leave our comrade in that bed. Is that clear?"

They all nodded.

"Go into the hospital, sign in under an assumed name and make the visit. After you have visited for a reasonable time, leave and find your way to the cafeteria. It will be closed, but one of the doors at the south entrance will be left taped by one of our people who is employed in the kitchen of the hospital. Go into the cafeteria and from there, using the rear stairway, find your way to the basement, then to the sub-basement and from there to the west boiler room. Is that clear?"

Everyone nodded.

"We will meet in the west boiler room at 9:00 post meridian, Sunday the 7th of February. The man in charge of the boiler room is a compatriot and sympathizer of our cause. There will be no problems. All of you have the times for carrying out your entry into the hospital and your descent into our temporary headquarters. Everything must be on time. We will remain there that night and the day of the action. At five minutes before seven that evening, at the height of the demonstration, we will begin our ascent. At eight o'clock we will strike, swiftly and with efficacy. I have no more to say. From now on we are on our own until we meet in the west boiler room. If any changes are to be made, all of your have the new list of restaurants. After Sunday the list becomes useless. If one of our group is missing from the rendezvous in the boiler room, we will have to go ahead without the person. Let us go over our assignments once again. I will, of course, be the anesthesiologist. Comrade Maritza?"

"Operating nurse."

"Comrade Tomás?"

"Heart specialist."

"Comrade Ricardo?"

"Heart machine technician."

"Comrade Enrique?"

"Intern."

"Good, during this part of the action only comrade Enrique and Maritza will speak, since they are the only ones who will not be detected when they speak English. Is there anything more? Any questions?"

Everyone shook his head. Tomas, however, wished to be heard.

"Yes, comrade."

"This is a brilliant plan, my commander," he said. "No one will suspect that we are to remain in the building after we liberate the young comrade."

"That is true. Comrades, let me wish you good luck and tell you once more how proud I am to be working with such dedicated compatriots. Let us see how the imperialist giant reacts when we are finished. Our victory will be one more thorn in the face of the paper tiger."

The other members of the attack group nodded in agreement.

They were silent as if pondering the significance of their roles. They got up, one by one, shook their commander's hand and left.

El Falcon remained behind, still troubled by his dream. This had never happened before an action and he was truly bothered. He walked to the kitchen where the group's mascot, *Pantera*, was munching on a piece of blood sausage. He knelt down and petted the large cat, speaking to it as softly as one would a loved one.

"It is of no importance to me," he said. "But did you participate in that debauchery last night? We can drop all protocol, please be honest. You and I understand these matters only too well. You are like me. Sly and quiet, but efficient. Tell me the truth. Do not be evasive, my son. Do you think the plan will work?"

The cat purred and let out a deep meowing. El Falcon laughed at the deep rumbling inside the cat's throat.

"That is a very good answer, my friend," he said. "Do not concern yourself for your health while we are gone. Someone will take care of you. There will be daily meals. But please do not let up your guard. Always be alert and do not give the enemy an inch. Goodbye, old friend."

El Falcon stood up, put on his coat and went outside. He locked the basement door and, once upstairs in the street, disappeared into the night. For the next two days he would visit with his family. He had not seen them in five years and his grandchildren were nearly grown. He then would prepare himself for entrance into the hospital to visit his old friend Betancourt and play a few tables of dominoes.

There was no fear in him. He had been in the city two months and nothing had yet gone wrong. Either the police had more important things to worry about or they were very close. In either case, it did not matter. Close or far, he would foil them again.

CHAPTER 26

In which the protagonist becomes a hero, gets a chance to view his past, has a further realization about athletics, and suffers a mental breakdown which lands him in the hospital.

After his first week with Maritza, his plan to leave New Amsterdam College was completely forgotten. He felt elated that he found someone like her and that the Puerto Rican students on the campus very rapidly saw in him a powerful symbol of their advancement in society. Any inroads made by one of their own in a sport which they considered the domain of Americans, meaning White Americans, were to be fully explored. Pleased to hear that someone named Armando Martinez had made the school's hockey team, they began attending the games in increasing numbers. This enthusiasm eventually swept over to the other campuses in the city. Disregarding school loyalties, they came to cheer Armando Martinez. Rather than a novelty, his playing hockey became a cultural accomplishment. Even the more radical students warmed to the idea and saw his playing as a possible vehicle for raising the consciousness of their less fortunate fellow students, whom they viewed as drowning in a sea of capitalistic propaganda.

This being the state of affairs, the Bronx Ice Palace, where the school played its home games, was suddenly invaded by Puerto Rican college students. They brought their younger brothers, sisters and cousins, whom they hoped to impress with the notion that anything was possible if one really tried, an idea which they often did not believe but thought supremely important to disseminate. So they came to watch their lean, handsome and graceful folk hero in-the-making. Boisterous, filled with a hope that in the eyes of society their image would improve, they came. As soon as he would step out onto the ice, they would go into a frenzy as they pointed out to the uninitiated that he was number ll, the one with the moustache and curly hair sticking out of the helmet. Coeds waited near the locker room before and after games, hoping he'd noticed them and say hello. The girls' boy-friends, despite seeing their positions threatened, felt no animosity towards him, but made it a point to shake his hand whenever they had the opportunity.

In one of the first games of the season, a City College player was checked into the boards by him, took exception to the clean but jarring contact, dropped his gloves and attempted to drive his fist into Garboil's face. Garboil was able to slip the punch, but without thinking, instinctively, followed suit and pushed the opposing player. They clutched and grabbed and eventually ended up on the ice with Garboil on top. Neither did any damage to the other, but the encounter caused considerable excitement on the ice as well as in the stands. *Dale duro, Armando*. Hit him hard, they shouted. When the commotion was over and he and the other player had been sent to the penalty box for five minutes, the crowd began accusing the referee of ethnic prejudice. The radical students, as part of their consciousness raising campaign, were particularly virulent in their verbal attack, citing the referee for Yanqui, monopoly-capital inspired refereeing. Although the spectators had no idea what the group was talking about, they knew passion when they saw it and joined in, calling the referee an imperialist pig, bourgeois honker and a capitalist pork chop.

After Garboil served his penalty and came back on the ice, he was greeted with a roar of approval from the crowd. The noise in the arena was deafening. On his next shift on the ice, he and the centerman broke in on the defense, two on one, worked a neat give and go, and Garboil snapped a blistering wrist shot into the upper right hand corner of the net for his first goal of the season. Once again the arena exploded and his reputation was established. New Amsterdam College won the game 5-2 and Garboil was so elated that he had almost forgotten about Maritza when he came out of the locker room. The mob wouldn't leave him alone, congratulating him, touching him, showering the adulation on him that he had only seen displayed towards stars. It took nearly twenty minutes for him to reach the lobby of the arena and, in his hurry to leave, was down the street and heading for the subway train before Maritza caught up to him.

By the next game, students had to be turned away and the management of the rink began making preparations for building a second set of stands at the far end of the arena. More significantly, a cheer had developed in which Armando Martinez was being urged to hit the opposition harder. Armando was shortened to Mando, like the Mexican boxer, Mando Ramos. The word *mando* in Spanish is also the first person singular of the verb *mandar*, meaning not only to send but to command or rule. More than a cheer, the crowd developed a chant, repeated over and over to a conga rhythm, a dance which perhaps their parents had danced, but which they only knew from watching Bugs Bunny cartoons on television when they were children. The students now took to bringing congas, cow bells, maracas, *claves* and tambourines to the games and chanting: DA-LE DU-RO MAN-DO. The implication was not only that he hit the opposition, but that they, as a body, were commanding him to do so.

Needless to say the opposition resented the din which this percussive and frenzied chanting produced. The few opposing fans who came to the rink to watch the games began cowering in a small section of the stands, opposite the New Amsterdam College Puerto Rican Rooting Section and Charanga or NACPR-RSC as it was described in the school newspaper by one of the sports correspondents.

Some of the more pugnacious opponents took to calling the team, which wore as its symbol a golden hawk, the New Amsterdam College Cucarachas. In the third game of the season, Moose Martorelli, the captain of the team, was checked into the boards by a Brooklyn College player, who made the mistake of asking Moose if he was the head cucaracha. "Bafangoo sorella," Moose explained and proceeded to illustrate physically an aspect of the game of hockey which the player had evidently not fully grasped: talking to the opposition disparagingly can sometimes lead to injury. They carried the player off the ice on a stretcher. On his nose the player now sported a knot the size of a golf ball, the result of his valiant attempt to break Moose's fist with his nose.

What had begun for Frank Garboil as a need to fulfill a dream had turned into a whirlwind of adventure. The adulation he was receiving from the fans and the respect which each day he earned from his teammates were the perfect fuel to fire his desire for recognition as the true athlete he had always believed himself to be. He now skated with complete abandon, never thinking of physical injury, letting his inner drive push his body relentlessly in every situation. He skated as hard at the beginning of a game as he did at the end. That drive inspired his teammates to emulate his efforts and excel as well. By the seventh game of the season Garboil was the second leading scorer in the Metropolitan College Ice Hockey Federation. The coach moved him up from the third line to skate with Kevin O'Brien at center and Billy Dankowski at right wing. He was now on the first line. The three became known as the MOD line, christened thus by the sports editor of the newspaper.

At the end of November, after routing Queens College, Armando Martinez was leading the league in scoring. That night he pumped in four goals and set a school single game scoring record by assisting on four other goals. The eight points gave him, after his first eleven games, 23 goals and 25 assists for 48 points, a phenomenal scoring pace. New Amsterdam was in first place in the eastern division of the league with a record of 8-1-2. In the locker room after the game, as he removed his equipment, dodged tape balls and listened to the animated and often ribald humor of his teammates, Kevin O'Brien asked him if he'd like to go out and eat.

"My father and mother wanna take us out," he said. "My girl, Kathy, is in from Boston and I want you to meet her. It'll be fun. The old man won't admit it, but he wants to meet you. He won't say anything directly but he's impressed."

"I thought your Pops was down on you?" Garboil said.

"Not since he started reading about us in the paper. He's a sports nut. I asked Billy D. to come, but he's gotta go somewhere with his girl. Com'on, man."

"Can I bring Maritza?"

"Sure," Kevin said. "The old man invited both of you. 'Ask the Spanish kid to come and bring his girl,' he said. I asked him if he didn't mind and he said: 'No problem at all, Kevin. No problem at all.' You'll get a chance to see a minor railroad executive up close. The old man likes you and he's really a nice guy. A little too conservative for my taste, but a heart of gold. No kidding. And like I told you, he likes you. He says you gotta lot of heart, style too. He's big on style, but it's the heart that really gets to him. He loves people with no sense," Kevin joked. "He grew up in this tough Irish ghetto here in the Bronx and he's always talking about it. Don't mind him if he starts talking about his old neighborhood after a couple of drinks. So how about it?"

"Sure, I guess so," Garboil said, heading for the showers.

When they finished dressing he and Kevin emerged from the locker room, their hair damp and their faces still flushed from the game. They carried their equipment bags and sticks and wore the new maroon and gold jackets with leather sleeves and the large stick-carrying Golden Hawk on the back. Their names had been embroidered on the front of the jackets. High up on the sleeves, on either side, were their uniform numbers and their positions. The school had received considerable publicity and the coach had ordered the jackets. They arrived the previous week and were handed out before the game.

The fans loved the jackets, but most of the players felt uneasy about the expensive jackets and thought them appropriate for a more reputable hockey school than New Amsterdam. On the front of Garboil's jacket, embroidered in scripted gold thread, was the name: MANDO.

Maritza was waiting for Garboil outside in the lobby of the arena and, as soon as she saw him, rushed up and kissed him on the cheek. She was dressed in a pants outfit and the maxi coat which she'd worn on their first date. She was smart, thought Garboil. She'd caught on right away that the hockey establishment tends to be conservative and did not want to embarrass him and ruin the image of what he represented by wearing her traditional garb of student radical. The only sign that betrayed her alliegance to politics was a small pin of the Lares flag on the lapel of her coat.

"That was fantastic, honey," she said. "You guys are too much together," she added, kissing Kevin. "It's too bad Billy's not political."

"Listen," Garboil said, "Kevin's parents wanna take us out to eat. Is that okay with you? Kevin's girl's down from Boston."

Maritza looked suspiciously at Kevin, but Kevin laughed and said it was okay.

"Com'on, they're waiting in the car," he said.

Outside the rink the temperature had dropped some ten degrees in the past hour and the wind was blowing up from the Hudson River. Maritza took Garboil's arm and hugged herself to the sleeve of the jacket as they walked. Garboil was still up from the game and hardly felt the cold except in his lungs when he breathed. His head was clear of any thoughts and his body only experienced the pleasurable, tired feeling which comes from playing a sport all out. When they reached the parking lot, a small blonde girl rushed up to Kevin and kissed him on the mouth.

"Wow, I bet your team could go up and wipe out B.C. and B.U. and Northeastern and Harvard and everybody up in Boston," she said.

Kevin was slightly embarrassed by the suggestion. He introduced his girlfriend to Garboil and Maritza. Once inside the car he completed the introductions. Driving across the George Washington Bridge to New Jersey, Mr. O'Brien asked Garboil if he had thought about what he'd like to do after he finished college. Garboil answered that he hadn't given it much thought.

"You've got a great future ahead of you," Mr. O'Brien said. "Are you thinking about the pros?"

"No, sir," Garboil answered.

"You should," Mr. O'Brien said. "There's a lot of expansion going on in the game and this is only your first year playing college hockey. You have the size, the speed and you understand the game better than a lot of pros I've seen."

"Thank you," Garboil said.

Kevin was elbowing him in the ribs and he almost laughed. They both knew the caliber of competition in their league and had no further dreams of going beyond college hockey. Of all the college hockey in the United States, they were at the very bottom rung. Mr. O'Brien drove on chattering about the sports credo. Eventually, they stopped at a steak house somewhere in New Jersey. There was a piano bar, candles on the table and a lot of red velvet. They sat at a large corner table and, after they had ordered dinner, Mr. O'Brien began talking about his old neighborhood. Garboil listened to him and felt as if he were being transported back in time to his years growing up. Everyone in the restaurant seemed far away, including Maritza.

"If you wanted to play hockey," Mr. O'Brien was saying, "you had to settle for roller hockey in the street. Now, that was the game. A couple of kids played hockey, but most of them played football. Where did you grow up, Armando?" he said, searching Garboil's face.

"In the Bronx," Garboil said. "On Cypress Avenue, near St. Mary's Park."

"Did you hear that, Peggy?" Mr. O'Brien said, touching his wife's arm. "Now, that's what I call a coincidence. It's a Spanish neighborhood right now, right?"

Garboil nodded but everything had become peculiar and his head felt hot and cold all at once.

"Are you all right?" Maritza whispered, sensing his discomfort.

"I'm fine,"he said.

"That was some neighborhood when we lived there, wasn't it, Peggy?"

"Yes, Charlie," Mrs. O'Brien said, smiling understandingly.

When they were finished eating and back in the car Garboil fell immediately asleep. When he woke up the car was in front of a large house in the suburbs and he was alone with Maritza.

"What's wrong?" he said.

"Nothing," Maritza said. "Kevin thought it might be a good idea if you came up to his house and rested before he drove us back to Manhattan. Let's go inside," she said, pulling him forward as she opened he door. "Com'on."

"That's all right. I'll stay in the car."

"Oh no, you don't. You have to be as brave now as when you play," she said. "It's the least you could do after they bought us dinner. Kevin's mother's making coffee. It's okay. It's just a house. People live in it. You have to expose yourself to this kind of thing."

Kevin had now come out of the house, opened the door of the car and was urging him to come inside. But he felt so tired and his head felt as if some dizzying thing had gotten into it to disorient him.

"Com'on, man," Kevin said. "I'll show you all my trophies and pictures going back to when I was in Mite hockey and Little League. I was a born jock."

Garboil got out of the car but still felt woozy. He didn't recall getting hit particularly hard during the game, certainly not on his head; in practice either. He walked into the house and sat down. It was a lovely home, everything neat and comfortable and so well cared for. It reminded him of those first months with Joan and visiting her house, except that this house seemed friendlier, not as austere and museum-like as had her parents' house. On the mantle there were pictures of the family and the decorations were mostly mirrors and store-bought landscapes.

Mrs. O'Brien brought coffee into the living room. Garboil drank some and felt a little better. Perhaps it had been the two bottles of beer he'd had with dinner. But something else was wrong and he felt puzzled. He didn't feel sick, but something odd was happening and he couldn't figure it out. It was as if time had stopped and he were moving backwards and everyone else were going on without him. Mr. O'Brien insisted the three of them go down to the den and see Kevin's trophies. They walked downstairs to the basement which Mr. O'Brien had fixed up as a den, but more as Kevin's own personal Hall of Fame, complete with his first skates in a glass case. In different cases there were uniforms and equipment, layed out on blue velvet, little typed tags indicating the year. Mr. O'Brien showed Garboil a book in which he had kept the records of every game Kevin had played since he was five years old. There were over a dozen cases and the paneled walls were covered with pictures of Kevin wearing the uniforms of six different sports. In the hockey pictures Garboil recognized some of the people from the youth hockey league in which his sons had played. He wanted to sit down although he wasn't tired. Kevin handed him a picture of himself at the age of ten. Kevin was wearing the Stars hockey uniform with the same number Peter had worn at the same age. His heart tugged oddly in his chest and he felt a shooting pain in his head. What was it?

"Wow, I've never seen a kid with so many trophies," he managed to joke, handing the picture back to Kevin.

"Oh, he was a pisser, this one," said Mr. O'Brien, tousling Kevin's red hair. "He wanted to play everything. He was just like the kids I useta coach back in the old neighborhood. We had a football team that went undefeated three years in a row. They played everything, too. Intense athletes, if you know what I mean. They hated to lose."

"What was the name of the team?" Garboil said.

"Oh, first the Shamrocks and then the Rebels. There were a few new kids in the neighborhood. Good players. We changed the name of the team. The kids changed the name. They voted or something."

"Why don't we go back up, Dad," Kevin said. "It's getting late."

They walked back upstairs and Garboil sat down next to Maritza. He looked at her and for the briefest of moments did not recognize her. She seemed quite at ease talking to Mrs. O'Brien and Kathy.

"We were talking about the old neighborhood," Mr. O'Brien said. "Peg, do you remember Tommy O'Hara?"

"The policeman?"

"No, no, Peggy," Mr. O'Brien said. "Mousey O'Hara. Little scrawny kid. Had a big fight with your sister Maureen one time. It made me think of it with Armando here and everything. Well, I saw him the other day. He was walking down the street with his wife and kids. Good looking children. Oh yeah, very nice looking children. He married that Spanish girl your sister was making such a big fuss about. The oldest of his kids was about twelve years old and looked just like Mousey, except Spanish."

Garboil guessed that this was Mr. O'Brien's way of saying that he and Maritza were welcome in his house. But it was all coming together now and he felt his body begin to shake slightly. There was a small headache, a pinpoint of pain, directly above his right eye. Kevin's father was Charlie O'Brien, who had married Maureen Rattigan's big sister, Peggy. And the man hadn't recognized him, hadn't even mentioned Gypsy. Garboil wanted to ask him if he'd known a kid named Frankie Garboil. He wanted to break the spell and tell them he hadn't meant to disappoint them, to mock their trust in him. He couldn't get over the idea that back then he had made no impression on Charlie O'Brien. Perhaps Charlie had recognized him and was waiting for him to get deeper into the mess he had created before denouncing him to the school authorities and the police. Scenes of those days came back to him vividly, each detail as if it were happening before him and Charlie O'Brien was instructing him on the football field. He had been a very good player and Charlie should've remembered him, but he'd made no connection between Gypsy and himself today.

He studied the man and found no malice in his face. Charlie was enjoying reliving his youth and seeing his son excel in sports. It was an honest, courageous attitude, and his recounting of those days was an homage to days long gone. There was no wishing to turn back the clock, no regrets, only a desire to retell a story, to keep a myth alive, at times disguising the truth, shaping it to convey a message secretly to those who understood the language in which the myth was told. And yet all he could feel was regret and a deep ball of pain which was growing minute by minute inside of him. As he sat on the couch of the O'Brien's home, he wanted to tell them, not so much Charlie O'Brien and Peggy Rattigan, but Kevin and Maritza and the small blonde girl, that they were right and no one over thirty should be trusted. He thought of his sons, Joey and Peter, and wished they were near him when he told on himself, when he revealed that he was a phony, a class-A fraud.

"I think we better go," Maritza said. "I think this one's caught a cold." She stood up and, with absolute poise, shook Mr. O'Brien's hand and thanked him. She then smiled warmly at Mrs. O'Brien and whatever secrets had been shared between them when the men had been downstairs were expressed by a sudden embrace and kisses on the cheek, the older woman patting Maritza's back.

Together with Kathy, Kevin drove Garboil and Maritza back to Garboil's apartment. Once inside the apartment, Maritza put him to bed, gave him aspirin and slept on the sofa. During the night she heard him moaning as if he were having a nightmare. The next morning he was fine and in good spirits, but appeared distant to her. She decided not to pressure him and let him come out of whatever he was feeling on his own. She suspected that he had been shaken badly by going into a middle-class home.

It was Sunday, they had a chance to sleep late and lounge around the apartment if they wished. She cooked breakfast and about noon they walked down to Riverside Park and watched the boats on the river and the joggers and dog walkers. There was a touch-football game going on below, on the softball fields, and he watched for a while, commenting on the plays and what they should've done, but he still felt odd about what had transpired at the O'Brien's home the previous night. He couldn't tell Maritza any of it. Not because she wouldn't understand, but because there was no way he could continue to play, and he owed that much to his teammates. The team was now on the way to a championship. If he had dropped out before the schedule began, it wouldn't have mattered. If he revealed himself now, the team would have to forfeit all its games and there would be a scandal which would center, not on his eligibility, which was intact as far as playing hockey, but on the fact that he was there under false pretenses. And the Puerto Ricans? They would be shamed, outraged that they had been duped again. He couldn't quit now, because he was on a team and he felt needed. He could be replaced, but it would weaken the team and that wasn't fair to them. He would do it slowly then, breaking away over a period of time.

"Is something the matter?" Maritza asked.

"No, I'm just a little tired," he said. "It must've been the game last night."

"Something happened at Kevin's house, didn't it?"

"No, nothing happened," he said, walking away from her.

She followed and told him that she also had a hang-up about going to White people's homes, that it made her uptight and start behaving like what they thought Puerto Ricans were supposed to act like. He denied that such had been the case.

"Well, you seemed pretty nervous and then you told Mr. O'Brien that you had grown up in the Bronx," she said. "You told me that you grew up in the Lower East Side. You see? You just wanted to impress him and you felt put down when he went into that number about it being a Spanish neighborhood now. That's another thing. Like I useta get bent all out of shape whenever anybody said Spanish when they meant Puerto Rican. Wait until you get into that."

"I can't wait," he said, a little too sarcastically even for his own liking. He stopped walking and faced her. "I'm sorry. Did I really say I grew up in the Bronx?"

"Sure, ask Kevin when you see him."

The following week went by quickly. The team practiced every day and on Saturday traveled to Flushing Meadow Park to play Fordham University. It was an eleven p.m. game against a relatively poor team. There wouldn't be many people at the game at that time of night, but as usual there would be a significant diehard group of fans from New Amsterdam College, anxious to set up their frenzied chanting and beating of drums. The chant had crossed ethnic lines and now everyone used DA-LE DU-RO MAN-DO to urge the team on.

Kevin drove down to pick Garboil up at his apartment at 9 p.m. Maritza had decided to remain behind and catch up on the school work she had neglected. Garboil laughed and kidded her.

"I bet you have one of those secret meetings," he said, as he said goodbye to her at the door.

"No, really," she said. "I have to study."

"Okay, I believe you," he said and then kissed her.

Two weeks before he had asked her if she belonged to any militant groups outside the school.

"You mean like the Young Barons?" she said, and he'd nodded and she'd shaken her head and he hadn't thought about it again. She explained that almost every college in the area had a chapter of the United Front for Total Caribbean Independence and sometimes the Central Committee, of which she was a member, got together to plan a demonstration, but that it was mostly a political group. Sure, there were a couple of ultra-radicals in the groups, but the political wing was unaware of their comings and goings and would disclaim any acts of violence committed in the group's name.

Now, as she closed the door to the apartment, he headed down the stairs and once outside got into Kevin's car. They talked about hockey all the way to the rink. At ten o'clock they went into the locker room and began changing. By the time he'd started lacing up his skates, the room was full of the usual horsing around which goes on before a game of little importance or challenge. No matter how hard everyone tried to get up for such a game, someone was always throwing tape or cracking wise about someone else's girlfriend. No one ever talked about Maritza, at least not in front of him. Word had gotten around that he'd been in Vietnam and, whether out of fear or respect, his teammates steered away from controversy with him. He wondered if he'd come out of a Puerto Rican bag and defend her honor. He was sure he would, but couldn't decide if he'd do it to keep up the charade or because he'd truly feel insulted. They respected his aloofness and quiet demeanor. Leadership by example it was called. And yet they were not beyond ribbing him indirectly. He watched some of the players, still in their jocks, doing a Conga and talking in Spanish accents like Bugs Bunny. Gwas op, Dack, they were saying and he laughed.

Moose Martorelli finally exploded. His captaincy was a position of great honor and responsibility and he felt obliged to keep order.

"Whyn'tcha stop fuckin' around, Riley," he said, to one of the other defensemen. "You don't know what's gonna happen when we hit the ice. You go into the game screwing around like that and the next thing you know they get a couple of quick goals and start thinking they're hot shit. Pretty soon they're ahead and start skating harder and we've gotta settle for a tie or maybe even lose a game we shoulda won. So get dressed and knock off the bullshit. That goes for you too, Dankowski. And the rest of you stars. This ain't the NHL, but that don't give you no excuse for screwing around before a game. Rules are rules."

A few minutes later the coach came in and made the usual speech about giving a hundred and ten percent and, if that didn't get it, reaching in and giving some more. He reviewed the lines for the game and reminded them not to take the opposition lightly. At a quarter to eleven they went out on the ice for warm-ups. At eleven o'clock the national anthem was played and the puck dropped. As soon as the puck hit the ice Garboil broke down his wing, took a pass from Kevin and passed the puck ahead to Dankowski flying down the right wing. Dankowski took the puck in full stride, wound up and let go one of his explosive slap shots. The puck rose about a foot at the last minute, struck the goalie in the face mask, hit the post and went in. Garboil, skating in for a rebound, saw the puck go in, raised his stick and went by the net. As he went by he saw the blood streaming from the goalie's mask and he circled back.

Players were crowding around the unconsious goalie. One of his teammates was attempting to remove the mask, which had shattered near the eye hole, the fiberglass looking like a dented fender. The Fordham coach and trainer were out on the ice immediately and an ambulance was called. It was a half hour before it arrived. The trainer removed the mask, wiped the blood, revealing a meaty hole where the eye had been. When the ambulance arrived, the goalie had regained consciousness and was smiling bravely, but one of the attendants was overheard saying that it looked like the eyeball had been disconnected from the socket and the cheekbone shattered.

The coaches conferred and decided to continue the game. The second string Fordham goalie came in and after some practice shots proceeded to get bombarded by a barrage of shots. Dankowski scored a hat trick before the first period was halfway through. At the end of the period the score was 7-0.

Fordham came out hitting in the second period and, in a scuffle in one of the corners, one of their players became annoyed by Dankowski's persistence and slashed violently at Dankowski's arm with his stick. Dankowski went down in a heap, holding his right arm. Martorelli was immediately on the scene and leveled the Fordham player with a straight right hand. The player jumped up and began swinging at Martorelli. Everyone paired off and began scuffling. Garboil, who had been perturbed by the injury to the goalie, skated up ice and away from the melee. He had seen sports injuries before, but nothing like the one to the goalie. Beanings, broken legs so that the bone showed through, but never anything so awful as that gaping red hole where the goalie's eye had been.

Garboil stood leaning against the boards, watching the action until the extra Fordham player came over and began jawing at him about their goalie. Garboil shrugged his shoulders and this angered the Fordham player who dropped his stick and gloves and made a grab for him. Garboil shook his head and told the player he didn't want to fight, but the player held on. Finally dropping his gloves, Garboil grabbed at the other player's jersey and they held each other off.

After the penalties were sorted out, Martorelli had been kicked out of the game, Dankowski had gone to the locker room and the referee warned both benches about further violence. At the end of the second period the score was 10-1. In the locker room, Coach Malinowski was furious. He was pacing up and down the room between the players. He was talking very loudly and cursing.

"I want you guys to go out there and bury those bastards. You skate as hard in the third period as you did in the beginning of the game. I want all three lines to skate and hit, hit and skate like you were in a championship game. Who the hell does that guy think he is sending his players out to injure my guys. You saw him. Son of a bitch."

No one was paying the least attention to the coach. Billy Dankowski had changed into street clothes and was on his way to the hospital for x-rays. His father had come into the locker room and was now carrying his bag and sticks as he had probably done since Billy was six years old and couldn't carry his own equipment. Dankowski's arm was in a temporary sling which the trainer had rigged up. Martorelli was in street clothes and began putting his equipment in his bag.

"Take care of that arm, Billy," the coach said. "We'll see you at practice on Monday."

Garboil spoke the words but they didn't seem to be his. "Coach," he said. "Why don't you give the fourth line a chance to skate? The score's 10-1 and with Billy hurt we'll have to use another right wing. You might as well send the whole line out. Maybe Kevin and I can take care of killing penalties."

It was as if he had slapped the coach in the face. The rest of the players thought it was a good idea and nodded their agreement. The idea, however, had not originated with the coach and it angered him.

"You scared to go out there, Martinez?" he said. "I didn't see you assert yourself too much with that fairy you were figure skating with out there. You're scared, aren't you? Admit it. When the going gets tough you bail out, right?"

"No, sir," Garboil said, recalling how his football coach in college preferred to be addressed.

"Don't you no sir me, Martinez. If you're scared, come out and say so and you can turn in your uniform. We don't have any room on the club for nervous nellies."

"I just thought you should give the other guys a chance with the score like it is. They'll get some game experience and it might make the Fordham players calm down. Somebody could really get hurt worse. Those guys on the other team have pride too, you know?"

He knew he was saying the wrong things, but the words continued to pour out of his mouth.

"And since when did you get appointed assistant coach?" Malinowski said. "You wanna coach, Martinez? Why don't you sit out the next couple of games. I mean that."

It was at that point that Garboil's thirty-three years of suppressed anger boiled over. He didn't even think that it was a blessing in disguise to be suspended. If he had, it would've been the perfect opportunity to begin easing himself out of the situation. He stood up, removed the unstrapped maroon helmet from his head and heaved it against the concrete wall on the other side of the room. The helmet made a crushing noise and fell shattered to the floor. He stomped away and kicked a locker, slashing open the metal with the blade of his skate and in the process tearing a gash on the side of his skate boot. The other players backed away and when Kevin tried to restrain him from doing himself any further damage, he pushed Kevin away. Garboil now picked up a stick and began smashing the bench on which he and the other players had been sitting.

"Who in the hell do you think you are, Malinowski?" he screamed at the top of his voice. "You just saw a kid lose a fuckin' eye, one of your own players gets his arm broken and you want us to go out there and continue this fuckin' bloodbath. Why don't you go out there and try skating and playing this game. You can't and that's what the problem is. You don't know shit about this game. This ain't football and you ain't Vince Lombardi. And you know what? I quit! You wanna suspend me? Great! You do that because it doesn't matter. I don't wanna play this lousy game anymore."

He tried removing his jersey, but it wouldn't come off and he was now tearing wildly at the golden hawk on the front of his uniform. It was as if the bird had suddenly come alive and was attacking him. He felt dizzy and his head was so hot. His eyes burned and there was a terrible pain deep in his chest. His teammates tried to restrain him but he hit out at them, screaming for them to leave him alone, to not touch him. He couldn't control himself and his rage continued to pour out of him in wild screams and pounding of the lockers with his fists. His knuckles were skinned and bleeding when Moose Martorelli finally came over and began talking to him very softly until he was able to calm him down. Only Moose seemed to understand that such great rage was being produced by intense pain.

Throughout the entire episode, Malinowski stood impassively aside, looking at the scene and what he considered an obvious weakness in the character of the team.

The team finally left the locker room for the start of the third period. Garboil was left by himself, sitting on the floor against the wall of the shower room. He surveyed the destruction he had caused. He had smashed his helmet, shattered his sticks, ruined his skates and made a fool of himself. He looked down at the bright maroon jersey, half ripped off his chest, the golden hawk folded over as if dead. He looked at his right skate and saw the exposed sock, blood soaking through.

And then the pain hit him all at once and he began sobbing, recalling vividly for the first time, hearing the shots and seeing his mother crumpled beside him, her chest spouting blood. He felt the tears flood his eyes, blurring his vision. His chest burned and, as the sobbing became more intense, he heard a boy screaming. He seemed far away and in need of help, but he couldn't move from where he sat. Some powerful force held him down rigidly, forcing him to stare straight ahead at the past, unable to affect the present. Everything became very clear, but he could do nothing to protect himself from the increasing pain. Minutes later he blacked out. When he woke up he was in a hospital room, a turbaned doctor shining a small flashlight into his eyes.

CHAPTER 27

In which we observe how medical and police science join hands in a plan to bring about the capture of FUCIT and thwart their attempt to rescue Armando Martinez.

On Friday afternoon Dr. Dieter Kopfeinlaufen visited his patients to reassure them that he had not deserted them. He returned to his office, ordered lunch to be brought upstairs and at one o'clock sat down to review the week's events. He would devote the next four hours to writing descriptions of the salient aspects of progress made or not made during the week.

"Our star patient, Armando Martinez, has made a tremendous break-through," he wrote as he munched on a liverwurst on pumpernickel sandwich, such as his *mutter* used to make for him when he was a little boy. "There is no longer a complete Frank Garboil. That identity has quickly faded in the past week and Armando Martinez is well on his way to complete recovery. It will be a comforting balm for his psyche to receive his due recognition. A war hero, a dedicated student, a superb athlete and a young man deeply in love. The pressures on him obviously too great for him to handle, but the resolution of the problem has been as anticipated. Rather than recall his war experiences, he relived them symbolically through hockey.

"Having viewed the damage his company had inflicted on the enemy during the beginning stages of the battle," Kopfeinlaufen wrote, as he continued to munch on his sandwich, "the young soldier suffered an extreme trauma, causing him to totally block any recollection of the events. A subsequent trauma, caused by seeing one of his comrades wounded, seriously produced a further amnesiac reaction.

"It is significant to note that his reaction at being asked by his commander to return to the front line was to suggest that less experienced troops be sent in. The final blow to the young soldier's ego came when the commander questioned his courage.

"Our staff has thoroughly analyzed the character of the Puerto Rican male. The conclusion we have come to is that this one fact, the questioning of his manhood, produced the breakdown and the need to exchange his Puerto Rican identity for one more suitable to his purposes, that of hiding the shame of his cowardice. We have received further corroboration on this point. It now appears clear that in order to deal with the psychic pain caused by his war experiences Armando Martinez adopted the identity of an accepted member of the dominant society, a man respected in the academic community, socially secure, emotionally sound and sexually adjusted in the modern sense. It will be several months before Armando is totally ready to accept his identity, but our work with him is nearly finished."

Kopfeinlaufen closed the file on Armando Martinez and moved on to the one on the Ponchartrain triplets. One thing puzzled him about the Martinez/Garboil case. There was no doubt that Martinez had painted an extremely flattering picture of Frank Garboil: married man, a bit neurotic but no more so than most people. It didn't make sense when in effect Kolodny had said, in his report, that Garboil was a homosexual. Perhaps Armando Martinez' entire psychological configuration, his going to war, his athletic prowess, his sexual agility were all a cover up for his own homosexuality. An interesting angle. As he pondered this question and began to write in the Ponchartrain triplets file, the phone rang.

"Doctor Kopfeinlaufen speaking," he said.

"Doctor, this is Deputy Chief Inspector Mullvaney of the Division of Special Investigations for the Borough of Manhattan."

"Yes, Chief Mullvaney. How can I be of help?"

"Doc, we have a little problem on our hands. Nothing to get alarmed about. Can I drop by and see you this afternoon?"

"Well, I'm quite busy Friday afternoons. I catch up on my paper work. I'm sure you must know how it is."

"Yeah, sure. Like I said, it's nothing big and it won't take too long."

"Ah, it is some civic function of the Police Department."

"That's it," Mullvaney said.

"Well, perhaps you could tell me over the phone."

"I can't do that, Doc. It's going to be a surprise and there's no telling who might be listening. It would spoil the fun if the news got out."

"Yes, of course. I understand perfectly. Please come up then."

Siren blaring, Mullvaney rushed to Stuyvesant Hospital and made it to Kopfeinlaufen's office just as the doctor had described how each of the Ponchartrain triplets was playing out the part of the personality which they swore to be. It was indeed as he had thought. Brought up in an extremely sheltered and austere environment, the triplets had developed only one personality and not three as the doctors in Montreal had diagnosed. "A most unusual case," Kopfeinlaufen wrote. "Pierre Ponchartrain is the id, Jacques the superego, and Maurice the ego." It was quite clear. The only problem left was to have them begin talking to each other.

Kopfeinlaufen stood up as Mullvaney came in the door. Smiling openly, he came out from behind his desk and shook Mullvaney's hand.

"Good afternoon, Chief Mullvaney," he said.

"You remembered my name," Mullvaney said.

"In my profession it is a very important part of the job to remember names. Please sit down and tell me how I can help you with this little surprise."

"Please close the door, Doc."

Kopfeinlaufen closed the door and returned to his desk.

"No one can hear us now," he said, eager to learn why Mullvaney had come to see him with such urgency.

Mullvaney stood up, took the telephone apart, checked under the desk, felt behind pictures and diplomas on the wall and sat back down.

"I'm sorry to have to go to all this trouble but this is a serious matter."

"I know. Surprise parties are always that way. Is it the Mayor's birthday?"

"No, it's a little more serious than that, Doc. I didn't wanna tell you on the phone, but we have a mess on our hands. Nothing we can't handle, but major trouble if anything goes wrong. It's one of your cases."

"Ach, I knew it. It's Margo, the elephant lady. I tell her day in and day out about spraying the people passing by the hospital. Granted, Chief Mullvaney, the woman does not have a normal nose and her level of resentment of other people is enormous, but I thought we had made some progress. I must apologize."

"No, Doc, it's not your elephant lady. It's this Martinez kid you have here."

"Oh, that is different. You are here to plan his return to the school. That was the way things were handled in Vienna. The police was always involved in civic affairs. I'm glad to hear we have the same concern here in New York. I'm quite happy to report that the patient is completely recovered. Remarkable case. He has finally admitted that he is Armando Martinez, a Puerto Rican Vietnam veteran, student, hockey player and husband to be."

"Right, Doc. That's where we come in. That's the guy we're after. He's a member of a left-wing, communist-leaning organization. Very powerful group probably getting their signals directly from Cuba and Russia."

Kopfeinlaufen laughed uproariously.

"That is exactly what we have discovered." Mullvaney jumped up from the couch.

"He confessed?"

"No, Chief. Nothing like that. He has told us that his girlfriend got him interested in radical politics."

Mullvaney rubbed his hands as he listened.

"He suspects her of being a member of a group called United Front for Total Caribbean Independence," Kopfeinlaufen went on.

"Did he ever mention a man named El Falcon?" Mullvaney said.

Kopfeinlaufen thought for a moment and then shook his head.

"No, no one by that name was ever mentioned," he said.

Saying the name of his hated enemy angered Mullvaney, but he maintained his professional aplomb and listened as Kopfeinlaufen reported part of the information Armando Martinez had provided. When Kopfeinlaufen was finished Mullvaney knew little of any importance. Based on the doctor's testimony they had nothing new on Martinez or his girlfriend.

"I cannot tell you any more than I have. As it is, I have gone too far without violating my oath as a physician. Since it is a serious matter, we will treat this as an unofficial conversation. Do I have your word, Chief?"

"Absolutely, Doc. My lips are sealed and I really appreciate your help. Now, let me tell you the story. The young girl, Maritza Soto, is a dangerous criminal and she's involved with this group. As a matter of fact, she's one of the leaders. To make matters worse, El Falcon, their Supreme Commander, flew the coop a couple of months back and joined up with them."

"Ach, that is incredible, Chief Mullvaney," Kopfeinlaufen said. He was truly amazed by his own genius and was more convinced than ever that Armando Martinez had told the truth and revealed his fantasy world completely at the same time.

"The incredible part is that this revolutionary group is planning your patient's escape this Tuesday."

"That's not possible, Chief Mullvaney," said Kopfeinlaufen, suddenly alarmed. "We cannot allow any interference with the program."

"I know how you feel, Doc, but we have to stop these nuts before they take over the city. By the time they're through there'd be nothing left. Leave it up to them and they'd have the subway back down to a nickel, everybody on welfare, and communism being taught in the schools. I know your program here at the hospital's gotta run smooth like, but we gotta stop these terrorists before they can do any more damage."

"Chief, I don't mean my program. I mean the television program. We have already arranged it for eight o'clock on Tuesday. Howland Gosell is going to do a live program for national television on our patient's recovery. It's part of Wild Whirl of Sports."

"Can't you have it cancelled? You have to."

"That's impossible, Chief. It would take a presidential order to stop Howland Gosell and there's no way of telling if that would work. You've heard Vice-President Agnew talk many times. Television runs the government. It would be easier to stop a nuclear attack than to stop Howland Gosell."

"Well, Doc, what can we do? Do we let them take the patient?"

Although extremely concerned by this new complication, Dieter Kopfeinlaufen's brilliant and complex mind saw the situation as a blessing in disguise. Earlier in the afternoon, before Mullvaney had called, Kolodny had delivered his report and it was quite encouraging. What better proof of his patient's true identity than having his own people attempt his rescue on national television. Ah, he thought, science and modern technology blending to produce the ultimate triumph of man. Dear, dear Friedrich was right. Man could surpass himself. He thought for a moment and then presented his plan to Mullvaney. They had to have the police on hand in case anything went wrong, but they must not appear to be police.

"The matter is quite simple, Chief Mullvaney. This is a moment of great medical significance. There is nothing to prevent me from bringing several of my colleagues to observe medical history in the making. I have already received many requests for data on my findings concerning the case. There is plenty of room in the psychiatric environment we have created for the patient. A few more doctors, as observers, would not be in the way and may prove invaluable in an emergency. They would swing quickly into action in order to suppress any problem which might arise. I am convinced of that."

Mullvaney tried to follow the plan, but it was becoming obvious that Ramirez' book on this man was lacking. What the hell was he talking about? How could more doctors help? And then it hit him. Of course it would help if the doctors were his own men dressed as doctors. That was it. It was worth a try. He'd suggest it and see how the doctor took it.

"Doc, I don't mean to question your judgment, but in case of an emergency, it would be a good idea if the doctors knew a little bit about police science. These U.F. people can play rough."

"Yes, of course," Kopfeinlaufen smiled. "Do you have any ideas?"

"Well, Doc, I only have top men in my Division. All of them took courses in First Aid. They can set bones or break them. That's a joke," Mullvaney chuckled.

"I understand, Chief."

"All of them are very competent. They can give mouth to mouth, deliver babies and I even have one guy who did a trach job with a can opener and a fuel line. It saved a priest's life. The poor guy had swallowed his tongue."

"That's an excellent suggestion, Chief," Kopfeinlaufen said, pleased with himself. "We have uniforms here and plenty of stethoscopes. But you must make sure your men do as little talking as possible and then only in whispers. You have been in hospitals. Doctors are always conferring with each other and you never know what's going on. At all times your men must look very bored. That we also learn in the medical profession. The more critical a situation the more we must appear as if everything is routine. It is done to ease the relatives' worries. So please remind your men of these things."

"Bored, right?" Mullvaney said. "My men won't have any problem with that. Don't worry about a thing on that score."

"How many men do you think you'll need, Chief?"

Mullvaney thought for a moment.

"Let's see," he said. "There's gonna be a big demonstration outside the hospital, so the Front is gonna maybe use two men to spring the Martinez kid. Maybe three, at the most four. That means we'll need five men, including myself."

"Good, Chief. You must give me the men's measurements so we can fit them as soon as possible. They will be wearing white and wear black name tags. I need their names so that we can make up the tags and identification cards. I will also need small photographs for their identification cards. We have a very strict security system here at the hospital, particularly on this floor. We will have everything ready Monday afternoon. Oh, one more thing."

"Yes, Doc."

"The TDE, the Total Detraumatizing Environment, where we keep the patient and where the television show will take place is air tight, and a constant supply of oxygen is pumped into a vent to provide a healthier environment for the patient. The more oxygen which we provide the brain, the easier it is for the patient to regress. There must be absolutely no smoking in the TDE. Once the door is closed the room will be air-tight."

"I understand, Doc," Mullvaney said. "Air-tight. No smoking."

Mullvaney was pleased with himself. That's what they'd have on El Falcon, an air-tight case. He stood and came over to the desk. Kopfeinlaufen stood up and the two men shook hands.

"Doc," Mullvaney said, "the City of New York ain't gonna forget this. The Mayor is gonna get a report when this is wrapped up."

"Thank you, Chief," Kopfeinlaufen said. "Always happy to cooperate."

Mullvaney walked out of Kopfeinlaufen's office convinced that this time he'd capture El Falcon. Kopfeinlaufen returned to his file on the Ponchartrain triplets. Why did they not speak to each other? Perhaps they had nothing to say, since they each knew what was going on with the other two.

Kopfeinlaufen began writing.

CHAPTER 28

Wherein we are treated to a television sports spectacular, witness a fierce battle as it is played out in the form of a hockey game, observe the effects of not paying attention to chemistry lessons, endure the presence of a truly obnoxious sports announcer, and are once again amazed by El Falcon's knack for disappearing.

The crew of Wild Whirl of Sports began arriving at Stuyvesant Hospital shortly after five o'clock Tuesday afternoon. Across the street from the hospital a group of students had just finished taking some large signs out of a Volkswagen mini-bus and were preparing to start marching up and down the sidewalk. Prominent among the signs were the slogans LET MARTINEZ GO and FREE MANDO NOW. Around the corner about one hundred demonstrators had set up a chant of FREEDOM in low humming voices. The group would later grow to more than a thousand, the unnerving humming serving as a bass rhythm to the rest of the demonstration.

The producer of the program, a middle-aged, short-haired man was now issuing out personally whispered instructions to the television crew as they moved hurriedly from their vehicles into the hospital. The mood was one of tension, with seething tempers barely under control. The appearance of the camera crew produced loud boos from the students across the street. The students had hoped to appear on the six o'clock news and air their grievances. The cameras, however, were wheeled inside the hospital and into an elevator.

Although the crew had been briefed about the size of Frank Garboil's room and where they would set up their equipment they were still amazed by the enormity of the converted solarium and its uncanny resemblance to a hockey rink, its gleaming white floor marked off with circles and lines such as on an actual playing surface. On the walls there were banners from every National Hockey League team and suspended from the ceiling were large American and Canadian flags.

The boom man, an avid hockey fan, deposited his equipment in a corner of the room, picked up a stick and, finding a soft rubber puck, began taking shots and raising his stick high every time the puck rippled against the cords.

Garboil watched the rotund little man, perhaps only a few years older than himself, not pitying him but understanding now better than ever what drove grown men to become so obsessed with a game, any game. He was able to concede that hockey still had a strong appeal for him, but no longer felt the drive to prove himself. He wanted to be near his sons and watch them play. He wondered if he'd ever looked as ridiculous as the boom man.

One of the prop men, a young Puerto Rican in mod clothes, came over to Garboil and shook his hand.

"Hey, man, you was too much when you was playing at New Amsterdam," he said. "My name's José. My cousin, Alma, goes to City and she got me to go to a couple of games. How you doing?"

"I'm doing okay," Garboil said.

"Oh, man," José said, "this is a bitch of an assignment. They usually got me working the news, but my man Victor got sick and they asked me off the set to come over here. This Howland Gosell is one weird dude, man. Everything's gotta be perfect otherwise he starts hollerin' and carryin' on. He won't show up for a while, but when he does watch him real good. He's all into announcing sports and whatnot, but the man don't even walk right. You know what I mean? Like if he was out in the playground and you threw him a ball the thing would probably hit him in the face and he'd trip over his feet. It's comical. You dig?"

José did a few quick dance steps and stuck out both of his hands, palms up. Garboil smacked them and thought about Billy Perez and Big Papa and Ray and One-eyed Pete. He wondered why they hadn't come to see him in the hospital.

"Jive, that's what this dude Gosell is, man," José said, sliding closer to Garboil. "He does a beautiful show once he's sitting down, but the rest of the time he's spastic."

"A retard," Garboil said, recalling the catchall word for any poor athlete. The word convulsed José, much as it had the guys in the neighborhood. He bent over, unable to contain his laughter.

"That's it, man," he said. "Beautiful! Wait till he gets here. But don't laugh or nothing or he'll catch a fit and cook you on camera; make you look real bad."

"When's he coming?"

"About an hour before the show. Mucho limousine and whatnot. Hey, man, you going back to school when you get out?"

"Yeah, sure, man."

"You gonna play, right? Cauze I'ma tell you somethin', bro. Those white boys ain't shit without you. You understand what I'm saying?"

If he only knew, Garboil thought, he would probably want to kill me. What was it about himself that convinced everyone that he was Puerto Rican? Yes, he had black, curly hair and a moustache and brown skin, but there had to be something else which produced such a startling effect on other Puerto Ricans. How could he be so convincing to them?

"Yeah, well, as soon as I get myself out of this jive hospital I'll start skating again and see what happens," he said.

"I hear you, bro. I seen you play and you got that thing going nice, man. And don't listen to none of those jiveass people, telling you that you're crazy. You ain't any crazier than the next guy and they got you in this nuthouse. These people just joggin' with you cauze you got into playing hockey and you're good. There's a lot of folks behind you, you being a veteran and whatnot."

"Thanks, man," Garboil said.

"That's all right, man. You're Mando to the people. Listen, I gotta go set up the shit before the man gets here. I'll catch you later and when ole Howland starts going at you just tell it like it is."

"I got you, man. Take it light."

The room was rapidly turning into a television studio. One technician was installing a small, remote control camera inside the net. Once it was in place, another technician tested it on the monitor. The boom man was still taking shots. On the monitor he appeared bloated and even more out of shape. The two large cameras had been set up in each of the near corners of the rink, behind the boards of the playing surface. The director was instructing José and another prop man how to set up the table where the interview was to take place.

Garboil's thoughts turned to Ingrid Konkruka. With Maritza not coming to visit him his attention had shifted to Ingrid. He was certain she was in on whatever El Falcon was cooking up. FREEDOM 2/9 8 PM the message had read. A cold fear suddenly invaded his body. It wasn't possible. He looked at the calendar behind him and saw that indeed it was February 9. Whatever El Falcon had planned and the television program for Wild Whirl of Sports would be taking place at the same time. Where was Ingrid? Her advice that he not panic had been valuable as long as she was present, but he hadn't seen her in three days and now the closer it got to eight o'clock the more nervous he grew. He recalled the last conversation he'd had with Ingrid.

"What the hell am I gonna do if the U.F. manages to get me out of here?" he'd said. "I can't go back to New Amsterdam."

"Don't worry about that," she'd reassured him. "You have my address and there's a set of keys taped to the bottom of your bed at the pillow end. No matter what happens come there right away. We'll think of something. One way or the other you'll get out. Just put on your best performance and things will work out.

Kopfeinlaufen is convinced that you're recovered. And he's convinced that you're still in love with that girl, Maritza."

"Yeah, that was pretty convincing."

"Well, are you?" she'd said, and he'd sensed a tinge of jealousy in her question.

"I don't know," he'd said. "I don't think so."

Now, as he watched the television crew make its final preparations, he wished he could summon up the courage he'd found during the previous year. He tried to concentrate and work up some of the driving energy he'd felt but all his mind produced were economic graphs, formulas and some quotes from Thorsten Veblen.

When he tried thinking about his life all that came out were doubts. He shouldn't have left his job or Joan or the children. Did he love Maritza? Did she love him? If she did, why hadn't she come to see him at the hospital? He definitely should've written to Joan. She'd told him she and the boys would be at her parents' home. But he'd made no attempt to contact them and she had no way of contacting him either.

He looked at the clock. It was now six o'clock. The room was now ready and the television crew was sitting around, talking and smoking. Every once in a while one of the men looked over to him, but for the most part they ignored him. He went into the bathroom and began changing into his New Amsterdam College home uniform, which had been delivered that morning on loan from the school. With it was a note from Coach Malinowski wishing him good luck. This was the first time he'd heard from anyone at the school. Even though it had been explained to him that for the therapy to work he had to be isolated and have no contact with his previous environment, he wished he could see Kevin and Bill Dankowski and Moose and the rest of his teammates. But that was crazy. He couldn't go back and play hockey after everything that had happened. He looked at the new white jersey with the Golden Hawk on the front and the number 11 high up on the sleeves but felt none of the excitement he'd once felt about the uniform.

Meanwhile, in the street outside Stuyvesant Hospital, Charles Mullvaney and his men were about to make their entrance into the hospital. Mullvaney had spent the entire weekend briefing his men and going over their plan to prevent the escape of Armando Martinez, but more to the point the capture of El Falcon. The cat operation had been a disaster and although it led to important intelligence on drug traffic, the numbers racket and other illegal activities, nothing had been picked up on the further plans of the United Front. Ramirez had finally suggested that the cat Mullvaney was after was too intelligent, had sensed a trap and had stayed away from the cuchifrito lure.

The five detectives parked their car down the street from the hospital and, dressed in white doctor's uniforms, each carrying a black bag, marched through the crowd of demonstrators and the considerable number of spectators that had congregated in the vicinity. The crowd now threatened to spill out into the street and disrupt traffic. Fearing that the demonstrators would storm the hospital and attempt to remove Martinez, the uniformed police had set up barricades from one end of the hospital to the other. Luckily, television crews from the local stations and independent networks had arrived and were beginning to set up interviews with some of the leaders of the demonstration. The presence of the TV cameras calmed tempers somewhat but the crowd was still in an ugly mood.

As Mullvaney and his men moved through the crowd, Sam Marconi periodically reached for his gun, but it wasn't there. A cold sweat broke out on his forehead and his hands felt clammy. He had pleaded with Mullvaney to let him carry at least his small Berretta on his person but Mullvaney had insisted firearms be carried in the black doctor's bags. Marconi argued but to no avail. He now felt an overpowering urge to retrieve the small pistol from the bag.

"This is a delicate undercover mission," Mullvaney had said. "All of you men were taught self-defense at the Academy. Use it if you have to. How the hell's it gonna look if we have a big shootout in the middle of a hospital. Use your weapons only as a last resort." Marconi didn't like it and had looked at Cahill for support.

"Chief," Cahill had said. "It's gonna look worse if five cops get shot."

"Use your intelligence, Cahill," Mullvaney said. "Both Ramirez and Chota briefed us on El Falcon and there is no one in the department more familiar with his MO than yours truly. He's a genius at escape and doesn't think he needs guns for this kinda thing. He's a proud son of a bitch. He can disappear whenever he wants, and to use a gun takes the challenge out of the situation. I don't like what he stands for but I gotta respect him. Don't get me wrong. If he tried to get away and I had no choice I'd plug him. He's never used guns and I don't think he's gonna start now. It would be like Willie Mays suddenly wanting to play softball instead of baseball. The man is a commie through and through, but he's a professional. He's not gonna change his MO for this operation, so forget your worries."

Mullvaney, usually on edge during the waiting period of an operation, was cool and fatherly towards his men. He had waited so long for this second chance and now that his confrontation with El Falcon was to take place, his concentration was on making sure everything went smoothly, or as smoothly as these things could go. So many things could go wrong in an operation like this one. Marconi was still unconvinced. He was shaking his head and looking behind him every couple of steps. Mullvaney once again encouraged his men to approach every aspect of the operation with calm professionalism.

"When we go into the hospital," he said, "let's look as serious and concerned as we can. Make believe we're about to do major surgery on the Mayor."

"I don't like it, Chief," Marconi said, fidgeting with his doctor's bag. "I'm Italian, not Japanese. This is suicide."

"Just relax, Vito," Mullvaney said.

When they reached the front entrance of the hospital, the five men made their way through the throng gathering at the barricades. They showed their hospital identification to a police lieutenant not in on the operation who did not question their authenticity as doctors, and Mullvaney and his men went into the hospital.

The crowd had grown considerably in the past hour and, because it was not yet well-coordinated, it began to take on the aspect of a mob. People of many different social and political persuasions had begun a number of debates, so that for a person uninitiated to the issues there was no way to determine what the plight of whales had to do with the Gross National Product or those two issues with a woman's right to abortion or those three with whether the Catholic Church should come out in favor of gay rights since there were avowed, albeit celibate, homosexual priests in their midst.

Small incidences of violence had taken place, including knocking a policeman off his horse and kidnapping the mount, an action carried out by an animal rights group. Several scattered Puerto Rican groups were shouting slogans in Spanish and displaying posters in the language, but for the most part each group was using the issue of Armando Martinez for its own gain. The day had been unusually warm for February, but now that it had grown dark a cold wind had moved in, forcing some of the demonstrators to begin building fires in trash cans. The police ignored this violation, but the command post called in a fire engine just in case of more serious conflagrations.

Mullvaney and his men went directly to Kopfeinlaufen's office, where they were introduced to the rest of the staff as doctors from hospitals in different parts of the city. The only one who did not believe the story was Ingrid Konkruka. Helen Christianpath and Rapudiman Kohonduro were so wrapped up in the idea of being interviewed on television that they really did not care who the men were. Ingrid, on the other hand, felt apprehensive about the men's presence. She didn't know why, but there was something familiar about the way these men moved. Doctors they were not. They usually gave her an imploring look, much as if they wanted her forgiveness. At least two of them had given her lewd, suggestive looks, filling their eyes with her bosom and holding her gaze for more than was proper upon first meeting a person.

At seven o'clock, Dr. Kopfeinlaufen, along with his staff, led Mullvaney and his men to Frank Garboil's room. As they entered the room, Howland Gosell was in the middle of a heated discussion with the director of the show. Gosell was diminutive, nearly under five feet, although on television he'd looked much larger. In spite of the makeup that he already had on, it was apparent that he was nearly, if not over, seventy years of age. The skin on his face was wrinkled, but covered with cosmetic powder and coloring so that his complexion resembled that of a cadaver that has been prepared for display. More significantly, exactly as José, the technician, had described, Gosell appeared to have little control of his arms and legs, which moved seemingly independent of the wishes of their owner. His only saving grace appeared to be his voice which, even at a normal level of speech, resounded and filled the room. As if that were not sufficient, Gosell spoke with a pomposity and arrogance that made most men wish to seize the little man by the neck, lift him up to their own level and spit in his face. He looked up to the director of the show and began berating him.

"This is an absolutely impossible situation," he was saying while gesticulating wildly with his arms. "In all my years of dealing with people in the industry I have never seen a more blatant display of incompetency on the part of men who are so-called professionals. I ask you, Irving, is this the level at which you expect me to conduct an interview of such monumental importance?"

"But Howland," answered the cowed director, "we tried to get a different table. Maybe we can cover it up with the Wild Whirl of Sports banner."

"A splendid idea, Irving," said Howland Gosell. "For once in your erratic career you have shown a glimmer of potential intelligence."

Kopfeinlaufen directed Mullvaney and his men towards the far end of the room, behind the backboards and to the right of the scorer's table and scoreboard. Several seats had been placed and Mullvaney ordered his men to sit down. Although their view was partially obstructed, they had a clear line of sight to the door of the room. Upon entering the room Ingrid Konkruka went directly to the bathroom to see how Garboil was progressing.

"Are you almost ready?" she said.

"I've been ready for the past half hour," Garboil answered. "I didn't want to go out there yet. Is Howland Gosell here?"

"Sure, he's out there right now. Does he have back trouble or something? He ought to see a chiropractor or something. I've watched his shows but I never realized how disjointed he is. Maybe that's why he's so obnoxious all the time. Are you excited?"

"No, not really. I should be but I'm not. That always happened to me when I played. This last year anyway. Before that I used to have cramps and nausea, but this last year I would sit in a daze like I was being hypnotized. After the game I'd collapse inside and shake while I was taking a shower and then at night I'd have nightmares about monsters chasing me. I'll be all right. Just give me a few minutes to put on my shoulder pads and jersey and I'll be right out."

"All right. I'll be cheering for you," Ingrid said, and went out of the bathroom.

A few minutes later Kopfeinlaufen walked in and asked Garboil to stand up.

"You look wonderful, Armando," he said. "Your school will be so proud of you. I brought you a present. A brand new Koho stick. We must make a little showing of your anger to show how you deal with your aggressions on the goalie, meaning me. You must take the stick and come in yelling wildly, but without shooting the puck. Mr. Gosell insisted that we use a puck, but I explained that it would be medically contradictory for me to be trying to cure you of this illness and for you to accidentally injure me with one of your shots. He did not understand but that's to be expected. He is in grave need of psychiatric help. I am telling you this confidentially, but the man is in deep, deep trouble. He has a very serious Olympian god disorder. The aggression must emerge verbally. Of course this is national television so that you cannot use foul language, at least in English. I think it will be all right if you choose to express yourself in Spanish. I discussed this with Mr. Gosell and he thinks it would add a touch of color to the program. What do you think?"

"I don't know, Doctor," Garboil said, as humbly as he could. "Cursing is cursing. A lot of my people are gonna be watching."

"Fine, whatever you decide. I'm going in to change right now. You can go out there whenever you're ready and warm up. It's almost seven-thirty."

Garboil nodded and went out of the bathroom. He almost expected to hear cheering as he had whenever he came out of the locker room at the New Amsterdam games. The only applause came from José, the technician, who allowed his emotions to get the best of him when he saw the uniform. Howland Gosell gave José a piercing look and he stopped applauding. When Gosell looked away, José made a face and stuck out his tongue.

Gosell came forward and, as if he were winding up to pitch a horseshoe extended his hand towards Garboil. Startled by the odd move, Garboil took a couple of steps back before realizing that all Gosell wished to do was shake his hand. He removed his right glove, stuck it under his left arm and shook hands with Howland Gosell. He managed his best crooked smile, more out of embarrassment at the odd little man, and went into his shy jock routine.

"Good evening, young man," Gosell said. "I have followed with keen interest and more than a jaundiced eye your exploits of the past months and hope that you live up to the public's expectations."

Garboil feigned not understanding what Gosell had said and responded with several moronic nods and the most subservient "yes, sir" he could muster.

"Good, let that then suffice to set the tone for our future dealings," Gosell said.

Garboil looked at Helen Christianpath at the scorer's table and smiled weakly. She held up a peace V-sign and returned his smile. Rapudiman Kohonduro, in his referee's shirt, whistle and turban, acknowledged Garboil's presence with a slow, tiny bow of his head. Ingrid Konkruka gave Garboil a thumbs up salute when he looked her way. A cheer went up from the television crew and the camera turned to her. In the monitor she appeared more beautiful and appealing than ever. Howland Gosell coughed loudly once and the crew once again went back to their work.

Outside Stuyvesant Hospital the crowd had grown to more than two thousand people. They now lined both sides of the avenue.

One portion of the crowd had begun marching quietly around the hospital, which took up an entire city block. The policemen on duty, more than five hundred strong, had become edgy in the past hour and were beginning to grip their nightsticks with more force and fiddle with their guns. It was now seven forty-five and in fifteen more minutes the crowd would surge into the street and disrupt traffic going up First Avenue. On the other side of the hospital, as of yet unknown to the police, several hundred people had sat down in the middle of the Franklin D. Roosevelt Drive, completely stopping traffic in both directions. By eight o'clock the traffic would be backed up to the Brooklyn Bridge to the south and the Fifty-ninth Street Bridge to the north.

From the demonstrators' point of view everything was progressing according to plan. Before speaking with his grandfather at the medium's home, John Chota had organized his people well and every major liberal and left-wing political group in the city, plus the ones on most of the college campuses, was well represented. There was a small cluster of right-wing counter-demonstrators, but they were of no consequence and whatever message they were trying to get across was drowned out by the larger group.

Meanwhile, in the depths of Stuyvesant Hospital, the attack group of the United Front for Total Caribbean Independence was making its last preparations for the ascent and eventual rescue of Armando Martinez. The two days spent in the sub-basement of the hospital had not been pleasant. It had been difficult to get much sleep with the furnace blasting away and rats running back and forth along the pipes. They were huge rats with bulging, hungry eyes. Whenever the group had its meals, which consisted mostly of plantain chips, canned Vienna sausages and fruit nectars, the rats congregated above them, dozens of them, to observe the group eat. Several of the rodents looked as if they would attack any minute and once a rather grizzled one lost its footing and landed among the group, immediately scurrying away before the group realized what had happened.

Everything that could have gone wrong did. Besides the inconvenience of not being able to sleep well, Tomas, the oldest member of the group, had an allergic reaction to the basement and sneezed continuously. Enrique, the young man in the group, discovered that he was claustrophobic and did nothing but talk about being outside. Maritza, just that morning, began menstruating. Fortunately, she had come prepared. Her cramps, however, were of such intensity, she wished she hadn't come. The only thing that drove her on was rescuing Armando, seeing him again.

Besides the petty annoyances of living in such close proximity to each other, of being watched by rats and existing on a meager diet, Ricardo Ortiz, the other member of the old guard, turned out to be suffering from chronic flatulence, which he discharged with malodorous and remarkable regularity.

During the early hours of Monday morning, Ricardo, because of his condition, and Enrique, because of his claustrophobia, were given the responsibility of securing a wheeled stretcher and a plasma unit. Additionally, El Falcon asked them to obtain two cylinders of ether. The stretcher and plasma rig were no problem at all. Ricardo Ortiz, looking very much the part of a hospital porter, wheeled the stretcher from the neurosurgical floor. When asked by a doctor where he was taking it, Ricardo explained that it had to be repaired. The doctor had not asked about the plasma. The plan to obtain a heart machine had been scrapped at the last minute, since none of them knew what it looked like. The problem of obtaining ether was quite another matter. Young Enrique Morales, likewise dressed as a hospital porter, well briefed by El Falcon on the location of the anesthesia, could not gain access to the room. The room was solid, reinforced steel, triple-locked and evidently rigged up to an alarm system. Recalling the floor plan of the hospital and gifted with great imagination and courage, Enrique managed to gain entrance to a suite in the dental wing of the hospital. The offices, as well as the operating rooms, were deserted and most of the doors open. Working with a small pencil flashlight, he located a large cylinder with a facial attachment and a hose, everything mounted on a wheeled cart. He searched the other two operating rooms and found similar cylinders, each marked with the designation "N_2O Anesthesia." Enrique wheeled the first cylinder out of the operating rooms, into the elevator and down into the sub-basement. He returned twice to retrieve the other two cylinders.

"What you got there, Chico?" asked the elevator operator, a sleepy Black man, on Enrique's last trip down.

"Is emptee," Enrique said, in his best Puerto Rican accent. "Day axe me to breeng eet down so it go in dee molneen."

At that time of night the elevator operator did not much care who came or went as long as the elevator wasn't too much in demand. He asked Enrique for his floor. Enrique explained that he wished to go to the sub-basement and the elevator plunged directly there. Enrique thanked the elevator operator and wheeled the last of the carts down the hall and towards the hideout. He knocked on the door twice, counted to ten and knocked once. The door opened and he pushed the cylinder in.

"Good work, comrade," said El Falcon. "Is that the last of the ether? Comrade Maritza tells me that you have brought down two other cylinders, so that we are in luck. I was planning on using only one cylinder of anesthesia but perhaps this is an omen. We will bring all three. Excellent, comrade."

"I ran into a small obstacle, my commander," Enrique said, apologetically. "I could not enter the anesthesia room, but I was able to enter the dental section of the hospital. That is where I found the three cylinders."

El Falcon looked at the chemical notation and nodded.

"It is anesthesia," he said. "The words are printed there. Very well, we are well-stocked. Let us get some rest. Ignore the rats. I will stand guard. The more sleep we get, the more alert we will be at the critical moment."

The day had gone slowly. Each member had taken turns listening to a portable radio with an ear plug in order to learn how the demonstration was proceeding. By six o'clock that evening, the demonstration had made the news and by seven-thirty, when the attack group held its final briefing, the demonstration was being reported as massive and potentially dangerous. Even several stories below street level they could hear muffled slogans being shouted out in the street.

At seven-thirty Don Alfonso del Valle, El Falcon, stood up.

"Comrades, let me once again remind you of the great importance of our mission. It is not only a mission of great humanitarian import but one of major political significance. If we are successful, and of this I have no doubt, we will manage to shame the imperialist pigs into admitting that we are a force with which they must contend. I will be handling the anesthesia. If there is an emergency, I will open the valves, releasing the gas. As soon as you smell the odor, put on your gas masks. All of you know your assignments. Carry them out thoroughly and do not think of personal gains. Think only of freedom. Please, put on your operating gowns, caps and surgical masks."

After the members of the group were dressed, El Falcon looked at his watch and signaled for a time check. It was now seven-forty-nine and thirty seconds. Each of the members of the group checked his watch and made the necessary adjustment.

"Let us begin," El Falcon said. "Comrade Maritza, you will go first. Each one of us will follow at five minute intervals. We will meet in the designated area, that is, the hall leading to the solarium where they are holding our comrade. At approximately 8:20 we will etch our names in the history of our struggle. Good luck, comrades."

El Falcon went to each of the members of the attack group, shook his hand and embraced him. When he came to Maritza, he paused momentarily, looked at her and nodded.

"You are the most courageous young woman I have ever met," he said and then shook her hand and embraced her. "Please be extra careful," he added.

Maritza Soto thanked El Falcon, adjusted her face mask and went out of the basement room. She rang for the elevator, got on and went to the eighth floor. She bought a Pepsi-Cola from a vending machine and sat down in one of the staff lounges to watch television. As fate would have it, the theme for the start of Wild Whirl of Sports came on. She watched for several seconds and then, being alone in the lounge, switched channels. Had she watched another few minutes, she would have learned the content of the program and it is quite likely that the action of the United Front would have been aborted. In keeping with their plan, each of the members of the attack group followed a different procedure on different floors.

Upstairs, Garboil's room had been moving with efficient precision. Howland Gosell, microphone in place on his shirt, was seated behind the announcer's table, near the entrance to the bathroom, labeled with a sign: "locker room." The director had counted off the seconds to eight o'clock. At precisely eight he pointed to Gosell, who underwent a total change in facial expression. From the grumpy, disagreeable martinet he was, he turned into an amiable but concerned critic, a confidant and personal friend who could clarify the issues as one sat at home.

"Good evening, ladies and gentlemen, and welcome to Wild Whirl of Sports. Tonight we bring you a story of near tragedy. Yes, near tragedy because, were it not for the tireless efforts of one Dieter Kopfeinlaufen, psychiatrist, sports enthusiast and human being, a young man of exceptional potential might not be with us tonight.

"Of course I am referring to Armando Martinez, Vietnam veteran, college student, hockey player. A simple lad of Puerto Rican origin involved in as bizarre a tale as has been witnessed or recorded in the history of sports.

"Raised in the streets of New York with crime, addiction, prostitution and general degeneracy rampant, he raised himself from the moral turpitude of this existence to serve his country in time of war. He survived that war and returned to fulfill a lifetime ambition to study Economics at New Amsterdam College of the City University of New York. Let us then meet this young man up close and personal."

The screen now turned to a quick montage of shots showing Garboil in different hockey games, skating hard, checking, scoring, celebrating victory, the file footage from those games which had been covered by a local television station when New Amsterdam began to receive attention from the media. There were a few shots of Garboil and Maritza walking hand in hand at the school. Garboil looked at the monitor which had been set up away from the scorer's table and liked what he saw. Somehow, his apprehensions about the upcoming program had disappeared and a calm had taken over. The feeling was quite similar to what he experienced when he played. The narration was filled with superlatives on his hockey skills. An interview with the coach of the New York Rangers added credibility to the story.

The interview embarrassed Garboil.

"What is your opinion, Coach?" Howland Gosell asked.

"There is definite potential there, Howland," the coach said.

"Let me come right to the point, Coach. Would the New York Rangers draft this young man?"

"Of course, Howland, as you know the draft is a very complex process and I for one do not make those decisions. The young man has three more years of college hockey. Should he decide to continue his career, we would definitely scout him under game conditions and make a determination based on those reports."

"There you have it, ladies and gentlemen," Gosell said. "Words of praise from a man who's been involved in hockey for nearly forty years. And such is the mettle of this courageous athlete. We will be talking to this remarkable youth later on in the program."

The camera has now turned back to Gosell. Sitting next to him is Kopfeinlaufen. He is dressed in goalie equipment, over which he is wearing a doctor's white gown.

"Seated alongside of me," Gosell said, "is the aforementioned Dieter Kopfeinlaufen. Good evening, Doctor, and welcome to Wild Whirl of Sports."

"Good evening, Howland," Kopfeinlaufen said. "It is a pleasure to be here with you tonight. It is an honor to appear on your show."

"Let me cut you short, Dr. Kopfeinlaufen, and get right to the heart of the matter in this amazing story. You have employed what can best be described as a total approach to Armando's problem."

"Yes, Howland. We, as you can see, have created a total hockey environment. We keep the temperature constantly at thirty-two degrees and have sealed the room completely to maintain it sterile. Oxygen is pumped in through special vents to facilitate the oxygenation of the brain and therefore produce quick healing."

"Please elaborate, Doctor."

"Well, emotional illness is no different than any other illness. In each case infection sets in and the body does not have the required anti-bodies to combat the illness. We are constantly exposed to insanity in all forms, but not all of us become susceptible to it. Those of us who do fall prey to differing mental and emotional illnesses need the same care provided for other illnesses."

"Are you saying there is a close relationship between the fighting of mental illness and sports?"

"Absolutely. The metaphor is an appropriate one. The illness is the opposition and we, the medical profession, are the home team."

"Absolutely remarkable, Dr. Kopfeinlaufen. Is it safe to say that, in the case of Armando Martinez, the home team is winning the game?"

"There is no question about this, Howland."

"Doctor, let me be blunt. What do you hope to accomplish and how did you come up with this remarkable place?"

"Well, Howland, as always the point of departure is simply that the patient has suffered great psychic trauma. In the case of Armando Martinez, the trauma was caused by his war experiences. To his credit he was able to deal with those experiences in the best way possible, that is, to suppress them and learn to cope. Had he not been able to deal with them, his Total Detraumatizing Environment would resemble a battlefield. As it is, Armando was able to cope and live a relatively normal life at a conscious level. Unbeknownst to him, however, his subconscious was quite active, as it is in all of us. When he began to play ice hockey, with its speed and the life-death urgency which the hockey establishment seems to thrive on, the original trauma began to surface in the patient."

"What you're saying, Doctor, borders on an indictment of the hockey establishment."

"No, Howland, I am strictly speaking in medical terms. Competition is healthy and there is no better sport for young men to pursue than ice hockey. I am, however, talking about the non-players and their driving of young men to surpass their emotional limits and capabilities."

"Are you saying that hockey is more stressful than war?"

"In many ways it is. In war there is always the possibility of death, but in hockey death comes in the form of defeat."

"As it does in every game, Doctor," Gosell said.

"Aha, Howland, but with one exception. In hockey there is constant movement and tremendous emotional investment made. Scoring does not occur that often, but when it does, it happens suddenly. Very similar to a battle."

"I am not entirely convinced of this metaphor which you have created, Doctor, but let us proceed. How were you able to determine that your so-called detraumatizing environment should take the form of a hockey rink?"

"Yes, the reoccurrence of our patient's condition, of the battlefield trauma, took place during a hockey game. For us to even tap the subconconscious, it was necessary to begin at the first layer of trauma. In this hockey game there were a number of injuries, one so serious that it produced a cathartic reaction in our patient and left him in a total condition of helplessness regarding his identity. Our task was to bring the patient to a realization that, in his mind, he had used hockey as a metaphor for the recreation and resolution of his battlefield experiences, but more significantly for the resolution of the battle raging within him and the guilt that he felt about being Puerto Rican."

"Are you saying that Armando Martinez did not want to be Puerto Rican?"

"It's more complicated than that, Howland. To be Puerto Rican is a very tough proposition. We are dealing with a strong-minded people whose men are taught from infancy to defend the honor of their women, but whose country has never known independence. How can this problem be resolved in the individual, other than through a negation of his identity? It is a question which has tremendous implications, Howland, and which in time may produce an epidemic of mental illness for the entire Puerto Rican population. Our patient was convinced that he was someone else, an Economics professor at a nearby college. He must be commended for wishing to better himself, but his desire was nothing more than an elaborate escape mechanism constructed to avoid dealing with his identity. You see, once the trauma was uncovered and dealt with, Armando was left with the realization that he was indeed Puerto Rican. Now that he has accepted this, we can release him and he can proceed with the business of being himself."

"A remarkable accomplishment, Doctor. Thank you very much. One last question. What we are about to see after we speak with Armando will be a demonstration of the treatment you employed?"

"Yes, Howland."

"In other words we will see a recreation of the illness in the form of actual bodies attacking the system, and the medical profession, your staff, combatting this illness."

Kopfeinlaufen smiled enigmatically and answered in the affirmative. If everything went according to what Mullvaney had said, the United Front would arrive shortly and Mullvaney's men would engage them. What better way to show the world his great accomplishment and the fact that his patient had been treated and cured than for his people to appear and attempt his rescue. His name, Dieter Kopfeinlaufen, would be entered in the annals of psychiatric history alongside those of Freud and Jung. Triumph at last.

"Thank you again, Dr. Kopfeinlaufen. Ladies and gentlemen, you heard it. We will pause for some commercial messages and return with the subject of tonight's program, Armando Martinez, followed by a demonstration of the treatment which brought this young man back from the depths of mental illness to a condition of normalcy."

The screen faded and commercial messages for a number of assorted products, including headache remedies, vitamins and allergy treatments appeared. Two minutes later Howland Gosell appeared once more.

"Welcome back, ladies and gentlemen," he said.

The cameras then switched their attention to the middle of the ice-like surface where Frank Garboil stood in full hockey uniform, sliding a puck back and forth on his stick. Dr. Kopfeinlaufen signaled him to come forward and Garboil came over to the table. On his skates he appeared well over six-foot tall. His black moustache gave him a fierce and determined appearance. Before reaching the table, he turned around, wound up and fired a booming slapshot which hit the post, made the familiar pinging sound and went into the net. On the monitor the scene looked very much like a scene in an actual hockey rink. The floor glistened like ice and was almost as slippery.

Garboil turned, came over to the table where Howland Gosell was seated and took a seat.

"Ladies and gentlemen," Gosell said, "seated beside me is the picture of determination and courage. Armando Martinez, star left wing of the New Amsterdam College Golden Hawks, welcome to Wild Whirl of Sports. In the archives of sports history and lore, there has never been a comeback the likes of this one. One is reminded of the dynamic James Piersall, one-time outfielder of the Boston Red Sox, a gifted athlete, who battled his emotional unrest and returned to the diamond and displayed once again his baseball playing talent. Armando, how do you feel?"

"I feel fine, Mr. Gosell," Garboil said.

"Armando, I know this has been a terrible ordeal."

"Yeah, an ordeal and a half. Wow, man. A real bleep."

"Yes," smiled Gosell, uncomfortably. "Now that you've recovered, what would you like to do?"

"I wanna go back to school and tell my teammates and the coach that I'm sorry I got sick. I know I gotta lotta catching up to do, but I know I can do it."

"Anything else?"

"Well, yeah, like I wanna say hello to everyone. You know, my family and my teammates and fans up at New Amsterdam and especially to the guys on the block. They know who they are. How you doing, Pete, Billy, Ray and Big Papa. And like I wanna thank the doctors here at the hospital and the rest of the staff, because if they didn't help me, I don't know what I was gonna do."

"Ladies and gentlemen, you heard it directly from this young man, who stands before you as the essence of what it is that separates sports from the rest of human endeavor, the uncommon courage and determination of the true athlete, of the human being who does not let adversity stand in the way of his ambition, of a drive which puts all thought of defeat aside for the sake of an ideal, which at times may be ephemeral but always timeless. This young man does not need the inspiration of the great Vince Lombardi. He has the desire, the will and the spirit required to triumph in the arena of life. Armando, your team is now in second place in its division. Your scoring punch has been sorely missed. Do you honestly think you can regain your skating form, timing and strength in time to help them finish first and go into the playoffs?"

"Yes, Mr. Gosell. I think if I can leave the hospital, I can start skating and training again."

"Armando, let me call your doctor over and ask him point blank on national television how he evaluates your chances of getting back into top form before the playoffs start." Gosell motioned to Kopfeinlaufen, who waddled over. "Doctor, as you can see this lad is ready to resume his athletic career. He is willing and able to begin work as soon as you release him. When, in your learned opinion, will he be able to leave Stuyvesant Hospital?"

"Howland, it is quite possible that he can leave the hospital tonight. In fact, barring any complications, certainly this week, but tonight is a definite possibility."

"Remarkable, Doctor. Simply remarkable. Ladies and gentlemen, let's pause for some commercial messages and we will return immediately with a demonstration of Dr. Kopfeinlaufen's treatment of Armando Martinez."

The screen faded once again and commercials appeared. As the commercials were being shown, there were last minute preparations and directions were given to the camera crews. On the bench, behind the boards, Mullvaney and his men sat impassively, except for Marconi, who was still edgy. It was now eight-thirty and nothing had happened. He always had trouble waiting and each time he had to wait something bad had gone down. He watched the director count the seconds and, when the commercials were over, point to Gosell.

Outside in the street, the demonstration had reached its apex and quickly turned into a full-scale riot, with the demonstrators battling the police. Mullvaney and his men were unaware of this. The one radio they had was on Mullvaney's person and only to be used in case of extreme emergency. The Commissioner of Police, however, was conferring with the Mayor on the possibility of using tear gas to disperse the crowd.

Down the corridor from the solarium where Wild Whirl of Sports was now on the second half hour of its special on Armando Martinez' recovery, the attack group of United Front was marching towards its ultimate confrontation with history. Maritza was pushing the stretcher while the older men and Enrique pushed the three cylinders filled with anesthesia. Several of the television crew not operating the equipment saw the group arrive with its equipment, made way for them to enter the room.

They thought little of the green-gowned and masked individuals, assuming that they were part of the staff which was about to demonstrate the treatment.

El Falcon was surprised that there were so many people present, but he was aware that the treatment which the young man was undergoing was strange and that the imperialists would stop at nothing. The fact that so many people were required to brainwash the young comrade was proof of his fighting spirit. He looked at the other members of the group and signaled them to proceed. The group moved into position on the opposite side of the ice from the scorer's table. On the screen, the viewers once again saw Howland Gosell.

"Ladies and gentlemen, the moment you have been waiting for. As you can see, Dr. Dieter Kopfeinlaufen is dressed in ice-hockey goalie's equipment, perhaps symbolic of how he has saved young Armando Martinez from suffering. He and Armando, and I assume the staff, since I see that a number of new medical personnel has entered the room, appear ready. Seated on one side are the doctors, five of them, members of the staff. Seated across with anesthesia equipment, and dressed in green, is the rest of the staff. Is that right, Doctor?"

"That is correct, Howland," smiled Kopfeinlaufen.

"Explain the method for our audience, Doctor."

So that is how they hoped to accomplish their end, thought Kopfeinlaufen, glancing over to the other side of the room at the attack group. Very ingenious and very daring. He looked at Mullvaney, but he and his men were oblivious that what they were there to prevent was very close to occurring.

"It's very simple, Howland," Kopfeinlaufen said. "Armando was suffering from great hostility towards himself and therefore towards his people. Part of the treatment consisted of revealing himself slowly, allowing his psyche to express itself freely, so that whenever he reached a point of frustration, he was able to direct his agression, verbally of course, towards an authority figure, mainly me. Unlike his experiences of hostility in the game of hockey, or for that matter war, here he was asked to vent his anger verbally, to articulate his physical and psychic frustration."

"Is that why you're wearing goalie equipment?"

"Exactly. I will now take my position at the goal, signal Dr. Kohonduro, who is my assistant, and serves as the referee, and to the timekeeper, Miss Helen Christianpath and also to Nurse Konkruka, who is in charge of the scoreboard. Every time Armando releases a burst of anger, he is rewarded by Dr. Kohonduro with a score. If he avoids the issue, he is assessed penalties, which can range from being denied reading the sports pages to watching the New York Rangers on television."

"Very well, Doctor. Proceed, and the best of luck."

Kopfeinlaufen waddled away from the announcer's table. As he passed the bench where Mullvaney and his men were seated, he paused for a few moments.

"They're here, Chief," he said.

"Who's here?" Mullvaney replied, suddenly startled.

"The people you're looking for. Across the way."

"How do you know that?" Mullvaney said.

"No one should be here except my staff and your men."

"Son of a bitch," Mullvaney said. He glanced across the room and back to Kopfeinlaufen. "Son of a bitch," he repeated. "You're right. It's him. El Falcon in the flesh. Even with all that crap on I know it's him. What the hell do you think he's up to?"

"I don't know, but get ready."

"What about the program? It's going pretty good. Howland Gosell is better in person than on TV."

"Don't worry about the program, Chief. Just make sure you are at your best. Who knows, being on national television and saving our patient from kidnapping may earn you a promotion. Think about it."

Mullvaney thought a moment and then nodded his agreement. Kopfeinlaufen waddled away towards the net as Mullvaney huddled with his men. To El Falcon and the attack group standing across the room, the scene appeared to be nothing more than a group of doctors conferring with each other. And yet there was something odd about the men, something vaguely familiar about them, a certain dullness in their eyes. El Falcon didn't know what set the men apart, but was at once on his guard. Now the group would have to attack immediately, swiftly. It was certainly an elaborate way to brainwash a person. The sooner they got the young comrade away from the lights and cameras, the better it would be.

The only person in the attack group who knew that everything was not as had been expected was Enrique. Himself a sports enthusiast, he recognized Howland Gosell instantly. As with most sports fans, however, he became a spectator and totally caught up in watching the inner workings of the television program. When he finally got around to telling El Falcon that perhaps the television cameras weren't part of the treatment, Mullvaney and his men had been alerted by Kopfeinlaufen. El Falcon immediately gave the signal for the attack group to spring into action.

At that precise moment Kopfeinlaufen reached the net. He raised his hand and air horns went off, followed by recorded wild cheering from the sound system. Dr. Kohonduro, standing in the middle of the rink, dropped the puck. Frank Garboil got it on his stick, moved towards the goal and was about to let loose with a barrage of insults when he felt someone grab his arm. Garboil turned and was momentarily startled. He recognized the piercing eyes of the man who had brought him his lunch and the message that the escape was to take place. A sudden fear gripped him at the thought that in being rescued by the United Front he would be branded a revolutionary. But who would? Frank Garboil or Armando Martinez? He wished suddenly that he could start over again at the point that he decided he wanted to play ice hockey and somehow redirect his life once more.

Also at that precise moment, Mullvaney and his men came over the boards and converged at center ice. To the viewers at home, this coming together of the two groups appeared quite normal. Enrique coughed and addressed Dr. Kohonduro.

"Good evening, my name is Dr. Morgan," Enrique said "We have orders to take the patient downstairs for emergency surgery."

"What surgery?" Kohonduro said. "I know nothing of any surgery. This must be a mistake."

"It's no mistake," Enrique replied.

"It has to be a mistake."

"You're mistaken. It's not a mistake. Tests were taken early this morning and they show that the patient needs immediate heart surgery."

"Then it is definitely a mistake and you are very mistaken."

"No, it's you who's mistaken and there's no mistake about that."

"Doctor, I think you're making a terrible mistake."

"We're taking the patient and if you try and stop us, you're gonna add another mistake to your first one," Enrique said.

The older members of the attack group wheeled the stretcher over to the middle of the room and urged Garboil to lie down on it. Kopfeinlaufen watched the scene with controlled amusement. At this point, Mullvaney ordered his men to seize El Falcon. Marconi had retreated to the bench, opened his bag and grabbed his pistol. Already numbed by what he had thus far seen, Garboil now noticed that Maritza was with the attack group. He stood with his mouth open, too shocked to move, but suddenly aware that he was erect.

"Don't worry," she said, "We'll have you outta here in no time."

Garboil shook his head and gazed into Maritza's eyes. How lovely she was and how much he wanted her. Maritza returned his look, but out of the corner of her eye saw Marconi.

"They're cops," she shouted. "It's a trap, he's got a gun."

She grabbed Garboil's hockey stick and with an upward swing hit Marconi's wrist. The pistol flew out of Marconi's hand

and skidded across the floor. Both groups began sliding after the elusive gun. Angry that Maritza had the advantage of a hockey stick, Mullvaney's men grabbed sticks of their own from the half dozen which the hospital had purchased as part of its program to rehabilitate Armando Martinez. The hockey sticks now in control of the opposition, Ricardo, Tomas and Enrique seized two brooms and a mop which they found standing against the wall near the bathroom.

Mullvaney ordered the door locked. Cahill immediately went to the entrance and locked it. He warned the television crew not to open it. The crew, assuming that they were witnessing part of what they'd come to film, nodded politely and continued watching the action.

The two groups, now being described by Howland Gosell as the doctors, who were dressed in white, and the illness, which was dressed in green, were engaged in a fierce struggle to control Marconi's pistol. It was at this point that El Falcon thought it judicious to use the anesthesia. He slid quickly across the floor and began opening the valves. He opened one, heard the hissing sound of the escaping gas but did not smell the familiar odor of ether. In quick succession he opened the next two cylinders. He achieved the same result. The hissing sound but no smell of ether. While he was checking the valve, the action shifted to his side of the room along the near boards.

Enrique had captured the puck on a broom, but was checked violently against the boards by Cahill. A scuffle immediately ensued which caused all three cylinders to be knocked over. The clatter of the bomb-like, metal cylinders striking the floor shook the room and Wild Whirl of Sports experienced technical difficulties for nearly a minute as a cable was reconnected. What proved more relevant than the interruption of the program was that two of the cylinders had their valves broken off, releasing the entirety of their contents, which contained not ether but nitrous oxide. By the time the cable was reconnected, the air-tight room was filled with the gas. The effects were instantaneous.

The properties of nitrous oxide are naturally anesthetic, but whereas ether causes the patient to lose consciousness, nitrous oxide merely blocks off the pain, leaving the person in an euphoric state. Dental patients, on whom it is often used, have at times reported pleasure. It appears that the greater the pain, the further removed from it the patient becomes.

Some people report experiencing sexual release while under the influence of nitrous oxide, while others boast of mystical experiences, and still others claim to see the future. In the majority of cases, however, the feeling of euphoria, of well-being, is universally experienced. A small percentage of people have an adverse reaction and a still smaller percentage of people become addicted to the gas. Some dentists have been known to use the gas in order to relax. It is safe to say that in the privacy of a dental office or in an operating room, patients can experience the effects of the gas and enjoy its salubrious effects with the benefit of a supportive environment.

Since there are no studies on the effects of nitrous oxide on a group, what next took place may give us an indication as to the properties of the gas when employed liberally on a gathering.

The first ones to succumb to its effects were the members of the attack group. The old men were immediately overcome with youthful vigor and wished nothing more than to assert their manhood. Having finally come in contact with the hated enemy, they desperately attempted to capture Marconi's pistol. Each time they drew closer they were assailed by Mullvaney's men, who meted out violent body checks that rattled the old men's bones. Neither Ricardo nor Tomas, however, felt much pain. The more they were hit, the more vigor they felt until finally, during a skirmish in front of the net, one and then the other passed out from sheer exhilaration.

Maritza, after a few minutes of inhaling the gas, decided this was a life-and-death struggle and saw herself once more battling in the mountains of the Island with Armando by her side, the two of them swooping down to attack a convoy of North American soldiers and single-handedly destroying it. The joy that she felt could not be measured. If death came at that point, she thought, it would be sweet and wonderful. She then saw herself in a casket, her body draped in the Puerto Rican flag, but a smile on her face because her mission had been accomplished. The image brought tears of joy to her eyes and her heart expanded to embrace all people. It was like a huge Coke commercial. At that moment, however, with the pistol on her stick and moving gracefully along the boards, she was suddenly hit with a violent check by Cahill, who piled on top of her and attempted to put his hands under her blouse. Garboil, who up to this point had experienced a heightening of sexual desire from the effects of the nitrous oxide, slid over and shouting wildly began beating Cahill. Badly out of shape, Cahill passed out laughing, his mind drifting away as he ran in some faraway park of his childhood and realized that, more than anything else, what he'd always wanted out of life was to be loved by his mother.

The crew of Wild Whirl of Sports, having prepared themselves for a serious program, were finally overcome by the madness and could do little to control themselves. They too began acting strangely and falling to the floor convulsed with hysterical laughter. As soon as Kopfeinlaufen saw the cylinders, he knew they were nitrous oxide and prepared himself for what was to take place. He went into a self-hypnotic trance which carried him back in time to a conversation with Sigmund Freud. Seated in Freud's library in Vienna, they shared several lines of cocaine and discussed a number of subjects, including Kopfeinlaufen's own theory of assigning symptoms to a patient and then curing them. Freud agreed that it was a novel idea, but one which could cause alarm if published and which could bring him undue financial difficulties in the form of law suits from irate patients.

Rapudiman Kohonduro also went into a trance. His was a deep, meditative one in which he chanted an obscure sutra of hinayana or provisional mahayana origin until his brain was a mass of treacle and he saw an incarnation of himself as a cobra slithering through a jungle of orchids. He sat in the lotus position in the middle of the room repeating his mantra and unifying himself with the universe, his mind merging with the cosmos, the orchids becoming more beautiful and the cobra of his life growing until it and the orchids were one. As he sat, a beatific smile came over his face and he had a profound orgasmic release and saw his penis as a huge cobra from which orchids were being sprayed upwards into the heavens.

For Ingrid Konkruka the effects were instantaneous. She felt hot and sexual and immediately began removing her nurse's uniform. In the process of climbing up on the table from which she was operating the scoreboard, she tripped several switches, causing the air horns, cheering, national anthem and ice rink organ music played at rapid speed to come on all at once. By the time the national anthem was over, she had shed every stitch of clothing, loosened her hair and was motioning for the technicians of the television crew to come and get it. At least seven of them came rushing over. "Line up," she said. Dutifully, they made a straight line. Kopfeinlaufen, finally seeing the massive size of Ingrid's breasts, came over and attempted to get to the front of the line. "I am the Chief of Psychiatry of this project," he said. "Please step aside." "No way, José," said the technician at the head of the line. José, who was last in line, heard his name called and came forward. A separate melee ensued and Kopfeinlaufen ended up being struck on the head. As he went down, Ingrid's nursing instincts took over. She jumped down from the table, went to the fallen Kopfeinlaufen and tried to help him. Taking advantage of the situation, Kopfeinlaufen opened his mouth and attempted to suckle himself on her breast. She slapped him and he passed out. That out of the way, Ingrid invited the technicians over to Garboil's bed, where she began giving them Swedish massages.

Helen Christianpath was not at all affected by the laughing gas. She remained at her post praying for the salvation of all involved. Also unaffected was Howland Gosell, who went on describing the action as if indeed everything that was taking place was exactly as it had been planned and explained by Kopfeinlaufen.

"Ladies and gentlemen," he said, at one point. "You are presently viewing the most amazing display of medical treatment I have ever encountered. Some sort of gas has been introduced into the atmosphere, lending to the proceedings an air of jubilation. Rather than a psychiatric therapy session one is reminded of a winner's locker room after a championship victory."

For Charles Mullvaney the scene turned into a nightmare worse than what he had experienced with the cats. Soon after the gas was released he ordered his men to seize El Falcon, but none of them paid the least attention. Marconi; was hell-bent on getting his gun back; Fried wanted to back up Marconi; Johnson, who constantly bitched about discrimination against blacks in the police department, went after the director of the television program and began berating him for not hiring any black technicians on a program that made its money in part from black athletes. As for Cahill, he was as useless as tits on a frog. He would have to capture El Falcon himself.

Fighting his way through the chaos on the floor he was finally able to reach his adversary. After so many years of sleepless nights, of planning his capture, here he was.

"At last we're face to face, amigo," Mullvaney said.

"Sí," answered El Falcon. "Gwat jew gwan, fahget?"

"You, El Falcon," Mullvaney said. "Take off your mask."

"Go fuck youlself, jew peeg."

Surprisingly, Mullvaney was not angry. He felt a warmth deep inside of his chest, an expansive feeling of Catholic brotherhood in which every one growing up was freed from the guilt of masturbation. He attempted to throw a friendly arm around El Falcon's shoulders, but El Falcon shrugged him off and put his hand up authoritativily, informing Mullvaney that he had gone too far.

"You're making it tough on me," Mullvaney said. "I have to take you in, so why don't you make it easy on yourself and come along peacefully."

"Nebel," El Falcon said.

"Okay, have it your way, pal," Mullvaney replied. He went into the waistband of his pants and began pulling out a gun.

What he saw next would stay with him for the rest of his days and cause him to become addicted to heavy tranquilizers. As he pulled out the gun, he saw the mask on El Falcon's face turn yellow and slowly become a beak. The protective glass over the eyes turned to an amber color, and behind them he saw brilliant, piercing eyes which saw inside of him and ripped every ounce of courage from his heart. His hand froze as he watched the man before him grow beautiful brown and red feathers. Mullvaney blinked and before his eyes was a huge hawk. It emitted a piercing hawk cry, spread its wings, flicked them twice and it was aloft, circling the room and then apparently exiting out of a window, which was either closed or open, but most likely closed, as he recalled. Before he could draw his gun and shoot, El Falcon was gone and Mullvaney, finally experiencing the effects of the gas, fell into a stupor of exhaustion and shame. It was no use. He saw his life as a complete waste and remembered how miserable everything had been growing up. Without any inhibitions, he began sobbing. After some ten minutes of uncontrollable crying, he was suddenly attacked by an overwhelming feeling of horror. He saw himself and his men captured by the United Front and then transported by them to the Soviet Union or, worse, to Cuba, where they would have to exist on a diet of rice and black beans for the rest of their lives. He crawled over to the sideboards, managed to get himself over them and, switching on the two-way radio he'd carried, called for additional units.

"Polar bear two," he cried into the radio, "this is polar bear one, don't know how long we can hold out."

Out in the street Lieutenant Gordon Marquand, doing backup for Mullvaney's men, heard the distress signal and swung into action with his men.

"Jesus, the Chief was crying," he said. "He must be shot. Let's go. On the double. Bring everything. Shotguns, tear gas, everything."

By the time Marquand and his men got upstairs, everyone except Helen Christianpath and Howland Gosell had passed out. Frank Garboil had ended up under his own bed, fast asleep. He had gone there to help Ingrid Konkruka, thinking that she had been stripped of her clothing and was being raped. As he got near the bed he was hit and knocked out by one of the Wild Whirl of Sports cameramen. Garboil's disappearance led to the headlines claiming the success of the United Front in rescuing Armando Martinez from the hospital.

After Marquand and his men got upstairs, opened the door to the solarium and saw everyone on the floor, they almost ran back out, fearing that a massacre had taken place. Marguand saw no blood, so he ventured further inside. What he did see was everyone contentedly dozing, smiles of pleasure etched on their faces. When he saw Howland Gosell, he pointed his gun at him and yelled for him to freeze. This frightened Gosell and he too passed out. Marquand then went to Helen Christianpath and asked her what had happened. She explained that the avenging angel had finally caught up with the sinfulness of the people and God had rained death upon everyone. She had a smile of satisfaction on her face. "Including that harlot," she said, pointing to the bed where Ingrid Konkruka was lying on the bed in a perfect "Playboy" magazine pose. "Oh, my God," said Marquand. "Holy Mother of God, I shoulda been a priest."

After it was all over, the police were credited with the arrest of four members of the United Front. El Falcon, however, had made a daring escape, carrying with him Armando Martinez. Marquand's men had revived everyone and sorted out each person's part in the chaos. Garboil came to slowly and much to his surprise heard his escape being discussed. He remained quietly under the bed and emerged only after the police and television people had left and the United Front members, including Maritza, had been taken away. The only persons left in the room were Dr. Kopfeinlaufen and Ingrid Konkruka.

When they saw him come out from under the bed they looked at each other and then began to applaud. They came over and began asking him questions. Garboil shook his head and said he couldn't remember much of what had taken place. Kopfeinlaufen suggested that they keep the matter of his presence in the hospital quiet until morning and he would then contact Mullvaney and inform him.

Garboil didn't care. He was too exhausted by what had taken place. More than ever before, he was convinced that the world and not himself was crazy and that he must do everything in his power to leave the hospital.

The following day, preparations were being made at the hospital for Garboil's release and departure. Two days later he was discharged with Kopfeinlaufen's blessing and some advice on how to deal with problems of time.

CHAPTER 29

In which Mullvaney finally puts the pieces of his investigation together, the protagonist is confronted with what appears to be his true identity, is offered gainful employment and is seduced in the process. We are also treated to some measure of suspense as Chota pays Maritza an unexpected visit.

Dressed in street clothes for the first time in nearly two months, Frank Garboil entered Dr. Kopfeinlaufen's office at noon, two days after his attempted rescue by the United Front. The doctor shook his hand, patted his back and offered congratulations on his remarkable recovery. Garboil smiled half-heartedly and thanked the doctor.

"That's quite all right, my boy," Kopfeinlaufen said. "Very hard work but there was never any doubt in our minds," he added, sweeping his hand about the room to include the other members of the staff. "One piece of advice. Try to remember who you are. Don't try to be someone else again. Good luck, Armando. I guess you'll be going back to school."

"If they take me back," Garboil said, looking down at his shoes and feigning embarrassment. "What I did was pretty stupid."

Kopfeinlaufen smiled paternally.

"Don't worry, my boy. It happens to the best. We've had calls from the administration and from your coach. Of course they'll take you back."

Garboil nodded and shook hands with Dr. Kohonduro, Helen Christianpath and Ingrid Konkruka.

"I guess you'll be going back to Minnesota," he said when he came to Ingrid.

"Saturday evening," she said. "Goodbye, Armando. And good luck. If you're ever up my way, come by and say hello."

"I might do that," he said.

He turned and went out of the office, checking once again his pocket where he carried the keys and address to Ingrid's apartment eight blocks from the hospital. Walking down the corridor towards the elevator, he felt giddy and carefree. He had won. Somehow he had managed to turn a corner in his life. For the first time in as long as he could recall, he was truly free. In the elevator he began humming, ignoring the stares of the other passengers. But his troubles were far from over. By the time he reached the hospital exit he was being followed. Mullvaney had finally seen the entire picture and it wasn't a pretty one.

"Look, Cahill," he'd said, earlier that morning in his office. "This had to be a professional job. Put a tail on that Martinez guy. They're letting him out today. I have a feeling he's working for the agency all right. The trouble is those guys are not too sharp and I think he's moonlighting for the other side."

"The Ruskies, Chief?" Cahill said, moving forward in his seat.

"It's just a feeling, Cahill. A hunch."

"A double agent, right?"

"You got it. Why else would the U.F. botch up the job? These guys are no dummies. If they had sprung Martinez it would've been obvious to the Agency that he was working for the other side. Instead, the U.F. screwed up the operation on purpose."

"You want me to put Chota on him?"

"No, no. Leave him out of it. He's in no shape. I put him on medical leave yesterday. Any leads on El Falcon?"

"Nothing, Chief. Zero. Disappeared into thin air like he always does. Chota still thinks the medium was right."

"What, the words?"

"Right, Chief."

"Horseshit. How in the hell can words make someone disappear. Chota ran the whole thing down to me. Says there's a guy named Vega involved. Some asshole werewolf."

"Warlock. A male witch, Chief."

"Whatever. Johnny's a good kid, but he gets carried away sometimes."

"I don't know, Chief. I read that in California they use mediums and ESP people to solve cases. When Chota told the medium about his bird dreams it clinched it for her. Her theory's that El Falcon turns into a hawk to escape."

Mullvaney was visibly shook by Cahill's words. He wiped his forehead and shifted uncomfortably in his seat. There was no way he was going to tell anyone what he'd seen. They'd have him up there at Stuyvesant Hospital with the rest of the loonies.

"Yeah, yeah," he said, with as much bravado as he could bring up out of his quaking belly. "And a little green man knocked up Rosie O'Grady. The Porto Ricans are worse than the Irish with their fucking superstitions. What about those other U.F. creeps?"

"Out on bail, Chief."

"Jesus, Mary and Joseph. We had enough on the bastards to crucify them. They would've gone up for life. The way things are shaping up, they'll get good citizen awards from that Protestant dingbat down at City Hall. Just put a tail on Martinez and stake out that girl's apartment. He's liable to head up there looking for her."

"Anybody in particular, Chief?"

"Yeah, have Argento stay with him."

"And uptown?"

"Kelly and Washington."

"Right away, Chief."

Cahill left the office and Mullvaney began shaking. The bastard had turned into a bird; and his eyes burned into him, amber eyes, dead eyes, but eyes alive with fire. For three days he had not been able to sleep and his nerves were shot. He went into the desk, opened a bottle and popped another of the tranquilizers he'd taken from his wife's vanity.

Meanwhile, up in the Bronx, John Chota had also spent another fitful night. Nightmares of huge birds lifting him up and dropping him from great heights interrupted his sleep at least six times during the night. On each occasion he woke up just before hitting the ground, his body cold and in spasms of overwhelming fear. After the third nightmare, he swallowed a couple of sleeping pills but they did not take effect. Finally, at about eight that morning, totally exhausted, he collapsed into a nearly catatonic sleep.

He woke up at three that afternoon, his mind racing and his thoughts jumbled. He shaved, showered, had some Rice Crispies and turned the television on to watch afternoon cartoons. As soon as he sat down, however, his mind began acting up again. One minute his mind was blank and the next he was back in his nightmare. Without any will of his own his mind was blank once more, except for tiny explosions going off in the distance, as if somewhere in his head a shootout were taking place. Why had Mullvaney taken him off the case? He was no longer trusted. On top of that he'd put him on medical leave the day before and ordered him to see the chaplain for counseling. Nobody believed him about El Falcon. But the spiritualist couldn't be wrong. They did it with words. But what words? he'd said. She hadn't known. There was a brujo involved, she'd said. His name was Yunqué, a manwitch. Magic words, she'd said. Secret words. Bastards. A hawk. A man that turned into a hawk. A hawk that turned into a man. Were there two? A man and a hawk? No, it was one. And the manwitch. That made three of them. But how? Words. His mind was on fire. If anyone knew, it had to be the bitch Maritza. She'd lead him to the brujo and he'd get it out of him. He'd go and see her right away. He had a score to settle with her, so he might as well kill two birds with one stone. The phrase annoyed him. But it was true. He'd have to kill her. There was no way she'd lie still. But she'd squirm before he blew her away. He got up, turned off the TV, opened a drawer and removed a silver plated pistol. He held it in his hand and then slid the magazine in place. Whether she wanted to or not he was going to have her. He debated whether or not to carry his badge. At the last minute he decided against it.

At six that evening, John Chota started out to find Maritza Soto. He went to her grandmother's apartment, but Maritza had just left. Where to? Her grandmother didn't know. He then called several members of the United Front and the Young Barons. No one was talking on the phone. Nobody wanted to meet. Everyone was spooked after what'd happened at the hospital. At least three people had left for the Island. At nine o'clock he went to Garboil's apartment. No one was in. For the rest of the evening he wandered in and out of bars, drinking and growing angrier. Everything he saw reminded him of birds. At 94th Street and Broadway things came to a head when he went into the Aguila China, the chinese restaurant with the eagle on its sign. He ordered shrimp fried rice and started an argument with one of the chinese-cuban waiters, accusing him of being a communist and threatening to have the place closed down. When the owner came over, Chota demanded to know why the hell he'd picked up a goddamned bird as a name for a restaurant. The owner told him, if he didn't get out of the restaurant, he was calling the police. The threat sobered Chota immediately and he left, but not without first screaming at everyone that they were nothing but communist bastards.

At one in the morning, more crazed than drunk, he made his way back uptown and knocked on Garboil's door again. From inside Maritza asked who it was. Chota managed to steady his nerves enough to tell her it was Pancho Miranda and that he had an urgent message. Not yet aware that Pancho Miranda was in reality John Chota, an undercover cop for the New York City Police Department, Maritza opened the door and let him in. She was about to go to bed and was dressed in pajamas, her breasts quite prominent beneath the shirt. Chota's mind was a blazing inferno of disconnected images, as he saw himself on top of Maritza. And then it happened, her skin sprouted feathers and she became beaked and her eyes had that hawk-like quality.

On his way uptown to Ingrid's apartment Frank Garboil surveyed the tempo of the city. Nothing had changed. People hurried as if driven by an unknown, frenetic force, all of them pursuing some forgotten dream whose only thread of reality was the unbridled animal energy they experienced. He could understand a little better what caused people to reach for the unattainable. Once inside Ingrid's apartment he sat down to ponder his next move. The walk in the brisk winter air had augmented his resolve to get on with his life. During the week he'd try to get his job back at Frick University. He was certain that he'd be a better teacher because of his experiences the past six months. Eventually his thoughts turned to Maritza Soto. The prospect of seeing her again both attracted and caused him apprehension. There was no way to explain to her what had taken place within him in the hospital. He'd have to tell her that he was not Puerto Rican, that his name was not Armando Martinez. That much he owed her. There was no telling what her reaction would be, but the possibilities disturbed him. He'd have to think of something to deal with her outrage.

In the meantime, he thought, he would begin enjoying his new freedom. He walked around the apartment, scrutinizing everything as if to learn more about its resident. On the window seat in the living room he saw an object which caught his attention. It was a small stone carving of a seal. He picked up the smooth, almost abstract sculpture and was examining it when he happened to look out into the quiet brownstone-lined block. Across the street, standing in a doorway, was a man. He couldn't be sure, but it seemed to be the same one who had been standing outside the hospital when he came out. He put the thought out of his mind and turned to more productive matters. He counted his money. A little over ten dollars. Not much but he still had over five hundred dollars left in the bank. Tomorrow he'd get his bank book and buy himself a suit. He wanted to look his best when he went back to see John Bacon at Frick. The reaction he next felt was similar to having his wind knocked out by a blow to the solar plexus. The rent hadn't been paid on his apartment for two months. Perhaps all his belongings, including his bank book, had been thrown out into the street. He immediately got ready to leave and head uptown.

However, at that moment a key turned in the door and Ingrid Konkruka came in. He stood still, feeling awkward in her presence. She came over and hugged him. He was immediately erect and his concern with the apartment had vanished.

"I finally made it," she said. "I thought I'd never get away."

Being without a woman for two months made him totally vulnerable to Ingrid, but the ardor with which she had pressed her body against him, the passion in her voice, embarrassed him. Sensing both his discomfort and arousal, she broke away, went into the kitchen and asked him if he'd like a beer. He said he would and sat down on the couch. She returned to the living room and handed him a pilsner glass filled with beer. He drank it with an animal thirst which surprised him. He had never been much of a drinker, particularly of beer. The taste seemed new to him, almost as if he'd never tasted beer before that time. It was another sign, he thought, that in some way he'd broken with the past, that he was finally free. He and Ingrid talked for some ten minutes, her voice becoming more and more intimate, his desire growing with each word. She was magnificent. Now that she was not at the hospital, he allowed himself to see how truly stunning a woman she was. She wasn't truly as big as she was imposing in her beauty.

"Do you know that there were times in the hospital when I almost couldn't control myself," she said. "Those back rubs were murder on me. A few times I came back to the hospital late at night to get in bed with you and always turned back at the door."

He was flattered.

"I wish you hadn't," he said.

"It wasn't the time, Frank," she said.

"And now?" he said.

She laughed throatily.

"We've got a lot to talk about. Let me shower and change. I'll fix something to eat and then we'll talk."

She stood up and asked him if he'd like another beer. He nodded and she went back into the kitchen, returned with an opened bottle, poured it and then went into the bedroom. Garboil sat back and thought about making love to Ingrid Konkruka. The beer he had consumed made him feel light-headed and without a care. Behind the perfect exterior of the blonde amazon who had helped him retain his sanity, there appeared to be a woman who needed him. They had been through quite an ordeal together and now they'd have a chance to let go. But it didn't appear she was just interested in a quick roll in the hay. All his relationships with women had been like that. They all wanted something he couldn't give, a surrender of a part of himself which he wasn't sure even existed. But that wasn't true. That had not been the case with Maritza. With her there had been no pressure and he'd given something of himself that was quite different.

The realization caused a wave of guilt to wash over him. He was being disloyal to Maritza and cursed himself for the feeling. He struggled with the emotion for more than twenty minutes and was almost to the point of apologizing to Ingrid and leaving the apartment when he decided that the guilt he felt was exactly what Maritza was demanding of him and therefore the relationship with her had been no different than all others.

A few moments later, Ingrid came back into the living room. She was wearing a long, loose fitting silk dress which clung to her body. She had let her blonde hair down so that it fell about her shoulders, framing her face, causing the sculpted lines of her face to appear even more exquisite than ever. Whatever the perfume was it blended perfectly with her looks, creating an exotic fragrance which surrounded her as an aura. She was utterly feminine, quintessentially woman, her professional decorum totally absent. She came to the couch and kissed him lightly on the lips, her breasts nearly covering all of his chest. Rather than desire, Garboil felt an overwhelming awe, much as if he were in the presence of a sacred being. She smiled at him, stood up and seemed to melt back across the room and to the kitchen. From there she chatted with him as she prepared their supper. When they were seated at the table and were halfway through the meal, she spoke more seriously to him.

"I don't want to pry, but I imagine you're ready to change your life quite a bit after what you've been through," she said.

"Yes and no," he said. "I was thinking of getting my job back at the school."

"I thought you hated teaching," she said. "Wouldn't you want something more challenging?"

"I'll do better this time around. Did you have something in mind?"

She shrugged her shoulders.

"I don't know. Government work, maybe."

"What?"

"Sure, the government employs economists in some of their agencies."

The remark puzzled him. In the candle light, the soft music playing and the wine making him sink deeper into himself, he suddenly felt the same fears he'd felt while in the hospital. She was truly a beautiful woman, but there was something wrong going on at that moment. He didn't know what, but something was definitely out of place.

"Life is strange, isn't it, Frank?" she said, reaching across the table for his hand. "I feel as though it was inevitable that we met."

"It seems that way," he said, holding her hand. "I really don't believe in chance. In many ways I'm a fatalist. A determinist, more accurately."

She caressed his hand with her long, smooth fingers and then brought her hand back to her side of the table. She was silent for a moment, her face growing dark in mood as she pushed the food back and forth on her plate.

"I suppose you're right," she said. "But I wish things could be different."

"Like what?"

"Like us," she said, looking at him.

"I don't follow."

"Well, I just don't know how long it'll last."

Her statement implied something which he could not grasp.

"It'll last as long as we want it to last," he said, but the words had no conviction to them. There was something definitely amiss. But why was he revealing his feelings of mistrust.

"What about the girl?" she said, looking into his eyes.

So that was it, he thought. She wanted to protect herself. Why hadn't he realized how love struck she was.

"I've thought about her," he said. "I won't deny it, but it wouldn't be fair for me to see her again. I'm not a kid, you know. Fourteen years older than her. And there's no way I can explain the truth to her. No way."

"Did you love her?"

"Sure, I suppose I did," he said. "Maybe I still do," he added, hoping the noble intent of his words would add to the finality of his decision.

"Good," she said. "That's perfect. If you love her, it'll make it easier."

The words shocked him and he looked more intently at her, trying to fathom the significance of her statement.

"Good? Easier?" he said. "I thought. . ."

"What?"

"I don't know. I thought you were. . .well, you know, that we were getting closer."

"We are," she said, reaching once more for his hand. "That's coming, if things work out."

Now his pride was hurt. What was she doing, holding out?

"If what works out?" he said.

She thought for a moment, a professional mask slipping back over her face. "Well, you'll probably be upset as hell after everything that's happened, but we talked it over and decided to make the proposition right away."

What did she want to do, charge him for a roll in the sack?

"Proposition? What are you talking about?"

"Coming to work for us," she said.

"C'mon, Ingrid. I don't know anything about psychiatry."

"It won't be that kind of work."

"What then? You've got me totally confused."

"I know. I'm really sorry. These things get so complicated when emotions get in the way. The thing is that we want you to stay with Maritza and more or less let us know what's going on with them. It would be ideal if at some point you could become a member of the United Front."

Frank Garboil stood up, put his napkin on the table and shook his head.

"I don't believe it," he said. "I just don't believe it. It's incredible. You're one of them. You're a cop."

"Please sit down and let me explain," she said.

"Yeah? Who's we? Who? I should've known. We, right?"

She stood up and came over to him but he walked away.

"I can't tell you everything, but you'll be paid better than at Frick. Twice as much, and you'll be taken care of for life. No hassles ever. We can give you whatever you want, Frank."

He was on the verge of hysteria, his mind flashing back to the scene in the locker room when he quit the hockey team and ended up in the hospital.

"What you mean is that you want me to spy for you," he said, his voice shaking with anger. "Who the hell are you? What am I supposed to do? Go back and play hockey and play the young Puerto Rican stud?"

"That's part of it, but not for long."

"Not for long? Not for any time, sweetheart. I'm through with all that."

She sat on the couch, completely in command, her figure imposing even when seated, the Nordic aloofness so prominent that he perceived her not as a woman but as a neuter being. A new fear invaded him, a question posed itself and loomed above everything else. What was she? They had caught him again and he'd never be free this time.

"Yes, not for long," she said. "Just long enough to reestablish your credibility with everyone. We can arrange for you to get medical dispensation, not to play, if that's what you prefer. A heart murmur which was overlooked in the preliminary physical examination. A flare-up of some debilitating Southeast Asian tropical malaise, which you contracted in Vietnam."

He wanted to scream that he'd never been in Vietnam, but realized just in time that she was laying out a scenario and not insisting that he was Armando Martinez. She went on speaking and, although he understood everything, part of him was closing up rapidly.

"Something big is shaping up," she said. "We need to know what.

Did you ever hear the word pitirre? Did Maritza ever mention it?"

"No, I've never heard it," he said, haughtily, quickly, trying to make her believe he knew, but wouldn't provide her with any information. "What does it mean?"

"It's the name of an underground organization on the Island. We don't know what they're planning, but there's been a lot of activity in the past few months and we want to find out what it's about."

Garboil shook his head, came over and stood in front of her.

"You're some sort of CIA fink, aren't you?"

Ingrid laughed, her cool demeanor unaffected by the insult.

"Yes, something like that. But the more you find out, the deeper you'll be involved. It's up to you, but I'll tell you one thing. You'd never regret coming to work for us. Never."

"It's no good," Garboil said. He let his shoulders slump and his arms hang at his sides. "Why me? I just did the whole thing with hockey to stay alive. Jesus!" He sat on the edge of an overstuffed chair and pulled at his hair with both hands, the mixture of rage and chagrin at having been deceived choking him. "I would've died inside if I had kept living the way I was. Half inside my head and half out. I would've dried up in a couple of years." He paused and looked at her, trying to penetrate the icy coldness around her. "Did you ever feel like you were dying, like your heart was shriveling up because you weren't free, because you couldn't call your life your own?"

"I'm sorry," she said. "We know what you've been through and that's why we decided to approach you after all this time."

"This is crazy. All this time? You make it sound like we've known each other for years."

"Ever since you were in the Army. Do you remember survival school?" she said.

"My God, that was fifteen years ago. I was a kid." He leaned back on the chair, his body sapped of energy. The room appeared to be spinning and Ingrid's hair looked on fire. "Jesus! You know, I tried talking about it in the hospital, but nothing came up."

"You had an accident and nearly died, Frank. It was a climb and you fell about seventy feet. There was a loss of memory for nearly a month. The doctors had a rough time putting you back together. Not physically, because the brush growing on the side of the cliff slowed down your fall and there were no broken bones. But you did bash your head a good one. If it hadn't been for your helmet your skull would've been crushed."

"I don't remember any of it," he said, more distressed than ever.

"I know. A lot of things were erased and other things took their place at our suggestion."

"Like what?"

"The hockey. That was the trigger. I was all you talked about while you were delirious. Everything that happened after that was our doing. Our fault if you want to call it that."

"You're lying," he said.

"No, Frank, I'm not. I'm sorry, but it's the truth."

"And Joan? My wife?"

"That was a convenient accident. Predictable but convenient."

"Predictable?"

"Yes, we pretty much figured it would eventually happen. I wasn't working on the case at the time, but I've read your entire file.

Given your attraction to certain women, it was bound to happen sooner or later."

"What women?"

"Oh, Wasp types. Good families, well rooted in America. That type. All American, goody-two shoes with *Ladies Home Journal* leanings."

"That's nonsense."

"Not really. Every woman you've been involved with fits that profile." "Bullshit! What about Angela Piscatelli? She was Sicilian."

"Right."

"So?"

"That's when we knew you were breaking away and ready to become the real you. We knew you'd eventually leave your wife. It happens in most controlled marriages. When that happened, everything went according to schedule."

"I don't believe you. This is more of Kopfeinlaufen's work."

Ingrid laughed.

"Kopfeinlaufen is an infant, Frank," she said. "True, he works for us, but his part in this operation is minor."

"What about Maritza? She's certainly not a Wasp."

"That's what clinched it for us. We knew you were ready."

"And does she work for you?"

"I wish she did. She's a bright kid and has got more guts than most men. Very passionate, but bright as they come."

Garboil stood up and sat back down. His mind was racing in a dozen different directions. He looked at Ingrid and attempted to draw on every reserve of courage that he had.

"I'm going to be totally honest with you," he said. "I don't believe a word you've said. I did what I did on my own. I just wanted to play ice hockey. The desire was in me ever since I was a little kid. I just wanted to play. It was that simple."

"We knew that. We also knew that your predilection for a certain type of woman expressed your need to belong to the society and that it was a sublimation of some deeper need to prove yourself as a man. When your relationship with that type of woman failed, culminating in your wife leaving, that part of the regression had been completed. It was then that we decided to start the process of bringing you back to your real self. The hockey was a deeper, more primal way of proving to yourself that you were an American."

"You're nuts. Why not football or baseball? They're just as American. In fact, more so. I played those sports."

"Precisely, but that's a good question and it took us a long time to figure it out. But it goes hand in hand with your choice of women. Hockey may be the national sport in Canada, but in the U.S., for the longest time, it was a sport for the upper class at Ivy League colleges. Do you see? In excelling at it you could claim your rightful place and eventually regain the respect of this country. You're right. It was something you had to do in order to survive. Once you had gone to your limits in playing out that need, you broke through to your real self and ended up in the hospital. What's ahead of you in working for us may seem cruel, but in the long run it may mean the freedom of more than two million people. Your people."

"What? What the hell are you talking about now? My people?"

"The Puerto Ricans."

It was as if an explosion had occurred inside of him. A deep rage rose up in his chest so that he was nearly out of control. And then it passed as suddenly as it had come. Gone was the hysteria and in its place there surfaced a cold hatred of the woman before him. Her beauty, her imposing figure and the kindness and understanding which she had displayed while he was under her care in the hospital had been replaced by an ugliness of spirit which sickned him. Beneath her beautiful exterior was a killer of dreams, a destroyer of souls, some impersonal machine that fed on the hopes of people like himself. Who was she that she could have so much power. He spoke very slowly, the words cold, matching the iciness he experienced when she spoke.

"I want you to listen to me and I want you to listen carefully," he said. "Things have gone as far as they're going. After the trip I've been on, trying to prove to everyone that I'm Frank Garboil, you're telling me that I'm the other guy. Of all people, you'd be the last one to try and convince me of that. You're the one in that nut house who believed I was Frank Garboil."

Ingrid smiled and shook her head in apparent sympathy.

"You are Frank Garboil," she said. "But we had to put you through the entire experience to make sure you could handle being Puerto Rican. Being Armando Martinez was a trial run. You took to it so well that we figured you could now be confronted with the truth about your identity. You were brought to New York when you were less than a year old, but there's no doubt about your origins."

Garboil felt the same icy hatred as he listened to Ingrid. It was as if his life, from the time of birth until this very moment, had been fabricated for him in some bureau in Washington, D.C.

"And my parents?" he said, almost inaudibly.

"Most of it is exactly as you told it."

The anger rose up again, blinding him momentarily.

"I see," he said. "What isn't?"

"Try to relax. That is the one thing which worried us the most. Once you surfaced, we knew that you would become much more emotional. I've always argued against genetic propensity towards emotionalism, but you're disproving that. We didn't alter too much. Except for your parents' background. They're both Puerto Rican, born and raised on the Island."

"That's crazy. Why was I made to think they weren't?"

"Several reasons. One was Kopfeinlaufen's idea. The business about a Puerto Rican being unable to adapt to a cold climate and to play ice hockey. I thought it was utter nonsense. Very unscientific, but the Department bought it. The other factor was arrived at pretty much by consensus on the part of our staff. Not the staff at the hospital but at the Department. They felt that you would've broken down irreparably if you had to admit that you were Puerto Rican. According to them, and this is based on studies they've performed, Puerto Ricans rank about a minus 20 on a world wide acceptability scale. The bottom of the scale is 25. Australian aborigenes, pygmies, etc. rank 21, 22 and so on. I don't believe any of it, of course."

"Of course," he said, sarcastically.

"What it means is that in a random sampling of citizens in over 100 cities in the United States, who were asked if they could change their identity, what would they like to be, even without first answering the question more than 20% responded that they would be anything other than Puerto Rican. But like I've said, I don't believe in any of those statistical studies."

"Who came in first? Swedes?"

"No, we came in second. The British were first, of course."

"Yes, of course."

"To be expected."

It was laughable, he thought. They were now trying to convince him that he was indeed Puerto Rican."

"And my name?" he said. "What is it?"

"Oh, that stands. It's Garboil, all right. We didn't change that. Francisco Eduardo Garboil."

"And my mother was shot."

"Yes."

"And she was not an Eskimo."

"No, she was not."

"And my father died a couple of years later and I went to live with relatives."

"Not relatives, just friends of your parents."

"Spiritualists?"

"Yes."

"I still don't believe you."

"How can I prove it?"

"What about Bones Friedenberg? Remember him? The big time bookie. And Benny the Letter Thief. That's how I got Armando's identity."

"They work for us, Frank. We knew once the hockey business was triggered and you contacted Friedenberg the rest would follow. You can pick up the phone and confirm it. I'll get you the number."

She moved to get up.

"Bones?" he said.

"That's right. He's one of our best people."

It all came back to him. Bones had offered him a job and talked about the President as if he knew him. Never mentioned his name but alluded to knowing him. Everything was so crazy. He had to leave the web Ingrid and her people had woven about him.

"What's to prevent me from leaving here?" he said.

"Nothing," she answered. "But where would you go? I doubt that you'd last the night out there. Once you leave I'd have to put the word out. I have a job to do, as cold and impersonal as that sounds. Once you leave you're on your own and our department has no control. All I can do is report that you're a stray and no longer under our protection. I don't mean to sound ruthless, but this is the big time. You're mature enough to understand that. Even if you got away for a while, there's no way you'd work again. Everything's sewed up. Forget going to work at a college. There's no school in the U.S., Canada or any place else, other than the communist block, where we don't have some influence, where we don't have someone on the payroll. It's that important, Frank. Do you know what would be facing your people if we weren't in the picture? The Island would be annexed by Cuba in no time and that means control by the Soviet Union. Do you want that for your people? I like you and in a way I feel badly for you. This is the hardest assignment I've ever had. You have guts and daring and have proven that. We wouldn't have risked bringing you forward if we didn't think you could do the job. But we can't let you go. You're like a time bomb now. We took a chance. If we turned you, you'd be great. If we couldn't, then we'd have a major enemy on our hands. It's your choice. It's not much of one, but it's still yours to make. It's either come to work for us or oblivion, the big sleep as they say in our circles. Permanent vacation."

A feeling of resignation was beginning to envelope him as he listened to Ingrid. Any hope of freedom was becoming dimmer as she revealed the absolute control they'd had over his life. The choices were once again being made for him. His life passed before him in quick motion and he tried recalling at what point he could have changed things permanently. He could not accept that he was not the man whose identity he had fought so desperately to defend. He was American, had been so all his life and that too had been destroyed. That he was after all Puerto Rican seemed a just punishment for deceiving Maritza and the rest of them, Ray and Billy Perez and Big Papa and One-eyed Pete. But it hadn't been his doing, had it? It had been neatly arranged by them, by that anonymous them who had tormented him as long as he could recall. Somehow, he didn't know in what form, he would avenge himself.

"I guess I have no choice, do I?" he said. What do I do, go out and purchase a trench coat and a gun or does that come with the job?"

"No, nothing like that," Ingrid said. "Just go back to school and continue to do what you were doing. If you need a divorce from your wife, we can arrange that. Whatever you need we can provide for you. I'm glad you decided on the saner course. We'll start on your paper work tomorrow. Welcome aboard. I'm not much of a sentimentalist, but I really believe our work is the noblest any human being could do. The threat of communism is a real one, Frank. So we have to be there. It can get messy sometimes, but rock bottom the work is noble and necessary."

"I guess I'll have to learn as I go," he said. "And you? Staying in New York?"

"Until things are a little more stable."

"Then I'm free to go," he said.

"If you want to, but I was hoping you'd stay," she said. She appeared feminine again. "I meant what I said about the way I feel about you. Your relationship to the girl won't interfere with what happens between us. Not from my end, anyway. I won't place any demands on you. Whenever you want to be with me, all you need to do is call. I'm not sorry I had to put you through all this. It's my job and I love doing it, but if you could find it in yourself to put your feelings aside, I'd make it up to you. I'm still a woman, you know."

How could she do it? She was a master at turning it on and off. She appeared totally vulnerable now, harmless, in fact.

"What about all that nonsense about not being able to conceive? And reaching an early puberty?"

"I did reach puberty early. Ten or eleven. I don't remember. Two years later I caught an infection and they had to remove my reproductive organs."

"I'm sorry to hear that," he said, but he wasn't.

"I would like you to make love to me, Frank," she said. I don't care if you don't love me, or even think badly of me. In my work there's no way I could become attached to any man, but if there was going to be one, you'd be on the top of my list."

"That bad?"

"No, that good," she said and smiled at him.

What the hell, he thought. If he was going to try and figure out how to get out of this new mess, he'd might as well gain her confidence.

"All right," he said. "As long as you put it that way, I'll do my best." He felt cold and empty in spite of the actual physical desire he was once again experiencing. "It'll be the first time I'm doing it for patriotic reasons."

He expected her to be hurt by the remark, but she was amused and happier than ever. She came over to his chair, knelt in front of him and put her head on his thigh. He touched her face and her breasts, feeling her grow warmer under his touch. Soon after they were in the bedroom. She was unlike most large women he had made love to, who because of their size were fearful of appearing aggressive and instead became passive. She was an athletic and skillful lover and so wanton in her need for him that he almost forgot her coldness of heart. But he could not and he made love to her with the violence that only deep hatred can summon, wishing to hurt her more than to give her pleasure.

He held back his own release for an eternity, his body aching with the need to be done like some unimaginable torture. With each violent thrust he saw himself destroying the system which had duped him. In his mind he pictured the destruction of sacred monuments, symbols which spoke of the inhumanity of the country: he was fucking the Washington and Lincoln monuments, the Tomb of the Unknown Soldier, JFK's eternal flame, and that part of it hurt because he had seen some hope in himself, but it didn't matter anymore; fucking the Pentagon, his sperm flooding the Grand Canyon, spraying the Rocky Mountains, the entire state of California, the Mormon Tabernacle Choir, the Alamo, Chicago, Illinois; Detroit, Michigan; Kansas City, Missouri; the Boston Pops Orchestra; the New York Philharmonic;

spraying his sperm, his juice, his cum, his scum, his jive, his jivejuice and then wiping himself with the American flag with its fifty stars.

At the moment of climax he saw himself as a giant, his penis the size of a telephone pole. Beneath him, her face contorted, her robes up about her hips, the Statue of Liberty, her legs spread and her torch at her side, screaming: FUCK ME! FUCK ME, YOU WILD SPIC!

When it was over he rolled quickly off Ingrid and lay on the bed, his heart frozen solid while she ran her hands over his chest and kissed his face, murmuring who knew what, except that as he was falling asleep it sounded like the Star Spangled Banner and then it made him cry because he remembered Mickey Mantle blowing bubbles out in center field during the playing of the anthem when he first came up to the Yankees and that was such an innocent time and everything was going to be all right even though his mother had died so long, so long ago and he was going to be a good boy and the Star Spangled Banner was such a beautiful song so long ago.

CHAPTER 30

In which the protagonist escapes the warmth and comfort of his new jail, is pursued by law enforcement officials, eludes them, has an opportunity to play hero by rescuing his beloved from certain death and in the process observes the demise of this tale's rat.

Rather than emerging slowly out of deep slumber, Garboil was awake instantly. It was as if he had been suddenly jarred and, although the room was not overly warm, his body was drenched in perspiration and his heart was pounding in an uncommon rhythm. An overwhelming fear seized him and for a moment he felt paralyzed. One part of his mind urged him to bolt out of bed and run as far as he could. Another cautioned him to proceed slowly, stealthily. Battling his nerves, he slid out from under the covers and to the floor, moving his body an inch at a time and hoping that Ingrid wouldn't wake up. Naked, on all fours, he groped about in the dark until he found his clothes, collected them and then crawled out of the room. He dressed quickly, found his parka and let himself out of the apartment.

Downstairs in the lobby he recalled the man who had been watching Ingrid's building earlier. He peered out from behind the curtained door of the brownstone and, seeing no one, ventured out, his heart still beating in a manner which disturbed him.

It was nearly one in the morning when he stepped out into the street. The temperature had dropped considerably and a raw, biting wind was blowing in violent gusts. The cold had a glass-edged quality that made the skin on his face feel brittle. He began walking, looking left and right, his breath coming in short bursts as if he had been running. He hurried on, not yet knowing his purpose but driven by the anxiety and ever present danger which he now felt pursued him. As he turned the corner and headed west, he saw a man crossing the street in his direction. Ingrid's words, her warning, upset any confidence he may have had and made his fear grow. He now walked more quickly, debating with each step whether he should run. His instinct was to hide, to find a small opening into which he could crawl and be safe. He was sure the man following him was the same one he'd seen across from Ingrid's building, the one who had been in front of the hospital.

When he reached Third Avenue he turned around. The man was still following him. Which way should he go? Should he continue up the street and find a place to hide or keep going until he reached the subway station? Perhaps there would be a policeman on duty at the station. The thought made him angry. What was he thinking? Whatever was going on, they were sure to be in on it. He would be running from one into the arms of the other. They all worked together, herding people as if they were sheep, making sure the strays kept pace with the flock. A policeman would be no help.

The street was deserted, the shops on Third Avenue closed. No bars or coffee shops to duck into and be with people. They wouldn't dare strike then. Not with people around. Perhaps they had ordered the shops closed. It was perfect. A quiet, tree-lined street on an early winter morning. A few shots from a silencer-equipped gun and his life would be over. The official findings would note that he was the victim of a mugging. That's how they operated. Human life meant nothing to them. They didn't have to close shops, just follow him until the right time and then blow his brains out. No feeling, no remorse. Just another assignment for a professional, who after completing the job would go home and get into bed and in the morning his wife would cook him breakfast and he would take the kids to school and go to the office and write a report.

Without thinking further he found himself running, the blood pounding in his head and his bowels on the point of emptying, such was his fear. When he reached the subway stairs, he stumbled and fell headlong, tumbling down and scraping his forehead. He picked himself up as the train pulled into the station and a few passengers exited. The fear growing with each second, he vaulted the turnstile and managed to board the train before the doors closed. He was dizzy and nauseous as he slumped into a seat, his entire body drenched in sweat and his breathing labored.

A couple of black teenagers sitting across from him looked his way and laughed. He closed his eyes and opened them suddenly at the thought of having to fight them off if they decided to start something. He returned their stare and they glared at him and laughed once more. When would his breathing become normal again? He stood up suddenly and, without looking at the teenagers again, went into another car. An old man was reading a newspaper. As the train rumbled uptown, Garboil thought about Maritza. She would never understand any of it. But he'd try to explain. They obviously wanted her out in the street again, even though she'd been caught with the others. The case would never be tried. He was sure of it. Insufficient evidence, some technicality; a campaign mounted by the liberal community to exonerate her part in it; the entire thing orchestrated by them in order to use her and him. But now that he wouldn't play along, she was in greater danger than before. Now she too was expendable. He had to find her and warn her, explain everything; that he was not Puerto Rican; that he was sorry he had deceived her. It was their trick, he'd say. Oh, God, he was scared. Everything was so confusing. They now wanted him to believe he was Puerto Rican. He wasn't. He was Frank Garboil. American. Yanqui. Gringo. Whatever derogatory remark or name they chose, that's what he was. She was in danger and so was he. The knowledge that he had to find her and warn her, protect her from them if necessary, calmed him considerably and his heart resumed beating regularly again. The running had helped release some of the tension, but his legs ached.

At a quarter to two that morning, he exited the train at 110th Street and Lexington Avenue, the heart of El Barrio. He followed a couple of people up the stairs and ducked into a tenement. He remained there several minutes, huddled in the hallway. A police car cruised slowly down the street and he froze, watching intently to determine whether they were looking for someone. The policemen stared ahead, obviously making their rounds. When the squad car was gone, he stepped outside and looked up and down the street. The wind was blowing more strongly now and the sky was red as it is before snow. No one was in the street and yet he felt the danger stalking him. By will alone he made himself begin walking north. He had to reach her, even though his overwhelming desire was to hide. Each shadow from the crumbling tenements made him shudder, each howling of the wind was like a scream, each doorway a new obstacle to controlling his fear. When would it come? Would he hear the shots or would he just feel the burning pain and then the blackness. Before he reached the housing project, three blocks from the subway station he was again sweating profusely. Where were they? He wouldn't hear the shots. They would use a silencer. Maybe he'd hear the whooshing sound of the silencer. Where were they? God, let them come now. Would he fight if they gave him a chance? They had to be around. They had to have radioed ahead. How would they know where he was headed? Was the old man reading the newspaper in on it? Were they watching him even now? He went on and his legs ached and his mind was scurrying about looking for some rationalization which would offer him release from the anxiety.

When he reached the housing project, he looked behind him into the desolate street and saw no one. In the distance he heard a fire siren screaming in the night. Once inside the lobby of Maritza's building with its tiled walls written on and already yellowed by time, he pushed the elevator button and waited. He could hear the elevator descending slowly, each second making his discomfort grow. Why were the elevators in projects so slow? He was certain their speed had been regulated to add to the frustration already felt in having to eke out a living under such trying circumstances. The blacks and the Puerto Ricans and the few whites who constituted the underclass of the city had to be taught patience. That was it. How could the city provide them with fast elevators when they were all so impatient? That had to be it. They had to be slowed down and taught that things could not march along as quickly as they wanted. Each second he waited, he felt greater and greater hatred towards whoever it was that decided to keep people oppressed. Again without any further thought, he pushed the door to the stairway and was racing up the eight flights of stairs. His lungs burned with the effort, but he pushed himself as he had pushed himself when he'd played for New Amsterdam. He could not stop now, even though his lungs and thighs seemed on fire from the effort. On the eighth floor he went directly to the door of Maritza's apartment and knocked, calling out her name. His voice sounded shrill with hysteria, despite his efforts to control it. When Maritza's grandmother finally came to the door and told him to go away or she'd call the police, he pleaded with her to open up.

"It's Armando," he said. "Please open the door. You remember me. I have to talk to Maritza. Tell her it's Armando." He heard her move the cover on the peep hole. "It's me, Armando. Remember?"

"Sí, sí," she said. "I remember. Maritza not home."

"Where is she?" he said. "I have to find her. ¿Donde está?

"She say you know where to find her."

He panicked for a second, thanked her and went flying back down the stairs. What did she mean? Where could she be? On campus? That was crazy. Where then? The twenty-four hour coffee shop on 14th Street where they had gone after walking around in the Village one Saturday night after a game? It was all crazy. Where? The apartment? No, it was bound to be empty.

Everything gone. The rent not paid and everything gone. But it had to be the apartment. He went through his pockets. The ten dollars and change were still there.

He rushed out of the building without looking to see if it was safe. He zipped up his parka, put up the hood but immediately felt the biting cold. His clothes were drenched and the moisture appeared to be freezing instantly. He hadn't gone a half block before he saw them. Two men now, across the street on the west side of the housing project. One was black and the other one white. This was it. America had equal opportunity when it came to getting rid of undesirables. They had finally come for him. He walked on, looking sideways to keep them in sight. They were still coming when he crossed ll2th Street. Far down the street he heard the uptown train approaching and he broke into a run, the gusting wind cutting his face, burning his eyes and making them water instantly. He felt a few flakes of snow. The men were coming fast now. He could hear them, their shoes clicking in the cold as they struck the sidewalk. They would shoot him. It would be like his mother. The shots would ring out loud and he'd smell the gun powder and faint and end up in the hospital again. No, in the morgue, because he would be dead, except that he wouldn't know it, so it didn't matter. Or maybe he would know it, but could do nothing about it. No one could tell him. Dead people became very secretive about their business once they died. The thought made him laugh crazily, the fear jumping inside of him like a caged rabid animal.

When he reached the entrance to the subway station he grabbed the light pole and spun down the stairs, conscious that he musn't stumble or fall. It was like going around the net at high speed, gauging the path of his skates to a millimeter to avoid the metal at the bottom of the net. He was crazy, he thought. They were right. He was a total loonie, no doubt about it. The thought brought on more hysterical laughter. As he hurdled the turnstile once more, he heard them on the stairs and almost gave up. The train was not a passenger train but the one which collected the garbage from the large bins at each station. It would sit there until each of the bins had been emptied. His mind had stopped working and only an animal instinct remained.

Suddenly, he was beyond fear and was now on the other side, no longer allowing thought to interfere with action. It was just like those other times when he had reached into himself during a game: seeing the ball clearly, its flight ever so slow it did not seem to be coming at eighty miles an hour, the bat striking; the pass play developing so that he felt as if he were playing against children; the goalie moving helplessly to prevent the puck from entering the net. Everything slow motion and him traveling beyond time at cosmic speed, making the past, the present and the future one, flying through time like an eternal comet, flying to infinity and back in the space of no time at all it seemed, knowing exactly what he must do now.

He ran to the front of the station, jumped on the small platform of the lead car, ducked down and waited. He heard the voices asking excitedly where he'd gone, describing his height and weight and clothing and the fact that he was Puerto Rican. Everything had happened too quickly and nothing but confusion remained in the minds of the transit workers. And then he heard them coming and he slowly let himself down into the tracks and under the train. He crawled beneath the undercarriage, the previous fear now transformed into animal cunning. He crawled slowly, hoping the train would not start up again, aware that he must not touch any part of the train or get his clothing stuck. His hands were raw and the dampness of the gutter between the tracks added to the cold. As he was nearing the end of the train, he heard one of the workers shout that they were done. The two men who had chased him were police officers and had just finished searching the train. There was some further talk about having to report that they had lost him and then the motorman blew the whistle on the train. He crawled free of the train, scrambled up on the wall of the tunnel and hid in a small, rectangular depression in the stone. For a moment he felt like jumping on the back of the train and escaping, but his animal instinct told him to remain hidden. He waited as the train pulled out of the station, heading uptown. They were still there, black and white, cursing, their faces angry.

In him now there burned a fierce determination to be free and he began edging himself away along the catwalk, deeper into the tunnel and heading for the station at 103rd Street. They were radioing their failure the last time he looked in their direction. He hurried on, hoping with each step that another train would not come. When he heard an approaching train and saw the lights, he calmly got down into the tracks, stepped over the third rail and clambered up on the catwalk on the other side of the tunnel. He was now on the downtown side. The roaring express train on the middle tracks sent a cold gust of air through the tunnel, but he felt no discomfort. He was beyond feeling, beyond pain, his mind absorbing each sensation easily, his body functioning so perfectly that he felt elated. When he finally saw the station lights at 103rd Street he stopped walking. There was no one on the platform nor on the one across the way. It was nearly three a.m. when he went out through the turnstile, past a token booth attendant who was reading and up the stairs into the street. Snow was now falling steadily.

He looked in every direction. A couple of people were huddled against a building at the top of the hill, on 102nd Street, but he didn't fear them. When they began coming down the hill, he knew they were after him again and he took off running. They'd never catch him, their bullets would not reach him. Up 103rd Street he went, heading west with the snow. Park, Madison, Fifth and into Central Park, the snow now falling heavily, big flakes close together. He never looked back. He was the wind and the snow and faster than time, he was.

When he reached the wall of the park, he went over it and was in the woods, climbing the steep hill near the garden next to the lake. A moment later Fifth Avenue was alive with sirens and screeching police cars and orders being shouted from a loudspeaker, but he was running ahead of them with the snow, running with the seal spirit of his mother, running free and the snow cool on his face. He ran for a half hour, fighting his way through the craggy terrain and thick woods of the park until he reached the other side.

There were no police cars to be seen, but he was again vulnerable. He crossed Central Park West, Manhattan Avenue, Columbus and then Amsterdam Avenue and was now in front of his building. He instinctively went through his pockets. No keys. It didn't matter. If Maritza was there, she'd let him in. He went up the three flights and suddenly stopped. It was as if a sixth sense had once again warned him to proceed more carefully. He inched himself forward along the hallway until he was next to his door. And then he heard the struggling and the sound of Maritza's voice, warning whoever it was not to touch her. He thought of crashing against the door, but knew it was steel and he didn't have the strength to break it off its hinges. That only happened in movies. He ran up the next two flights of stairs, opened the door to the roof. The snow had covered everything very quickly. Carefully, he made his way to the fire escape and let himself down until he was on his apartment's landing, thinking he'd have to break the glass. The window was partially open. Beyond the kitchen he saw Maritza in the living room. She was dressed in pajamas and was holding a knife. There was a small man in front of her but Garboil couldn't see his face.

"Put it down, Maritza," the little man said. "I don't wanna have to use this on you, but I will if I have to."

"You're crazy, Pancho or whatever your name is," she said. "Just get out and leave me alone."

"Just take off your clothes," the man said. "You've done that before. I've seen you with that Martinez bastard."

"You're the bastard," she said. "What did you do, sneak in here?"

"Yeah, I hid in there," he said, pointing to the closet. "It's a good thing you didn't have to get anything out of there, cauze I'd a blown you both away then. Maybe it would've been better back then. So take 'em off, puta."

"Your mother's a puta, faggot," she said.

"Take'em off, bitch."

"No, go ahead and shoot if you're gonna, pig."

He had a gun then. The fear returned immediately. Maybe it was fate. Maybe this was the night he'd have to be shot. Jesus! Before he knew what he was doing, he'd removed his parka and shoes. There was barely enough room under the opened window for him to crawl under without having to open it further and make any noise. The cold hit him and it was like he was being scalded. Carefully, he crawled in head first into the darkened kitchen and stood up. Maritza saw him and their eyes met for a moment, recognizing him instantly even in the semi-darkness. At that moment her eyes were like those of El Falcon, brilliant with courage. He took another step and hit the plastic trash basket next to the stove.

Everything happened very quickly then. The man turned quickly around and at that very instant Maritza slashed at him with the long butcher knife. The blow was a downward one, delivered with all the anger and strength she had, so that the blade hit the wrist of the gun hand and the small pistol crashed to the floor and under the sofa. Rather than going after it, the little man turned around and headed for the kitchen. Garboil stepped aside and, the fear choking him, struck the man with a metal chair from the dinette set. The blow caught him on the side of the face, crushing the right cheekbone and blinding him instantly in that eye. The little man reeled against the wall, saw the window and scurried under the bottom pane and out into the fire escape. Maritza had come into the kitchen screaming and slashed at his leg as he went out. And then, a moment later they heard a scream and the muffled sound of the little man's body hitting the bottom of the well created by the two buildings. A dog barked several times and then everything was still and he was standing still and everything was as if nothing had happened. Snow was blowing into the kitchen. He went to the window, retrieved his parka, but could not find his shoes, and guessed that they had fallen with the man. The heavy snowfall had turned into a blizzard, blinding him even as he pulled in his parka. By the time it was finally over the next afternoon, nearly eighteen inches had fallen.

"Oh, my God," Garboil said, closing the window and locking it. "We should do something."

"Shh, turn on the lights," she said. "Will he come back?"

"I don't think so," she said. "If he does, he's crazier than I think he is."

Garboil turned on the light in the kitchen. There was blood spattered on the wall, the stove and the floor. He immediately found a dish rag and wiped everything clean. When he finished, he took the rag to the sink and ran water on it until all the blood was gone. He wrung it out and then deposited it in the trash can. He washed his hands again and then dried them on a dish towel. When he turned again to Maritza, she was still standing in the middle of the kitchen. The knife was still clutched in her hand and she had a glassy stare in her eyes. He went to her, pried her hand open and took the knife and placed it in the sink. And then she collapsed sobbing into his arms, her crying making her body move spasmodically against him.

He held her until the crying stopped and then he turned off the light in the kitchen and the living room and took her to the bedroom and made her lie down. She told him everything then, explaining how the group had trusted John Chota, which he said was his real name, even though everyone had been suspicious of him, as the case was with everyone new, adding how difficult it was to trust anyone, when it came to the struggle, even if you'd known the person for years; but that they had been right and yet never expected that he was an under-cover cop; that he had told her when she had refused his advances, because he'd made up his mind to rape her and then kill her, so it didn't matter if she knew who he was; that she had let him in because he was part of the group and she considered him pretty harmless, always going along with everyone's suspicions that he had been involved in drugs, but never imagining that he was a pig, which showed her where she was at in terms of judging who the enemy was.

When Garboil asked her why the window had been open, she explained that the apartment had been too warm, not an uncommon occurrence in buildings in which the superintendent was a Latin. For once he was thankful for Victor's insistence that they roast. Garboil held her close to him, knowing that the danger he'd felt was genuine and that his concern had been for her safety.

For John Chota the end came slowly, painfully and as sadistically as he imagined Maritza's death was to be. As he went out the window, he was aware of the blindness in his eye and the throbbing pain on the side of his face. The snow was falling so heavily that he could not see clearly from his other eye. His only concern was to escape over the roof, get his other gun and return. He'd have to hunt both of them down, now that Maritza knew he was a police officer. He'd have to come back and get them that night.

It had been stupid to let her know. And who'd hit him. It had to be Martinez. Had he been there all along? How had he come in? Had he learned the flying trick from El Falcon? He cursed all birds as he started up the fire escape. His foot hit Garboil's running shoe, buried in the snow on the step. He slipped backwards, hitting the railing, so that before he was aware of it, he was flying through the air and plummeting downward. He'd tumbled over the hand railing, tried desperately at the last minute to grasp the edge of the fire escape, but the blizzard had made everything slippery with ice. His right wrist badly injured by Maritza's knife, he had no chance.

The fall was three stories plus the basement level. In spite of the height, the fall did not kill him nor did it render him unconscious for very long. His body was found three days later after the snow melted, revealing the fetally curled-up form. Neighbors had thought it was the body of a child. They called the police and they came and removed Chota's body, not suspecting who he was.

The autopsy revealed that Chota had suffered a broken right ankle, a dislocation of the left hip, severe lacerations of the right cheekbone, loss of vision of the right eye, a major laceration of the right wrist, a minor one on his left leg and total damage to his larynx. The medical examiner determined that, unable to call out for help or climb out of the well created by the surrounding buildings, death had been caused by exposure to the severe cold.

The official police department report was that John Chota had died in the line of duty, allegedly in the pursuit of an undetermined perpetrator. At the funeral, Mullvaney swore to redouble his efforts to capture El Falcon and the rest of the trash that polluted the city. He knew Johnny had done his best and he was obviously trying to help capture Armando Martinez and the girl. Even when he'd been pulled off the case, he was still trying. That was the kind of stuff that great cops were made of. He'd requested an inspector's funeral and he'd gotten it with Ramirez' pull down at the Commissioner's office. The first inspector's funeral for a Puerto Rican and Johnny Chota definitely deserved it. That night he went home and got completely drunk and cried because the kid had been like his own son.

By the time the many forces had been mobilized to apprehend Armando Martinez, a.k.a. Frank Garboil, which they had finally surmised was his real name, and his accomplice Maritza Soto, the two of them, now considered armed and extremely dangerous, had dropped totally out of sight. In spite of law enforcement efforts to cover all exits from the city, including airports, they were nowhere to be found.

CHAPTER 31

In which the protagonist and his beloved have their first serious argument, of all things about identity, after which he determines to become a Puerto Rican again and in order to do so enlists the assistance of a former teaching colleague.

After sitting in the darkened apartment for nearly a half hour Maritza asked Garboil to turn on the lamp on the night table of the bedroom. Garboil turned it on and then said he should check on Chota. Maritza warned him to be careful. Wielding one of his hockey sticks, Garboil went to the kitchen window and without opening it looked outside. The snow had piled up considerably and still fell heavily, obscuring even the closest objects. From the bedroom Maritza asked if he could see anything. He said he couldn't and was going to open the window. When he did, he stepped back quickly, shocked by the intensity of the blizzard. It was as if someone had thrown a bucketful of snow in his face. He quickly looked up the fire escape and then down below but could see nothing in either direction. He closed the window and then locked it. One thing was certain, he told Maritza after returning to the bedroom. Even if Chota had survived the fall, there was no way he was going to climb out of the place where he had fallen. Still feeling the rage, she said she was glad because the longer Chota was trapped, the more time they had to get away.

Maritza had dressed again and was packing their belongings. She stopped suddenly and noticed that his face was scratched and his clothes were damp and grimy and immediately said he had to get out of his clothes and take a bath and change. He obediently went into the bathroom and began filling the tub. He stripped, got into the tub and began soaping himself. The soap burned his face where the tree branches had scratched him as he made his way through the park in the dark. When she came in with towels he felt embarassed by her presence. His nakedness didn't seem to affect her; she was all business now as she urged him to hurry. In spite of her apparent need to be moving she sat on the toilet seat and began talking, telling him everything that had gone on with the group during those times when she had to go off to meetings. It was as if she had a need to unburden herself of the knowledge, to expiate her part in the failed attempt to rescue him. He listened attentively, trying to understand her passion for the struggle, touched by the other members' willingness to risk their lives for a cause.

Once out of the tub and dressed it was his turn to confess. Haltingly, he told her that he was not Armando Martinez, that his real name was Frank Garboil, an economics professor, married and the father of two children. He was separated from his wife and had been so when he met her. He even told her that he was thirty-four years old. She said she understood, but seemed abstracted from the reality of what he had layed out before her.

"It doesn't matter," she said. "What counts is what we have."

Confessing that he was not whom she thought him to be should have cleared up matters once and for all between them. Gone would be the lies, the deception and pretense which at times prevented them from being closer to each other. Although hurt by the knowledge that she had lived a lie with him, she seemed to understand his motivation.

"Now you know why we wanna be free from Yanqui domination," she said.

He nodded his head several times but truly could not comprehend her concern with the issue of independence. Nor could he accept that she was not having the reaction he had expected. From her standpoint, it seemed, their bond to each other had been solidified by his openness. After what had happened to John Chota or Pancho Miranda, or whatever his name was, they needed each other more than ever. If Chota survived the fall, he'd never admit to his superiors what had transpired. But she felt he was cunning enough to have the police come after them. One way or the other, now that they knew his true identity, he'd try to avenge himself.

"They're already watching me," he said.

He explained about Ingrid without mentioning their lovemaking, since it would serve no purpose for her to know. It was so unimportant and he felt nothing but disgust and regret about the time he spent with her. But something was not right. Revealing his true identity, rather than freeing him, had produced quite a different effect. After all the weeks of insisting that he was Frank Garboil, he now felt empty and without purpose. What would he do? Run off somewhere with her and hide and help her struggle? Because that's all he could do to help her. What motivated her to want to fight such a useless battle? The idea of further violence sickened him. The little man hitting the ground below had been horrible, his scream so filled with the knowledge that he was about to die. Now that he had participated in the violence would he have to learn how to kill with purpose? He sat on the bed and let his head fall between his hands. In the light of the lamp he appeared completely crushed. Maritza took his hand and then kissed his cheek.

"What is it?" she said, tenderly. "The pig? It was an accident. It was his fault. Forget it, okay."

"It's not that," he said. "Not really. I mean, it is but there's something else I can't put together."

"Something else you haven't told me?"

"No, I've told you everything. I just don't feel right. Something's missing from all this. Something not resolved. It's like it doesn't feel right being me again. Like Frank Garboil doesn't exist anymore." She attempted to dissuade him from the idea, but he insisted, sinking deeper into his depression. At one point he went as far as saying that he felt as if Frank Garboil had died.

"Don't say that," she hissed at him, gripping his arm so tightly that her nails dug into his flesh. "Don't ever say that."

"Well, that's how it feels," he said, momentarily shocked out of the emotional stupor into which he was falling.

She stood up and began pacing.

"It's just not the right time for all this," she said." We have to leave. For all we know there's a million cops out there waiting for us. If they come up here, that's it. Whatever happened to the pig, like they'll try to blame us. I'm not going to jail. I have my piece and the one the pig left behind. If you hate violence so much, shut your eyes, because they're not taking this prisoner of war alive."

"You have a gun?"

"Yeah, I have a gun," she said, angrily. "What am I supposed to do, let these people run all over me? Does that shock you?"

"I guess I am," he said. "I'm sorry," he added, meekly.

"Sure you are," she said, stopping to face him. "I'm gonna tell you something, since we're getting honest and whatnot." Her voice was hurt and angry. "I love you as much as I ever have. Whatever you are. You saved my life and were as brave as anyone could've been, but right now you're being like very indulgent and selfish and we can't afford to go into a big psychological number about your hangups. Whether you like it or not, here's the way I look at it. You got bored with your life as a like nondescript, anonymous, turned-off, white intellectual and you decided to become a Puerto Rican. Good for you."

"That was planned by them, I told you," he said.

"Whatever. So you get a chance like to be a Puerto Rican and like you do such a good job that you take in a whole student body, some pretty hip people, a whole revolutionary group and me. Great. But it didn't suit you so now you're back to the same point in your life. Still bored with existence and wanting to take one more look at your belly button. Except that this time, half of the cops in New York City are gonna be looking for you. On top of that, you're feeling guilty about some friggin pig that almost raped and killed your old lady, again me. Pretty friggin indulgent and like pretty friggin selfish. Maybe you were better off as a Puerto Rican. Because believe me, honey. Like for whatever reason we don't suffer from a lack of identity. If anything we seem to have too much of it."

He was up off the bed immediately.

"That's it," he said, as if he'd suddenly woken up to a great truth. "That's what's missing."

"Now what?" she said, watching him screw up his face with new determination.

"I'll be a Puerto Rican again."

"Oh sure," she said, her hands on her hips, her shoulder turned to him in derision. "You gotta be joking."

"I did it before. Who's to know?"

"I will," she said.

He was suddenly taken aback, the wind out of his sails, so to speak.

"But you said it didn't matter."

"It doesn't," she said, "but it'd be like we were living a lie. It's gonna be bad enough trying to keep the cops away, but now I'd be worried that you'd give it away."

He walked over and took her face in his hands and told her how he'd try harder this time around.

"I just got scared, that's all," he said. "I didn't understand what it really meant to be a Puerto Rican."

"And now you know, right?"

He hesitated.

"Not everything," he said. "But I'll learn. I'll study even harder this time. In a year's time I'll be the best Puerto Rican you'll ever know. I mean it. I can do it."

She looked at him with such contempt that he'd almost sat back down on the bed from the force of the rage he felt in her.

"What are you talking about?" she said. "What do you plan on doing? Is that what you think the Puerto Rican Studies Department at New Amsterdam is all about? You think that's why I'm majoring in it, so I can go around teaching turned off-white boys how to be Puerto Rican." Her anger was immense, her eyes growing bigger and her body growing larger with the outrage. "I can see it now. I graduate, open up an office in midtown and advertise in the "Voice" and "The Times": LEARN TO BE A PUERTO RICAN. SIX WEEKS TO WISDOM IN THE WAYS OF THE SPIC. LEARN LATIN DANCING, RAPPING TO CHICKS, MACHO BEHAVIOR UNDER STRESS, ROLLING A JOINT IN THE WIND, and all kinds of other neat tricks that'll help you get over."

"You know that's not what I'm talking about," he said. "I'll really try to find out more about your people and respect the struggle and learn to speak Spanish better."

"It's not the same," she answered.

"You mean you have to be born a Puerto Rican to really know."

"That's right," she said, sullenly.

"I see," he said, walking away from her. "In other words there's something special about being Puerto Rican, right?"

"Yeah," she said, defensively, without conviction. "Damn right there is."

"What?" he shot back at her. "What?"

"I don't know," she said. "You'd have to be one to understand."

"Thanks," he said.

"Don't mention it," she replied and turned her back on him.

In the time they'd known each other this was their first fight and neither one enjoyed the distance that was being created by the angry words. They knew it was the wrong time to create a rift between them. Until they were away and clear of the mess in New York, they had to do everything they could to protect each other.

"I'm sorry," she said, sheepishly. "I shouldn't have said what I said. I don't know what being a Puerto Rican is about. I just know that we're being messed with. That's all."

"Me too," he replied. "It seemed like a great idea, me being Puerto Rican, when I thought of it."

"Maybe it still is," she said, shrugging her shoulders. "What do I know."

"What?" he said, not believing she had changed her mind.

He began laughing and shook his head. The laughter made his insides hurt.

"Sure," she said, turning and smiling at him. "The trick would be pulling it off again. This time for good. No changing your mind this time."

"I wouldn't. You'd be really proud of me. I promise."

"I know, I know. I trust you. But how? You can't go back to New Amsterdam. I can't even go back after this thing with Chota."

They thought for a long time, spinning off ideas about restructuring their lives as a young, typical Puerto Rican couple. The idea of going to the Island was dismissed immediately on several counts. No matter how menial the work, they'd be displacing someone in the work force and, once there, they'd stand more of a chance of being found out because of the language. No, it was best that they stay in New York. It was the last place they'd look for them. They'd get regular jobs, fall into a regular routine and in a few years emerge once again in the struggle. He'd get a job in banking and she could start school all over again as he had. They'd move to Boston or Philadelphia or Chicago, places that had Puerto Rican communities and then after a while she could go to law school and in a few years they could start a family. He'd get a divorce and they could get married. But what names would they use? Not their own.

It didn't make sense, he thought. How could they pull something like that off? The business of the cop still haunted him. If they were caught, they'd have to answer questions and who knew what would happen then. There had to be a way to turn time back and restructure the past. It was done to history all the time. Events that were reported as news in one way to protect the security of a government, later, when it was no longer important, were revealed as different. What was truth anyway? It was relative. All of it based on social contracts. As long as no one was hurt, what did it matter? She was right. The important thing was to be free and, as corny as it sounded, to lift the human spirit and soar above all the petty differences that destroy people.

"Holy cow," he said. "That's it."

"What is it?" she said.

"El Falcon," he said, gleefully, the heaviness apparently dispelled and his face beaming with satisfaction.

"No way," she said. "He's gone. There's no way he's gonna be of any help. Not for a while, anyway."

"No, not him."

"Who, then?"

"Vega."

"Who?"

"The writer. I told you about him. We taught together at Frick. Didn't this guy Chota or Miranda or whatever his name is or was mention him?"

"Yeah sure," she said, puzzled. "He talked about some other writer and said he had the goods on him and El Falcon both because he was helping El Falcon. "He was ranting and raving but he didn't mention your friend."

"Sure he did. You told me. What did he say? Tell me again."

He mentioned a guy named Yunque. He said an espiritista told him this guy was helping El Falcon and Chota was gonna find him and do him in and make him tell how he helped El Falcon appear and disappear."

"Yunque, right?"

"Yeah."

"It's the same person, Maritza. Yunque's his mother's last name. Listen, if he can make El Falcon appear and disappear, he's capable of a lot more."

"Yeah? Like what? Making a Puerto Rican?"

"Sure."

"Oh sure. What is he a forger or a plastic surgeon?"

"Just a writer. I told you about him. You'd have to meet him to understand. If he helped El Falcon he can help us."

"I don't know," she said.

"C'mon, if he was helping El Falcon he's gotta be part of the movement."

"Don Alfonso never mentioned him."

"Of course not. It musta been really secret stuff. Vega's okay, really. Hard as hell to get along with. You know, a little weird."

Like what?"

"Well, like you never know what's really going on with him. He's always playing some kind of game. One minute you think he's super smart and then he'll say something that really makes you wonder and then you get the feeling he's just playing with your mind."

"And he's gonna help us?" she said, not at all convinced.

"Yeah, he could."

"Sure, like I really want my mind played with at this time."

"It's worth a try. C'mon, I've told you about his books. Remember me telling you about all the Puerto Ricans not really being from Earth but from another planet and having a real tough time adapting."

"Yeah, that was pretty hip," she said, but was not convinced that they should go seeking his help.

"And he's Puerto Rican," Garboil said. "Weird but Puerto Rican. C'mon, let me give him a call. I haven't spoken to him in about two years, but it's worth a try. If he was helping El Falcon, he can help us."

"Maybe he's the one that finked on us about the escape plan."

"Vega?"

"Yeah, Vega."

"No way, Maritza."

"Yeah? Maybe we'll get up there and like that's when the cops are gonna grab us."

"Not the way he feels about P.R. Let me call him."

She thought about it and then nodded reluctantly.

"If we're gonna get caught," he said, "we might as well find out who's who. "If he rats us out," he went on, recalling the phrase that was used on the block for describing betrayal, "then we can tell everyone."

"If we live," she said.

"Don't worry," he said. "He'll help us."

Garboil went to his desk and from one of the drawers pulled out an old address book. After looking rapidly through it, he dialed the number and waited. After a few rings a strong, masculine voice answered the phone.

"Internal Revenue Service, Joe Bacciagalup speaking."

"Vega?" Garboil said, immediately recognizing his friend's voice. "Yeah, who's this?"

"Vega, this is Frank Garboil. I'm sorry to be calling so late."

"That's all right. How's it going?"

"Okay, I guess. I need to speak to you."

"Right now?"

"I know, I know. It's almost five in the morning, but I'm in kind of a jam." "Where are you?"

"In my apartment. Not too far from you, if you're still in the same place on a 102nd Street."

"Same place still."

"240 West l02nd Street, apartment 65, right?"

"You got it."

"I got somebody named Maritza with me. You don't know her. Can she come?"

"I don't know. Can she?"

"What?"

"Just a joke. Sure, bring her over. Make sure she wipes her feet outside, I have parkay floors. Another joke. Or are they butter?"

Garboil chuckled and shook his head. Same old Vega, he thought.

"Okay, thanks," he said. "And I'm sorry to be cutting into your writing time."

"No problem, Frank," Vega said, more seriously. "I just finished marrying off Nelson Monserrat and Rosaura Caraballo. He's getting ready to run for City Council as part of a grand scheme for the year 2000. By tomorrow she'll be pregnant with their first kid. How soon can you be here?"

"Ten minutes," Garboil said.

"Are you hungry?"

"Yeah, as a matter of fact," Garboil said.

"You're out of luck then. See you then."

Garboil hung up the phone. There was a smile of satisfaction on his face as he began gathering some more of his belongings: some clothes, toiletries and his bank book. When Maritza removed Chota's gun from under the bed, he asked her for it. She shook her head, but he insisted and she handed it to him. He took it, holding it as if it were a dead mouse. With a towel he wiped it clean of fingerprints and asked her to open the kitchen window. When she did so, he tossed it out into the blizzard. It made no noise as it hit down below. He now asked for her own gun. He appeared so sure of himself that she handed it over immediately. He followed the same proceedure of cleaning it and then tossed it out.

When they were ready to go he looked once around the apartment as if to take in everything, recording it all for memory. Whatever happened to them, now he could always recall the happy hours they had spent together in the apartment and the trust they had developed and, most of all, their lovemaking.

CHAPTER 32

In which the protagonist and his lady fair come face to face with their maker, engage in significant and often poignant dialogue, strike a deal with him to ensure their safety and wellbeing, which concludes the remarkable comeback of the hero.

Out in the street the snow and wind had not abated. Garboil and Maritza could hardly see more than a few inches in front of them, there was no definition between sidewalk and street, and parked cars appeared as similarly carved mounds of snow. There were drifts a foot or more against the buildings. They encountered no one as they walked. The one cab that came trudging up Broadway, its chained wheels singing its muffled song, did not appear interested in a fare. Fighting against the wind, it took Garboil and Maritza nearly fifteen minutes to walk the four blocks to their destination.

They rang the doorbell downstairs in Vega's building and a few minutes later, cigarette in hand, Vega met them at his front door. The apartment was huge, high-ceilinged and well-lit. The two men shook hands and Garboil introduced Maritza. Vega nodded approvingly and invited them into the dining room where he had set out a mushroom omelet, a watercress and scallion salad, soft rolls and herbal tea.

"We might as well have breakfast," he said.

Garboil thanked him and Maritza looked suspiciously around her, but both sat down and ate. When they were finished eating, Vega cleared the dishes, returned from the kitchen and motioned them to follow him into the living room where they sat down.

"What can I do for you?" Vega said, once they were seated.

"Do you know El Falcon?" Garboil said.

"El Falcon?" smiled Vega, through a cloud of smoke.

"Don Alfonso Del Valle," Maritza said, not disguising her annoyance.

"Let's say, I know of him," Vega said. "Why?"

"There are rumors that you helped him escape," Garboil said. "That you can help him appear and disappear."

"And?" Vega said.

"And we'd like you to help us," Garboil said.

"How?" Vega said. "Would you like to disappear?"

"Let's go," Maritza said, getting up. "I don't feel like being played with."

"No, sit down," Garboil said.

Maritza sat back down. She looked straight at Vega, challenging him to continue his game. Vega returned her look with equal intensity.

"People say that you helped him by turning him into a hawk so he could fly away," she said. "I know that's all bullshit spiritualism. They say you gave him words so he could turn himself back and forth from man to hawk."

"That's possible," Vega said, knocking another cigarette out of the pack on the end table next to him.

"Then you admit it," Maritza said.

"No, I simply said that it's possible that people are saying those things," Vega replied, lighting his cigarette.

"Then you're saying that it's impossible to just use words to make someone fly," Maritza said.

"No, I didn't say that either," Vega said.

Then it is possible," Maritza said.

"Sure, it depends on who's using the words and what they are."

"So, did you?" Maritza said, growing more annoyed.

"Very possible," Vega said.

"That doesn't tell me anything," Maritza said.

"Excellent," Vega said.

"He's a real winner," Maritza said to Garboil.

"Anyway," Garboil said, "that's what the police think. "They also believe you're behind the actions of the United Front at Stuyvesant Hospital. Were you down there?"

Vega laughed and ground out his cigarette. He immediately lit another.

"Next they'll start saying I'm El Falcon," he said.

"Are you?" Garboil said.

"C'mon, Frank," Vega said, shooting Garboil a look of disbelief.

"He's not El Falcon" Maritza said, frowning at Garboil "I've met him and he's nothing like him."

"I was simply attempting to ascertain the veracity of certain statements being circulated," Garboil said. "The problem is that we've managed to immerse ourselves totally in this situation, Vega. The police are after us and we've managed to implicate ourselves. An undercover operative very likely died tonight and we happened to witness the tragedy."

"What tragedy!" Maritza shouted. "He tried to rape me! And why are you talking like you swallowed a damned dictionary."

Grave concern was suddenly etched in Vega's eyes.

"Who was it?" he said. "John Chota?"

Maritza instinctively reached for her gun, but it wasn't there. Upon hearing Vega mention Chota's name, a look of surprise came over Garboil's face and he shook his head.

"You see," Maritza said. "He's one of them."

"How did you know his name?" Garboil asked.

"Please don't concern yourself with that," Vega said. "If it's a question of my keeping quiet about what happened, don't worry about it. As far as I'm concerned you don't even exist."

"Thanks," said Maritza, sarcastically. "The problem is that we do exist."

"Only on paper," Vega said.

"What do you mean only on paper?" Maritza said.

"Exactly what I meant," Vega replied. "School papers, police reports, social security rolls, bank statements. Nothing more."

"Is that all we are to you?" Maritza said.

"Not to me, to the society," Vega said.

"Oh, you pious, pompous . . ."

"Maritza, hold on for a minute," Garboil said. "Vega, the problem, as far as I'm able to analyze it, centers around my identity, of me being who I am or as it turns out who I'm not. Anyway, in a rather absurd flight of fancy, I adopted someone else's identity. A Puerto Rican young man who was killed in Vietnam . . . Armando Martinez. You see . . ."

Vega cut him off.

"I know," he said.

"How?" Maritza said. "This is crazy."

"Yeah, how?" Garboil said.

"I just do," Vega said. "Go on, Frank."

"She's a little nervous," Garboil said. "She thinks you're involved with the police and you're gonna turn us in."

Vega did not look at Maritza but spoke directly to Garboil.

"Please inform her that a vivid imagination is good for only two things. One is the writing of fiction and the other is going crazy. Inform her that unless she has more than a passing interest in writing, then she ought to be extremely concerned about her mental health. Please make her aware of that, Frank."

Garboil laughed nervously.

"That's real funny," Maritza said, grabbing a cigarette from the pack next to Vega. "Can I have one of these, Mr. Amateur Shrink."

"Sure," Vega said, and immediately reached to light her cigarette. She inhaled deeply and then blew the smoke out angrily.

"I see what you meant, Frank," she said. "He does enjoy fucking with people's minds."

"Did you say that about me, Frank?" Vega said, playfully.

Garboil felt immediately on his guard. There was no way to contradict Maritza without making the situation worse and he felt he owed his friend an explanation.

"I didn't use the word 'fuck,' " he said.

Vega laughed uproariously.

"It's a perfectly good word to use for what I do," he said. "The only problem is that that particular human activity, whether expressed literally or metaphorically, should be the domain of adults. Children should not be exposed to it. I'm very sorry, Miss Soto."

Maritza could not contain herself.

"Oh, fuck off, you Prasp bastard," she said.

"What?" Vega said, genuinely shocked. "Prasp?"

"Yeah, Prasp," Maritza spit out. "Puerto Rican Anglo Saxon Protestant."

Vega roared with laughter.

"That's great," he said. He looked admiringly at Maritza and for the first time his face appeared to soften. He liked her spunk, the toughness and fire in her eyes. He looked at Garboil and smiled. "You seem to be in good hands, Frank."

"Thanks," Garboil said.

"Now he's gonna be charming?" Maritza said, crossing her arms. "Where did you go to school, Princeton or Yale?"

"Neither," Vega said. "N.Y.U. I'm a violet at heart."

A tiny smile appeared on Maritza's lips and she looked away.

"Look," Vega said to her. "I've already given you my word. If that's not good enough, there isn't a hell of a lot I can say or do. I don't know how much I can do to help you, but I've always liked Garboil. I don't have too many friends, but I'm sure if I were in the same situation, he'd try and help me. So tell me what I can do."

Garboil looked at Maritza but was unable to determine what she was thinking. She still looked upset, but there was now a more relaxed look in her eyes.

"Anyway," Garboil began once more. "I took on this young man's identity in order to play hockey. One of the best parts of the whole thing was meeting Maritza, but being Puerto Rican was enjoyable. You know, like being able to let go and not talk like she said, like I swallowed a dictionary. I couldn't do that if I was gonna pull the thing off. So when I got my own identity back, it didn't feel right."

"Are you saying you want to be Puerto Rican again?" Vega asked.

"Yeah," Garboil replied. "Does that seem strange?"

"No, I don't think so," Vega said. "It'd probably solve about ninety percent of the problems in this country if everyone wanted to be Puerto Rican. Look at it this way. Except for a few privileged people, there's no real advantage in being either black or white. In fact, it's a disadvantage. There's laws for apparently protecting, but really screwing, both groups. If everyone was Puerto Rican, then the whole black-white issue would disappear. There would still be a few diehard racists, but in a couple of generations they'd be gone."

"That's pretty stupid," Maritza said.

Vega lit another cigarette and thought for a moment. He got up, walked around the room, sat back down and then an enigmatic smile etched itself under his thick moustache. Behind his glasses there appeared a look of absolute mischief.

"How do you know you haven't been one all along?" he said, looking at Garboil.

Garboil looked puzzled. Maritza was equally confused.

"That's impossible," Garboil said.

"I don't think so," Vega replied. "The way I remember it, your mother and father had a bodega in the Lower East Side. There was a holdup and your mother was shot. They were a typical Puerto Rican couple trying to make it in this country."

"You're crazy," Maritza said.

"Thank you for the compliment," Vega retorted.

"Go on," Garboil said. "Let him finish, Maritza."

"Don't listen to him, Frank," Maritza replied, but there wasn't as much of the vitriol in her voice as before. She turned to Vega and shook her head, almost pleading this time. "Why are you trying to fuck up his head, man. He's been through a lot. He really trusts you and you're running a game on him. He's not Puerto Rican. His mother was an Eskimo. He told me himself. She was shot, but she wasn't Puerto Rican."

"Yes and no," Vega said, calmly.

"Yes and no, what?" Garboil said.

"Yes, she was shot, and, no, she was not an Eskimo. Not exactly, anyway."

"Sure, sure," Maritza said. "He's playing with your mind, Armando. I mean, Frank. Let's get outta here."

"No, wait," Garboil said, and turned back to Vega. "How do you know that?"

"My father knew your parents. He used to take me down to Orchard Street to shop for clothes and to get my glasses when I was a kid. Same hometown."

"Which?" Maritza said.

"Cacimar," Vega answered.

"Aha, you're wrong," Maritza said, standing up. "My grandmother said there's no such place on the Island. No town like that. Maybe some barrio or some place up in the country, but definitely not a town. Frank told her that's where his parents were from the first time he met her, but he was pretending to be Armando." She turned to Garboil. "Why did you tell her that, Frank?"

Garboil began to explain, but he caught Vega's eyes move almost imperceptibly to ask him not to attempt answering.

"I don't know," Garboil said to Maritza. "I think you told me Cacimar was some Taino Indian chief, who died fighting the Spaniards. I think that's where I got it."

"Yeah, Cacimar was a cacique. He died up in El Yunque." Maritza said, puzzled by Garboil's response. "But his mother was an Eskimo," she insisted, pointing at Garboil.

"In a matter of speaking she was," Vega replied. "To help out with their dream of returning to the Island and building a house, she sold coconut ice. You know, *helado de coco.*"

"So," Maritza said.

"Well, a few other people sold *helado* down there," Vega said. "All of them men. In those days women didn't go out in the street and do that kind of thing. But she and her husband really understood each other and didn't much care what other people thought, so she decided to go ahead with her little business. She was a very smart lady."

"Woman," Maritza corrected.

"Woman," Vega said. "Anyhow, she understood the power of successful advertising as a way of counteracting the competition . . ."

"The sexism," Maritza said.

"That too," Vega said. "So she contacted Porfirio Vizcarrondo, El Pintor, to do her cart that she sold the helado from. Porfirio did all the signs and landscapes for the bodegas and barber shops down in the Lower East Side in those days. Porfirio was an advertising genius. Frank's mother explained the problem and he came up with a great idea. What do you think he painted on the cart?"

Maritza was silent, suddenly at a loss for words. But Garboil brightened immediately.

"An igloo," he said.

"Right," Vega said. "An igloo with a palm tree in the background, an Eskimo woman next to the entrance to the igloo and the words COCO ESKIMO written in icy blue letters on the snowy, white background. Not only was the recipe for the coconut ice great, but now it had distinctive advertisement. Frank's mother sold from early March into late October, when it was already chilly. People took to calling her La Eskimal, the Eskimo lady. She didn't mind as long as the nickels and dimes kept coming."

"Bullshit," Maritza said.

Maritza's comment did not affect Vega. More significantly neither did it affect Garboil. He was suddenly dazed, his mind numb, his eyes seemingly hypnotized by Vega's explanation.

"Sol," he said.

"What?" Maritza said.

"His mother's name," Vega said. "Isn't that right, Frank?"

"Yes, that was her name," Garboil answered. "Not Summersun. That was my father's doing. He wrote poetry about her. 'Eres como un sol de verano, cálido y benigno,' he said, in perfectly accented Spanish. And they shot her," he added, sadly. "But I don't remember it."

Maritza had been moved by hearing Garboil recite the verse and looked at Vega suspiciously, but more warmly, her mistrust melting slowly away, her need to find out more about Garboil supplanting the resentment she'd felt towards Vega.

"It was a holdup," Vega said. "They were closing the bodega one night. January, I believe. Totally senseless. They didn't move quickly enough when they were asked to open the cash register."

Garboil's hands were sweating and he felt nauseous.

"And my father?" he said, almost in a whisper. "He told me he was from Europe," Garboil said, almost in a whisper. "He told me he was from Europe somewhere and that he'd traveled a lot."

"No, he was Puerto Rican," Vega explained. "French and Spanish background. He married your mother late, but he was in the Merchant Marine for quite a few years before that, so he did travel quite a bit."

"But why did he lie to me?" Garboil asked, suddenly overcome with grief.

"To protect you," Vega said. "That's what my father said. I can't figure it out. I really don't know the real reason."

"Protect me? From what? From being Puerto Rican?"

"I guess so," Vega said. "Maybe he figured you'd be better off. You were only six when your mother was killed. The experience triggered an amnesiac reaction. He tried giving you a new past."

"And my name?"

"Oh, it's Garboil all right," Vega said. "French. From the time of the pirates and corsairs."

"French?" Maritza said.

"Sure," Vega said. "There are plenty of French names on the Island. Italian, too. And Dutch, German and even Russian and Polish."

"I don't remember any of it," Garboil said, shaking his head. "But if you knew all about this, man," he said, looking at Vega, "how come you never said anything? How come you let me go on living a lie?"

"I didn't think it would add anything to our friendship," Vega said. "I don't make friends with people that often and I definitely don't make friends based on the fact that they're Puerto Rican. I never thought of breaking into what you'd created as your own life. I knew the whole story and didn't think it was my business to go against something your father had done. We were friends, you understood what I was trying to do in terms of my work and that was enough for me. I'm sorry. If I thought it would've helped, I would've told you."

"That's okay," Garboil said, dejectedly. "The worst part of it is that I don't even feel Puerto Rican. I'm not even sure I can pull it off again, except that I don't think I have a choice this time."

"Why should we believe you?" Maritza said, challenging Vega once more, this time without an edge of sarcasm in her voice. "How do we know you're not making the whole thing up like they did?"

"You don't," Vega said. "You're absolutely right. I could be making the whole thing up, but I'm not. On top of that, harsh as it may sound, I didn't come looking for you. You came to me and I'm doing the best I can. You're not in a pretty situation."

"That's right, Maritza," Garboil said. He turned once again to Vega. "What can we do? They're gonna come after us."

"Tell me what you want and I'll see what I can do," Vega said. "Do you want to go on fighting or do you want to give in and do it their way. It's up to you."

"We wanna keep fighting," Maritza said.

"I don't know," Garboil said. "I don't know if I'm cut out for all the revolutionary stuff. It makes me ashamed to admit it but I don't think I'm ready to go to war about the whole thing."

"Can you teach us how to make bombs?" Maritza asked.

"Sure, if that's what you want," Vega said.

"And get the materials for the bombs?"

"I can put you in touch with the right people."

"I don't know," Garboil said.

"How about weapons?" Maritza said.

"It can be arranged," Vega said.

"To shoot people?" Garboil said. "I don't like it. I just wanna work and have a nice quiet place to come home to and rest. I don't wanna hide for the rest of my life."

Maritza stood up and banged the wall with her fist.

"We have to fight," she said. "Don't you understand that, Frank? We have to. There's no excuse now. You're Puerto Rican and you have to. I have to. Otherwise we'll lose it once and for all."

"Lose what?" Garboil said.

"Everything. The Island. Our culture, our language, our dignity and ourselves."

"What about us?" Garboil said. "They'll kill us eventually. And if they don't, we'll end up in jail. What about what we feel for each other. How long do you think that's gonna last before it's gone because of the pressure? What if we have a child? A baby. Don't you know how I feel about you?"

His words pierced her, hurting her so deeply that tears flowed from her eyes and she dug her nails into her palms until she couldn't bear the pain. She sat back down, not disappointed in him, but wishing there was a way out of the situation. He was right. He wasn't cut out to be a soldier. Some people were and some people were not and it didn't seem to have so much to do with courage as it did with a difference in principles. But they had to go on fighting. There was no getting around that. He was right. Eventually she'd want his child, their child. But she wanted the child to be born in a different world. She'd want the child to be able to say that he or she was Puerto Rican and have that mean something concrete. She wanted to tell the child that somewhere in the middle of a beautiful sea there was an island of wondrous mysteries where people were kind and generous and loved each other, a place where people respected each other and cherished freedom above everything else.

"Can we do both?" she said, meekly to Vega.

"You mean fight and live a peaceful life?"

"Yes, something like that."

Vega thought for a moment and nodded solemnly.

"It's very dangerous," he said.

"It doesn't matter," she said.

"I only know of one way," Vega said.

"What is it?" Garboil said.

"Becoming invisible," Vega said.

"Please don't joke anymore," Maritza said. "Please."

"It's no joke," Vega said, seriously.

"Would we be able to see each other?" Garboil said. "Yes, of course," Vega said.

"What about other people?" Maritza asked. "Could they see us?"

"Yes and no," Vega replied, lighting yet another cigarette. "It depends on you. You would both have to rid yourselves of the idea that being Puerto Rican is such a big deal."

"Wait a minute," Maritza said, suddenly defensive once more.

Vega ignored her outburst and went on.

"With Frank it won't be so difficult," he said. "As it is, you can hardly tell that he is. But with you," he said, pointing his chin at Maritza, "it's going to take a lot of doing. Right now you stick out like a sore thumb."

"Now I've heard it all," she said. "I'm supposed to get rid of the idea that I'm Puerto Rican, right?"

"Wrong," Vega said. "You can keep all of what that means to you and protect it and cherish it and celebrate it, but you have to stop wearing it like a 'I'm Puerto Rican and I'm proud' button. In the bigger scheme of things nobody cares."

"I do," she shot back.

"I know," Vega said. "And it's going to eventually get you into all sorts of trouble. If you really mean what you said about having to fight you're going to have to get serious and become invisible."

"Are you invisible?" she said, once again defying him.

"Pretty much so," Vega said.

"And you like it?" she said.

"Yeah, I do. It gives me time to do my work. I don't get invited anywhere to represent Puerto Ricans because I'm an extremely poor public speaker. I think most things are comical, especially when they have to do with a few people having power over a lot, and on top of that, I can't stand bullshit and, although I may not always say how I feel, it always comes across that I think most of what some of these clowns want to put across as being best for the people, is going to screw the people. Left, right, middle. It doesn't matter. None of them can mount a popular movement worth a damn, but they can talk real pretty. If their hearts were in the right place, people would go for a socialist democracy in a minute. I really believe if people understood how it was going to benefit them, they would want independence. And the issue of the United States. That can be dealt with in terms of world opinion. The U.S. doesn't want to let go, but it has to. And we have to be willing to let go too. But that doesn't mean we can't maintain friendly relations with the U.S."

"Right," Garboil said.

"And you like being invisible," Maritza said.

"That's right," Vega said. "There's definite advantages in it."

"What about the disadvantages?" she said.

"Good question," Vega said. "That's where the danger comes in. You can get so caught up in being invisible that you start thinking you're not Puerto Rican."

"Are you starting again?" Maritza said. "I thought you said that was the whole idea."

"No, I never said that," Vega said. "What I said was that you had to get rid of the notion that being Puerto Rican was such a big deal. Christ, some of our people are a walking Puerto Rican Day Parade 365 days out of the year."

"It's the only thing they have," Maritza said. "It's their identity, their dignity, their pride."

"Bullshit," Vega said. "Identity and dignity and pride has to be a little more than a few buttons, some slogans and a scowl. What you fail to see is that all that nonsense is also propaganda. As long as people keep making us believe that all we have is a complaint, then we don't have to really make an effort to do anything else but posture. What you both have to decide is what you want to do and then do it. I never forget I'm Puerto Rican, but I don't announce it every other sentence. Most of what gets us in trouble has nothing to do with being Puerto Rican. Most of it is plain and simple neurotic behavior and, because it's happening to us, we think it has to do with being Puerto Rican. Do you follow me?"

"No, I don't follow you," Maritza said. "And the more I think about it the less I want to be invisible."

"I think I understand it," Garboil said. "In my case what I have to guard against is blending back into non-descript, turned-off, white society. If I do that, then I become invisible, because I'm going against what I really am, which is Puerto Rican, and everyone can see it. Am I right?"

"Yes, one hundred percent right," Vega said.

"What I have to do," Garboil said, "is learn to speak Spanish better, find out what the issues are concerning the Island and learn more about our culture. Nobody's going to care that much except me. To the Puerto Ricans, I'll be one of them and therefore they won't notice the difference and to Americans . . ."

"North Americans," Maritza interrupted.

". . . North Americans," Garboil went on, "I'll be Puerto Rican and therefore harmless and therefore invisible."

"Right," Vega said.

"That's crazy," Maritza said. "You're asking me to give up all my ideals. You're trying to make us commit cultural suicide. That's like what's his name's book."

"Ellison," Vega said. "Right," Maritza said. "INVISIBLE MAN."

"Not quite," Garboil said. "That was different. That was imposed on him by the society. In this case we're choosing . . ."

"I'm not choosing anything," Maritza said.

"All I'm suggesting," Vega said, "is a little more discretion. Excuse me for saying this, but you have to take this entire matter of independence more seriously. We're not talking about the United Front or the Young Barons or Counts or whatever they are. I suggest you shelve the rhetoric, stop posturing and have a more definite commitment. Go to law school . . ."

"What?" she said. "How did you know I wanted to go to law school? The only person I ever told was Frank. Did he tell you?"

"I'm sorry," Vega said. "I was just using that as an example."

"Why?"

"Because you have a sharp mind and great determination and you like to argue and don't back down."

"And I'm not planning on starting," she said.

"I don't want you to," Vega said. "I'm glad you're thinking about studying law. It's a good start. Become as straight as you can. The better the cover that you create, the more invisible you become. Study what this country is really about and then beat its brains out at its own game."

"No way, man," she said. "Like I've heard about as much as I wanna. You're trying to co-opt my efforts."

"I'm sorry you feel that way, Maritza," Vega said. He was serious then, the pain was so evident that she was suddenly frightened. "Let me tell you something. I hadn't been to the Island in nearly ten years. It makes me sick to go there, because what I remember of it happened as a child and what I know now clashes with that memory. So I went there and went up into the mountains, where I'm from, and it struck me how well suited the place was for fighting a guerilla war."

"That's right," Maritza said. "Hit them and hide and run and hit them some place else."

"Right. Perfect terrain for it. There's only one problem."

"Supplying the people," she offered.

"Correct," Vega said. "You'd have to stash away arms and ammunition for the next twenty years before you could mount any kind of offensive. And all this country would have to do is throw a blockade around the Island once they got wind of it and that would be the end of it. At best, all that could happen is a few romantic escapades and a considerable loss of life. Not theirs but ours. So the battle is here, isn't it?"

"Yes, I've always said that," Maritza replied. "It's on us, here. That's why I can't understand how becoming invisible is gonna solve anything. There's only a few of us as it is."

"Because the solution has to be a political one," Vega said. "One that's fought on the basis of world opinion. For that you have to become invisible and let the issues speak for themselves. You have to put your ego aside and really think and fight whatever it is that keeps you personally from being free."

"That sounds pretty individualistic," Maritza said.

"No, no, no," Vega said, growing exasperated. "On the contrary. If you put your ego aside, really give it up for a great ideal, like freedom for others as well as yourself, then you're striking a blow for collective freedom. You have to start thinking of your own self. You have to give yourself up, Maritza. You have to. Really give it up if you mean what you say about independence. Nobody is ever totally free. For example, all of us will eventually die. There's no need to hasten the process for any reason whatsoever. Without life, there's nothing much that can be done. All that martyrdom nonsense is Christian cant. All of that crap is predicated on Christ on the Cross indoctrination. Mark my words, you'll see the Church involved more and more in armed revolution. What more of a contradiction would you want? But at the same time, how fitting that the Church help people martyr themselves. Perfect. The hypocrisy is overwhelming. And the other camp is no better. Martyrdom for the sake of the state is political cant and no less Christian, except that it's couched in Marxist terms. Forget it. Enslavement to doctrine. If you want that kind of life, you can have it. I don't want it. I believe in people and their capacity to unite and do good. Do you understand?"

"I think so," she said, almost in a whisper, as if to assent too loudly would jeopardize her political standing. "I just don't know."

"I hate to repeat myself," Vega said, "but nobody is absolutely free, ever. It's restricting enough that we're going to die, but that doesn't prevent us from doing the things we love doing. It's the same politically. No nation is ever truly free. They all depend on each other, don't they? Even if Puerto Rico were free tomorrow, it'd have to depend on other countries. Even if it were one hundred percent economically self-sufficient, it would have to depend on other countries for trade and human contact. That's the way it is. Twenty-five years from now, if the whole world is not blown up, in which case none of this is really important, economic and political lines will be even more indistinguishable than they are today. The important thing will be economic power and that is why it's so important that people wield that kind of power. I don't think there's a greater romantic alive than myself, Maritza. And yet I think, like all things, romantic fantasies grow outmoded. The idea of an armed battle against the U.S. is as romantic as you can get. Even little skirmishes and bombings in order to draw attention to our plight and raise the consciousnes of the people are a waste of human resources and part of the martyr mentality and very romantic. Except that it's outmoded. What is truly courageous is to believe that we can beat them by being smarter, more sensitive, more secure in ourselves. Don't you think we're smarter. Don't you think so?"

"Yeah, I suppose," Maritza said. She resembled a young child, finally capitulating to a truth, resigned to its inevitability. "And you think we can?"

"Yes, I think we can."

"And you really think we're smarter?"

Vega smiled openly at her, his heart filled with great love for this brave child that his friend had brought to him.

"Yes, I know we are," he said. "Smarter about life and therefore capable of learning other things. And we can get smarter if we apply ourselves. Name another country, with the exception of Switzerland, which has avoided wars and loss of life to the extent that we have. Other than conscriptions into the wars of the United States and individual, pathological violence against ourselves through drugs, we've done all right. Not great, but passably. We'll eventually take over this city. That's the history of the Spanish speaking people. Wherever they've gone they've endured and won out. Time is on our side. The mistake is thinking that it has to happen today. Any protracted war is a matter of patience, you know that. New York will be the first totally bilingual city in the United States. Mark my words."

"No, I believe it," she said. "But what about the Island?"

"That'll come as we achieve greater power," Vega said. "But let's get stronger here first. Become invisible, but not so invisible that you become null. Being a human being is a very private and lonely thing. Once you strip away being Puerto Rican, you're faced with that same loneliness everyone has to share with himself. The sooner you accept the loneliness, the better off you'll be."

Maritza nodded thoughtfully. It made sense, but there was something missing, something not clear.

"I couldn't do it," Maritza said. "I'm sorry. It's too scary."

"You have to," Garboil said, taking her hand. "If you don't, then we might as well turn ourselves in right now. If you want, we can go out shooting," he added, and she knew that he meant it.

"No, that won't do," she said, more pensive than he'd ever seen her. "Not anymore."

"Look, let me put it this way," Vega said. "The worst thing one human being can do to another is to strip him of his or her humanity. Do you agree with that?"

"Yes, of course," she answered. "And it's done to our people constantly. Here and on the Island."

"Precisely," Vega said. "That's why it's so important to become more human. Don't you see that?"

"They won't let us," she cried.

"They don't have that kind of power, Maritza," Vega pleaded. "They really don't. We're the ones that give them the power. We can just as easily take it away. The more human we are, the more power we have. The more Puerto Rican we are, that is, the more we emphasize the superficiality of our reality, the less time we have to look into ourselves and find solutions."

"But I am Puerto Rican," she said. "I can't deny that. I might as well kill myself."

"I'm not asking you to deny it, or forget it, or put it aside," Vega said. "Just accept it and start working on finding out what being a human being is all about."

"But being Puerto Rican is so beautiful," she said, her voice suddenly choked with emotion. "I don't have anything else," she said and then began crying softly.

Garboil moved closer to her on the couch and held her and she began crying openly, the sobs so agonizing that tears came into his own eyes. When she was finished crying she wiped her eyes and said she was sorry.

"That's all right," Vega said. "Nothing to apologize for."

"And I won't disappear?" she said. "If I become invisible, I won't just vanish?"

"No, you won't vanish," Vega said. "I'll make sure of that."

"Couldn't it be something other than invisible?" she said.

Vega thought for a moment.

"All right," he said. "Camouflaged. You can be crypto-Puerto Ricans. Like Frank was for a long time. Like the crypto-Jews of Spain after they were supposedly kicked out. Not invisible but camouflaged. Keeping our traditions alive and continuing to work for independence."

"What do you think?" she said, to Garboil.

"It's up to you," he said. "I think it'll be all right."

"Okay," she finally said. She felt very tired and sleepy and small, but somehow safe.

"When do we start?" Garboil said.

"Right away, if you want," Vega said.

"The sooner the better," Garboil said. "Is that okay, Maritza?"

"Sure," Maritza said.

Vega stood up and motioned them to follow him. They walked down the long hall of the huge apartment, past a couple of bedrooms where children slept, and into a large room with a double bed.

"You need rest," Vega said. "I'll take care of the details. There's a bathroom in there. If you need anything I'll be down the hall. I might as well get started."

"Thank you," Garboil said, extending his hand.

"You know what they say, buddy," Vega said. "A friend in need is a jerk indeed. Really, don't worry."

Garboil laughed and pushed at Vega's arm. "I'm sorry I was so nasty," Maritza said. "Thanks for your help."

"My pleasure," he said, bowing curtly. "Now get some rest and I'll see you later."

They closed the door, undressed, turned off the lights and got under the covers. Through the curtained window they saw that the sky had lightened and the snow still fell heavily. With their bodies against one another for the first time in more than two months, but too tired to feel any desire, a feeling of peace enveloped them and they held each other, drifting . . . drifting . . .

Before finally succumbing to the tiredness of mind and body which now overwhelmed them, they heard the steady tapping of a typewriter down the hall . . .